Books by David Westheimer

SUMMER ON THE WATER
THE MAGIC FALLACY
WATCHING OUT FOR DULIE
THIS TIME NEXT YEAR
VON RYAN'S EXPRESS
MY SWEET CHARLIE
SONG OF THE YOUNG SENTRY

Song of the Young Sentry

Song of the Young Sentry

by David Westheimer

LITTLE, BROWN and COMPANY   Boston   Toronto

LIBRARY OF CONGRESS CATALOG CARD NO. 68-24237

FIRST EDITION

Published simultaneously in Canada
by Little, Brown & Company (Canada) Limited

PRINTED IN THE UNITED STATES OF AMERICA

For Chuck Williams

Song of the Young Sentry

‡‡‡‡‡‡‡‡‡‡ **CHAPTER 1**

Six of them never came up.

Three of the survivors clung desperately and with dazed gratitude to the green breast of the indifferent sea. One of these, Steven Lang, the navigator, had neglected to check the inflating bottles of his life vest before the mission and only moments before had discovered there were none. Now, with the Mediterranean Sea tugging at his flying coveralls and heavy GI shoes, size 10D, he was pleading in a small voice for Bernard Moran, the copilot, to let him hang on.

Paul Smith, the assistant radio operator, bobbed a few feet away from them in his yellow Mae West, bright-eyed and grinning with shock, immersed in an expanding rosy tincture of his own blood.

James Allen Byrd, the pilot, had not come up yet. The pink wings of his desert-camouflaged Liberator bomber were, for the moment, holding the flight deck which imprisoned him in a tenuous suspension between surface and deep.

Everything in back of the wings — guns, ammunition, emergency rations, the tail gunner's loaded dice, the tail gunner himself and the two waist gunners — was still settling leisurely toward the bottom to join one of the Macchi 202 fighters which had shot them down.

The flight deck was seven inches below the surface when, after an interminable thirty-second wait, Byrd's russet head popped out of the escape hatch. It remained there, swiveling around with glazed gray eyes.

"Jaybird!" Moran shouted. "Get out!"

"Come on, Bernie," Lang said desperately. "Let me hang on to you."

Moran looked at him as if only now aware of his presence, swiftly unbuckled his Mae West and thrust it at Lang, saying, "Here, you son of a bitch."

Then he swam swiftly to the wreckage, pulled Byrd out of the escape hatch and, when the pilot stared at him without comprehension, pulled the cords inflating Byrd's life vest. With Byrd safely afloat, Moran unzipped his flying boots and tore them off, sinking beneath the water as he did so. He struggled back to the surface, gasping, and held lightly to Byrd as he trod water.

Lang watched him, petulant despite his shock and fear, thinking, you're holding on to Jaybird, how come you wouldn't let me hold on to you and how come you called me that. I didn't ask you to give me the God damn Mae West, all I wanted to do was hold on. Showing off, is all.

Shortly thereafter the flooded flight deck dragged down the pink wings, bearing with it the bodies of Harold Bertram, the bombardier; the radio operator and the aerial engineer, two of them having been killed in the air and the

4

third smashed by the top turret, which had wrenched loose on impact with the water.

The four survivors floated in the gently breathing sea two hundred yards off the Italian shore at a point which Lang estimated to be somewhere south of Salerno. Exactly how far south he could not say, having abruptly lost all interest in navigation when Italian fighters knocked out number three and four engines and the B-24 bomber had begun its controlled but rapid descent toward the distant beach.

The beach had proved too narrow and rocky for a landing, and Byrd, with Moran keeping the plane straight and level by sheer strength of his legs on the rudder control bars, had set down in the sea.

It had been a rending, untidy landing and the four surviving crewmen floated in a littered seascape. Papers, charts, the comic books of Paul Smith, who was nineteen, and bits of debris were strewn over the surface and in the midst of the litter the grotesque geometrical figures of the nosewheel and the bomb-bay fuel tank bobbed placidly.

Pulling the dazed pilot behind him, Moran paddled back to Lang and Smith.

"Must have hit his head," Moran said. "He ain't said a God damn word."

"I didn't want your Mae West," Lang said. "I just wanted to hang on."

Ignoring him, Moran turned to Smith. Smith's eyes had lost their abnormal glint and the water around him was no longer pink.

"How you doin', Junior?" Moran asked.

Worried about everybody but me, Lang thought. I could be hit, too, for all he knows.

"Fine, Lieutenant," Smith replied unconvincingly. "What you think they gonna do to us?"

"Nothing. Just take it easy."

Moran looked toward the shore.

"A rowboat's coming out," he said.

All except Byrd turned to watch.

"Nuts," Smith said, genuinely disappointed. "Is all we get a rowboat?"

"What you expect, a Chris-Craft?" Lang demanded angrily.

"No, sir," Smith said, his tone disrespectful.

They waited silently for the clumsy little boat to reach them, grateful to be alive but each wrapped in his own somber thoughts.

There were two men in the rowboat. One was in uniform, a carabiniere with a rifle hanging from his shoulder. The other was a ragged, grizzled civilian plying the oars.

"Allo," the carabiniere shouted as they drew near, following with a question in Italian.

The civilian stopped rowing to stare at the Americans and the carabiniere nudged him with a boot toe. After a brief and friendly exchange of insults the civilian resumed his methodical rowing and drew alongside Lang and his companions.

Disregarding the proffered hand of the carabiniere, Moran pulled himself into the boat with muscular ease, then reached down and plucked Byrd out of the sea. He sat the pilot down in the stern and with the carabiniere's help pulled Smith into the boat, both of them being careful not to bump his legs. The civilian made a sympathetic clucking sound and shook his head when he saw Smith's youth and wounds.

Lang waited for Moran to reach down to him, angry at being the last to receive attention although Smith was only a sergeant and he was a first lieutenant, but Moran was now helping the carabiniere arrange Smith as comfortably as possible in the bow with his neck and shoulders propped against a thwart and his legs straight out.

Realizing no one intended to help him, Lang seized the side of the boat and tried to pull himself aboard as Moran had done. He raised himself until his chin was level with his hands and found he could go no higher. As he hung there, the motion of the boat wrenching his shoulders and straining arms, a forgotten humiliation of junior high school days crossed his mind. A fat, overgrown boy of thirteen, he was competing in a rope-climbing contest with other members of his gym class and had dangled a foot off the floor, unable to pull himself another inch higher. The gym teacher had begun laughing and soon the whole class of almost fifty boys, most of them smaller than himself, was laughing and jeering. Even now, nine years later, though he was drenched, frightened and in the hands of the enemy, the memory rankled.

But now fifty schoolboys were not laughing and jeering. No one was paying any attention to him at all. Byrd was sitting quietly where Moran had deposited him and Moran and the two Italians were looking down at Smith. Smith's upper body was clad in a yellow Mae West and a khaki United States Army shirt, his lower half in white drawers stained with excrement and British battle dress trousers bunched down around his flying boots. There were two small blue-black holes through his right calf and high up inside his left thigh a deep clean wound gaped pink as an open mouth.

Lang stared queasily, then looked away, briefly ashamed of having spoken angrily to Smith in the water. His sense of injustice at his own predicament quickly reasserted itself.

"Hey!" he cried sharply.

Everyone looked at him. The carabiniere made a gesture of dismayed apology and leaned down to grasp Lang's wrists. His slung rifle slipped off his shoulder and slid down his arm. It hit Lang on the head.

"Oh, God damn!" Lang cried, blinking.

The carabiniere apologized profusely and the civilian looked on with deep concern. Moran was the first to laugh, then Smith. The Italians, observing this reaction, and seeing Lang was uninjured, permitted themselves a grin. The civilian had only three teeth, two above and one below. They did not meet. The carabiniere handed his rifle to the civilian, who held it gingerly, as if fearing an explosion, and took a fresh grip on Lang's wrists.

Heaving and grunting, he hauled Lang's hundred and eighty-three pounds half into the rowboat and left him draped over the edge, his face directly above a basket full of gaping anchovies. Lang stared at them and they stared back, cold, unwavering and aghast.

Lang averted his face.

With the last of his strength he pulled himself into the boat and maneuvered his way past the anchovies. Rising from hands and knees, he looked for a place to sit. There was none. Moran was sitting beside Byrd trying without success to get him to say something. The carabiniere stood facing them, astride the anchovies. The fisherman sat between the oarlocks and Smith occupied the entire bow. Lang stepped over an oar, tripped, scraped the back of his hand on an oarlock recovering his balance, and crouched uncomfortably beside Smith.

The fisherman began rowing, breathing out gusts of garlic which mingled with his sweat. The odor, the motion of the rowboat and the tension which knotted his stomach made Lang abruptly ill and he leaned over the side and vomited. He felt better immediately.

"You okay, Lieutenant?" Smith asked.

Lang felt a quick surge of friendship for the youngster, grateful that someone had at last expressed concern.

"Yeah," he said. "How you feel?"

"It didn't even hurt," Smith said incredulously.

"Good," Lang replied, wishing he could think of something reassuring to add but too concerned with his own predicament to do so.

Everything had changed the moment the plane hit the water. Before that happened he had been a first lieutenant in the United States Army Air Force, the highest eminence he had achieved in all his twenty-two years. Now he did not know what he was, except that he was a prisoner of war. He was filled with vague dread but mingled with his foreboding was a strange and undefined sense of triumph explained only partially by the fact that he had survived and six of the crew had not.

In the stern, Byrd leaned forward suddenly and spewed out a gush of sea water, drenching the carabiniere's leg.

"Lordy," Byrd said.

It was the first sound he had uttered since the crash.

The carabiniere cursed, apologized for his outburst, and started to mop his trouser leg with a handkerchief. Instead of doing so he offered the handkerchief to Byrd, who only stared at it.

"Thanks," said Moran, taking the handkerchief.

He wiped Byrd's face.

"You okay now, Jaybird?"

"Lordy," said Byrd again, with a hint of returning awareness.

But he did not answer Moran's question and the journey toward shore continued in silence except for the heavy breathing of the carabiniere and the fisherman. The fisherman was breathing heavily from exertion, the carabiniere because his pants were too tight. He was plump for a wartime Italian.

After the crash the silence had been so sudden and pervasive that Lang had thought himself deafened. Now he found his hearing acutely sensitive. The air was astir with small sounds, some near, some far, but all distinct. The oars creaked in the oarlocks and small waves lapped against the boat. Sounds of conversation floated out to sea from the beach. Farther inland, dogs barked, birds sang, a cow lowed, a goat bleated and an ax bit leisurely into wood. The woodchopper was deaf and had not heard the crippled plane smash into the water nor been told of it by his neighbors hurrying to the scene.

Everyone else in the area was waiting on the beach, a curving black line of children, women and old men and, a little distance away from them in a self-consciously official stance, a carabiniere sergeant.

The boat scraped upon the sand and the fisherman shipped his oars and climbed over the side. When he had pulled the boat as far as he could unassisted, the carabiniere in the boat picked his way past Lang and Smith, poised himself on the bow, took a deep breath and, urged on by his sergeant, leaped heavily to the beach. Even with his help and that of the sergeant, the fisherman was unable to draw the heavily laden rowboat upon the beach.

Moran leaped over the stern and pushed. Though he was short, only five feet six, he was immensely strong and the rowboat grated over the sand until only a foot of it remained in the water.

The black line of spectators murmured at Moran's display of strength, then fell silent again. No one among them moved.

Byrd climbed over the side and stood looking around with a puzzled expression on his face. The sergeant led him solicitously a few feet higher on the beach. Moran plucked Smith out of the boat and carried him in his arms to where Byrd stood. Lang, finding himself alone with the anchovies, scrambled after him. Lang, Moran and Byrd grouped themselves around Smith.

The Italians on the beach remained mute and immobile. They did not even appear to be breathing except for one old man with his mouth open making sounds like a kettle. But they stared, all of them. Their eyes clung to the four Americans, unblinking, as if they were gods spewed up by the sea.

Lang saw this and his undefined sense of triumph resolved itself.

He was a hero.

A veteran of twenty-three combat missions shot down in the service of his country, a battle-hardened flying officer who filled these Italian civilians with wonder and admiration. He straightened and pulled in his stomach but the soaked flight coveralls clung to his body and betrayed his undeniable corpulence.

10

He looked at the hand he had scraped on the oarlock. He was not just a hero, he was a wounded hero and no doubt would get the Purple Heart when he got back. The thought destroyed his mood. When he got back. When would he get back, and what was to happen to him before he did?

Lang was completely unprepared to be a prisoner of war, having often and in frightening detail considered the possibility of being killed but never of being captured. Would they torture him for information? Would he get enough to eat? Would anybody back at Group or back home know what happened to him? And would anyone care, except his mother and father?

"Are we all that got out, Bernie?" Byrd said to Moran, lucid at last.

Moran nodded somberly. He had searched the line of Italians for a pretty face, found one and had been studying it, wondering what sort of social arrangements a prisoner of war might be able to make in Italy.

Byrd sighed.

"Lordy," he said, full of anguish.

It was as near as he ever came to swearing.

Seeing Byrd's grief, Lang now for the first time felt sadness for the death of his crewmates. Before he had been too preoccupied with himself. He had never gotten along with any of them, particularly Harold Bertram, the bombardier, and he knew even the enlisted men called him by his nickname "Blubberbutt" behind his back; but they were members of the same crew and now they were dead.

Despite this unaccustomed emotion he felt more a hero than ever. He had come through alive and six of them had not. And, for the first time in a very long while, he felt he had been favored by luck. Lang had always considered himself a singularly unlucky person.

Byrd knelt beside Smith and examined his wounds. Moran was again studying the only passable face in the crowd.

"Looks pretty clean," Byrd said. "Hurt much, Paul?"

"No, sir," Smith replied. "Not very. Captain? What they gonna do to us?"

"Don't you worry," Byrd said, patting his shoulder reassuringly. "First thing they'll have to do is get you a doctor."

Byrd got to his feet and turned to the carabiniere, who was describing to an entranced audience his epic rescue and capture of the American fliers. The fisherman, to whom he had given a cigarette for his assistance, was blinking his eyes through a cloud of tobacco smoke and nodding his head in confirmation. The sergeant was content to observe, his condescending expression clearly indicating everything had been done at his instruction.

Before Byrd could get the carabiniere's attention, Lang stepped between them and thrust out his scraped hand.

"Hey, Jaybird," he said. "Look."

Byrd looked and nodded absently. Moran shook his head incredulously. Lang expected the copilot to say something ribald, as Moran usually did when he disapproved of him, but Moran said nothing.

"You," Byrd said to the carabiniere. "Soldier."

The carabiniere broke off his recitatif and turned to face Byrd attentively.

"This man needs medical attention," Byrd said, indicating Smith. "Doctor."

"Si," the carabiniere said, nodding. "Dottore. Subito."

He pointed toward a small square stone building on a rocky promontory a quarter mile up the narrow beach and indicated they were to go there.

"We'll need a litter," Byrd said.

The carabiniere shrugged uncomprehendingly and looked at his sergeant. The sergeant shrugged also.

"Litter," Byrd repeated authoritatively. "Stretcher. Ambulance."

The carabinieri, who knew no English, shook their heads and exchanged helpless looks. Byrd indicated with signs what was wanted. They shook their heads and smiled apolo-

12

getically, indicating the wounded man would have to be carried. The sergeant, a strongly built man, pantomimed he would make a chair of arms with Byrd but Moran nudged him aside, picked Smith up as he had done earlier and began walking toward the stone building without a backward look. The plump carabiniere hurried up ahead of him to lead the way and the sergeant fell in step with Byrd and Lang.

Byrd walked with his head high and his back straight. Lang walked head down. His head seemed terribly heavy to him. He was apprehensive, his joints ached and he was extraordinarily tired.

And he no longer felt like a hero.

Not yet twenty-three, Lang was the youngest surviving officer of the *High Flying Flora*, the Egypt-based Liberator bomber now strewn over the bottom of the Mediterranean Sea with the bodies of six of its crewmen after an attack on the harbor at Naples. It was December, 1942, and American bombers had only recently begun attacking the Italian mainland.

The crew had been Lang's third. When combat crews were formed after preliminary training in Florida that summer, the pilot to whom Lang was assigned as navigator had refused to accept him. It was not a matter of Lang's competence. He was an excellent navigator. It was simply that the pilot detested him. He had not been alone in this feeling toward Lang.

Lang went overseas with another crew, navigating the Southern Route from West Palm Beach through Trinidad, Brazil and Africa to his bombardment group's new base at Ramat Jonas in Palestine with unimpeachable skill. He had flown three combat missions with it before asking to be reassigned. The other officers and even some of the enlisted men, he explained to the squadron commander, were always picking on him.

His request would have been blasphemously denied had not Byrd's navigator just been indefinitely grounded with an inner ear disorder. Byrd was an element leader and his crew had to be kept at operational strength.

Even though Moran had immediately nicknamed him "Blubberbutt," Byrd had measured him by his skill as a navigator and Lang had never regretted the change; until an hour ago, when he had stared out of the Plexiglass window by his chart table in the nose of the *High Flying Flora* into vast empty sockets which a moment before had contained two engines.

Now, benighted on an unfamiliar shore, he did not blame himself for having made a change that ended so disastrously. He blamed the bad luck which had always pursued him and he blamed his former crewmates whose indignities had forced him to ask reassignment.

He felt a twinge of shame at this disloyalty to Byrd, who had always treated him fairly and who was not responsible for his present misfortune. On the contrary, he believed he owed his life to Byrd's skill as a pilot. But Jaybird should have said something about his wounded hand. He could have at least done that.

As he plodded along the beach in the sharp late afternoon sun he was as oblivious of all life outside himself as a newborn infant swaddled in shock and silence. The plummeting sun was like the mouth of a tilted bottle spilling iridescent red ink over the water but he was even less aware of it than the carabinieri, who had seen the sun set on the Mediterranean too many times to be impressed.

The other Americans were hardly more aware of externals than Lang. The perceptiveness which had followed the initial shock of crash and capture had now given way to numbness born of fatigue and withdrawal into the fastness of self. Even their dead were forgotten for the moment.

And none of them knew any more than Lang what to expect of the future. Several months earlier they had been briefed meticulously on evading capture, finding assistance and getting back to Allied lines. They had been issued detailed maps on silk handkerchiefs and printed messages promising cash rewards to those who assisted them. But the maps were of

Egypt, Libya and Tunisia and the messages, called "goolie chits," were in Arabic. Of the other escape materials which had been issued to them, all had been mislaid or lost in the crash except a compass in the guise of a button which Byrd had sewn at the neck of his flight coveralls. They had not been briefed on evasion in Italy or on the treatment of prisoners of war anywhere.

CHAPTER 2

Their wet flying suits were taken away and replaced with blankets. Though his teeth were chattering, Byrd refused to get out of his suit until he had seen Smith made as comfortable as possible on a wooden bench before a twig fire burning in a brick alcove. When he did remove it he pulled the button compass covertly from the collar and put it in his mouth. When Moran stripped, the carabinieri openly admired his physique and parts, making jokes which transcended language about the latter. Moran cursed them cordially in bad Spanish. Like his companions, he knew no Italian but he had picked up a little Spanish in his civilian occupation. He had been a used car salesman in Los Angeles before the war.

The Italians were amused by this and one of them

16

clapped Moran on the back and collected cigarettes from his companions to pass around. Lang, who did not smoke, shook his head.

"God damn it, Blubberbutt," Moran ordered, "take one."

When Lang did so, Moran plucked it from his hand and stuck it behind his ear. He lit the other with a twig from the fire and took an eager drag.

"God Almighty!" he cried. "It goes down like razor blades and horseshit!"

Byrd took the burning twig from him and lit Smith's cigarette. Moran stopped him when he held it to his own.

"Three on a match," said Moran. "Bad luck."

"Is that a fact?" Byrd said, lighting up and taking a cautious drag.

The Italians watched as he blew out a plume of smoke and looked thoughtfully at the cigarette.

"It's not so bad," he said.

The carabinieri seemed pleased with his approval.

It was dark when the doctor came, escorted by a dapper little Italian officer in a well-tailored gray gabardine uniform. The doctor was a civilian in a wrinkled and ill-fitting black suit with a Fascist party button in the lapel. While he was attending to Smith's wounds the officer began questioning the others in a mixture of Italian, French, and labored English.

"Don't give anything but your name, rank and serial number," Byrd ordered.

He told the officer in college French they would give no other information. The officer scowled and said, "Why does country so rich make war on country so poor?"

"To get the cigarettes," Moran said. "We're wild for Wop cigarettes."

"Knock that off, Bernie," said Byrd.

The doctor left Smith groaning on the bench and came to the officers, a bottle of iodine in his hand. Iodine hurt, Lang thought, but his wound should be treated because you never knew when a cut might get infected. When he was a child his mother had told him stories about little boys who lost hands and even legs when they let their cuts and scratches go untended. He thrust out his hand, gritting his teeth. The doctor swabbed it with iodine. The sting was less than his childhood recollection.

"Can't beat iodine for a wound," he said.

"Wound my ass," Moran said.

The doctor stared at the three of them, his face sour and spiteful. He said something to them in Italian.

"What did he say?" Byrd asked the officer.

"For you the war is over."

"Not by a long shot," Byrd said quietly.

The officer did not understand his idiom.

"Andiamo," he said. "We go."

He opened the door and motioned them out.

"Just a God damn minute," said Moran. "What about this?"

He pointed down at his feet, clad only in white cotton socks. He had shed his flying boots in the sea. The officer shrugged, as if it were no concern of his, but the carabiniere sergeant brought him cloths to wrap around his feet.

Two of the carabinieri carried Smith out to a waiting open truck on the bench and slid him, groaning, into the back. The other carabinieri followed and all shook hands with the departing Americans.

It was cold outside. Lang looked up at the sky, ebon except where pricked with stars. A perfect night for navigation, he thought. If they had not been hit he might now be shooting his last three-star fix before reaching the coast and the flashing code beacons which would guide him to the airstrip in the sandy wastes of the Great Western Desert.

He felt a pang of almost unbearable despair and a deep longing for his cramped little nook in the nose of the *High Flying Flora* with its letdown table for his mercator chart and Plexiglass dome for shooting the stars. He knew and loved the night face of the sky better than that of any human except his parents and felt more at home with it, though he did not actually realize this and could not have put it into words. For he had never felt so complete and competent as in the night sky with a crew of ten men dependent upon him for guidance and perhaps for their lives and knowing that whatever they might think of him as a man they had implicit faith in his skill, even Moran.

He sighed.

Byrd did, too, and misinterpreting Lang's melancholy said, "They were such a great bunch."

"Huh?" said Lang adding, when he understood Byrd was speaking of Bertram and the others who had been killed, "Yeah. They sure were."

It was freezing in the jolting bed of the truck and Smith groaned with increasing frequency as his wounds chilled. Lang tried to keep his mind off the sound and the cold and the jolting by studying the sky, which was more familiar to him than his surroundings. Polaris was in clear view except where trees hung over the road or a hill intervened and he was able to tell in which direction they were moving despite the tortuous climbings and turnings. He kept Byrd informed as if the truck were a plane and Byrd still his pilot and was pleased that Byrd appeared interested in the information.

They spent the night traveling by seemingly aimless stages, stopping twice at military posts where they were placed on display and questioned desultorily. At one of them they were given used Italian uniforms to replace their blankets and Moran got some shoes. They were told "Per lei la guerra è finita" often enough to learn it meant "For you the war is over," and asked again in broken English why a country so rich made war on a country so poor. The uniforms fit indifferently. Moran's was too small in the chest, Lang's in the belly, and Byrd's too short in arms and legs.

The latter part of the night's journey was by train. When their escort led them to a compartment Lang pushed in ahead of the others and got a window seat. At home he had always taken the window seat on buses and streetcars so he could look out at the scenery. Moran sat next to him, crowding him with his big shoulders, and Byrd next to Moran, across from the escorting officer and soldier. Smith was in the next compartment with a guard, though he did not need one.

After the train got under way cold air poured over Lang from the loose window. He wondered if Moran might be persuaded to look at the scenery, abandoning the thought when he realized there was none outside the window, only blackness.

The cold had been harsh since nightfall but now it was vicious. Byrd pulled himself out of his stupor and went to have a look at Smith, stepping over the officer's legs and staring down his objections. He returned bleak with rage.

"The window's broken," he said. "Paul's freezing in there."

He looked grimly at the Italian officer, who was smoking a cigarette.

"It's like a refrigerator in there," he said. "Get him more blankets."

The officer blew out a trickle of smoke and looked at Byrd unmoved.

"I insist you do something for my wounded man," Byrd grated.

The officer merely huddled deeper into his greatcoat and blew out more cigarette smoke.

"C'est la guerre," he said indolently.

Moran, who had been aroused from an uneasy doze by Byrd's vehemence, leaned toward the officer and said, "You son of a bitch."

What are you guys doing? Lang thought anxiously. You're going to get us in worse trouble than we're already in. He shrank against the window, trying to disassociate himself from Byrd and Moran.

The officer reached for his pistol, found it hopelessly muffled by his tightly buttoned greatcoat, glanced at the soldier next to him and saw he was fast asleep, and assumed an attitude of great indifference.

"Give me your blouse, Bernie," Byrd said. "You, too, Steve."

"What for?" Lang protested. "It's cold in here."

Byrd merely looked at him. Lang meekly surrendered his blouse. Byrd took their three blouses to Smith. They passed what was left of the night wretchedly.

It was day when they left the train at Salerno. When Smith was brought out on his litter the civilians crowding the platform filled the air with murmurs of sympathy. Lang was jealous of the attention given Smith who was, after all, only a sergeant, but he was surprised and reassured to see that the enemy looked so much like Americans and were no less sympathetic. Until now he had seen only poorly clad peasants, rumpled soldiers and sleek, often unfriendly officers.

The sun was warm and restorative and, though his stomach ached with unfamiliar hunger, Lang smiled at the thronging civilians. Many of them returned the smile. He forgot he was wearing an Italian uniform.

Moran smiled, too, concentrating his attention on a striking blond girl modishly dressed in a knit suit, silk stockings and high heels. This interest was not lost on the little Italian soldier, who had slept through the entire journey despite the cold and was now explaining to a circle of civilians that the men in custody were not Italians but Americans, very brave and fierce, in whose capture he had played a considerable role. Now he nodded toward the girl, smiling, and said to Moran, "Bella ragazza."

"Bella who?" Moran demanded, wondering how the soldier knew the girl's name.

"Bella ragazza," the soldier repeated.

"Hey, Bella," Moran called softly. "Bella Ragatsa."

Lang observed the exchange in silent disapproval. That's all Moran ever had on his mind, he thought. To hear

Moran talk there was no such thing as a decent girl. And you'd think with one of his best friends dead just a day Moran would have more on his mind than getting fresh with some girl he didn't even know.

The girl lifted her eyes in surprise, gave Moran a flattered smile and departed with a companion, laughing. Lang felt as if she had betrayed him and womanhood.

"I'll be God damned," Moran said. "The little bastard really did know her name."

Byrd had been kneeling by Smith, shading his eyes from the sun and giving the youngster what encouragement he could. When an ambulance came to carry him away Byrd called Lang and Moran over to say good-bye to him. Lang was relieved to see Smith go. Now maybe Jaybird would pay some attention to other members of the crew.

The three officers were taken away in a police van. Despite the fact that they had been under guard in some fashion or other since their capture, for the first time they actually felt in custody. The van was windowless and the only light came through a wire grating on the back door, through which also came the tantalizing sounds of a busy city.

After a moment Moran grinned.

"This is the first time I was ever in a paddy wagon," he said. "In a foreign country."

"I never been in one before," Lang said.

He felt somewhat more cheerful. If they had them locked up in a police van they must consider them dangerous characters. Until now their captors had been notably lax and when Lang thought about it it seemed humiliating to be held so lightly.

"Have you really been in a paddy wagon before?" Byrd asked.

"Me and my old man," Moran said, not without pride. "We got in a fight at Ciro's. But they didn't book us. The other guys started it." He sighed. "My old man could sure go. The old bastard," he added fondly.

22

Lang was envious. To have the kind of father who would take you to nightclubs and get in fights with you. And to be the kind of son who got into fights. But he really wouldn't want that, to get into fights. He was afraid of fights and besides his father and mother both said it was wrong to fight. Not that his father didn't give him companionship, either, or disapproved of nightclubs. But his father was always urging him to make friends his own age and go out and have fun with other boys and girls, as if it were all that easy to make friends, at least friends who weren't always riding you or arguing with you and doing everything better than you except in school.

"Ciro's?" he said. "In Hollywood?"

"Yeah," said Moran. "On the Strip. Man, is he gonna tie one on when he hears about me."

"I wonder how long it'll be before our next of kin are notified we're safe?" Byrd said. "Flora'll be beside herself until she finds out."

Byrd, who had been a high school teacher in New Mexico before flight training, was the only married officer on the crew. The *High Flying Flora* was named for his wife.

My mom and dad will really carry on, Lang thought, feeling frustrated at being unable to let them know he was all right. But there was something pleasant about it, too. He remembered how, when he was little, and had been punished or denied something, he had wished he were dead so they would be sorry they had been mean to him, and how he had taken back the wish when he realized if he were dead he would not be around to witness their remorse. He would spare them pain and worry now if he could, but since he could not there was something attractive about being reported missing and possibly thought dead, and not being dead. And he thought particularly about the effect of this upon those he had not gotten along with, who had held him lightly or ignored him. The girls who would not go out with him or, if they had, would not do so a second time, would see him in a different light now. It almost made up for one of the great disappointments of his military career, that after he got his wings he had been sent straight to combat crew training instead of getting leave to show off his uniform and new second lieutenant's bars to everybody in Houston.

The van stopped, the back door was unlocked and they were hustled quickly into an imposing stone building on the edge of the sea. Lang paused for a moment, stricken with a sudden longing for home by the glint of sunlight on the water and the salt air which brought back memories of family excursions to Morgan's Point.

They were left unguarded in a small waiting room filled with chairs and benches. They sprawled wearily, eyes closed. Moran took off his shoes and kneaded his toes. Lang's stomach growled.

"I'm hungry," he said plaintively.

"I could eat a live skunk starting at the asshole," Moran said.

He looked thoughtfully at Lang.

"You know something, Blubberbutt? Wouldn't hurt you a damn bit to miss a few meals."

"Oh, yeah!" Lang cried angrily. "Why don't you just . . ."

"You guys quit arguing," Byrd broke in with an irritability that surprised both of them.

They had now been without food and virtually without sleep for thirty hours.

A tall, slender and shy officer came to lead Byrd away.

"This may be the first big interrogation," Byrd said. "If it is, remember. Just name, rank and serial number."

He left with the Italian.

"If it is an interrogation, you think they'll, you know, get rough?" Lang asked nervously.

"I hear they're worse than the Wogs," Moran said slyly. "I hope you saved your goolie chit."

24

"You're just trying to scare me," Lang said.

He leaned back and closed his eyes. Moran was just saying that. The Italians hadn't been mean to them so far. Except not giving them anything to eat. He wished he had a can of C rations from the case which had gone down with the plane and the chocolate bar from the emergency pack in his parachute.

Byrd had been gone almost half an hour when the tall officer returned and summoned Moran. Moran slipped on his shoes and limped away, leaving Lang angry and apprehensive at being alone. Byrd must have told them I was just the navigator and Moran was a pilot, he thought, yet knowing it could not be true because Byrd would only tell them name, rank and serial number. Unless he had been tortured. Lang's skin contracted, as if he had been suddenly dipped in ice water.

He tried to lose himself in sleep, but tired as he was he could not and when the door opened to admit the tall officer he sat up stiffly. He followed the officer reluctantly down a broad hall to a heavy door. The officer knocked, opened the door and stood aside politely, motioning Lang to enter. Lang inhaled deeply and did so. The door closed silently behind him.

He was in a sunny, spacious office overlooking the Mediterranean and a quay at which small boats were moored. Despite his fears, his attention was drawn to this scene before his eyes made a furtive inspection of the office for signs of brutality or instruments of torture. He saw instead an impressively appointed office with heavy carved furniture and pictures of King Victor Emmanuel and Benito Mussolini on the wall. A stocky, gray-haired colonel was seated at a broad desk at the back of the room. For a moment Lang thought he had seen the man before because he so closely resembled a colonel of the previous night. A few feet to the colonel's left, facing Lang, stood a slightly rumpled officer whose dark eyes twinkled behind steel-rimmed glasses. Behind him sat a third man bent over a stenographer's pad. This man did not look up and all Lang could see of him was a mane of glossy, well-groomed black hair.

Though none of the Italians was smoking there was the acrid scent of Italian tobacco in the air, reminding Lang, somehow, not of Italian cigarettes but of Moran.

"You will please salute the colonel," the rumpled officer said.

The colonel acknowledged Lang's salute with a careless flick of his hand.

"You will please to be seated," the rumpled officer said.

Lang slumped gratefully into the comfortable chair facing the colonel, his stomach bulging over the unbuttoned waistband of his breeches.

The colonel eyed him distastefully, then said, "Por lei la guerra è finita."

The interpreter saw from Lang's expression that he understood and said, "You speak Italian?"

Lang shook his head. The interpreter looked at him thoughtfully. He said something to the colonel, continuing to observe Lang from the corner of his eye. When there was no indication that Lang had understood his words he appeared satisfied with Lang's denial.

"Do you wish a cigarette?" the interpreter said, holding out a packet.

Lang started to refuse, remembered Moran's admonition and took one, afraid Moran would know it had been offered. The interpreter held out a lighted match. Lang shook his head and put the cigarette away.

The colonel began asking questions, observing Lang closely. The interpreter gave his undivided attention to whoever was speaking, turning from one to the other as he translated. The stenographer wrote furiously, never looking up.

"What is your position in the aircrew?" was the opening question.

Name, rank and serial number, Lang thought. That's what Byrd said.

"I don't know," he replied, hunching down in his chair and looking at the floor.

"What is the range and speed of your aircraft?"

"I don't know."

"What is your armament and from what altitude do you drop your bombs?"

"I don't know," Lang repeated doggedly, though a furtive look at the colonel told him the Italian was growing increasingly displeased with his answers.

At this the colonel lost his temper and shouted. Lang retired deeper into his chair.

"Do not say 'I don't know,'" the interpreter translated mildly, despite the heat with which the colonel had spoken. "The colonel says do you regard us as fools? We are aware you know these things."

He added helpfully, "If you will not say, say you will not say. It makes my colonel very angry to say you do not know."

The interrogation continued.

"Why do you bomb our cities?" the interpreter translated.

"I don't . . ." Lang began, stopping when the interpreter held up a cautionary finger. "We don't bomb cities."

"Really? How is it then the whole of your ten formations bombed only the city."

"We didn't have ten formations, only . . ."

This time he stopped of his own accord.

"Anyway, it was the harbor we bombed," he said truculently. "We don't bomb cities."

"You know that is false. You of all your crew."

"Me?" Lang demanded. "How come?"

"Because you are the bomb aimer."

"I am not!" Lang exclaimed indignantly. "I'm the . . ."

27

He stopped again.

"We have been informed to the contrary."

"Who said so?"

"One of your fellows."

"Lieutenant Moran?" Lang said, sitting up.

He would never have believed Moran could do a thing like that to him even if Moran was always riding him. But Byrd certainly wouldn't have said a thing like that, not even if he really was the bombardier. It had to be Moran.

The colonel and the interpreter exchanged looks.

"Si, Tenente Moran," the interpreter said quickly.

Lang realized they were trying to trick him. You couldn't trust these Italians.

"Do you not feel guilty for killing innocent people?"

"We don't kill innocent people. And Lieutenant Moran never told you I was the bombardier."

"Why are you so certain of this?"

"Because I'm the navigator."

That was stupid, he thought. But what the hell, it didn't mean anything if they knew that. It might even help. Now that they knew he wasn't a pilot maybe they wouldn't expect him to know much about the plane and would lay off.

The colonel pursed his lips thoughtfully when he received the information from the interpreter. He leafed through a clump of papers on his desk and removed a water-stained chart, which he unfolded and spread out deliberately.

Lang was horrified. It was the navigational chart which he had left thumbtacked to his table when Byrd ordered him to his crash station on the flight deck. He had chewed up his flimsy, a sheet of onionskin paper listing the colors of the day and the locations of lighted code marker beacons and emergency landing fields, but his other papers had been too bulky to dispose of even if he had had the presence of mind to try.

"From where did your aircraft depart?" the interpreter translated.

Lang thought furiously. They did not know because

28

there had not been room on the mercator chart to plot both Landing Ground 139, the advance base from which the mission had started, and the target. He had instead plotted the place at which they crossed the Libyan coast as the point of departure. He felt relieved and clever.

"I don't . . ." he began, adding quickly, "I can't tell you."

"You refuse to say?"

"Yes."

"We have ways of forcing you to say."

The sharpness of the colonel's voice prompted Lang to look up and the translation confirmed his fears. However, the interpreter appeared singularly unintimidating, even amused, and Lang said nothing.

"You know what the Japanese do to prisoners of war?"

The interpreter seemed to be experiencing some inner struggle as he translated. He suddenly broke into laughter.

Lang looked from the scowling colonel to the mirthful interpreter, not knowing which expression to believe. At the moment, the colonel looked capable of any brutality.

The colonel's glare, however, was directed at the interpreter, who hung his head.

"I won't tell you anything but my name, rank and serial number," Lang said defiantly, deciding the colonel was bluffing and even if he were not that he would not talk. Not unless they really got rough.

The colonel took this with unexpected good grace. He opened a folder and removed a small piece of paper which he handed to the interpreter as he spoke. The interpreter gave it to Lang, who accepted it gingerly. It was a clipping from an American newspaper, brittle from having been soaked and then dried. The clipping showed a photograph of Lang's group commander over an account of a raid on Navarino Bay. Lang remembered the raid well because of the intense flak.

"This was found in a purse taken from the body of one of your comrades. This is your commanding officer?"

What kind of jerk would carry something like that on him on a mission? Lang thought, and them was ashamed at having such thoughts about a dead crewmate.

He did not answer the question.

"If this is not your commanding officer, why would your sergeant carry it in his purse?"

"Maybe it's his old man," Lang blurted.

"Old man?" the interpreter said without translating for the colonel.

"Yeah. His father."

"Father," the interpreter said. "Momento."

He whipped a small black notebook out of his pocket and wrote in it.

"Old man. Father," he said with a pleased expression.

"But you appeared to know this man when you beheld his picture. Is this not so?"

"Maybe."

"So. He is your commanding officer."

"I didn't say that."

"But you know him so he must be your commanding officer."

Lang looked desperately for a way out of the trap into which he had gotten himself. He looked longingly out of the window where a small boat was just leaving the quay, then around the room. His gaze fell on the portrait of Mussolini.

"I know him," he said. "And he's not my commanding officer."

A transient smile crossed the colonel's stern features when this was translated for him. He said something to the interpreter which made him laugh.

"He is now," he translated.

Lang did not think that was so funny but he thought it best to smile.

"Whom do you wish to be informed of your safety? You have parents or a wife?"

"Mr. and Mrs. Walter B. Lang, 2906 Blodgett, Houston, Texas," Lang said gratefully.

"Texas," the interpreter said. "Tom Mix. Bang, bang."

He gave the colonel a look of apology for this lapse.

The colonel looked up from his papers.

"Comport yourself properly and you will find you will be well treated. You are dismissed."

Lang was relieved. It had not been nearly as bad as he had expected and they hadn't got a thing out of him but name, rank and serial number.

He reeled slightly when he got to his feet, cramped from his position in the chair and a little giddy from his hours without food or sleep.

Byrd and Moran were talking when he rejoined them. Probably about him, Lang thought.

"How'd it go, Steve?" Byrd asked.

"Nothing to it," Lang replied nonchalantly. "All I told 'em was name, rank and serial number."

"Good."

"You get a cigarette?" Moran said.

"Yeah."

He took it out of his pocket and handed it Moran.

"Good going," Moran said.

"Did anybody fall for that line about next of kin?" Byrd asked.

Moran and Lang exchanged glances.

"What do you mean?" Moran asked.

"They try to get the name and address before your next of kin get the official notice. They can use it for propaganda and getting information out of your folks."

"You never told us that," Lang protested.

"Darn it, I said just name, rank and serial number."

"I told 'em, too," said Moran. "I thought the old bastard was just being nice. He said they'd let my old man know I was okay."

The words, "old man," gave Lang a guilty feeling. He wondered if what he had said in the colonel's office had told them what group he was in. But hell, they knew anyway. They knew it had to be a picture of the group commander. Unless they'd really fallen for his story about it being the sergeant's father. That had been a pretty clever thing to say on the spur of the moment like that. He wondered if he should tell Byrd about it. No. Jaybird would just find fault with him.

"From now on just name, rank and serial number," Byrd ordered. "Understand?"

Moran put the cigarette Lang had given him in his mouth, then behind his ear.

"I was so hungry the cigarette they gave me in there made me drunk as a fool," he said.

"What they trying to do, starve us to death?" Lang said angrily. "That colonel said they were going to treat us good."

"This is a heck of a note," Byrd said, getting to his feet.

He went to the door and threw it open. The soldier guarding it came to attention.

"We want food," Byrd demanded, pointing to his open mouth. "Something to eat."

The guard spoke to a passing soldier, who hurried off and returned with the interpreter.

"You wish something, gentlemen?" he asked.

"We want something to eat," said Byrd curtly. "We haven't eaten in twenty-four hours."

"Thirty-one," Lang corrected.

The interpreter's face fell.

"But this is unthinkable," he said.

He went to the door and spoke to the guard.

"You will have food," he said when he returned. "Only do not expect so much as in your own country. We are poor in Italy."

"Why does a country so poor make war on a country so rich?" said Moran.

32

The interpreter looked puzzled.

"That's not funny, Bernie," said Byrd. "Tell me, what happens now?"

"Two weeks of detention for . . . how do you say . . . quarantine. Then a prisoner of war camp. There you will be well treated. Italians like Americans."

A soldier brought in a wooden bowl containing a few small apples, crusty brown loaves the size of hamburger buns and slivers of cheese of a size usually seen on cocktail toothpicks. The three Americans turned to stare avidly at the food. Lang was bitterly disappointed.

"Is that all we get?" he demanded.

The interpreter sighed.

"We are a poor country," he said.

He left them and Byrd divided the food into three portions. There were seven apples, three buns and three slivers of cheese.

"Who gets the pile with three apples?" Lang asked hopefully.

Moran grinned at him.

"Let's Honest John for it," he said.

Lang scowled. Moran had taught him to Honest John his first week on the crew. There had been six of them at the makeshift bar in the officers' mess at Ramat Jonas and Moran had proposed they Honest John for the drinks. He put six numbered slips in a flight cap, the man getting the highest number to stand treat. Lang had drawn number six. He discovered later that Moran had written 6 on all the slips and the others had known it. Lang had never Honest Johned again.

"I put the smallest apples in the three pile," Byrd said patiently. "Take whichever pile you want."

Lang hesitated. The three apples were more than the two apples but you had to think about the extra core.

"God damn it, Blubberbutt!" Moran said. "Why are you always so scared of gettin' screwed? Take a friggin' pile before we starve to death."

Lang took the three apples.

They wolfed the food with ferocious intensity. They ate the apple cores and gnawed the cheese to the flinty black rind, then picked the breadcrumbs from their uniforms with dampened forefingers and licked them off. Lang, still ravenous, ate his cheese rind. Byrd put his in a tunic pocket. Moran studied his cheese rind thoughtfully.

"Very rich Americans," he said, and put it in his pocket.

A crowd had gathered around the police van when they emerged from the building, frayed old men and stringy women in dark shapeless dresses. They moved forward and set up a cry at the appearance of the Americans.

"They're cheering us," Lang said incredulously.

The crowd surged toward them and the soldiers pushed through it, closing around the Americans. The civilians hissed. Some shook fists. Lang thought they were mad at the soldiers for shoving them around. A wrinkled little woman carrying a string bag slipped by a soldier and spat at Moran. Then Lang knew the civilians were not cheering them and he tried to hide behind a soldier half his size. He scrambled into the van first. As the van moved off, honking, the hissing and threats increased in volume and pebbles rattled off its sides.

They were all very quiet for several minutes.

Moran looked at the saliva still dribbling down his blouse.

"Ah, yes," he said ruefully. "Italians like Americans."

CHAPTER 3

It was not yet dawn when they reached the quarantine prison. They had left a train in a lonely station, and, unobservant as sleepwalkers, climbed into a collapsing bus that pitched and creaked over a rutty back road. It labored grimly up hills and along walled lanes, the rheumy headlights picking out skeletal branches thrusting from ghostly trees. The illusion that they were descending deeper and deeper into nowhere troubled Lang's apathy. The others slept.

They dismounted in a chilly, damp courtyard paved with brick, their breath pluming in the cold.

"Hey, Blubber," Moran said, yawning, "where the hell are we?"

Lang was irritated that Moran expected him to know

but flattered, too. The stars were clear and frostily bright but even his favorite star, Polaris, more brilliant than he had ever seen it before, told him nothing.

"About a hundred miles from Rome," he said, guessing wildly. "Southeast."

They were led into a long, deserted and dimly lit hall. The empty dimness, the unrelieved masonry walls and the clatter of a guard's hobnailed boots on the stone floor were ominous to Lang. His foreboding intensified as they went deeper into the building, up and down short flights of worn stairs through a maze of halls in which he saw no other beings.

They entered a small, disordered office. At the back was a plain wooden desk covered with neat piles of documents. Behind the desk, his hairy big-knuckled hands palms down before him, sat a gaunt Italian with deep-set eyes and an air of grave concern. There was a fresh razor nick on the angle of his long jaw, as if he had just shaved. Though his uniform was the ordinary serge of an enlisted man it fitted as if tailored.

Their escorting officer gave him their papers and, pointing in turn at the prisoners, standing in line like schoolboys called to the principal's office, said, "Capitano, tenente, tenente."

"Capitano, tenente, tenente," the seated man repeated, looking from Byrd to Moran to Lang.

They did not respond in any way. It had happened too many times before in too many places on too little food and sleep. The escorting officer shook hands with the man behind the desk and left them. They did not say good-bye or even look his way. When he was gone it was as if he had never existed.

The Italian leaned back in his chair and studied them at his leisure. The square of darkness in the window behind him was fading to gray.

"Capitano, tenente, tenente," he said in a low voice, as if establishing their identities for all time. Raising his voice to conversational level, he said in a careful, rehearsed manner, "You will remain here a short time only. You will be treated with full courtesy. Military discipline is observable at all times."

This ignited a spark of interest in Byrd, who pulled himself erect with excruciating effort. The Italian noted it with approval.

"Military courtesies are also observable," he continued. "I am maresciallo. You must salute when you enter into my office."

He waited a moment and when there was no response said kindly but firmly, "Please to salute now."

They stared at him blankly, then Byrd said, "Oh."

He saluted, followed raggedly by Moran and Lang. The maresciallo returned the salutes with grave courtesy.

"Excellent," he said. "You will have good care here. That is my promise. But you must obey all rules. Now you will be taken to your quarters. Good morning, my gentlemen. Please to sleep well."

He summoned a soldier who, surly and still half asleep, led them to a hall lined with heavy doors in another wing of the building.

He unlocked one and stood aside, saying, "Capitano?"

Byrd stepped forward. The soldier motioned to him to enter. When Moran and Lang moved to follow the soldier shook his head violently and barred their way with a stubby arm. He banged the door shut, locked it and, after looking in on Byrd through a peephole with a sliding cover, conducted them to the next door. Lang went inside without being bidden. Moran waited stolidly for the soldier to close the door behind Lang. Instead of doing so the soldier pushed Moran after him.

"Hey," Moran protested, torn out of his stupor. "Don't I rate a room of my own?"

His last words were spoken to the door. A key turned

in the lock, a small aperture appeared in the door, an eye gleamed, the aperture closed and footsteps clicked down the hall. Moran looked glumly at Lang.

"If it ain't bad enough to be a prisoner, I had to draw you for a roommate."

Lang did not answer. He was looking around the room. The sun had risen, bathing the room in cheery light. It was clean and contained two substantial beds, two chairs and a desk. His sense of foreboding vanished.

Moran stripped back the heavy blanket covering the bed nearest the window. Lang held back the protest which sprang to his lips. He had wanted the bed by the window.

"Jesus," Moran cried. "Real sheets."

He sat down on the bed to remove his shoes and sank into a soft mattress.

"And a real mattress!"

He massaged his feet, sighing.

"I been wanting to do that all night," he said gratefully.

Lang was suddenly aware that his own feet itched maddeningly and he sat down on the other bed. For a moment he forgot his feet. He could not recall ever having felt such luxurious softness before.

Moran stripped quickly to his underwear and slipped between the sheets. He gasped.

"Cold as a well-digger's ass in Butte, Montana," he cried, gingerly stretching out full length.

Lang unlaced his shoes with clumsy, unresponsive fingers and began rubbing his feet. The rough material of his socks chafed and he took them off. His toes were mottled with red and white patches.

"Moran," he called, frightened. "Something's wrong with my feet."

But Moran was already asleep.

With an angry look at him, Lang pulled the socks back over his burning feet, took off his uniform and slid, shivering, into bed. The sheets were icy and his teeth chattered. After a few minutes he felt warmer. He fell asleep thinking, If the food matches the beds, this place won't be so bad. Except I got Moran for a roommate.

They were in quarantine for more than two weeks, during which they followed a routine which seldom varied. Early every morning the surly guard who had first shown them to their rooms would pound the door until it rattled, inspect them from the peephole and conduct them, one at a time, to the incredibly foul lavatory with a seatless toilet and a grimy washbasin which was their only bathing facility.

Later they were brought hot water by a muscular little soldier who came banging down the hall shouting "Acqua calda" in a stentorian but not unmusical voice. With the water they brewed tea, using a scrap torn from their underwear as a tea bag. The tea came from a Canadian Red Cross parcel issued to them with quiet pride by the maresciallo. None of them had known such things were provided for prisoners of war and they were moved by the kindness of the maresciallo and the Canadian Red Cross.

Twice a day they were brought food by the same merry little man, a ladleful of thick hot vegetable soup in which a scrap of meat floated occasionally, a slice of coarse bread, a sliver of cheese and a dab of boiled greens. Occasionally, after a few moments of tantalizing hesitation, the guard would give them extra soup. Moran had a way of coaxing him which Lang envied but could not duplicate. He would sidle up to the guard, who was shorter than he but proportionately broad, get the little man to flex his arm and then feel his bicep admiringly. The guard would test Moran's bicep in turn. His admiration was profound and sincere. Sometimes when he knew Moran was watching he would do acrobatics on a horizontal iron bar beside a bocce court under their window where the off-duty guards bowled and argued endlessly. Moran would applaud.

The third guard they saw regularly was a middle-aged

man with a seamed, kindly face, who took a fatherly interest in them. He would often come into the room at mealtime and tell them the Italian names for what they were eating. Almost as often he would then walk around the room telling the Italian names for the furniture and for objects visible through the window. Neither Lang nor Moran learned much from him, though out of courtesy they pretended interest. They were never able to decide what his exact duties were but because, unlike the other two, he carried a rifle slung over his shoulder, assumed he was supposed to see that they did not escape.

Moran named him Pop. He called the surly guard Mac-Nasty and the merry one Laughing Boy. Lang liked everything about the names except the fact that Moran had thought them up.

Once they had arisen for the day they were obliged to make their beds and were not allowed to lie in them until it was time to retire for the night. Moran often ignored this rule, as he did others, including not urinating out of the window when the night guard did not come to let him out quickly enough. The surly guard, MacNasty, would tiptoe along the hall to their door, stealthily open the peephole and, if he found Moran lying on the bed, fling the door open and fill the air with threats and curses.

Moran would grin and say, "Same to you, Mac."

They visited the maresciallo's office two or three times a week, occasionally encountering Byrd there. There was always a good deal of business to transact in the office and the maresciallo permitted them only a minimum of conversation with one another. He issued them cigarettes at the rate of five a day per man from a tin box he kept locked in his desk, books from a fifteen-volume library which he explained with glowing pride he had assembled on his own initiative, and food from their Red Cross parcels, which he also kept locked away. They had to sign for everything with a dip pen which he cleaned meticulously after every use. On their first visit Moran and Lang forgot to salute and, somewhat aggrieved, he reminded them that military courtesies were observable.

They discovered later that *maresciallo* meant warrant officer. Warrant officers did not rate salutes from officers and Lang was indignant. Moran was amused.

On fair days they were allowed a half-hour constitutional in a neglected back garden from which, over a low stone wall where lizards sometimes played in the December sun, they could see a long vista of green valleys and hazy mountains. Lang spent much of this period on a concrete bench, basking and exposing his toes, now covered with chilblains, to the sun. Moran's feet no longer bothered him and he walked up and down furiously, looking caged and impatient. He was penalized one outdoor period for speaking to Byrd, who chanced to be exercising at the same time. Prisoners were forbidden to speak to each other unless they roomed together.

There were no bathing facilities for prisoners, the only water available being that brought to them hot by the guard they called Laughing Boy and the trickle from the tap in the noisome lavatory, at which they washed their hands, faces and eating utensils. One morning Moran requisitioned the hot water over Lang's protests and bathed from his soup dish, using his undershirt as a washcloth. Rid of his own aroma, he found Lang's offensive and insisted that Lang do the same next day. Afterward, Lang was glad he had done so but would not admit it to Moran.

Their second day in quarantine Laughing Boy brought them extra hot water, a battered safety razor, a blade spotted with rust or blood, a molting shaving brush and a flinty piece of soap. Lang rushed to be first to use the razor but the dull blade pulled so painfully at his five-day beard that he surrendered the equipment to Moran after one tentative stroke. Moran shaved recklessly, cursing and shifting his weight from one foot to the other. When Laughing Boy returned for the equipment and found Lang still unshaved he grew angry and shouted at him. The din brought first MacNasty and then Pop running to the room and in the end Lang was forced to shave.

Moran drew up a chair and watched. Lang shaved as recklessly as Moran had done, determined not to add to Moran's amusement by showing pain. Despite the dullness of the blade he managed to cut his face in several places. Moran applauded when he finished. Lang turned his back on him.

"Maybe I'll ask Jaybird to put you in for that Purple Heart you been bucking for, Blubber," Moran said.

You think you're so damn funny, Lang thought.

The same day they were given a sheet of paper and an envelope for letters home. Lang wrote his letter with extreme care. He did not want his parents to be needlessly alarmed yet he wanted them, and through them everyone he knew in Houston, to know just how rough and heroic it was to be a prisoner of war. And he wanted to sound brave and cheerful while making it abundantly clear it took a special breed of man to be so under such trying circumstances. The maresciallo gave them stamps, for which they were required to sign his ledger.

From time to time they were visited by Sergente Roberto Tedesco, who implored them to call him Bob. Tedesco, he explained with some embarrassment, meant German in Italian and he did not like Germans. They would not have known he was Italian had he not been in uniform. He could easily have been an American, a rather carefully educated one, for his English was unaccented. He was tall and broad-shouldered, as Americans were supposed to be, and had fair hair.

Tedesco did not get along too well with Moran, who called him a stool pigeon and threatened to throw him out of the room, but he seemed to take an almost instant liking to Lang. Lang was immensely flattered by this. He could not recall anyone ever having taken an instant liking to him. It was true Tedesco asked a lot of questions about B-24 production and bombing techniques but even Moran admitted he never pressed for the answers, or seemed particularly interested in

42

the subject. He appeared far more interested in matters of a more personal nature. Was it true an ordinary workingman in the United States could have his own house, an automobile, a radio and a machine for washing clothes? What was the cost of a small apartment in Houston, how many suits of clothes did Lang own, did American girls like Italian men and did Lang think after the war an Italian would be unpopular in America? Moran would not discuss even these innocent topics with him, so Lang had Tedesco's exclusive attention.

Byrd intercepted Lang outside the maresciallo's office one day and dressed him down for talking with Tedesco. He had seen the two of them from his window laughing and talking in the garden.

"I don't tell him any military secrets," Lang protested. "Mostly I just tell him about home and he tells me about when he was manager of the Excelsior Hotel in Rome before the war."

"Darn it, Steve," Byrd said severely, "how can you be so dumb? Don't you know he's picking up dope to help him pass for an American? And he's lying about being manager of a big hotel. He's too young."

Lang did not believe that Tedesco was pumping him for information for any motive other than a personal interest in America and he did not mind if Tedesco had lied about his civilian station in life. He had exaggerated his own civilian accomplishments a bit in their conversations. But he was careful after that not to speak with Tedesco where Byrd might see them.

Having Moran for a roommate was the only thing which Lang found really oppressive about the quarantine prison. Though he was confined to one room except for walks in the garden and occasional visits to the maresciallo's office or the lavatory, he did not find the confinement particularly unpleasant. He had no duties or obligations and no one to answer to. The maresciallo treated him with the same grave courtesy he showed Byrd and Moran and Tedesco regarded him as a gallant airman and supreme authority on America and, even more satisfying, preferred his company to Moran's. Though there was never enough food, he liked what there was and even welcomed the chance to lose a few pounds, something he had never been able to do on willpower alone. He would have liked occasionally to soak in a hot tub but it was a luxury he could live without, and he preferred not bathing at all to taking cold showers, which he had been obliged to do at Ramat Jonas. His chilblains itched but this would have been so anywhere and here he could sit and nurse them as much as he pleased without being accused of pampering himself or trying to avoid combat missions.

And he had his simple pleasures, few enough but sufficient to help him pass his days tolerably except for Moran's abrasive presence. There was tea to brew in the morning and lunch and dinner to be eaten. There was Bob to talk with. There were books to read, though he was not overly fond of reading and the maresciallo's scrappy library offered little inducement to change. He could watch the off-duty guards bowl in the bocce court beneath his window and listen to them sing. And he could daydream as much as he liked. Best of all, he could daydream.

Daydreams had been a refuge since childhood. When things went badly they could be altered in the boundless privacy of his mind. His aspirations could be realized there and his desires satisfied. And in them he was liked.

In his daydreams he was not overweight, but lean. And no one dared or wanted to call him Blubberbutt. Tex, perhaps. In them he did everything well, not just navigate a B-24. It was he who had scornfully thrust a life vest at Moran, and he, not Moran, who had saved Byrd, and he, not Byrd, who had seen that Junior Smith was tended to, who was insolent in the face of danger and resolute in adversity. And he who would devise an escape plan, part cold cunning and part reckless daring, which would free them all from this place despite the guard in the hall and the one on the roof they could hear stamping his numb feet at night, and lead them to an airfield and steal a plane and navigate them all to LG 139 and a hero's welcome.

And he at whom Bella Ragatsa had smiled in the station at Salerno and who had eager girl friends in Los Angeles and Lakeland and Haifa and that tall nurse in Cairo. And Serena the Butterfly Girl. Especially Serena the Butterfly Girl because Moran had not had her first or ever. All Moran ever had to do with her was the note he had sent backstage to her at the Haifa nightclub where she danced, signing Lang's name to it to embarrass him. And it had embarrassed him when she came to their table, not wearing the gauze wings from her act or bathed in the changing colored lights now but unbelievably beautiful and desirable anyway, embarrassed him so that he had blushed and stammered and they had all laughed at him. Even Serena. But she had not laughed unkindly and had turned the tables on Moran by telling Lang how much she appreciated the way he risked his life every day in the air as she could tell from his wings and all, and how much she regretted she could not accept his thoughtful invitation to have a drink with him because her brother, who was her partner, was very strict about such things, and how she hoped he would always stay as sweet and shy as he was right then. And then she had kissed him on the cheek.

That part was not daydream, nor the way the lights reflected in her sparkling black eyes and shimmered on her gauzy wings when she danced, as agonizingly beautiful and ethereal as a real butterfly. But the part that was daydream was better.

He dreamed it now. He had not gone to the nightclub with Moran and Bertram but alone. And no note had been sent backstage. Serena, whirling, dipping and floating in her wings of gauze, splashed with colored lights, saw him sitting alone, alone as an eagle, his sweetness and shyness shining in his face, and had been drawn irresistibly to him as he to her, and there was no strict brother, only Serena the Butterfly Girl and Steven the Eagle, and she took his hand and led him from the nightclub to the beach, lapped with the silken waves of the Mediterranean and bleached by moonlight, and they walked, hand in warm hand, nearer to floating than to walking, she in her wings of gauze, he with his wings of silver until, without speaking or even thinking they sank to the soft, warm, gently hissing sand and kissed, ever so gently, and . . .

And Moran's hateful voice split the dream and let in a world that was only one cold room with a locked door and a barred window.

"Hey, Blubber, four bits says I can guess what's on your mind. You got a hard on big as my arm."

Lang looked at him, one long, hard, hurt and murderous look, then slowly turned his face to the ceiling.

I hate you, Moran, talking dirty about something beautiful but you wouldn't understand because you think all girls are alike and just for one thing, and taking my cigarettes just like you had a right to them even if you do let me have extra Klim from the Red Cross parcel, and making me read the maresciallo's bum books when I don't want to just so you can have somebody to talk to about them, and getting the extra soup from Laughing Boy and always making fun of me and never being afraid of anything and the girls always liking you and everybody always liking you and why don't you just leave me alone.

Tears, shameful and unpreventable, squeezed from his eyes and slid across his face.

Now he'll really make fun of me, Lang thought wildly, why did I have to do that, that's all he wants, for me to act like a baby so he can pick on me some more.

"Hey, Blubber, what's the matter?" Moran said, puzzled and concerned.

Lang did not answer. He raised an arm, hiding his face and wiping away the tears with his shoulder.

"I didn't mean to . . . Hell, there ain't nothing wrong with having a hard on. I've had one on since we got here."

46

Lang looked at him again.

"Why don't you just leave me alone?" he said tightly.

"Okay, okay. Don't get your bowels in an uproar."

That night when Laughing Boy gave Moran extra soup he shared it with Lang and not until next day did he say anything at which Lang could take offense. And not once did he say anything about having seen Lang cry.

They were allowed to spend Christmas Eve with Byrd, who was so grateful not to be alone that he hugged them both. Lang was stirred deeply by this, not merely because Byrd for the first time had displayed any affection for him but also because of the revelation that Byrd, even Jaybird the brave, the unshakable, the good soldier, could know loneliness.

"Am I glad to see you jokers!" Byrd said.

They saw each other regularly, in the garden or in the maresciallo's office, but Lang knew what he meant. Being together, not seeing. Because now, for the first time since he joined Byrd's crew, he and Jaybird, and Moran, were truly together.

Their dinner was brought to Byrd's room and in addition to double portions there was a special Christmas ration of boiled chestnuts, tangerines and a tall bottle of thin red wine. Moran did not like the chestnuts, which had the texture and taste of wet sawdust, and gave his portion to Lang without being asked, and without offering them to Byrd first. There were two tangerines each. Lang resolutely did not compare the sizes of his portion and the others'.

After dinner they played hearts for a while with a deck of worn cards Moran had signed for in the maresciallo's office. Byrd joined with Lang to catch Moran with the Widow, the queen of spades, and Moran cursed them both with impartial gusto. For half an hour or so they laughed and made jokes, then Byrd, and after him Moran, fell silent and moody. Lang, exhilarated by the wine and camaraderie, looked from one to the other, puzzled and dismayed by the end of laughter, wanting desperately to hang on to it but not knowing how.

"Hell," said Moran, throwing down his cards. "Let's quit."

"Okay with me," Byrd said.

"Aw, fellas," Lang protested. "That's not fair. Just when I'm going for the Widow and all the hearts."

"Okay, Blubber," Moran said. "You win. Me and Jaybird get stuck with twenty-six points apiece."

"But I don't want to win," Lang said desperately. "I want to *play*."

"I really don't feel like it any more," Byrd said apologetically.

Bursting with unspoken protest, Lang watched Moran gather the cards and square them into a deck with the dexterity of a gambler.

Byrd lay on the bed, folded his hands behind his head and looked up at the ceiling. Moran put his hands in his pockets and stared morosely out the window. Lang sat where he was, trying to think of something to say which would help recapture the earlier mood. But nothing came to him.

"I wish Hal was here," Byrd said. "Hal and the others."

"Yeah," Moran said, turning from the window. "He was a great guy."

"He sure was," Lang said, for the moment really believing it though Bertram had despised him and he had hated Bertram for that.

"What I wish is, the whole damn bunch of us was back at Kabrit instead of this God damn dump," Moran said.

Kabrit was their permanent base on the Suez Canal. They had moved there from Ramat Jonas in Palestine.

"I guess Flora'll have the tree decorated and everything," Byrd said with a sigh. "And the baby's asleep."

Lang looked at his watch. It was ten-fifteen but seemed much later.

"Unh unh," he said. "It's not but two o'clock in New Mexico right now."

48

"Blubber, how you figure that stuff out in your head like that?" Moran asked admiringly.

Lang shrugged, cloaking his pride with diffidence.

"You know what I told Colonel Pizer?" Byrd said, sitting up. "I told him you were the best darn navigator in the group."

"You did?" Lang said, blooming.

"Hey," Moran said, holding up his hand. "Listen."

Down the hall a British Lancaster crew was singing "Sixpence."

The three of them crowded around the window, listening. The words were different from those they had learned in the cadets, obscene.

"They shouldn't use that kind of language," Byrd said. "Not Christmas Eve."

"I kind of like the English translation," Moran said.

When the song ended, Moran said, "Let's us give them one," and began singing "Home on the Range." It was a song the crew of the *High Flying Flora* often sang over the interphone on the way back from a mission.

They stood in the window, arms around shoulders. This is great, Lang thought, singing at the top of his voice, his eyes shining.

The inside guard, who was a little drunk, watched them through the peephole as they sang and the outside guard stopped his pacing and looked up. On any other night they would have ordered silence, as they often did with the noisy British, but tonight they did nothing.

When the song ended the British applauded and one of them sang a dirty limerick.

When he finished, Moran sang one. For several minutes they sang dirty limericks to one another, their voices resonant in the frosty night. Byrd sang a clean one when his turn came around. There was silence again for a minute, and Byrd said, "I know what. How about 'Silent Night'?"

He began singing. Moran and Lang joined him, and then the British. Midway a new voice intruded, stronger, richer, more musical, and Italian. It was the outside guard. The prisoners stopped their own singing to listen.

"Jesus Christ, that's pretty," Moran whispered.

Lang wanted to cry.

When the guard finished no one said anything. They looked at each other. The evening was over. Moran took out a cigarette and opened the window to drop it to the guard.

"Merry Christmas!" he shouted.

The guard began yelling threats and snatched his rifle from his shoulder. Prisoners were not allowed to open their windows after dark. Moran dropped the cigarette at his feet.

"Merry Christmas anyway, you little bastard," he yelled cheerily, and slammed the window shut.

The inside guard unlocked the door and motioned that it was time to leave. They shook hands.

"Maybe next Christmas . . ." Byrd said, not finishing, not having to.

"I sure as hell hope so, Jaybird," said Moran. "Come on, Steve."

He called me Steve, Lang thought.

He could not remember ever having been so happy before, or so sad.

Back in the room, as a special concession to the season, Moran let Lang eat a heaping spoonful of powdered milk from their one-pound can of Klim. Lang had grown very fond of it and had promised himself when he got home he would always have a can around. Powdered milk tasted to him like the Horlick's malted milk tablets his mother had given him for a while instead of candy when he was a child and the family doctor told her he should lose weight. He had lost none but he had learned to like malted milk tablets.

Now, in bed, with the dissolving powdered milk like a ball of putty in his mouth, he thought of Horlick's and his parents and home with exquisite nostalgia. It was only his second Christmas away from home. The first had been at navigation school in Georgia. It was right after Pearl Harbor and there was no Christmas leave but his parents had come to visit him. He yearned for Christmas at home, the tree, the stocking, the presents, fireworks.

He got up on his elbow.

"Hey, Moran, you know what?" he called across the room. "I wish we had us some firecrackers."

Moran, who had been drifting into sleep in the arms of Zelda Yelkin, whose rent he had paid in Haifa when the group was based at Ramat Jonas, opened his eyes resentfully.

"Firecrackers?" he said incredulously.

"Yeah. Back home we always shoot firecrackers on Christmas Eve. It just don't seem like Christmas without 'em."

"Jesus Christ!" Moran cried derisively.

He turned over on his face and pulled the pillow over his head in an emphatic gesture of rejection. Lang was deeply hurt. For Moran to be like that after acting so nice all evening. Christmas Eve was absolutely ruined.

Two days after the New Year they were told to prepare to leave for their permanent camp in one hour. They assembled in the maresciallo's office to go over their accounts.

"Accounts?" Moran demanded when the maresciallo got out his ledger. "You mean we have to pay a bill like this is a hotel?"

The maresciallo explained that as prisoners of war they received pay equal to that of Italian officers of the same rank. Lang and Moran were entitled to nine hundred and fifty lire a month, equivalent to perhaps forty-five dollars, and Byrd somewhat more.

"It is not given to you in the hand. It is placed to your account. Please to examine and say if all is not correct."

They found they had been paying for their cigarettes, extra bread, the razor and soap with which they shaved, Moran's deck of cards and even the Christmas wine, chestnuts and tangerines. Lang wondered if Moran intended paying him back for the cigarettes. If I'd known I had to pay for them I never would have taken them, he thought, feeling swindled.

He remembered there were still a few spoonfuls of Klim in the bottom of the can back in the room, all that remained of the eleven-pound Red Cross parcel. He told the maresciallo he had forgotten something and asked permission to return for it. The maresciallo sent Tedesco with him.

Lang ate the powdered milk faster than he liked — he preferred letting it dissolve voluptuously on his tongue — and asked Tedesco to let him into Byrd's room. He found Byrd had left not only powdered milk but also a blackening half inch of corned beef in the bottom of a tin. Tedesco waited while he ate it. There was a little tea left and Lang gave it to him.

"Don't tell the maresciallo," Tedesco begged. "He said if he catches us with any Red Cross goods he'll send us to the Russian front."

On the way back to the office he said shyly, "I've taken down your address, Stefano. After the war I'll write to you and we can be pals. Okay?"

"You bet," said Lang.

He could not remember the last time anyone had wanted to be pals with him.

Tedesco rode to the station with them. Before Lang climbed aboard he shook Tedesco's hand and said, "Don't forget to write."

Moran burst into laughter.

"Jesus, that was funny, Blubber," he said admiringly, when they were inside the car. "And you never even cracked a smile."

CHAPTER 4

Lang squirmed on the hard bench between Byrd and Moran. They were always being left somewhere in the middle of the night without anything to eat or a place to sleep, he thought. Across the depot office from him their guard slept on another bench, flat on his back, his carbine clutched to his breast. A corporal stamped and sorted papers at a desk and an iron stove burned cheerily in the corner.

Lang dozed.

Moran awakened and lit a cigarette.

"Hey, Blubber," he said in a low voice.

"Huh?" Lang grunted, swimming up through a murk of sleep.

Moran inclined his head toward the sleeping guard.

"Watch that guy," he whispered. "He's playing possum."

"What are you talking about?" Lang demanded peevishly.

"That little bastard over there. He's just waiting for everybody to fall asleep so he can escape. Somebody better stay up and watch him."

The corporal looked up from his paperwork and, seeing them whispering and studying the sleeping guard, shifted warily.

"If he starts for the door, trip him," Moran said.

"Cut it out," Lang said. "I'm sleepy."

Just because you can't sleep, he thought. You're not half as funny as you think you are, Moran. He closed his eyes again but could not sleep. His feet itched maddeningly. He went to sit on the floor by the stove and tore off his shoes and socks. Moran raised his head and sniffed the air.

"Who died?" he said.

Lang scowled and massaged his toes. The corporal took a little round can from his desk and brought it to Lang. Lang drew back suspiciously from the black, foul-smelling contents. The corporal dragged his chair up and, as if to reassure Lang, removed his shoes and socks and smeared his own mottled toes with the ointment.

"Buon'," he said.

Lang rubbed the ointment on his feet. The itching stopped. The corporal motioned Lang to keep the can.

"Gratsey," said Lang.

"Prego," the corporal said. "Parla Italiano?"

Lang shook his head.

"Look out, Blubber," Moran called. "He's in with the guard. He's trying to get on your good side."

"Why don't you just shut up?" Lang demanded.

Byrd awakened. He stretched, breaking the gesture abruptly when his gaze fell on the bare feet of Lang and the Italian.

54

"What's going on?" he said.

The corporal put his shoes back on and Lang did the same. It was light outside now. Lang was ravenous. He wondered how long it was until breakfast. And still their guard slept.

Before long their officer escort of the previous night came for them, shaved, rested and looking as if he had enjoyed a good breakfast. He awakened the guard by kicking the bench and jerking a thumb at the Americans.

"Andiamo," he said.

"You son of a bitch," Moran said, standing up with a groan. "I bet your ass didn't grind a hard bench all night."

Lang gave the corporal a shy wave of farewell.

"Arrivederci," the corporal said. "Buona fortuna."

"Hey, Blubber," said Moran. "Tell him to write."

The cobbled streets still glistened with the night's rain but the sky had cleared. A couple of hundred yards up the street was a stone church streaked with years and rain. The officer began running in place and motioning for them to follow him.

"He wants to show us up," Byrd said. "He knows we're beat."

"Screw him," Moran said. "I wouldn't run to catch the next plane to L.A."

The officer ran nimbly backward a few steps, coaxing them.

"Shucks," said Byrd. "Let's take him up on it."

He began running with a fluid sprinter's stride, splashing in the puddles. The officer whirled and ran after him.

"Come on, Blubber," Moran yelled, following them.

Lang hesitated, looking at the guard. The guard shrugged. Lang ran after Moran. His feet were burning again and he was tired but he did not want to be left behind. The guard, finding himself abandoned, ran after Lang, his short legs churning, his rifle swinging.

Seeing Byrd was pulling away, the officer quit skirting

the puddles to splash recklessly through them. Moran was like a charging bull at his heels, laughing and whooping. Lang lumbered after them, his shoes slipping on the cobbles. The little guard passed him. Lang ran faster. He could not be last. Moran would never let him forget it if the tiny Italian beat him.

He ran with his head down. He heard feet pounding, and Moran's wild shouts. With a burst of speed, Moran passed the officer and Byrd, reached the church, stopped and leaned against the wall, laughing and panting. Byrd was next, and then the officer. The Italian tried to keep from panting, his eyes bulging with the effort.

The guard was a few steps ahead of Lang, and Moran shouted, "Come on, Blubber, you can beat him!"

Lang groaned. He felt as if a fist were clutching his windpipe. His feet burned and his eyes were misted with tears. He threw his head back and gasped for air like a fish. Damn Moran, damn that Italian bastard, damn everybody. He was going to come in last, he knew it. He always came in last. He put all his strength into one agonizing burst and passed the guard.

Not last.

"I knew you could do it, Blubber," Moran cried, pumping his hand.

Blood sang in his ears, like a crowd cheering. But his shoes were filled with live coals and the fist clenched tighter on his throat. I'm suffocating, he thought wildly, I'm going to die. He leaned forward, retching. Moran held his head.

"You'll be okay, Blubber," he said. "You're just winded."

The fist eased its grip. Why can't Moran be like this all the time? Lang thought. Why did you have to be in trouble before he'd quit picking on you?

Lang looked up. The officer was watching him, grinning with malicious pleasure. Lang pulled away from Moran's supporting arms and drew himself erect.

"Yeah," he gasped. "Winded is all."

The officer's breeches and shoes were splashed with mud.

Lang was glad.

He was breathing normally by the time they reached the heavy wooden gates of the prisoner of war camp. It was on a stony meadow a quarter mile beyond the station and several hundred yards removed from any other habitation or ground cover, fronting on the road. The camp was surrounded by a thick, ten-foot wall over which peeped the tops of flat-roofed buildings. The camp was girt on three sides by a seven-foot barbed-wire fence ending at the road. Wooden sentry boxes were spaced on top of the wall.

Inside the camp another wall, seven feet high, divided the interior. A paved street led from the gates through which Lang's group had entered to another set of gates in the interior wall. On either side of the street was an ell-shaped building, one with washing flapping on a line outside, the other with a pole flying the Italian flag.

The officer hustled the Americans into the building with the flagpole and along a tiled hall to a room containing a black iron stove, a plain desk and two straight chairs. He gave their papers to a stocky black-haired sergeant behind the desk. As soon as he left, the sergeant sprang to his feet, smiling, and approached them with outstretched hands. His nose was slightly askew, giving his homeliness an engaging quality, and his hair was cut short, American style. He had a gold-capped tooth which glistened in the overhead light.

"Welcome to P.G. 203," he said, his accent American.

He seized Lang's unresisting hand and pumped it.

"Not that I like to see our guys in a fix like this but as long as you gotta be in the bag this is the best place for it."

"Who the hell are you?" Moran demanded.

"Mike Pellini. Just call me sarge."

"You American or Italian?" said Byrd.

"American. Just like you guys."

"Then what are you doing in that uniform?" Byrd asked, coldly suspicious.

Pellini laughed.

"You got one on, too," he said.

"You know what I mean," Byrd said, not smiling.

"I was only kidding. The Eyties claim I'm an Eytie because my folks were born over here. You ever hear such a crock? I was over here on a visit when the war started and it was join their army or go to jail."

"What they give you to eat here, Sarge?" Lang said.

"Well, it ain't no Howard Johnson but they do the best they can. Now before I take you in to the colonel I'll give you guys the gen. The dope," he added, seeing they did not understand.

"Sergeant," Byrd said. "Don't you know that an American sergeant doesn't call officers 'you guys'?"

"Okay, if you want to be like that," Pellini said, hurt. "I'm just so damn glad to see Americans. This place is mostly limey. Okay? Colonel Malvi's a right guy. Rugged but right. When we go in, I holler attention and you all salute him. Okay?"

He led them to another office, knocked once and ushered them in.

"Attention!" he bawled.

Colonnello Malvi was a middle-sized round man with spectacles and thin dark hair combed carefully across his bald crown. He put down the pipe he was smoking and stood up behind his ornate desk, smiling cordially. The smile vanished abruptly. He began shouting wrathfully and flinging his arms, his tirade growing increasingly shrill. Pellini leaned back apprehensively, though remaining at attention. Lang was frightened, too. Colonnello Malvi dismissed them with a furious wave of his arm.

"Wow," Pellini said, wiping his brow in an exaggerated

gesture of relief when he had closed the door behind them.

"What was that all about?" Byrd demanded.

"He's sore because your uniforms ain't marked to show you're P.G.s," he said, conducting them back to his office.

"It wasn't our fault," said Lang, defensively.

"He ain't mad at you, Lieutenant. He's mad at the dopes gave you the uniforms."

Pellini turned apologetically to Byrd.

"You're gonna have to take 'em off so we can mark 'em. The colonel says you gotta be searched, too."

They stripped naked and Pellini went off with their uniforms, leaving them with two soldiers who searched them head to toe, examining all orifices. Byrd hid his compass under his tongue. When the search was completed they were given blankets and left with a single guard. They huddled around the ineffectual iron stove. Moran held out his blanket-draped arms.

"Right back where we were the first day," he said. "Now some joker's gonna come in and want to know why a country so rich makes war on a country so poor."

He touched the stove gingerly.

"I pee hotter than this," he complained.

He flicked the stove door open and stuffed in coal briquettes from a small pile beside it. The guard watched in silence. The stove was radiating heat when Pellini returned with the uniforms. He scowled at the guard.

"This dope waste my coal?" he demanded. "I just get so much a week and it's gotta last."

"I wasn't watching, Sarge," said Moran.

Their uniforms had been marked with white paint, a band around the arms and legs, a circle on the back with "P.G." in the center and a smaller version of the same monogram on the left breast. Pellini explained that the P.G. stood for *prigioniero di guerra*, prisoner of war.

When he took them back to Colonel Malvi's office the

colonel smiled approvingly and shook their hands. He motioned them to stand at ease and made a well-rehearsed speech, translated by Pellini.

"The times are difficult and Italy is a poor country but you will be treated with every possible consideration. It is my attitude that you are my honored guests and if you conduct yourselves as guests you will find your detention in beautiful Italy not too unpleasant. For after all, here you are safe from war's dangers. For you the war is over."

Lang was delighted with Colonel Malvi's speech. Colonel Malvi was a nice man and Sergeant Pellini was a nice man and maybe it wasn't going to be so bad after all, just sitting out the war.

"The colonel wants to know if any of you guys collect stamps," Pellini said.

They shook their heads.

"Tough. He's got some Vatican albums he gives stamp collectors. He puts down their addresses and after the war he's gonna keep in touch. You oughta see his stamp collection."

"I'm dying to," said Moran.

Lang wished he had said he collected stamps. He would have if he had known Colonel Malvi was giving away albums.

Colonel Malvi took three flat round objects wrapped in gaudily printed silver gilt paper from a desk drawer, gave one to each of the prisoners and dismissed them with a benevolent smile. Lang unwrapped his as soon as they were out the door and, finding it was a cake with a hard white glaze of icing, devoured it on the spot. It was dry and disappointingly tasteless. The silver gilt wrapping had been cruelly deceptive.

Pellini dismissed their guard and conducted them personally to the inner gate. The soldier on duty there leaned his rifle against the wall when he opened it for them. Lang noticed Byrd's speculative look at the untended rifle and hoped his pilot was not contemplating anything rash.

The gate opened on a continuation of the street. The street passed between three pairs of substantial one-story buildings, terminating at a long boxy building at the rear of the walled compound. The broad open area between buildings, set here and there with leafless trees, was aswarm with men, some marching furiously up and down the street and others moving about with the aimlessness of waterbugs. At Pellini's appearance with the new prisoners all activity stopped and a cry went up, "Visitors!"

The men were clad in blankets and mismatched bits of British winter and summer uniforms. As they surged toward the gate, two tall men emerged from the crowd to approach the newcomers. The leaner of the two wore desert shorts, knee-length stockings and a battle dress jacket. He had a scar across his forehead and his knees were chapped. He wore the insignia of a British colonel on his shoulder tabs. The other man, heavier and softer looking, was dressed in a pair of blankets, one tied around his waist and the other clutched around his shoulders. A ruff of springy gray hair showed at the edge of his overseas cap and his shins gleamed naked and hairy between the blanket and knobby GI shoes. He clenched a curved pipe between his teeth. On his cap was a lieutenant colonel's silver leaf.

From behind the two colonels came questions and greetings.

"All right, you chaps," cried the British colonel. "No questions from the floor."

"Hi, Colonel," Pellini said ingratiatingly. "Brought you some buddies."

"Up your bloody arse, Pellini," someone called.

Pellini looked hurt.

"You've delivered them," the colonel said curtly. "Now muck off."

Pellini affected a grin.

"Be seeing you," he said, and left.

The colonel stared at the newcomers, baffled.

"Where the devil did you get those uniforms?" he demanded.

"Compliments of the management," said Moran.

"Yanks," the Englishman said. "Yours, Waterfield. Colonel Waterfield's SAO. I'm Colonel Townes-Baker, SBO."

What is he talking about? Lang wondered irritably. And when's breakfast?

"Captain Byrd, sir," Byrd said, saluting. "Lieutenant Moran, Lieutenant Lang."

"That's enough details for now," said Townes-Baker curtly. "We'll have the balance at interrogation. Milton, give me a call when you've got them sorted out."

"Come on, fellows," Waterfield said.

He reminded Lang of a scoutmaster he had once had who always called the boys fellows. The older scouts had made fun of him behind his back.

Waterfield led them into the building just inside the wall on the right and down a broad dim corridor to the last of six high-ceilinged rooms which it divided down the middle. The air inside was dank. Lang thought of the Polar Wave Ice Palace in Houston. He had only skated there once because his ankles bent and the tight laces hurt his feet. His feet were hurting now and he longed to remove his shoes and rub his toes with ointment.

The walls of the bay were lined with double-deck bunks placed end to end. By each bunk were two stools and in each half of the bay a long trestle table. Everything was of unpainted wood. The rude, simple furnishings were incongruous in the tile and plaster building, as if Waterfield's Boy Scouts were camping out in a public library.

There were twenty-three men in the room clad in blankets and United States Army uniforms except for one man in flight coveralls and another in Royal Canadian Air Force blues. Outside tall double windows overlooking a wintry courtyard a crowd had gathered and was staring in at the newcomers with good-humored interest.

"You two'll bunk there," Waterfield said to Lang and

Moran, indicating an empty frame by the corridor. "You'll bunk above me, Captain. Unless you snore."

"No, sir," said Byrd.

"Afraid I do," said Waterfield. "But RHIP."

Lang knew what that meant. Rank has its privileges. But what did SAO mean?

Waterfield put his hands on his broad hips and surveyed the jostling throng surrounding him.

"Okay," he said, the pipe still between his teeth, "who's got the bedboards?"

When there was no answer he removed the pipe and pointed it like a pistol.

"If I don't see three headboards and three full sets of bedboards in five minutes you'll all field strip your bunks for a showdown inspection. Bunch of pack rats."

He sounded exactly like Lang's scoutmaster.

There was an immediate scurry to bunks and a pile of short planks mounted on the table. Waterfield looked at his watch.

"Three minutes," he said, as if surprised to be obeyed with such alacrity. "Not bad."

Moran had been smoking. He took a deep final drag and threw the butt on the tiled floor. Everything stopped and every eye fastened on the smoldering cigarette. Lang had never seen Moran so disconcerted. Served him right, he thought, taking my cigarettes and then throwing them on the floor.

"Sorry," Moran said, retrieving the butt.

"I'm not worried about the floor," Waterfield said. "I just don't like my troops getting killed scrambling for a butt. Tobacco's the scarcest thing there is in here."

"Second scarcest," said the RCAF man.

"Sex maniac," Waterfield said. "You better save your butts, Lieutenant."

He sucked fiercely on his pipe. Lang realized for the first time there was no tobacco in it.

"Did they feed you?" Waterfield asked.

"No, sir," said Byrd.

"Not since yesterday afternoon," Lang added. "Except for the big cookie."

Everyone laughed. Lang was undecided about joining them. He was not sure who the joke was on.

"We call it Malvi's Cow Patty," Waterfield explained.

He turned with a sigh and got half a brown bun from a cardboard box under his bunk.

"Anybody else got anything for these men?" he said.

A chunky clear-skinned young man with dirty blond hair fetched a loaf somewhat larger than the colonel's.

"Where the fire you get that OR loaf?" Waterfield demanded. "If I catch you trading . . ."

The blond young man grinned in impudent silence.

"Doug Harbold, our messing officer," Waterfield said.

"Call me Dogass," said Harbold.

"This is Jaybird," Moran said. "I'm Bernie. This is Blubberbutt."

Lang scowled. Why did he have to go and tell everybody that?

Harbold sliced the bread with a sharpened table knife. Others brought oleomargarine and jam in cans.

Two identically undersized soldiers in blue coveralls came in overburdened with straw paillasses and bedding. Waterfield argued with them in a mixture of English and Italian. They shrugged and left.

"They only brought you two blankets each," Waterfield explained. "Issue's supposed to be three for men without greatcoats. I'll take it up with Captain Ribolla. Our settore officer."

After they finished eating Waterfield sent the RCAF man, Petitclerq, across the camp street to fetch Colonel Townes-Baker and conducted the newcomers to a small room at the front of the building. There was one double-deck bunk in the room, the usual table and several wooden stools. The colonel arrived shortly, accompanied by a wiry, bright-eyed English major in desert uniform with a muffler wound around his thin neck. His shock of bristly hair was like a bird's top-knot, which with his bright eyes gave his whole aspect a bird-like quality.

"Hudspeth, Evelyn," he said. "Major, British Army."

He shook hands all around with military ceremony.

That's a girl's name, Lang thought. Evelyn. And he pronounces it funny. E-velyn.

Townes-Baker sat down at the head of the table. The scar on his forehead gave him a raffish and faintly sinister air. Lang wished he had one like it, perhaps a trifle smaller. He was a little afraid of the colonel.

"Shall we get on with it?" Townes-Baker said.

The others arranged themselves around the table.

"Before we start, can somebody tell me one thing?" Waterfield blurted. "Who won the Rose Bowl this year?"

"We've been in quarantine, sir," Byrd said.

"Damn," said Waterfield. "I've got ten cigarettes bet."

"First of all," said Townes-Baker, "let's find out just who you are. Now and again the little buggers try to slip one of their own in amongst us."

Since there were three of them and they had come in together it was not difficult to establish their identities. Hudspeth asked particularly sharp questions, however, and Lang took a dislike to him. He felt the major did not trust him.

They were then questioned in, to Lang, boring detail about operations in North Africa and the Great Western Desert and what they had observed of Italian military measures and civilian attitudes. When these subjects were exhausted, Hudspeth extracted a folded paper from the lining of his greatcoat and spread it on the table. It was a meticulous scale drawing of P.G. 203.

"This is the guards' barracks," he said, pointing to the building in the forecourt with the clothesline, "and this the administration building," indicating the one with the flagpole.

"Offices, storage rooms and two solitary confinement cells."

Lang swallowed. He did not like the implications of solitary confinement cells.

"Now," Hudspeth said briskly, "what can you chaps tell us about the outer compound and the immediate surroundings of P.G. 203? State of the wire, number and activity of Italian personnel, etcetera, etcetera, etcetera?"

How did he expect us to notice all that? Lang thought irritably. No sleep, nothing to eat, and no time to see anything the way they'd been hustled into Pellini's office.

"Well," said Byrd, "the outside wire was about seven feet high, six horizontal strands and vertical strands every ten-twelve inches."

Lang stared.

"No change, then," Hudspeth said. "Any breaks?"

"No, sir. There's concertina wire at the base of the wall for about four or five feet out. None at the road, though."

"Nasty stuff," Townes-Baker said. "Had a man caught in it last month. Wog Simpson. Malvi's little buggers gave him a beastly time. Beastly."

"Only one guard at the entrance," Byrd continued. "Inside. One at the gate into here."

Hudspeth was nodding impatiently, hearing nothing he did not already know.

"He put his rifle down when he opened the gate for us," Byrd continued.

"Good point," Hudspeth said.

"There was a guard walking post between the wall and the wire," Byrd said, unimpressed by either Hudspeth's impatience or approval. "Gave us a real once-over when we came up the road. Three more in the outer compound who looked like they were on duty. Everything buttoned and carrying rifles. Four or five others I don't think were on duty. They were a mess."

Waterfield looked smugly at Townes-Baker during Byrd's recital.

Byrd was giving a summary of their encounter with Pellini when there was spaced rapping on the door.

"Captain Stagno," the lookout called from outside.

"Come in, Doc," said Waterfield.

A dark, very burly man in a white smock entered. He had heavy, crowded features. There was a large, perfectly round bald spot, like a tonsure, in the middle of his thick hair. A froth of curly blue-black hairs spilled out of his smock at the neck.

"Dr. Stagno," said Waterfield. "Cuts corns, heals warts and counsels on sex."

"Blow it out your ass, Colonel," Stagno said without rancour in a resonant bass. "I got two cases of jaundice and a bleeding hemorrhoid to get back to. Any of you men got any ailments?"

Byrd and Moran shook their heads.

"I got chilblains," Lang said eagerly.

"Keep your feet warm and dry and stay off 'em as much as possible."

"How'm I gonna keep 'em warm?" Lang asked plaintively.

The doctor looked at him without expression.

"Try tucking 'em under your armpits," he said. "If any of you have health problems, sick call's in the dispensary after morning brew. But I'll personally kick the ass of any man reporting sick with nothing seriously wrong. See you at chow, Milton."

He left.

"Any questions?" Townes-Baker said.

"Yes, sir," said Byrd. "This Italian sergeant tried to tell us he's American. Pellini."

"We're not sure," Hudspeth said. "But it doesn't follow he'd be posted here if he was sympathetic. I say, you didn't speak freely with him?"

"Of course not," Byrd said, for the first time nettled by Hudspeth's manner.

67

Lang cleared his throat. Everyone looked his way. He studied the floor.

"What's SBO?" he asked. "And SAO?"

"Senior British Officer," Townes-Baker said. "And Senior American Officer."

"Oh," said Lang, feeling ignorant and wondering if Jaybird and Moran had known or just did not think to ask.

"Well," Townes-Baker said. "I think that should do it." He paused. "Just one more thing. I don't suppose anyone would know if Carmen Miranda's made a film recently."

"Last one I saw was *That Night in Rio*," Lang said, pleased to know something the others did not.

"Good?" Townes-Baker asked.

"Terrific."

"Lucky beggar," Townes-Baker said wistfully.

When they returned to their bay they found someone had made their bunks for them. On each was a drinking mug, table knife, fork, spoon and forty English cigarettes.

"A whole week's issue," said Waterfield. "Make 'em last."

"I don't smoke," Lang said.

"Then you're in business," Waterfield said enviously. "Cigarettes are money here."

Lang looked reproachfully at Moran. If you hadn't made me give you all my cigarettes I'd have a whole bunch saved up by now, he thought.

"Okay, Blubber, okay," Moran said angrily. "How many I owe you?"

Lang wanted to pick a number, a large number, but he saw Byrd eyeing him.

"None, I guess," he mumbled.

He was furious with Byrd but tried not to show it.

Dogass Harbold joined them.

"Breakfast in the room, lunch and supper in the mess hall," he said, very businesslike. "I'll show you your places. Three brews a day. Breakfast, teatime and night."

"Teatime!" Moran said.

"Don't knock it till you've tried it," Harbold said. "We get one loaf a day. At lunch. But don't eat it then. Save half for tea, half for breakfast next day. Parcels day after tomorrow. Two men split one a week. S'posed to be one a man but we're on half parcels. Shortage of transport."

He turned suddenly to Lang.

"You don't smoke at all?"

Lang shook his head.

"Give you an OR loaf for ten cigarettes," Harbold said.

Lang shook his head again. He did not know what an OR loaf was and anyhow he was not going to rush into anything before he knew the ropes. Harbold might be playing him for a sucker.

Harbold sighed.

"You guys are in luck today," he said, brightening. "Meat in the soup this noon."

He left for the mess hall and within half an hour a shout of "Grub up!" at the back door aroused the room to action. Everyone rushed to his bunk to drag from beneath it a cardboard Red Cross parcel box full of open tin cans. They streamed out the back way, followed by the occupants of the front bays, each man with his box. The stamping, clank and rattle were like an exotic tribal dance. Lang, Byrd and Moran followed Waterfield.

Over the heavy back doors a notice was painted in black block letters.

ANYONE APPROACHING THE WALL AFTER CURFEW WILL BE FIRED UPON MINUS WARNING — MALVI, COL.

Between the back walk and the brick wall was a smooth heavy tripwire strung between wooden posts eighteen inches high. Small wooden signs dangled from the wire at frequent intervals. PASSAGE AND DEMURRAGE NO ALLOWED — MALVI, COL. The curfew warning was repeated on the wall behind each wing of the three buildings in the row.

The mess hall was in the far wing of the last building.

The wing was identical with Lang's except that instead of bunks and stools it was crowded with long wooden tables and benches. Harbold showed the new men their assigned places. Byrd was with Waterfield, Captain Stagno and others from the room. Moran was assigned to a table with other of their roommates and English officers. Lang was assigned to a table of utter strangers. Harbold had it in for him because he wouldn't trade his cigarettes, he thought.

The English officers introduced themselves when he sat down. He was between a dark, narrow man with the jutting features of a Bedouin and a fair, downy-cheeked officer with a face round and wise as a cat's, wearing a blue Royal Air Force blouse with a row of ribbons on the breast.

"Wog Simpson," said the dark man. "Leftenant, Royal Artillery."

The backs of his hands were striped with healing cuts. Wog Simpson. Lang knew the name. The man Colonel Townes-Baker had said got caught in the concertina wire.

The RAF man was Pilot Officer Perkins. He saw Lang eyeing his incongruously dressy attire.

"I'd planned attending the cinema directly I came back off the sweep," he explained. "I flew Spits off Malta."

A large chipped bowl from which an appetizing steam arose sat at the end of the table. At each place was a smaller bowl, five almonds, three dried figs, a wizened apple and a small brown loaf. Lang put the bread in his tunic and began eating the other things. When the introductions were completed, a large man wearing a blanket as a shawl, who had introduced himself as Major Feather, stood up behind the steaming bowl.

"Would you care to join me for luncheon, gentlemen?" he asked.

The bowls were passed to the head of the table, where Major Feather ranged them before him. He ladled out the soup with great care, dividing the bits of meat scrupulously. The meat was tortured little lumps of gristle which Perkins

70

soberly assured Lang was diseased bullock. Major Feather kept up a running commentary as he divided the soup.

"Captain Bromley, I believe you prefer the lean. Perkins, you fancy a bit of fat."

Holding the ladle over Lang's bowl he said, "Leftenant Lang, shall I carve you a slice of the rare?"

Lang did not think he was very funny.

The soup was blander than that at the quarantine camp, full of insipid chunks of some pumpkin-like vegetable, but it was thick and hot. Lang ate it with relish, saving the meat until last.

"Oh, I say!" Perkins cried, holding up his spoon. "I found a garbanzo."

"Good show," his companions cried in unison.

Lang's flaring envy vanished when he saw it was only a pea.

He gagged on a bit of gristle. He spit it back into his bowl surreptitiously and saw a wild-eyed officer with a wispy mustache staring at him from across the table. He smiled a feeble apology and the man looked away. Lang finished his soup quickly and passed his bowl back to Major Feather. He wanted to be sure he got seconds if there was not enough to go around again. The major was taken aback. Then he smiled, showing crooked teeth, and roared with mock ferocity.

"What, more!"

Lang winced, amid laughter.

"Oliver Twist," Perkins said. "You do know Dickens?"

"I had to read it in high school," Lang said, remembering the children in the workhouse got only one bowl of gruel.

He was angry and embarrassed. He had just met them and they were already picking on him.

The wild-eyed officer across from him remained seated when the others left the table. Lang chanced to look back just as he reached across the table into the bowl and popped the morsel Lang had discarded into his mouth. Lang swallowed to keep from retching and hurried to catch up with Byrd and

Moran, feeling a chilling premonition. If you could get that hungry here it must be a terrible place.

Back in the room, Lang sat on his bunk tending his chilblains while Byrd and Moran exchanged war stories with their roommates. He could hear laughter from the group surrounding Moran. Wherever Moran went, people always liked him. He wished he knew how Moran did it. They liked Byrd, too, but not the same way. They didn't warm up to Byrd the way they did to Moran. He wondered who he would rather be like if he had the choice. He could not decide.

Two Italian officers came into the bay and all conversation stopped. One of them, a captain, had kinky red hair and a pale, freckled serious face. His companion was only a lieutenant though years older, with graying hair and a seamed, driven face. Both saluted Waterfield. The older officer gave a Fascist salute, which Waterfield ignored pointedly. Waterfield called Lang, Byrd and Moran to his bunk.

"Meet Captain Ribolla," he said. "Our settore officer. He looks after us pretty good."

Ribolla saluted each in turn.

"My leftenant, Grasso," he said, indicating the older man.

Grasso saluted each in turn, Fascist style, clicking his heels together as he thrust out his arm. Then he reached into his tunic and brought out some pamphlets. Waterfield turned red.

"God damn it, Grasso," he said heatedly, "didn't I tell you not to try and peddle that Fascist junk in here!"

Grasso returned his glare defiantly. Ribolla looked faintly embarrassed. Waterfield turned to him.

"Ribolla, you know damn well Colonel Malvi said we didn't have to put up with his nonsense."

Grasso spoke rapidly to Ribolla. Ribolla addressed himself to Waterfield with the air of a man not fully convinced of his position.

"Tenente Grasso asking to know if you have fear your men learn of the truth," he said.

"Bull!" Waterfield said testily. "You don't even believe that garbage yourself."

Ribolla's expression was noncommittal.

"He can set up all the lectures he wants and anybody that feels like it can go," Waterfield said. "But I won't have him coming in here with that stuff."

Ribolla said something to Grasso in a quiet voice. Grasso scowled and began nosing around the room, where he was studiously ignored by the occupants.

"As I have say you many before, I must to support my Tenente Grasso," Ribolla said firmly. "He are of my army, not I of yours. But I speak him again not make propaganda within room."

"Yeah, I know you say me many before," Waterfield said with a sudden grin.

He gave Ribolla a cigarette and held a light for him. Ribolla inhaled luxuriously.

"I make with you change places," he said.

He pinched out the cigarette and stowed it away carefully in a silver case containing Italian cigarettes.

"There is one problem concerning blankets, Colonnello?" he asked, assuming a more official manner.

"The mighty mites only brought over two blankets per man. My new people don't have greatcoats."

"Do not fearing. I will see to the additional."

He shook hands all around and left, taking Grasso with him.

In midafternoon, at a call of "Brew up!" from the front of the building, one of Lang's roommates seized a jam bucket with a rope handle and raced down the hall. The others got out their drinking mugs and began feverishly slicing bread and spreading it with miserly portions from their arrays of tin cans.

The newcomers' table knives were too dull to slice the loaves. Someone loaned them a sharpened knife and others provided oleomargarine and an array of cans labeled meat roll, lobster paste and Golden Syrup. Someone gave Moran half a pilchard and Harbold gave each half a spoon of sugar, saying, "You can pay me back when you get yours."

Lang, Moran and Byrd ate together when the tea was distributed. Half the small loaf was like tinder to Lang's appetite and when he had finished his hunger raged more fiercely than ever. It took all his willpower not to eat the remaining half. The hours until the evening meal were interminable.

After dinner, which was pumpkin soup again without the meat, the distant hills were still sunlit but the camp lay in a pool of dusk. Lights came on on tall poles outside the wall, followed moments later by the naked bulbs over the back of each wing. The guards in their boxes on the wall tested their searchlights. The ceiling lights were not on yet and Lang's room was steeped in icy shadow. He could see his breath in the gloom, like cigarette smoke. When the lights came on, dim and yellowish, the room seemed somehow warmer and more cheery to Lang than by day.

His roommates occupied themselves darning clothes, writing letters and talking in loud voices of girls, food and military exploits. Byrd sharpened his table knife on a brick and Moran was in the center of a group telling stories. Lang felt alone and unwanted. He crawled into his bunk and removed his shoes. Eyes closed, he massaged his feet sensuously and suddenly was thinking of Serena the Butterfly girl. To his embarrassment he had an erection.

Later there was tea again. Byrd and Moran shared Colonel Malvi's cakes with him and he felt again the closeness of Christmas Eve at the quarantine camp. The feeling persisted until the lights went off at nine-thirty and he lay shivering in his bunk. He was cold and hungry and his feet burned.

Conversation continued between bunks for some time

74

after lights out, punctuated with laughter and snatches of ribald song. At last Waterfield shouted, "Knock it off, fellows, some of us are trying to sleep," in the same half-imploring tone Lang had once heard his scoutmaster use on an overnight hike and conversation gradually died. Lang could not sleep. He was uncomfortable and his future was menaced by uncertainties. And the room was never truly quiet.

Men snored, bunks creaked and rustled with restless twistings and turnings. A man groaned as if in agony, another muttered, "That's enough of that," in his sleep and once someone gave a wild, gasping snort of terror which brought the room awake. There was constant traffic up the center corridor to the latrine at the back of the wing, making a steady procession past Lang's bunk, which was on the aisle. The British had nails in their boots and their footsteps were loud in the cold still air. Those from the front of the wing were often in a great hurry and would run past Lang's bunk and let the door slam between the American bay and the latrine section of the building.

Outside the barracks Lang could hear the tread of a sentry walking his post and the creak of the sling as he eased his rifle on his shoulder. When at last he fell asleep it seemed he was awakened almost immediately by the flash of a light in his eyes as two whispering Italians made a bedcheck. He fell asleep again almost immediately thinking, in the moment just before oblivion, he was back home safe in his own bed.

He dreamed of a great flock of white birds.

They had taken off from their base at Kabrit on the Suez Canal and were flying low over the Nile delta as they always did when the target was Tobruk or Benghasi and they were striking from the desert. At first, in the dream, it was like any other mission. Bertram was in his seat at the bombsight singing on the interphone and Lang was relieved that it had all been a mistake and Bertram was not really dead. The tawny desert surrounding the airbase ended abruptly in the luminous checkered green of the delta. He could see paths and irrigation canals lacing the fields, splashing buckets, half-naked farmers and slow dun-colored animals.

Then, as always, the white birds began rising from the fields, frightened by the thunder of the low-flying bombers. At first only a few birds rose before the thunder. Then more, like puffs of smoke. They thickened below the *High Flying Flora* until only glints of emerald were visible through rents in the flapping billow of white feathers. And then even the glints vanished and the birds were a snowy undercast blanketing all the earth.

The air grew cold in the nose of the B-24. Lang knew if the flock did not disperse soon he would miss his final checkpoint before the trackless desert. It grew colder, as if they were at altitude. The air was clean and glittering as it always was at altitude and Lang knew with a great burst of joy, wondering how he could have forgotten something so important, that they were not on the way to bomb Benghasi but were flying home and he got on the interphone to give Byrd the new course.

No one answered.

And Bertram was not in his seat at the bombsight and he leaped from his perch on the navigation table and stared back at the flight deck out of the Plexiglass dome through which he shot the stars and there was no one there.

He was all alone in the plane, high above the earth, all alone in the glittering sky except for the great billowing undercast of white birds flying.

CHAPTER 5

The setting of Campo Concentramento Prigioniero di Guerra 203 had a certain charm, virtually all of which was lost on the eleven hundred British and twenty-six Americans and Canadians wintering there.

To the west was a broad, noble hill, its slope gridded with slumbering olives and its crown capped with a pleasant white village. At close range the village was neither pleasant nor white but none of the prisoners knew that with the possible exception of a Lance Corporal Derek Gorsely, who claimed to have been slipped out for one night dressed in Italian uniform for a hundred-cigarette bribe and a pledge of secrecy.

An archaic little tram, which the Americans nicknamed the Toonerville Trolley, ran along the hill, climbing into view above the camp wall and rattling along jauntily to disappear below the wall again, like a shooting gallery duck, to reappear reduced in size at the crests of more distant hills until it vanished completely. It was a cheerful link with the outside world and many prisoners would stand in the cold to watch it from the time it appeared until it slid behind the final hill.

To the north of the camp was a hazy sprawl of mountain, often veiled in purple. Colonel Townes-Baker, who had spent his holidays in Italy when in a position to select his own accommodations, said he thought it had a famous ski slope although he could not remember its name. He said that was of no importance, however, because on this holiday he did not have his skis along.

Nothing was visible over the wall to the south because of the flatness of the terrain but it was thought in the camp there was a cantina at a bend in the highway less than half a mile distant where the guards went for entertainment of varied nature. On crisp nights when atmospheric conditions were right the wind from the south flaunted tatters of music and female laughter. On such evenings there was great unrest in P.G. 203.

To the east were the tops of the two buildings in the outer compound and the Italian flag proclaiming the authority vested in Colonnello Filippo Malvi. Everything and everyone entering or leaving the inner compound came from the east although some of the prisoners were continuously at work attempting to dig new exits under the wall.

The six U-shaped buildings of the inner complex were divided into two sections, or *settori*, one on each side of the camp street. The buildings, called bungalows, were identical, comprising two wings divided into six large bays. There were several smaller rooms in front, facing the street. At the end of each wing was a latrine and washroom on opposite sides of the long center corridor.

Most of the wings housed prisoners. There were twenty-eight to thirty men in every bay except the American room in Bungalow 6, Settore II. The arrival of the *High Flying Flora* survivors brought its strength to twenty-six, the greatest number of men ever commanded on active duty by Lieutenant Colonel Milton Waterfield, who had achieved his rank in the reserves between the two World Wars.

A wing of the last building on Lang's side had been converted into a mess hall. The messing staff portioned out the Italian rations in a latrine which had been only partially modified by plastering over the facilities. The prisoners made jokes about the fitness of this arrangement but appetites were unaffected.

Part of a wing of the bungalow across from the mess hall was used for classes. An overage British subaltern, in civilian life a full professor at the University of New Delhi, had set up a school which the prisoners called P.G.U. Tenente Grasso was an enthusiastic supporter of the school, having been won over by the addition to the curriculum of a course in modern Italian history for which he provided the instructor and for which Colonel Townes-Baker provided a full classroom of reluctant volunteers for three one-hour lectures a week by an elderly retired high school teacher from Pantella, the village on the hill. Dr. Corbellini always put his Fascist party button in his vest pocket before entering the prison compound and sometimes distributed little cakes, cigarettes or pamphlets purchased from a fund Tenente Grasso had wheedled out of the party apparatus in Rome. The pamphlets were in great demand. The Italian issue for prisoners of war did not include toilet paper. There were also courses in military history, Chaucer, mathematics, French, Italian and other subjects. Major Evelyn Hudspeth taught military history, the most popular course.

A small room in front of the school wing was used as a music room. It was furnished with an old upright piano provided by Colonel Malvi out of his own funds in his continuing effort to keep the prisoners happy with their lot. On Monday, Wednesday and Friday mornings a second lieutenant from Nottinghamshire came to practice *"Liebesträume"* without

79

noticeable improvement and on Tuesdays, Thursdays and Saturdays three Scots in kilts made of blankets brought a bagpipe and performed Scottish dances for their own entertainment and that of anyone who cared to look in the window.

The washroom of the wing was used as a barbershop by a British corporal who gave shaves and haircuts for one lira each in camp money. He gave shaves only one hour a day before morning roll call because the straight razor was checked out to him for that period.

A Spartan dispensary and hospital were in the next wing. Captain Stagno was there every day, assisting the Italian military surgeon assigned to the camp. They argued endlessly in Italian about medicine and politics but remained on friendly, though guarded, terms.

Other Ranks, British enlisted men, occupied a wing of the bungalow across the street from Lang's. They were more crowded than the officers and worked endlessly at camp chores, which included making the officers' bunks. The officers did no work except washing and mending their clothes and, occasionally, a little tunneling. There was little contact between officers and Other Ranks and trading with the ORs was forbidden by Colonel Townes-Baker. The ORs were forbidden to trade with the guards by both Colonel Townes-Baker and Colonel Malvi. Some of them obeyed.

The kitchen was in the long building at the back of the compound. The cookhouse ORs prepared meals and boiled tea on a rank of huge coal-burning stoves in kettles so large they were moved about with hand cranes and pans so big two strong men were needed to take them off the stove. The food cooked in the kitchen was principally the official Italian ration but it was supplemented occasionally by tinned meat and vegetable stew and other items from Red Cross parcels which required heating, and by nonissue luxuries such as fruit and nuts which Colonel Malvi allowed the camp messing officer to purchase on the civilian black market with money held out of officers' pay for the purpose. Colonel Malvi did not take a profit from these transactions and was unpopular with civilian suppliers because he insisted on fair prices. The official ration comprised the daily loaf, vegetables in season, a coarse brown pasta and modest quantities of meat, sugar, rice, hard cheese and thin red wine.

There was a shower room at one end of the cookhouse, with its hot water boiler in the kitchen, and a theater at the other. Prisoners were allowed one hot shower a week in the white-tiled stalls. Those who missed it or were so fastidious they desired more than one bath a week used the icy taps in the washrooms. The camp orchestras practiced in the shower room because of its isolation and accoustics. There were two of them, a dance band and a group calling itself the Pantella Symphony. They had the same personnel. The instruments were gifts of Pope Pius XII, the International YMCA and the Red Cross.

The theater was a bare room with a shaky stage set on trestles. Prisoners brought their own stools. The orchestra played here. There were also plays and original musical revues. Colonel Malvi attended all opening nights and often donated costumes and make-up. He brought along his own folding canvas seat and Sergeant Pellini to translate for him.

Lang would not have found life in P.G. 203 overly oppressive had he not almost always been cold and hungry. The bay was unheated and his three blankets were thin and narrow, unlike the large fleecy Italian Air Force blankets at the quarantine prison. He was disappointed in the food, having had visions of spaghetti and meatballs, veal scallopini and other Italian dishes he knew in Houston restaurants.

However, because of the forced association he was more involved in the daily lives of his companions than at any other time in his life. He got exactly as much of everything as anyone, he went to the theater and the shower when his roommates went and, through his identification with Byrd and Moran, benefitted from their popularity and prestige. In his limited contacts with the British he was treated much like the other

Americans, the British considering all Americans rather peculiar and Lang merely an interesting variation on the national character.

He did not find the daily routine particularly disagreeable or monotonous. He rose at eight and breakfasted on tea and half a loaf of bread. Then there was morning roll call, parade the British called it, outdoors in good weather and inside the room if wet. And then there was lunch, and then teatime, afternoon roll call, dinner and finally, evening brew, which he took with portions of his Red Cross parcel. In between he might take a constitutional with Byrd and Moran, who gave him greater acceptance in the prison camp than they had at their airbase, watch Moran play poker or write home on the ruled postcards and letter forms provided by his captors. His messages were almost exclusively lists of things he wanted sent to him. Though none of the Americans had as yet received one, food and clothing parcels could be sent by next of kin every three months.

He signed up for a full schedule of courses at P.G.U. and shared classes in military history and Italian with Byrd. Moran took no courses. He was too restless to sit still except for poker. Once a week Lang went to the theater with Byrd and Moran, and after he overcame the initial shock of seeing obviously virile men playing women's roles enjoyed the performances immensely.

Lang's favorite day was Friday, the day he and Moran drew the Red Cross parcel they shared. He began thinking about parcel day on Monday and on Wednesdays, when he was out of Red Cross food, his thoughts became obsessive. Even Moran surrendered to the excitement of parcel day. They would bring their parcel back to the bay and spread out its contents on Lang's bunk. Parcels varied from week to week and there was always the chance of a pleasant surprise.

Lang liked having Moran for his parcel-partner. Moran did not like sweets, or milk in his tea, and traded Lang his half of a Cadbury bittersweet chocolate bar for five cigarettes and his half of the tin of condensed milk for fifteen, although the going rate for a bar of English chocolate was fifteen and for condensed milk sometimes as high as fifty. Lang's store of cigarettes mounted, for despite their negotiability and his hunger he would trade only with Moran. He was both shy and suspicious and was unwilling either to pay the going rate for anything or to bargain.

The first week he ate his food parcel in its natural state. Then he became aware that his roommates did interesting things with their Red Cross food on Tuesdays, when the cookhouse prepared personal teatime dishes for his bungalow. He learned to soak Canadian biscuits in water to be fried in olive oil and eaten with jam, and to make rissoles of bread, onions and curry powder, and even invented a dish of his own, tinned English bacon in layers with onions and breadcrusts. He cooked for Moran, as well. Moran was too impatient and indifferent to prepare food. Lang was delighted to find something at which he exceeded Moran. They ate together on cooking day and Moran was at his friendliest.

When he was not otherwise engaged, Lang sat in his bunk tending his healing toes and daydreaming. Sometimes he thought about Serena the Butterfly Girl or certain adventures he had had in the City Pensao in Belem on the flight overseas and the Mimosa Club in Beirut on leave but usually his thoughts were not romantic or erotic. He thought about going home a hero and even more often he thought about eating.

Crab bisque and steak and baked potato at Ye Olde College Inn. Hot dogs with chili and onions at James Coney Island. Shrimp De Jonghe at the Café Ritz and barbecued beef sandwiches at Kelley's at the stand-up side, and ribs and hot links and soft white bread soggy with sauce at Matt Garner's. His mother's raspberry jello with fruit and nuts and fresh whipped cream, and the éclairs and cream puffs his father brought him on the way home from the office, and the taffy man in the narrow alley next to the Iris Theater when he was a child, and the hot tamale man who had come around the neighborhood with tamales in bundles of three in a steaming lard can, and iced crabs and hot biscuits and fried chicken at the San Jacinto Inn, and hot roasted peanuts and french fried potatoes, and the tuna cocktails at Pross's in Haifa, the pastry and mousses at Groppi's in Cairo, and popcorn, and strawberry cream pie at One's-a'Meal, the dripping banana splits at Rettig's, triple-dip cones, his mother's cornbread and macaroni and cheese, and bread toasted in the oven with real butter on it in bubbling pools.

His hunger and the frustrations it caused pursued him even in sleep. He began having a recurring dream in which he found himself back in Houston in a grocery store closed for the night, Weingarten's or Piggly-Wiggly or the A & P. He was always in a rush because he had only a few hours' leave from P.G. 203 and in an agony of indecision because he could only bring back what he could carry in two hands. And the dream always ended before he made his choice.

On a raw rainy morning three weeks after his arrival Lang woke with a sense of foreboding. It was not until he was fully awake that he realized why. In a moment of recklessness the night before he had agreed to take a cold bath with Moran before breakfast. A British tunnel had cut the pipe to the shower room and there was no hot water that week. Lang would gladly have waited for the pipe to be mended but Colonel Waterfield had a standing rule, requested by Dr. Stagno, that everyone in the American bay bathe at least once a week. Stagno was a firm believer in cleanliness and, moreover, in cold baths for keeping the circulatory system in order. He himself took a cold bath every morning. He was the only officer in P.G. 203 to do so except an Australian in Bungalow 2 who had been blown up by a mine outside Tobruk and was said to be mad as a result of the experience.

From his bunk Lang could see the rain beating against the window. Even Moran would not undertake a cold bath on such a day. Relieved, he closed his eyes and entered his morning reverie. What to have for breakfast. Breakfast was an important function, for what he ate in the morning determined what he would have for afternoon tea and what, if anything, would be left for evening brew. And this morning, if he sweetened his tea to his liking, he could not afford sugar for afternoon brew unless he bought some from Moran for cigarettes.

Under his bunk was a cardboard box filled with opened tin cans. He knew the position and contents of each tin without having to look. There was one sardine, a sliver of tinned English cheese, browning remnants of meat roll and ham paste, an inch of sultana pudding, half a Canadian biscuit, a spoonful of Golden Syrup and half his Italian loaf from the previous day.

He decided to have the sardine and Golden Syrup with his half loaf, sliced very thin. If he had the Golden Syrup his brew need not be so sweet and he could save his sugar for teatime. Then he could have that day's loaf with what was left of the cheese and meat roll for tea and for evening brew the half Canadian biscuit, ham paste and sultana pudding. This left a blank for next day because parcels would not be out until the day after. If he grew really desperate he could trade some of his cigarettes. He now had ninety, more than anyone in the bay except Flight Lieutenant Petitclerq, the RCAF officer, who had received five hundred Sweet Caporals in a personal parcel from home.

"Hey, Blubber," said Moran's voice from the top bunk. "It's time to meet the monster."

Lang opened his eyes. Moran's inverted face hung over the edge of the upper bunk, grinning.

"It's raining," Lang said hopefully.

Moran vaulted from his bunk and stood over Lang.

"Off your ass and on your feet," he ordered cheerfully. Lang did not move.

Moran stripped the blankets from him. Lang was fully dressed except for his shoes.

"You don't waste much time getting ready for bed, do you, Blubber? Strip down and wrap up in your sheet."

He hovered over Lang, grinning but implacable. Lang rose, resigned. There was no arguing with Moran when he was in a mischievous mood. He stripped, hung the coarse sheet over his chilled shoulders and groped in his parcel box for his Red Cross soap. His roommates applauded and whistled as he shuffled toward the washroom.

There was a line waiting at the tap jutting from the wall three feet above the icy floor. Stagno was sitting under the tap, snorting and hairy as a bear, droplets glistening on his pelt like hailstones. Lang and Moran got in line.

When the water struck Lang's body he went rigid, as if it was charged with electricity. He tried to get up but Moran put a foot in his chest and pinned him against the wall until he was drenched in fire. Lang wanted to curse him but the icy water drove the breath from his lungs. He could only gasp. When Moran released him Lang scrambled to his feet and swung at his tormentor. Moran evaded the blow instinctively, a startled, ferocious expression on his face. Then he grinned.

"What was in that water?" he said.

Lang went to the end of the line and soaped up as he had seen others doing. He was aghast at what he had done, trying to hit Moran, but proud, too.

It was not quite so bad as before when Lang got under the tap to wash off the soap. He dried himself on the sheet and ran back to the room without waiting for Moran. He huddled trembling in his blankets, feeling scalded. The memory of the ferocious look on Moran's face haunted him. When Moran came back, toweling himself vigorously with his sheet, Lang turned his head away.

"See?" Moran said. "Wasn't so bad, was it?"

He sounded almost friendly.

The shivering stopped and Lang felt antiseptically clean. Then warmer. Then glowing. And ragingly hungry.

When the tea bucket was brought in he sliced his loaf paper thin and wolfed it down with the sardine and Golden Syrup, sweetening his tea recklessly. His hunger undiminished, he ate his cheese, meat roll and ham paste with the piece of Canadian biscuit. There were seconds on tea and he poured his into an empty condensed milk can to dissolve the sweet film adhering to the sides, added the last of his sugar and drank it with the sultana pudding.

It only seemed to whet his appetite.

He took all the empty cans out of his parcel box, tilted the box until the crumbs from three weeks of daily loaves rolled into a corner and pursued them with a dampened finger. He scraped the sides and bottoms of all the empty cans with his spoon and licked the last few grains from the sugar tin.

Now he had nothing.

Lang hovered between heady bravado and panic. He had shot the works, the way Moran might do, but he had nothing to go with his half loaf for tea or tomorrow's breakfast and tea. And no relief in sight until day after tomorrow's parcel. It was an eternity.

He brooded on his profligacy all during roll call, which was held indoors because of the rain. Each man stood at his bunk while a guard counted them aloud in Italian under Tenente Grasso's supervision. He would have to trade for something to go with the teatime half loaf and worry about breakfast when the time came. A memory of home cajoled him. Sometimes on rainy afternoons, when he was a child, his mother would make cocoa for him and with it he would have a slice of white bread spread with condensed milk.

Lang knew what he would have, what he absolutely must have, with his half loaf for afternoon tea. Without even thinking of the possibility of being cheated, he called across to Harbold:

"Hey, Dogass. You got any condensed milk to trade?"

Harbold was surprised. He had given up trying to get Lang's cigarettes.

"Silenzio!" Grasso shouted. "Interferite con il conteggio. The counting."

Harbold hurried over as soon as Grasso and the soldier left.

"Nobody's got condensed milk," he said. "It's two days until parcels."

Lang sighed.

"Anyhow, it costs like hell," Harbold said. "Up to fifty. You can get five OR loaves for a can of condensed milk."

Lang sighed again.

"But maybe I could find you a can," Harbold continued. "For a five-cigarette commission."

"What kind of sucker you think I am?" Lang demanded.

"Okay," said Harbold. "Find your own friggin' milk."

"You damn right I will."

Lang's sense of outrage was still unabated at lunch. There were to be onions fried in olive oil with dinner that night, and each table sliced a portion for the kitchen after lunch. As Lang sliced onions, his eyes streaming, he thought about bread spread with condensed milk and how Harbold had tried to make a sucker out of him. He would show Harbold nobody needed him.

"Hey, Perkins," he said, without looking at the flier. "You got any condensed milk?"

"Damn all. Why?"

"I thought I'd trade some cigarettes," Lang said guardedly. "If the price was right."

"I've a lovely tin of marge," said Wog Simpson, who was listening.

The scars on his hands were still livid. Cuts healed slowly in the damp cold of P.G. 203.

Lang shook his head.

"Come back to quarters with me," Perkins said. "There may be a tin about."

Lang did not want to go into a strange room but he felt obligated by Perkins's interest. And Perkins had not mentioned a commission. Perkins waited while he collected his cigarettes and conducted him to Bay 2, near the front of the bungalow. Lang was nervous. His palms were sweaty and his stomach in turmoil. It was something like stage fright. Perkins's roommates did not look up when they entered. They all seemed terribly preoccupied writing letters, reading, playing chess, mending. Lang was on the verge of asking Perkins to drop the matter when Perkins made his announcement in a loud voice.

"Chaps, my friend here has fags for milk."

Everyone stopped what they were doing and looked at Lang with undivided interest. Lang blushed.

"I say," said a chess player eagerly, "would English biscuits do?"

"I've a tin of cheese," said another.

Lang received offers of chocolate, jam, Golden Syrup, meat roll and Canadian prunes but no condensed milk. He was ready to leave, his disappointment mingled with relief, when a sturdy man in a blanket kilt dropped from an upper bunk and looked at him with dark, beady eyes, his thick arms folded across his collarless English woolen army shirt. Lang had seen him playing the bagpipes in the music room on Tuesdays, Thursdays and Saturdays.

"Jock Guthrie," Perkins said formally. "Leftenant Lang from the Yank bay."

"I know," Guthrie said. "How many cigarettes have you?"

"Ninety," Lang said. "But if you think I'm gonna give that many . . ."

Guthrie quieted him with a gesture, his stern face softening. He was a heavy smoker but his mother disapproved of tobacco and would not send tobacco parcels, only food and clothing.

Guthrie brought a cardboard box to the table and took out a carefully rolled shirt like the one he wore. He was one of the few men in P.G. 203 with two shirts.

"You may have the shirt for ninety cigarettes," he said.

"I got a shirt," said Lang.

"This is a proper British shirt," Guthrie said, "not your pitiful Eyetie sort."

"I thought you had some condensed milk."

Guthrie unrolled the shirt and produced a tin of milk. He balanced it on his fingertips before Lang's eyes and rotated his hand gently, as if he were a jeweler displaying a gem. Lang salivated. The Scot rolled the tin in the shirt again and put it in the cardboard box.

"Hey," Lang protested. "I thought you wanted to trade."

"So I do," said Guthrie, folding his arms and fixing Lang with an intense look. "How many?"

"What's it supposed to be worth?"

"What a chap can get for it. That's what anything is worth in the bag."

"Well, how many you want?" Lang said.

He had lost his nervousness and grown stubborn. He did not like the way the Scot was beating around the bush.

"Sixty is quite reasonable, I should say."

"Sixty!" Lang cried.

Everyone was looking at him but he did not care. Who did this guy think he was? Sixty. Dogass had said up to fifty.

"My parcel mate sells me his half for fifteen," he said belligerently.

"Then you've got a bloody soft-headed half section," Guthrie answered, unimpressed. "But to show you Yanks we Scots are not what you say I'll give it to you for fifty-five."

But Lang was angry now. Guthrie was trying to take advantage of him just because he was new in camp and did not know how to trade. He wouldn't have the milk if Guthrie gave it to him. The Scot saw he was losing his man.

"Fifty," he said.

Lang shook his head. You should have been nicer, he thought.

"I guess I'll just wait until parcel day," he said.

Perkins, his round face sly, lit a cigarette and let the

smoke drift toward Guthrie. Guthrie inhaled and gritted his teeth.

"Forty-five and be damned!" he roared.

"I should take it, Lang," Perkins said. "You'll not find milk at that price anywhere else."

"Okay," Lang said, regretting it immediately.

That was half his cigarettes and how did he know Perkins hadn't been in cahoots with Guthrie all along? But Perkins didn't seem like that kind of guy, and Dogass had said up to fifty.

"All Players," Guthrie said.

They went through the cigarettes together, weeding out the Craven As, State Express and other brands. Lang looked at the tin of milk with mixed emotions. It was all his but was it a bargain?

"You're a shrewd trader," Guthrie said, appearing to mean it, "but if you should draw a Scottish parcel with a tin of porridge, pop around."

As Lang was leaving, Guthrie called after him:

"If you see my wee haggis flitting about, will you send her home?"

"What's a haggis?" Lang asked.

"Ye dinna ken haggis?" Guthrie demanded. "The haggis is the national bird of Scotland. A bonnie bird."

"It's a sheep's stomach stuffed with unmentionables only a Scot would eat," Perkins said.

"There's the woods haggis and the water haggis," Guthrie continued as if Perkins had not spoken. "My Annie's a woods haggis. If you see her, speak to her gently and tell her to come home."

He bounded into his top bunk, kilt flying, and Lang went back to his room with the milk bulging in his tunic, bursting to tell Harbold.

Harbold was watching the poker game, his hands in his pockets. Moran was raking in a sheaf of counters made of cigarette boxes.

91

Lang took out the milk and held it up.

"Look what I got, Moran," he said, not looking at Harbold.

"Where'd you get it?" Moran asked, impressed.

"What'd you have to give?" Harbold said, trying to hide his surprise.

"Forty-five," Lang said nonchalantly.

"Forty-five! You got rooked."

"Oh, yeah? You said up to fifty. You said it was worth five OR loaves and that's fifty."

"I could get five OR loaves for it," Harbold conceded.

"Who from?" Lang asked.

"That's all right who from. You just gimme the milk and I'll bring you back five OR loaves."

"No," Lang said.

He could already taste the bread and condensed milk he was having for tea.

"Don't stand short," Moran said. "Five OR loaves is a lot of bread. I'll give you my half of the condensed milk for two of 'em Friday."

Lang calculated swiftly. Five OR loaves was fifty cigarettes. That was a five-cigarette profit right there. And if he got half a can of condensed milk for two of them that was another five-cigarette profit. If he could just hold out until Friday he would have condensed milk and plenty of bread to go with it.

"Okay," he said, handing the tin to Harbold. "Prove it."

Harbold buttoned the tin inside his shirt and left. Lang tried to watch the poker game but could not keep his mind on it. His thoughts clung to Harbold and the milk he had trusted him with, and the five loaves he would get if Harbold had not been lying. He would trade a few cigarettes for a spoonful of marge and jam and have a whole loaf for tea.

Dogass came back, grinning. He reached into his blouse and took out five loaves, one at a time, and laid them in a line on Lang's bunk. They were bulky, brown and crusty. Lang was dazzled.

"When old Dogass says five loaves, he means five loaves," Harbold said.

As he turned to leave a sixth loaf fell out of his blouse at Lang's feet. Harbold stooped quickly to retrieve it. He gave Lang a glance which was both speculative and challenging.

"Where'd you get that?" Lang asked.

"What do you care? You got your five."

"You got it for my milk," Lang cried in outrage. "You got six loaves."

"What if I did?"

"It's mine. You got it for my milk."

"The hell it is. I told you I'd get you five and I did."

Their voices had risen and attracted the attention of everyone in the room. Moran put down his cards and turned on his stool to watch.

Fearless with outrage, Lang grabbed at Harbold's blouse. Harbold pushed him away. Lang grabbed again. A crowd was gathering. Harbold knocked Lang's hand from his blousefront.

"You put your dirty hooks on my bread and I'll cream you," he grated.

"Knock him on his butt, Blubber," said Moran, who had joined the crowd.

Lang stared at Harbold, his fists clenched. He was two inches taller than Harbold and thirty-five pounds heavier but his belligerence drained away before Harbold's fierceness.

"Go ahead, Blubber," Moran urged.

Harbold waited, his fists doubled. The crowd moved back to form a circle. Lang looked down at the floor. Everybody wanted him to fight but he did not want to. He was afraid of Harbold. He stood frozen for an eternity while Harbold and the crowd waited. He hated them all, the crowd for wanting to see a fight, Moran for egging him on, Harbold for cheating him.

Byrd came into the bay and, seeing the circle of men, and Lang's troubled face, pushed his way to the center.

93

"What's going on?" he demanded.

Harbold looked at Lang.

"Nothing, Jaybird," he said.

The crowd murmured agreement. Moran said nothing but looked disgusted. People began to move away.

"What's the matter, Steve?" Byrd asked.

Lang could not look at him. He was grateful to Byrd for rescuing him but too humiliated to speak. Byrd studied him thoughtfully.

"You all right?" he asked.

Lang nodded. Byrd left him then, and Lang sat down beside his five OR loaves. He felt as if everyone was snickering at him but when he looked up guardedly no one was paying any notice. He began idly to arrange his loaves in patterns. Then he picked up one of them and nibbled at it daintily. Everybody was down on him except Jaybird. And Moran was disgusted with him. They all wanted to see him get beat up and nobody cared if he'd been cheated.

But nobody was going to cheat him again. He would show them all. He took a larger bite and chewed it slowly. A tear rolled down his cheek.

Nobody was going to cheat him again. Not ever.

94

╾╾╾╾╾╾╾╾╾ CHAPTER 6

Byrd took evening brew with Lang and Moran that night. In recent weeks his duties had prevented him from spending as much time with his crew as he would have wished. Colonel Waterfield had made him his aide and he went to staff meetings and took an active part in shaping policies and plans. He had also joined a tunneling crew. Waterfield, who at fifty was twenty-four years Byrd's senior and one of the oldest men in P.G. 203, had developed a fatherly affection for Byrd and was a little in awe of him. He liked having Byrd around at evening brew for discussions and reminiscences but tonight Byrd had excused himself.

After much inner conflict, Lang invited Byrd to share an OR loaf with him. Byrd accepted on condition he be allowed to provide the jam and margarine and the three of them leaned against Moran's upper bunk, eating and drinking tea. Moran drank tea but did not like it. Tea, he said, was for old ladies and limeys. Men drank coffee.

"What was that all about this afternoon, Steve?" Byrd asked.

Lang told him, shaping his account to give the impression he had refrained from fighting Harbold through self-control rather than fear. Byrd nodded approvingly. Moran did not agree.

"Dogass asked for it, God damn it," he said angrily. "When a guy tells you he's gonna whip your ass you oughtta make him prove he can do it."

"I don't know how to fight," Lang admitted reluctantly.

"I'll teach you," Moran said. "Now Dogass has got your number he'll be pushing you around all the time."

"There won't be any fighting in this bay," Byrd said firmly. "I'll talk to Harbold."

Lang shook his head. That would only make things worse.

"I wish I had hit him," he said with a flash of spirit. "The way he rooked me."

"The hell he did," Moran said. "He said he'd get you five and he did."

"You must have thought he rooked me," Lang insisted. "You said to hit him."

Byrd gave Moran a disapproving look. Moran shrugged, unrepentant.

"I saw you pushing and shoving at each other like two sides of a fat lady's ass," he said. "I didn't even know what the flap was all about. I just wanted you to get in the first lick. Sometimes that's enough."

"You were on my side against Dogass without even knowing he gypped me?" Lang demanded incredulously.

"Whose side you expect me to be on? You're on my crew. It don't make a rat's ass to me who's cheating who."

Lang could scarcely believe it. Moran didn't hate him. Moran even liked him better than he did Dogass, and Dogass was one of the most popular men in the room.

"Hey, Moran," he said in a burst of fellowship, "I'll give you two and a half loaves for your half the milk Friday. That's what it's really worth."

The conversation shifted to talk of home. Byrd wondered if their next of kin had received any of their letters yet, or even knew they were safe. His eyes brightened with moisture when he spoke of his wife and child. For a moment Lang felt tougher than Byrd. He did not get tears in his eyes when he thought about home.

While they were talking a voice said, "Hi, guys," and the nightly babble stopped abruptly. It was Sergeant Pellini, looking expectant and imploring.

"What do you want, Pellini?" Waterfield demanded from his bunk.

"I get lonesome for Americans out there with all those Eyetics, Colonel," Pellini said. "I get sick and tired of hearing nothing but Italian all day long."

"Go peddle your papers somewhere else," Waterfield said. "You're not going to pick up any gen here to take back to Malvi."

"He didn't send me," Pellini protested. "Honest. He'd eat me out if he knew I was in here."

He dug into a pocket.

"Look what I got, guys."

He held up an object. A gasp swept the room. It was a package of Chesterfield cigarettes.

"One of the Eyeties brought it back from furlough. All I want is one. You guys can have the rest."

No one moved or spoke, then someone said, "Shove 'em up your ass, Pellini."

Pellini was crestfallen. He looked wretchedly around the room for a face that did not show bitter disapproval. When he saw Byrd, Moran and Lang he smiled tentatively.

"I guess you guys are doin' okay, huh?" he said.

Lang felt sorry for him. He knew exactly how Pellini felt. He knew what it was like to be an outsider.

"Pretty good," he said, immediately sensing Colonel Waterfield's disapproval and regretting his impulse.

Pellini grinned, showing his gold crown. He came to the bunk holding out his cigarettes.

"How about a Chesterfield?" he said hopefully.

"Don't care if I do," said Moran.

He looked around the room defiantly.

"I'd reach into my mother's coffin for an American cigarette and if anybody here don't like it they know what they can do," he said, taking a cigarette and adding, with a glance at Waterfield, "unless you want to make it an order, sir."

Surprisingly, Waterfield smiled and said nothing.

Byrd refused the pack curtly but Lang, acting instinctively, took one to give to Moran later.

"If there's anything I can do for you guys . . ." Pellini said.

"You just did it," Moran said, lighting his cigarette. "Now beat it."

Pellini sighed.

"Well," he said. "So long."

He started to put the cigarettes in his pocket.

"So long, Sarge," said Lang.

Pellini looked at him gratefully.

"Here," he said, thrusting out the cigarette package. "You take 'em."

He pressed them into Lang's hand and left, looking smaller than when he came in.

"Jesus," said Moran reverently. "What'll you take for 'em?"

"I don't know," Lang said. "I don't know what they're worth."

He was thinking about what Jock Guthrie had said. In

the bag, things were worth what you could get for them. Silently he handed Moran the cigarette he had first taken. He did not know why he felt obligated to do so but he did.

"Gratsey," said Moran.

Lang offered one to Byrd. Byrd shook his head. Lang knew Jaybird was angry with him for accepting the package.

"Don't have anything more to do with Pellini," Byrd said. "He'll pump you for all you know."

"But I don't know anything," Lang protested.

"You know there's a tunnel in the latrine. You know Major Hudspeth is head of the escape committee. You know a lot of things Malvi'd like to."

"I wouldn't tell him anything like that."

"All the same, keep away from him."

"All right," Lang said reluctantly.

But it did not seem fair.

After lights out Lang lay thinking. It had been a remarkable day. He had made trades, turned a profit and learned Moran did not hate him. And he had seventeen Chesterfield cigarettes of indeterminate, but no doubt considerable, value. All that marred his day was Harbold. He wished now that he had hit Dogass. Jaybird would have stopped the fight before he got hurt. If only he had known Jaybird would come in at just the right time. But deep inside he realized that even if he had known he would not have had the nerve to hit Harbold. And he knew something else. Now that he had learned to trade he was, somehow, going to get even with Dogass.

Harbold was the bay's most active trader and the only one with OR loaves. He would watch Dogass. He could learn from him and one day perhaps even use it against him.

That night was the first in P.G. 203 he did not think either of home, his hunger or sex before falling asleep. And he did not dream.

Lang had never before lived in an economy of acute scarcity or had to fend for himself. Whatever he needed had been provided by his parents except the year between college and the Air Corps when he worked for an insurance company. Even then he had paid no rent at home. And he had never been hungry until stationed at Ramat Jonas, with its British rations and British cooks serving unpalatable lumpy porridge and tinned bacon warmed in the can on the stove. It had not been true hunger and he had been able to supplement his diet at the NAAFI canteen truck with sweet biscuits and tinned fruit and at a boardinghouse in Ramat Jonas with fried eggs, chips and sliced tomatoes.

He would have welcomed the lumpy porridge and glutinous bacon now and there was no NAAFI truck at P.G. 203, no boardinghouse to slip off to for fried eggs. There was only the limited Italian ration and the weekly forty cigarettes and half an eleven-pound Red Cross parcel. Only these things and whatever else a man's own shrewdness and tenacity could make of them. Lang had never been shrewd or tenacious nor, until now, ever needed such qualities.

After morning roll call, which was out of doors because the weather had broken, Lang studied the bulletin board in the front hall of the bungalow. There was one in every bungalow where officers lived, with notices signed by Colonel Malvi, an analysis of military news from *Il Popolo di Roma* and other Italian newspapers prepared by a committee of English officers calling itself the Central News Agency and, what Lang was most interested in, bids and offers for food, clothing and cigarettes. By lunchtime he had read all the boards in P.G. 203. Because it was the day before parcels, most of the bids were for food, not cigarettes.

On parcel day the market reversed itself and cigarettes were in demand. But Lang did not trade, except two American and three English cigarettes for Moran's half of the chocolate bar and the agreed two and a half OR loaves for Moran's half of the condensed milk.

Once a week the Italians set up a canteen where notebooks, pencils, razor blades, toilet paper, toothbrushes, washcloths, dried fig bars and other small items could be purchased for the camp money issued in lieu of officers' pay. Much of the pay went into the messing fund and that issued to the officers was useful only in the weekly canteen and poker games. Lang bought a notebook and pencil and began recording the prices quoted on bulletin boards. When he was ready to begin trading regularly he knew the going price for everything.

At first he restricted his trading to things he wanted to eat. His appetite varied. For a few days it might be chocolate, then condensed milk, then Canadian biscuits for frying in the cookhouse. He traded for Moran, as well, who also had occasional special hungers and a craving for tobacco, though not as great as Colonel Waterfield's or Jock Guthrie's. And at first he traded only in his own wing. As his confidence grew he expanded his sphere. He went to any bungalow that promised a bargain and became as well known in the camp as Byrd, who had the prestige of a staff assignment, or Moran, who was widely admired as a raconteur and prodigy of strength.

He enjoyed visiting British bays. Bargaining had become heady to him and few of the British called him Blubberbutt. He was more generally known as Leftenant Lang or the Yank. He particularly liked being called the Yank. It was almost as good as being called Tex.

Parcel day was his busiest, though the greatest bargains usually came the day before. On parcel day he would make his rounds of the bulletin boards with his notebook and retire to his bunk to study the market before spending the rest of the day visiting and trading.

After a few weeks his reserve of cigarettes grew low. In his infatuation with commerce he had been trading more than his weekly ration of forty. Now he began trading not merely to obtain food but also to take a cigarette or two profit wherever he could.

Captain Ribolla came to know him by sight. Lang was conspicuous for his bulk and his painted uniform but the Italian might never have bothered to inquire his name had he not observed Lang's frequent sorties between bungalows. One day as Lang was hurrying to read a bulletin board, his neck pulled down in his collar against the cold, Ribolla stopped him. He studied Lang with his un-Italian green eyes, his freckled face thoughtful.

"Name of you, please?" he said.

"Lieutenant Lang."

"You make always busy, no?" Ribolla said.

"Yeah," Lang replied nervously.

He had not spoken with an Italian since Pellini. He was afraid Byrd or someone would see him talking with Rosie Ribolla and suspect him of revealing camp secrets. And he was cold.

"You carry secrets, correct?"

"Secrets?" Lang demanded, wondering if Ribolla could read his thoughts.

"P.G.s have many of secrets," Ribolla said knowingly.

"I just trade stuff is all," Lang protested. "See?"

He opened his notebook with numb fingers and showed Ribolla his lists.

"Ah," Ribolla said. "You very businessman."

He shook a gloved finger at Lang.

"You not trading my soldati?"

Lang shook his head emphatically.

"Okay," Ribolla said with a friendly salute. "Good trading for you, Tenente Lang."

As Lang had feared, his conversation with Ribolla was noted. Byrd questioned him about it but was satisfied with his description of the encounter.

"Just be careful what you say to him?" Byrd cautioned. "Ribolla's cagey."

"Aw, he likes us."

"That doesn't keep him from doing his job."

Lang became so busy with his trading activities he stopped attending classes at P.G.U. Byrd urged him to continue with his Italian class, saying "If we get loose we'll be able to use it."

102

Lang's stomach contracted at the thought of being on the run in a hostile world.

"Moran's not taking Italian," he said.

"I know," Byrd replied regretfully.

Lang acquired a reputation among his roommates as a man who knew the market. They began coming to him for advice and information as often as to Harbold. Harbold was neither as methodical nor as dedicated as Lang, and Lang gradually eclipsed him except in the OR bread market.

Lang's ties with Moran grew stronger as Moran came to depend on him to divide the weekly parcel fairly, plan and prepare cooking day specialties and do his trading. Lang offered to do the same for Byrd, but his pilot cooked with Colonel Waterfield and traded only for foodstuffs which could serve as escape rations and did so at the going prices without bargaining.

Jock Guthrie sometimes came to visit or trade, always asking if Lang had seen Annie, his haggis, and became friendly with Moran as well. Moran would not trade with him.

"You won't catch me doing business with no Scotchman," he told the hard-faced Scot. "When I was peddling used cars the only guy I couldn't skin was a Scotchman. My old man always told me, 'Before you deal with a man named Mac, be sure he's Irish.'"

"I hae no doot you were a hard man," said Guthrie, who affected a burr when he was enjoying himself.

"I never stood short," Moran said.

Like the other Americans, Moran was curious about what Scots wore under their kilts.

"Nothing," Guthrie said.

"In this weather?" Moran demanded. "You'd freeze your tail off."

"A Scot's bum is impervious to cold. The Rock of Gibraltar is no more impervious to cold than the bum of a Scot."

One day when Guthrie bent over Lang's bunk to see what Lang had to trade Moran lifted his kilt. In an instant he was flat on his back with Guthrie standing over him, smiling, and saying, "And then you kick him to death."

Moran rose slowly, also smiling.

"I bet you can't do that again," he said, poised to grapple.

"I could, indeed."

"Well, let's get on with it."

Guthrie shook his head.

"I might accidentally break your neck," he said. "I'd no like that."

"I'd no like it, either," Moran said, lowering his arms. "I never even got a chance to see if you had anything under that skirt. Why didn't you get mad?"

"I try never to lose me temper," Guthrie said. "I am too dangerous when I'm provoked."

Lang was enormously impressed. Guthrie was not as strong as Moran but had thrown him easily. If Jock would show him how to do it he need never be afraid of Dogass or anyone else.

"Could I learn how to do that?" he asked.

"Probably not," Guthrie said. "A man must be quick. And you're too timid, old buck. You'd get the wind up and use too much force and break some poor sod's back."

"The hell I'm timid. I flew twenty-three missions."

"You lie!" Guthrie said, thrusting his scowling face close to Lang's.

Lang shrank back.

Guthrie laughed.

"You see, Blubberbutt," he said, "your reactions are all wrong. When a man makes a threatening gesture you're not to pull back. You move to counter."

"I wasn't expecting anything like that," Lang said, relieved but angry. "What'd you do if somebody did like that to you?"

"If it was a friend, I'd laugh and turn me back. If not, butt him in his bloody face."

104

"Hey, Jock," said Moran. "You ever kill a man? I mean with your bare hands?"

"Aye."

"Tell us about it," Lang said eagerly.

"A gentleman does not tell tales about girls he has stuffed or men he has pranged," Guthrie said.

In his covert surveillance of Harbold, Lang discovered the busy messing officer was saving sugar in a cocoa tin. One morning before tea Harbold slipped the tin inside his shirt and, after a furtive look to see if Waterfield had seen it, left the bay. Lang sprang from his bunk, slipped on his shoes and followed at a safe distance without pausing to tie the laces. He stopped just inside the bungalow door and watched Harbold hurry across the frigid yard to the OR wing. Lang went back to his bunk and waited.

Harbold returned while Lang was having breakfast and furtively transferred six OR loaves from his blouse to his parcel box. Lang tasted power and triumph. Everyone in the room knew Dogass traded with the ORs but he was the only one who had the proof. He would tell Jaybird, and Jaybird would tell Colonel Waterfield and they would catch him with the six loaves. And he would be even with Dogass for cheating him. But then Dogass might beat him up.

And why share his new-found knowledge that a cocoa tin of sugar was worth six loaves to the ORs? Sugar was worth more to them than to officers because with their access to hot water from the cookhouse they had more brews. Instead of telling on Dogass he would begin saving his sugar, too.

The Italian sugar ration was half an ounce a day and he had another ounce a week from his share of the tin that came in the British Red Cross parcel. Canadian parcels had a four-ounce bag but were issued infrequently. He began saving by going without sugar in afternoon and evening brew, hoarding it grain by precious grain. It was the first time Lang had ever practiced such denial except during the painful time when he was losing weight to pass his cadet physical. When

105

the brew was an Italian invalid's drink called Dimaltina or something similar from British comforts parcels there was no problem, but when Lang drank unsweetened tea it was with an acute sense of deprivation.

When at last he had saved a cocoa tin of sugar Lang slipped over to the OR bungalow, apprehensive but determined. No one saw him but the ubiquitous Ribolla. Lang hesitated at the entrance to the OR wing, looking back at Ribolla. Ribolla gave him his usual friendly salute. Lang was reassured. It was not an Italian rule not to trade with ORs, he thought, it was Colonel Townes-Baker's and Waterfield's, and it wouldn't matter to Rosie Ribolla what he did as long as he didn't break any Italian rules. Anyhow, the OR bungalow was in Settore I and Ribolla was in charge of Settore II. He went in.

The OR bunks were triple-decked and closer together than in the officers' bays. There were only four men in the room, one of them sick in bed. The others were out on work details. The first man to see Lang shouted, "Attention!" and his companions sprang to their feet. Even the sick man raised his head from the pillow a moment in deference to Lang's rank.

Lang was taken aback. This had happened to him only once before. At Ramat Jonas, Byrd had sent him to fetch the aerial engineer and everyone in the tent had come to attention. In his confusion Lang forgot to give them at ease, as he had been taught in preflight military training, and they had grinned, mockingly he thought, and gone about their business.

Now he remembered to say it.

"At ease, men."

But his voice was not as authoritative as he would have liked. The ORs stood at parade rest and looked at him expectantly. Lang took out the cocoa tin.

"Sugar," he said.

The three ORs all began speaking at the same time. It sounded very much like English but Lang could understand only isolated words. A suppressed argument developed, from which the ORs would turn from time to time to give Lang an apologetic look. Lang knew they were arguing about which one of them would trade what for the sugar but the details escaped him in their Welsh and Cockney accents.

The argument ended abruptly when another OR came flying in from a bay farther back and said, " 'Ere now, wot's orl the bloody flap?"

He had the single inverted chevron of a lance corporal on the sleeves of his neat battle dress jacket and was as clean as the other three ORs were sooty. His skin was clear and ruddy, his face looked freshly scrubbed and shaved. He had a carefully trimmed hairline mustache. When he saw Lang he said, "I beg your pardon, sir," and saluted. His hand was delicate and well tended.

"Oose time for bluidy sugar, Derek?" one of the ORs demanded.

"Lance Corporal Gorsely, Derek Gorsely, sir," the clean OR said to Lang with scrupulous courtesy, his diction like an actor's. "May I be of service, sir?"

"Lieutenant Lang from the American bay," Land said. "I've got this cocoa tin of sugar."

"Lovely," said Gorsely. "What would the leftenant like for it?"

"OR loaves. How many do you give for it?"

"The standard's six, sir."

Lang nodded.

"None of you chaps has six," Gorsely said to the three ORs. "I suggest you make up a pool of six amongst the three of you and divide the sugar accordingly."

"Good on yer Derek," said one of the ORs.

When the exchange had been made, Gorsely said, "Would the leftenant condescend to take tea with me?"

Lang hesitated. He did not want to linger in the OR bungalow and risk being caught.

"I've a lovely bit of New Zealand butter and jam, sir," Gorsely said.

"Thanks," said Lang, deciding.

Gorsely's roommates were at their duties and the two of them had the room to themselves. Gorsely brought Lang a thickly spread slice of bread and a tin mug of tea with condensed milk.

"With the leftenant's permission," he said, sitting down across from Lang with a mug of his own.

He studied Lang over his tea.

"Sir," he said carefully, "does the leftenant know there's a reg against trading with ORs?"

Lang scowled. What was this? After Gorsely had even helped him.

"If you report me I'll report you," he said.

"Good heavens, sir!" Gorsely protested. "I'd nothing like that in mind, I assure you."

"It's a good thing," Lang said.

"Actually, sir, there are many of us, both officers and men, who consider it deucedly unfair."

Gorsely did not talk like the other ORs. He sounded to Lang like some of the prissier English officers. He wondered if Gorsely had once been an officer and had been busted.

"Makes things difficult for all concerned," Gorsely continued. "We've extra bread, you've extra sugar. You've little use for camp money, we've damn all lira for toothbrushes and such. Of course," he added quickly, "the officers are most generous with lira pools to help us along. But there's no personal touch, sir. I always say it's the personal touch that's important. Doesn't the leftenant agree?"

"Yes," said Lang, wondering what Gorsely was getting at.

"What I've just been wondering, sir, is perhaps the leftenant might consider helping my chaps along with his chaps."

Lang looked at him uncomprehendingly. A look of

irritation crossed Gorsely's face so swiftly Lang was not even sure he saw it.

"What I mean, sir, I wonder if the leftenant would be kind enough to help us dispose of our surplus for officers' surplus."

"You mean be your go-between?"

"Precisely."

"I could get in trouble."

Lance Corporal Gorsely smiled knowingly.

"I hardly think an officer like the leftenant is afraid of a bit of trouble, if you don't mind my saying as much, sir." He paused a moment. "And, of course, we shouldn't expect an officer to lose by helping us. There'd be a bit of buckshee in it."

"If I helped you out it wouldn't be for any buckshee," Lang said indignantly.

"Of course, sir," Gorsely said placatingly. "But my chaps simply couldn't permit an officer to look out for them if they couldn't look out for him a bit. Fair is fair. May I be quite frank with the leftenant?"

"Say on," said Lang.

He'd heard Colonel Townes-Baker say that once and liked the sound of it.

"Actually I'm afraid Leftenant Harbold took care of himself rather too well, if you'll excuse my speaking so of an officer."

"Harbold?"

"Yes, sir. I'm afraid things have got a bit thick, if the leftenant knows what I mean."

"Do I? He traded a tin of condensed milk for me and held out a loaf."

"That's it, sir," Gorsely said, throwing his arms wide dramatically. "Things like that, sir. Makes it difficult for my chaps to make a proper trade. We need an officer who's thinking about the poor OR, not himself. A proper officer like yourself, sir."

What a break, Lang thought. He'd be in a position to make some great trades and get even with Dogass to boot. If he could just keep Byrd from finding out.

"I guess I could help you guys out once in a while," he said.

"Good show, sir," said Gorsely.

As Lang was leaving the OR wing he heard a voice which sounded exactly like Gorsely's saying, "Orl right, you bloody bastards, where's me bit of the bloody Yank's sugar?"

Harbold was standing in the middle of the camp street, his pale eyes bleak.

"What the hell you been doing in the OR bungalow, Blubberbutt?" he demanded.

Lang shriveled.

"Nothing," he said.

"Then where'd you get those lumps in your blouse? You been trading."

The nerve of the guy, Lang thought. He trades with the ORs all the time and now he's trying to act like it's his business if I do. And he doesn't know the half of it.

"You've had it, Dogass," he said triumphantly.

"What you mean?"

"I'm doing all their trading from now on."

"You son of a bitch!" Harbold cried, shoving his angry face close to Lang's.

Fearful, Lang drew back. Then he remembered what Jock Guthrie had said. He'd butt Dogass in the face and teach him to get tough with Steve Lang. While he was thinking about it Harbold punched him in the nose.

CHAPTER 7

During the weeks in which Lang was engrossed in trade he gave little thought to the world outside P.G. 203. Even at night, after lights out, the most difficult time for prisoners, when thoughts of home, sex and plenty made confinement palpably oppressive, Lang thought more often of his business dealings than of anything else. But as he prospered and his hunger eased, and his transactions grew routine, the old thoughts came crowding back.

On very clear nights, when the stars shone hard and burnished in the map of the sky, he longed to be high above the Mediterranean in the nose of the *High Flying Flora* bringing Byrd and the crew back from a shipping strike, peering out into the darkness for the wink of the beacon at Birg El Arab to confirm another perfect landfall in a friendly coast.

111

He often thought of going home a hero, ignoring the means of getting there and thinking only of the moment when he would walk in the door of his home to surprise his parents and see their faces illuminated with startled joy. And he would be a hero not only to them but to everyone who knew him, even those who had slighted him, particularly to those who had slighted him.

When the wind brought music and laughter from the cantina he remembered the City Pensao and the Mimosa Club, evoking in vivid detail all that had happened there. The girl in Belem had been shy and had not looked at him once the door of her room had shut behind them and had crossed herself before and after. She was soft and brown and wide across the hips. In Beirut the girl was a laughing little Turk with lean shanks and disappointingly small breasts. She had tweaked him impishly and mocked his clumsiness until she became intrigued with his innocence and began employing all her professional skills. Though they were whores, Lang thought of them with nostalgia and something close to affection because he had gone to bed with no other girl but one.

That was in Houston when he was eighteen. She had seduced him on a dare. The girl was a demanding slattern and the experience had been unsatisfying and disillusioning for him. It had not stopped him from lusting after other girls but he had never appealed to another girl enough to repeat the experience.

There were times when his fantasies of the tawny plump Brazilian and lithe Turk, or girls at home he had admired but feared to approach, were so demanding that he could not resist his rigid desire and he took relief in a manner he had been taught was shameful.

He thought sometimes of Serena the Butterfly Girl. Such thoughts filled him with ineffable tenderness until they grew erotic, then they filled him with as much shame as desire. For she was pure and not to be used in the same fashion as the brothel girls even in fantasy.

112

He dreamed of her one night, an enactment of the vision of her he had had in the quarantine prison. She came to him under a bright moon in the warm sand wearing only a melting smile and her dappled wings, and hand in hand they waded into the sea and made love neck deep in the lapping water.

He no longer dreamed of grocery stores.

It eased Lang somewhat to know Moran suffered more frequent and agonizing nocturnal fantasies than he did. Moran thought desperately of girls every night and would thrash about in his bunk in paroxysms of frustration, filling the room with the rustling of the Italian newspapers he had placed between his blankets for insulation. Lang wondered if Moran ever resorted to the same devices he did but the subject was far too private and shameful for him to discuss with Moran.

He wondered, too, if Byrd ever had such thoughts. He did not think so. Byrd was married. And he never sang dirty songs or told dirty jokes like the others or talked about sex like Moran did.

After he got to know Lance Corporal Gorsely better, Gorsely had sworn him to secrecy on his honor as an officer and told him of his visit to Pantella at the price of a hundred cigarettes.

"I shouldn't speak of such to an officer," Gorsely had said, "but I can tell a gentleman of your experience has an eye for frippit."

After that Lang would often gaze longingly at the village on the hill, knowing he would not have the courage to approach the girls there even if he had the opportunity to emulate Gorsely, but he did add ripe, faceless Italian girls to his nocturnal inventory.

Once he realized Harbold was not going to turn him in and that no one in the room seemed to know or care he was trading regularly with the ORs, Lang enjoyed his visits with Gorsely more than anything else he did in the camp. Gorsely treated him with flattering deference and always had something good to eat with tea. And he counted Gorsely among his friends. He had five now, more friends than ever before in his life. There was Moran, Jock Guthrie, Pilot Officer Perkins, Gorsely and Pellini. Though he seldom spoke with Pellini, fearing Byrd would find out, they always waved to each other when Pellini came into the prisoners' compound and when Pellini came to the American bay Lang smiled at him if no one was watching.

He did not include Byrd in his list of good friends because he did not feel really close to his pilot despite the fact Jaybird had always defended him and protected him. He was not sure this meant Byrd actually liked him.

Lang was not terribly sorry he was not closer to Byrd. As much as he wanted his pilot's approval, it would be too much of a strain to be close friends with anyone as selfless, brave and disciplined as Jaybird. It was better to have grateful friends like Gorsely and Pellini. He did not believe, as Byrd and some of the others did, that Pellini was only after information. On the few occasions when he managed to sneak a word with Pellini, the sergeant never tried to pump him.

On the contrary, Pellini told him things about the course of the war which did not appear in the Italian newspapers and gave him advance information about parcel shipments so he knew when the issue would be Canadian or New Zealand instead of the usual British and he could plan his trading accordingly.

One afternoon Pellini came through the inner gate as Lang was slipping out of the OR bungalow. He stopped Lang with a covert gesture and walked to the OR bungalow, taking up a position between it and the wall.

"Stay around corner of the building, Lieutenant," he said, "so they won't know I'm talking to you."

Lang stood with his back against the bungalow facing the camp street. Pellini remained around the corner of the building facing the wall between the prisoners' compound and the outer compound.

"You won't be wearin' the clown suit much longer,"

Pellini said. "Shipment of British battle dress just come in for everybody don't have complete winter uniform."

"Greatcoats, too?" Lang asked.

"Yeah."

The worst of the winter was over but the air was still raw when the sun was not out. A greatcoat would come in handy, Lang thought. You could hide a lot more under a greatcoat than under an Italian blouse. And he'd better warn Jock Guthrie so he could unload his extra shirt before everybody had one. He wouldn't tell Guthrie how he knew. It was now common knowledge he traded with the ORs but no one knew he talked with Pellini.

"Thanks," said Lang. "Need any tea?"

Despite the levies on parcel tea for the daily brews, there was always a surplus among officers. There was a great demand for tea among the Italians, however, and Lang sometimes provided it for Gorsely to trade.

"You sure you can spare it, Lieutenant?" Pellini said gratefully. "You can get a shack job in Pantella for a bag'a tea. Mamma mia, them Eyetie ragazzas. Hey, Lieutenant, you know Colonel Malvi wanted to let you have girls in here once a week but Colonel Townes-Baker turned him down? Said British officers didn't do that kinda thing."

Pellini snickered.

"I'll bet," he said. "Say, Lieutenant, you a friend of Major Hudspeth?'"

"Yes," Lang said.

He was not but Pellini did not have to know it.

"I got some gen about him. Colonel Malvi found out he's head of the escape committee and he's gonna have him transferred to one of them places for the bad boys next week. Without no advance notice."

"Yeah?" said Lang, not too interested.

He hadn't liked Hudspeth since the day he arrived and the major had been so snotty with his questions.

"So I thought maybe you might want to tell him."

Lang saw Captain Ribolla looking at him from across the compound. He bent down as if tying his shoelace.

"Ssh," he warned. "Rosie's looking this way."

"Jesus!" Pellini said in a low frightened voice. "He spot me?"

Lang stood up and brushed the dirt from his knee.

"No," he said, not moving his lips.

He felt bold and mysterious.

"Just stay back around the corner," he continued, still not moving his lips.

Ribolla walked on.

"All clear," Lang said.

Pellini made a sound of relief.

"That's all I'd need," he said. "Grasso's always after Colonel Malvi to get me transferred to the Russian front. That Fascist louse. So you'll tell 'em about Major Hudspeth?"

"Yeah. I'm putting the tea on the ground by the bungalow. You can pick it up after I go."

"You're an all-right Joe, Lieutenant. Listen, don't tell nobody who told you, hear? That friggin' Grasso'd try to get me shot."

It took Lang twenty minutes of aimless walking around the compound to decide he must tell Byrd. Byrd had ordered him not to talk to Pellini. But if Byrd ever found out he had not passed on important information he would be in worse trouble.

Byrd was out of the bay and Lang had to wait for him until teatime. He invited Byrd out for a walk and when they were outside said hopefully, "Jaybird, if I tell you something important you promise not to make me tell you how I know it?"

Byrd stopped walking and looked at him, his expression uncompromising.

"Please, Jaybird."

"All right," Byrd said, softening.

116

Lang told him what he learned, not revealing the source.

"You sure this is pukka gen?" Byrd said.

Lang was suddenly transfixed with doubt. Until this moment he had not questioned the truth of what Pellini had told him. What if the others were right about Pellini and it was some kind of a trap? But why would Pellini want to do a thing like that? And he'd been too scared of Grasso finding out not to be telling the truth.

"Yeah," he said.

"Good work, Steve," said Byrd.

Jaybird hadn't said that to him since the last time he guided the *High Flying Flora* back from a mission, Lang thought.

"You won't tell Colonel Waterfield or anybody I told you, will you, Jaybird?" he begged.

"Okay."

Lang was pleased with himself. He had given his information and kept out of trouble. But something was missing. He had done something special and only Jaybird knew what he had done. It continued to bother him after he went to bed. Moran was rustling above him in his nest of blankets and newspapers. Lang rose on an elbow.

"Hey, Moran?" he whispered.

"Huh?" Moran said sleepily.

Lang got out of bed and leaned close to Moran, the tiles icy under his feet.

"Guess what?" he whispered. "They're going to ship Major Hudspeth out and I'm the one who found out about it."

"Jesus Christ!" Moran said angrily. "You have to wake me up just to tell me that?"

He disappeared under his blankets, pulling the cover emphatically over his head.

Lang got back in his bunk, crushed.

It was decided Hudspeth would go into hiding for a

few days. Byrd informed Lang of the plan as a reward for having given warning of Malvi's intentions.

"What good will that do?" Lang demanded.

"Malvi's trying to catch us with our pants down on all our projects," Byrd explained. "Major Hudspeth's the only one with all the gen on all the schemes. We've got to keep him under cover long enough for him to brief a replacement."

"How you going to hide anybody in this place?"

"In our tunnel," said Byrd.

"Our tunnel? Why not one of theirs?"

Lang had heard the British had two going. If the Italians found Hudspeth hiding in the American tunnel his bungalow would get all the blame and Malvi would cut off the hot showers or something. Everybody knew how mean Colonel Malvi got when somebody broke the rules.

"Because Hudspeth will have to live with us," Byrd said patiently. "And the British are sealing off their tunnels for a while anyhow. One of them's been compromised and they don't know which. An OR heard Grasso tell Rosie he saw an Englishman sneaking out of a bungalow with dirt in his hair. We figure Malvi intends to pull a big search the same time he transfers Hudspeth. They'll hide all the stuff in the sealed tunnels. Maps, compasses, Italian money, civilian clothes, forged IDs. You know."

Lang nodded, though he did not know. He did know that some of the prisoners were busy in mysterious ways but only a hundred or so out of more than a thousand were actually involved in escape activities and he was not one of them. He was not in on any of the secret projects. Until now. He had set all this activity in motion and was not getting credit for it. He felt slighted.

"Jaybird," he said, "would Colonel Townes-Baker make me tell how I knew if he knew I was the one told you about Major Hudspeth?"

"I don't think so. He's so tickled about putting something over on Malvi I think he'd give you a medal."

118

"Really?" Lang said eagerly.

He would love to have a medal. That would really make them take notice back home.

"You know what I mean," Byrd said.

"Oh," said Lang, disappointed. "Well, anyway, if you want to you can tell him who told you. If you're sure it won't get me in any trouble."

Lang's reward was an appointment as Colonel Waterfield's runner and one of the newly arrived British uniforms so he would not be too conspicuous when he carried messages to Colonel Townes-Baker. The SAO and the SBO did not want to be seen meeting too often after Hudspeth's disappearance. Lang was not sure he liked the honor. If he had to do a lot of running back and forth it would interfere with his personal activities. And it would involve him in serious opposition to Colonel Malvi. If they got caught he would end up in the cooler. All you got to eat in the cooler was the Eyetie ration and they said Colonel Malvi had it in for you forever after.

Byrd and Moran also got new uniforms. It would have drawn attention to Lang if only his Italian uniform had been replaced. At Colonel Waterfield's direction they turned in only two of the daubed uniforms, wadded carelessly into a single bundle. The third was added to the escape material being hidden in the sealed British tunnels. The deception went undetected.

It was raining the morning Major Hudsepth went into hiding. He slipped over to the American bay before roll call, his bright birds' eyes agleam with anticipation, and disappeared into the latrine tunnel wrapped in blankets and carrying a can of water, a breadloaf, a chocolate bar and a can of emergency rations prepared from his own recipe. The tunnel was two by two by twenty feet and Dr. Stagno said there would be no problem about air.

The count was taken indoors as was customary on rainy days. The Americans were more boisterous than usual, overreacting to hide their nervousness, and Grasso was displeased with them.

"Simmer down," Waterfield cried testily.

They grew more orderly but after Grasso got his tally and departed they erupted into noisy horseplay. Colonel Waterfield got them quiet again, scolding in his scoutmasterish fashion. He sent Byrd to lift the square of tiles covering the tunnel entrance and check on the major after posting Harbold at the back window of the latrine to watch for roving guards.

After Captain Ribolla and the Settore I officer checked their tallies a bugle would blow to announce the end of roll call and free the ORs to leave their bungalow to go to the kitchen for the tea dixies. On this morning there was only silence after the customary interval.

"They've missed him," Colonel Waterfield said. "If you guys don't act natural during the recheck I'm going to kick myself some behinds."

They were quiet and watchful when Grasso came back to count them again. He appeared relieved to find the number tallied.

"What's going on, Grasso?" Colonel Waterfield demanded. "Where's our tea?"

Grasso shook his head angrily and left at a trot. Within minutes the bugle sounded, but not the call which announced the end of head count. It was the call which always presaged a full-scale search. An extra detail of Italian soldiers would come tumbling out of their barracks, form in the outer compound and march into the prisoners' compound, where they would cordon off the bungalows to prevent any movement between them. Other soldiers would patrol the corridors in every wing to stop movement between bays so that no one could be counted twice and cover up for the missing man. Because of this unvarying procedure, surprise searches seldom achieved their purpose. It never took the guards less than ten minutes to form up and deploy.

Colonel Waterfield advised everyone to have breakfast without morning brew.

"The next count may take a while," he said dryly.

The Italians went from bungalow to bungalow and from bay to bay checking off individual names on their rosters. Captain Ribolla personally supervised the recheck in Settore II. When he and his party reached Lang's bay the prisoners were herded together on one side and required to cross to the other as their names were called. Ribolla and Grasso scrutinized each face as the men crossed over. Lang's heart beat wildly when his name was called and he was certain the Italians would sense his guilty knowledge. He resolved he would not tell them what he knew unless they tortured him or did not give him enough to eat in the cooler. Captain Ribolla looked at him sharply. Lang stopped breathing.

"You having new uniform, Tenente," he said. "Much nice."

When the last name had been read, Ribolla said "All correct," and gave Colonel Waterfield a parting salute.

"Have we had an escape, Captain?" Colonel Waterfield asked.

Ribolla pursed his lips thoughtfully.

"Perhaps," he said.

"Wish it had been one of mine," Colonel Waterfield said. "I bet the SBO the first one to make it would be an American. A week's cigarette issue."

"I fear you have losed," Ribolla said with a wry smile.

Soon after he left the bugle blew, recalling the troops, and blew again, releasing the ORs.

"Let's get Hudspeth out of there," said Stagno.

Major Hudspeth was stiff and shivering when they hauled him out of the tunnel. Stagno put him to bed at once, wrapped in blankets. From the outer compound came a prolonged shriek, as if someone were in agony. Stagno ran to the window facing the inner wall and threw it open. The shriek

121

became words, Italian and hysterical. Stagno held up his hand for silence.

"They know it's Major Hudspeth," he said. "Malvi's just canceled the troops' wine ration and all furloughs. And I think he may need some toilet paper."

Colonel Malvi was vengeful and inconsolable. He cut off the Italian newspapers and black marketing purchasing privileges. For several days after Hudspeth's disappearance there were intensive searches and surprise roll calls, some of them in the middle of the night. During these, Major Hudspeth, who had taken up residence in the American bay, would be popped into the tunnel. Pellini was mystified by Hudspeth's disappearance and apprehensive until Lang assured him no one knew of his involvement. He told Pellini no more than that despite the sergeant's burning curiosity.

Colonel Malvi was still so displeased two days after the disappearance he did not attend the opening night of a new musical revue and took back the evening gown he had donated. The soubrette, a broad-shouldered Welshman whose only qualification for female impersonation was a passable falsetto, had to wear a hastily stitched costume made of two coarse bedsheets.

Hudspeth did attend the musical, going on the night reserved for Bungalow 6 with his cap pulled low over his forehead and a muffler wound around his jaws. Lang sat as far from him as he could, hoping if the major were apprehended at the theater he would not be involved.

It was one of the best shows yet, Lang thought, with British music hall comedy routines and some of his favorite songs, "The Couple in the Castle," "I'll Be Seeing You," and "We'll Meet Again." The last was performed by the most popular singer in P.G. 203, a tenor who in civilian life had been a tutor at one of the Oxford colleges and was noted for his ferocity in the final defense of Tobruk. Lang's eyes misted during the song and he wished desperately that he really had a girl to look forward to meeting again and not just girls about whom he made up fantasies.

Colonel Malvi was at last forced to report that Major Hudspeth had escaped. It was the first such blot on his record as commandant of P.G. 203. Hudspeth's bedding was collected and one ration was cut from the Italian and Red Cross issues. Lance Corporal Gorsely informed Lang that a team had come from Rome to grill the guards, Colonnello Malvi being convinced no one could escape without inside help.

"They picked up our best contact," Gorsely said sadly. "Found him with a rucksack full of soap and tea."

Major Hudspeth's presence complicated life in the American bay but gave it a welcome spice of deception. Residents of the wing took turns standing two-hour watches around the clock in a front room overlooking the inside gate. During night watches the man going off duty would take the bunk of the man relieving him, freeing a bunk for Hudspeth. The major took his meals in the mess hall except when roving patrols were active and received a Red Cross ration held out for him by the camp parcel officer.

Colonel Townes-Baker appointed Byrd to replace him as head of the escape committee despite opposition from some members of the British majority on the grounds of Byrd's nationality, inexperience and newness in camp. Byrd spent several hours a day being briefed by Hudspeth. He was required to commit to memory the names of everyone on the three tunneling teams and the names, locations and skills of everyone who could make maps, forge documents, tailor clothing or otherwise assist in escape schemes.

Hudspeth's nose turned red and dripped constantly from his frequent immersion in the dank air of the tunnel and he developed chilblains, to Lang's secret satisfaction. He disliked the major more than ever now that he was obliged to be on call to carry messages between Colonel Waterfield and Colonel Townes-Baker. Colonel Waterfield was friendlier now but

Colonel Townes-Baker's sinister air still frightened Lang and he always felt the SBO was measuring him and finding him wanting. Adding to Lang's resentment against the major, Stagno commandeered his foot ointment to treat Hudspeth's chilblains.

In the daytime Hudspeth could visit in his own bay but from curfew on he had to remain with the Americans. He was bored among them and wandered around the bay looking lost. One evening, having nothing better to do, he watched Lang prepare a dish for personal cooking day.

With a sharpened table knife Lang scraped a space on the board table free of dirt and grease. Then he brought out a parcel box in which he and Moran had been saving bread-crusts. Working with dexterity he had never displayed before except at his navigation table in the *High Flying Flora* he rubbed the softer bread into a pile on the clean area and grated the hard crusts on a cocoa tin punched with nail holes. Hudspeth watched, absorbed, while Lang produced two large onions and minced them on the table, mixed them with the bread and added a few drops of water and olive oil.

"Oh, I say," Hudspeth said reverently, "olive oil."

Lang did not think it necessary or wise to explain the olive oil was a gift of the ORs for whom he traded. He began kneading the mass with both hands.

"Rissoles?" Hudspeth said.

"Yeah," Lang replied, pushing the hair from his forehead with the back of an oily hand.

Conscious of the major's rapt attention, he kneaded in small quantities of Red Cross pepper, dry mustard and curry powder with a theatrical flair. He molded the mixture into six fat cakes which exactly fitted into a Klim can.

"Lovely," Hudspeth whispered to himself. "I say," he said hesitantly in a louder voice, "I don't suppose you'd care to trade one off, would you?"

Lang, who had been relaxed and a bit imperious, was suddenly alert.

"What for?" he said.

"What do you fancy?"

"Chocolate," Lang said. "You got any?"

"Thirteen bars," Hudspeth said. "Two of them Canadian."

Lang was filled with greed and wonder.

"Where'd you get all that?" he said enviously.

"Put them by. Splendid escape ration, actually."

"I'll give you a rissole for a Canadian bar."

"Really, Leftenant Lang," Hudspeth said stiffly.

A Canadian bar was worth up to twenty-five cigarettes.

"Give you two of 'em," Lang said, taking out a patty and displaying it as Jock Guthrie had once displayed his tin of condensed milk. "You saw all the curry powder I used. Smell it."

He held it under Hudspeth's nose.

Hudspeth licked his lips.

"Done," he said.

In the morning when Lang reported to Colonel Townes-Baker before roll call with Colonel Waterfield's report that the night had been uneventful, he found the SBO glaring at a litter of bread shards, his sinister, romantic scar livid.

"Bloody dull knife," Townes-Baker said more to himself than to Lang. "Now I'm buggered for breakfast."

"The ORs have lots of bread," Lang said, unthinkingly. "But not enough sugar."

"They receive the same issue as officers," the colonel said irritably, baffled by Lang's remark.

"I know, sir," said Lang, wondering how to extricate himself. "But they're always short. With all the brews they have."

"I shouldn't doubt it, Leftenant. What with the tea dixies turning up gallons short every time the OC turns his back. Why this interest of yours in the ORs' sugar?"

Though not by nature an intuitive young man, Lang

125

had developed a certain shrewdness in his dealings and he sensed more than a cursory interest behind the colonel's question. But he did not know if the SBO was trying to trap him or was in a mood to trade.

"Say on," Townes-Baker ordered.

Lang decided to risk it, but cautiously.

"Well, sir," he said carefully, "some of the guys say they could get, uh, five OR loaves for a cocoa tin of sugar."

"And I suppose if I had a tin of sugar you'd undertake to find such a chap?"

"Oh, no, sir!" Lang protested, fearing a trap after all.

Townes-Baker stood up and tucked his thumbs in the waistband of his shorts. He strolled to the window and looked out.

"Even with no questions asked?" he said, before turning around. He faced Lang squarely. "Leftenant, it just happens I've sugar out me ruddy ears and I'm that famished I would eat a dog's breakfast. If you can find five OR loaves for a tin of sugar, have at it."

Lang trotted to the OR bungalow, exchanged the sugar for six loaves with Gorsely, refused tea and trotted back to his own bay to deposit one of the loaves in his food box before returning to the colonel's room. He did not intend making the same mistake with Colonel Townes-Baker that Harbold had made with him. Now that he had taken advantage of the colonel in a trade the SBO no longer seemed quite so intimidating or sinister.

When he fetched the rissoles from the cookhouse at teatime he traded half the loaf for one of Moran's. He was out only one rissole for the Canadian chocolate bar and in addition had half an OR loaf. It was one of his better days. He astonished Moran by giving him a cigarette for nothing at tea. For a man who had sold used cars in Los Angeles, Moran was not much of a trader, Lang thought, and he did not feel he should take advantage of a crewmate.

Lang could not put Hudspeth's hoard of chocolate out

of his mind. The major grew so annoyed with Lang's constant importunities he began avoiding him. Lang had given up hope of ever making a deal when he overheard Hudspeth complain of boredom to Byrd.

"I don't know what I wouldn't give for a good book," Hudspeth said longingly. "Pity there's none in the bay."

"I know a guy's got two," Lang said, joining the conversation. "But not in this bay."

Pilot Officer Perkins had two borrowed books with him when he was shot down. He had intended returning them on the way to the cinema after the mission.

"Do you suppose you might get me the loan of one of them?" Hudspeth said eagerly, suspicions lulled.

"Waiting list's too long," Lang said, improvising.

"Oh, dear," said Hudspeth.

"What'd you give for one?" Lang asked casually. "To keep, I mean."

"For my very own? There's nothing I wouldn't give for a book of my own, I should think."

Lang shrewdly refrained from pressing for a specific commitment. He did not have a book in his possession yet. If Hudspeth was that hard up for a book he should be willing to give as many as ten English chocolate bars for one, Lang estimated, the equivalent of a hundred and fifty cigarettes. If he could get the book for a hundred and twenty-five it would represent a fair profit, though a hundred would be even fairer, considering the time he had already wasted on Hudspeth.

One of Perkins's books, *Dombey and Son*, was in deplorable condition. The binding was torn, the pages loose, and it looked quite as if it had been shot down and captured. He should be able to get it cheap, Lang thought. He offered seventy-five cigarettes.

Perkins smiled a pitying smile.

"I dare say Dickens would turn over in his grave at that price," he said.

"Look at the shape it's in," Lang protested.

"Don't be rude," Perkins said. "Or we'll comment on your shape. One hundred sixty-five."

On the verge of getting angry, Lang saw Perkins was teasing him. If he had the whiskers which went with his cat's face PO Perkins would be licking them. Somehow Lang did not resent Perkins's teasing. There was no malice in it as there had once been in Moran's.

"Ninety," he said.

"Charles is whirling," Perkins said gravely. "One fifty."

Lang threw himself on Perkins's mercy. He regretted not having read Dickens and other great English writers when he had the chance, he said earnestly, and he would never have as wonderful an opportunity to make up for it as now, when he was a prisoner with time on his hands.

"I am deeply moved," said Perkins. "One hundred thirty-five."

They settled on a hundred and ten.

That night Lang bided his time while Major Hudspeth, acutely bored, watched the poker game, the bridge game, a man darning some socks and another sharpening his knife before going to his bunk for the night and sitting there looking wretched, his nose red and runny and his eyes dulled by the daily hours in the tunnel. Lang strolled over and laid the book on the major's bunk.

Hudspeth's eyes regained a little of their old sparkle.

"Oh, I say," he said reverently, *"Dombey and Son."*

Lang was touched with cold apprehension.

"You've already read it?" he said.

"It's been donkey's years. I'd love reading it again."

"It's yours," Lang said.

Hudspeth stared.

"I bought it for you."

"I don't understand."

"You said you wanted a book. So I bought it for you. A real bargain. A hundred and fifty cigarettes."

"I haven't anything like a hundred and fifty cigarettes, my dear chap."

"Ten English bars'll do."

"Ten English bars? I'm afraid not. That's the better part of my escape ration."

"But I bought it for you," Lang persisted.

"My dear chap," Major Hudspeth said, as if addressing a child, "I don't understand why you persist in saying that. I most certainly did not ask you to."

"You said there wasn't anything you wouldn't give for a book of your very own," Lang said heatedly. "And quit calling me your dear chap."

Hudspeth's nose was running again and he blotted it on a sodden handkerchief made from a woolen shirttail.

"I'm sorry you misunderstood," he said, not sounding sorry at all.

"Nine?" Lang said.

Hudspeth shook his head.

"Eight?" Lang said desperately, feeling his world collapsing.

His entire operating capital was tied up in *Dombey and Son*.

"Sorry, old chap. I should like to read it, however."

"You've got a lot of nerve," Lang cried. "After I paid all those cigarettes."

"I should be willing to pay for the privilege," Hudspeth said frigidly.

"One bar?"

At least it would not be a total loss.

"Half," said Hudspeth.

"No," Lang said indignantly.

"Sorry."

It was not until late that sleepless night Lang admitted to himself he had made a mistake in buying the book before setting a deal. Maybe he could resell it or charge a reading fee.

And he most certainly was going to have to do more trading to rebuild his reserve.

The first thing in the morning Lang slipped across to the OR bungalow, his battle jacket concealing two cocoa tins of sugar, a sheaf of camp lira and a toothbrush. Before he had time to show Gorsely what he had brought the lance corporal said, "I've a bit of news for your chaps, Leftenant."

"Yeah?" Lang said without interest, anxious to begin negotiation.

"It's about Major Hudspeth, sir."

"They found out?" Lang cried, fearful his part in the deception might be discovered.

"Oh, no, sir. Colonel Malvi thinks the major showed him a clean pair of heels. That's the point, sir."

Lance Corporal Gorsely laughed.

"Oh, this is lovely, sir. The fact is, Malvi's going to announce Major Hudspeth has been shot trying to cross into Switzerland. Shake us up a bit, he fancies."

"How you know?"

"One of my chaps has a friend among the Eyeties. The Eyetie heard Colonel Malvi and Grasso planning the announcement. It's laid on for evening parade."

Lang left everything with Gorsely and hurried back to his own bay, realizing too late he had neglected to have Gorsely count the lira in his presence to forestall disagreement about the amount.

Byrd was out. Colonel Waterfield was sitting on a stool paring his yellowing toenails with his table knife and sucking on an empty pipe. Lang blurted out his news. Waterfield rubbed his nose with the bowl of his pipe.

"Who told you this, Lang?" he asked.

"Lance Corporal Gorsely, sir."

He hoped Colonel Waterfield was not going to ask how he happened to be talking to Lance Corporal Gorsely.

"This Gorsely, he reliable?" was all the colonel said.

"Yes, sir."

Waterfield started putting on his shoes and socks.

"Find Jim and bring him to the SBO's quarters," he said.

Colonel Waterfield was the only man in P.G. 203 who called Jaybird by his given name.

Lang found Byrd practicing Italian with one of the blue-coveralled soldiers. Colonel Waterfield and Major Hudspeth were already in Townes-Baker's room and the lookouts posted.

"What a clever bugger is Colonnello Malvi," said Townes-Baker after Lang had repeated his story for him. "Give us a turn if Evelyn actually had escaped, what?"

"Sir," Byrd said to the SBO, "how much longer you think Major Hudspeth should keep under cover?"

Hudspeth had been in hiding almost two weeks. He had finished transferring his secrets days before but Townes-Baker and Waterfield were enjoying the deception so much they had not considered ending it.

"Actually, I hadn't given it much thought," said Townes-Baker. "Why?"

"Dr. Stagno says his cold could turn into pneumonia if he has to spend much more time in the tunnel," Byrd said.

He did not add that the men in the wing had started grumbling about the two-hour watches they were required to stand, because he did not sympathize with them.

"Nonsense," said Townes-Baker. "You Yanks coddle yourselves too much."

"Jim's right," Waterfield said in a rare show of opposition to the SBO. "Just look at Evelyn."

Townes-Baker regarded Hudspeth's red, dripping nose and dull eyes. The major had deteriorated noticeably.

"I'm quite able to continue indefinitely," Hudspeth protested.

"Yes," Townes-Baker said musingly. He sighed. "Pity. But I suppose there's nothing else for it. It shan't be until after Malvi's little announcement, at any rate."

"Naturally," said Waterfield.

"Evelyn," Townes-Baker said, "when do you fancy going to the cooler? In the morning?"

"Doesn't matter, really, sir," Hudspeth said, wiping his nose.

Lang had been standing in the background, quiet and unnoticed, flattered to be present at this meeting of the brass. Now there flashed across his mind his childhood fantasy of being present at his own funeral and, thinking of the consternation it would cause if Major Hudspeth were to appear during Malvi's announcement, he chuckled. All eyes turned to him.

"Do we amuse you, Leftenant?" Townes-Baker demanded.

"No, sir," Lang said hastily, embarrassed by the attention and intimidated by the SBO's gruffness. "I was just thinking, it sure would be funny if Major Hudspeth was to come walking out right after Colonel Malvi said he was dead."

Townes-Baker stared at Lang as if seeing him for the first time. The incredulity faded from his eyes, his scar dropped to its normal position and, leaping from his stool, he slapped his thigh and shouted with laughter. None present had ever seen the SBO so demonstrative.

"Fiendish!" he cried. "Positively fiendish. What a lovely turn of mind you have, Leftenant Lang. I shouldn't have guessed it."

The others added their congratulations. Even Hudspeth. Lang was elated.

At roll call, Settore I lined up on one side of the street, Settore II on the other. It was agreed Hudspeth would hide in Townes-Baker's quarters until after Malvi's announcement and then present himself in full view of the assembled prisoners and Italian staff.

Lang's euphoria lessened as afternoon parade drew nearer. What if Gorsely had given him duff gen, he thought, wrong information. His tension increased during the count. Because of him a thousand men were waiting gleefully to see the Italians make fools of themselves. Even the cooks in their sooty uniforms had drifted out to the cookhouse veranda to watch the fun. The British gave little indication anything special was afoot but the Americans were less phlegmatic and Waterfield had to scold them.

"If one of you fellows ruins the show I'll make him permanent tea orderly," he growled in a low voice.

Upon satisfactory conclusion of a count the Italian officer in charge normally signaled Townes-Baker to dismiss the troops. Now, when the signal was not given, Lang breathed more easily. The inner gate opened and Malvi entered, followed by Pellini, who looked forlorn. Pellini must really believe Major Hudspeth had been killed, Lang thought.

The Italians snapped to attention and the prisoners, on Townes-Baker's bawled command, followed.

Captain Ribolla stepped forward.

"All officers and Other Ranks," he said in a loud voice. "Your commandant has a pronouncement of extremely importance to all. Please to make attention."

He stepped back. Colonel Malvi walked forward deliberately and swept the formations with a slow, stern gaze, his eyeglasses glinting in the sunlight. Lieutenant Grasso was smiling with anticipation. Sergeant Pellini, standing beside and a little behind Malvi, still looked forlorn. Malvi spoke gravely. Pellini translated at the end of each sentence.

"It is my unpleasant duty to inform the officers and Other Ranks detained at P.G. 203 of a needless tragedy," Pellini translated.

Lang turned to grin at Byrd. Byrd frowned a warning.

"In spite of my efforts to make detention as comfortable as possible, Major Evelyn Hudspeth, British Army, two weeks ago betrayed the trust I place in all of you."

"Hear, hear," a British voice muttered.

Malvi paused, annoyed.

"As I have advised you so many times," he continued

133

at last, "it is better you remain peacefully in my protection than risk the perils of a valiant nation vigilant and merciless in war."

Someone snickered and was elbowed by his neighbor.

"What I must relate to you saddens me, but as a soldier of Italy I must accept its justice and as your commandant point out to all of you that a similar fate awaits all who may attempt to follow the path of Major Evelyn Hudspeth, British Army. Yesterday at 0900 hours in the railway station at Chiasso, Major Hudspeth, being apprehended and attempting to flee, lost his life."

Malvi searched the formations again with his stern gaze, studying the effect of his revelation. The prisoners appeared frozen with shock. Grasso's smile broadened.

"Major Hudspeth was dressed in civilian clothing," Malvi resumed gravely, his words sounding more apologetic than stern in Pellini's translation, "in defiance of all rules of conduct and in his pockets were incendiary fountain pens for burning the homes of innocent citizens. In spite of such gangsterism I deeply regret the death of an English officer in my care. But be warned. Attempt no further escapes. Here you are safe. Outside you will meet the fate of Major Evelyn Hudspeth."

There was a long, dramatic pause. Then Malvi signaled the Italian officer in charge to dismiss the prisoners and began walking toward the gate. The OIC in turn signaled Colonel Townes-Baker.

"Settore I," Townes-Baker cried. "Eyes left! Settore II. Eyes right!"

On either side of the street the formations stood at attention looking back toward the cookhouse. The Italian officers, who were forming up their own troops to march out, stopped this activity and looked curiously at the long lines of prisoners. Pellini reached out and touched Colonel Malvi's shoulder. Malvi stopped and turned around.

Major Hudspeth had slipped out of the bungalow after

the count and taken a position behind the rear rank of prisoners at the end of the formation. Now he came around to the street and began marching toward the distant gate with the angular bent-arm strut of the parading British soldier. In one hand he carried his razor, toothbrush and comb rolled neatly in a towel. He wore a complete, clean uniform assembled from fellow prisoners. He had borrowed freshly blacked British Army boots to replace his broken desert shoes and the hobnails clacked smartly in the stillness. His face had regained its color and his eyes sparkled with their former keenness. His nose had faded from rosy to pale pink and no longer ran.

The prisoners remained silent and motionless except for a turning of heads to follow Hudspeth's progress toward the gate. Colonel Malvi, who was a bit nearsighted despite his glasses, watched Hudspeth's approach with puzzled annoyance. Grasso was livid, Pellini dazed. Ribolla scratched his head and stared at Colonel Waterfield.

When Hudspeth reached Malvi he halted, stamping his right boot in the British fashion. Colonel Malvi recognized him now. He, too, looked dazed. Hudspeth flung out his right arm and brought it to his temple in a vibrating salute. Malvi hesitated, then returned it.

Hudspeth cried out in a strong voice, "Hudspeth, Evelyn. Major, British Army. Present, sir."

CHAPTER 8

Tenente Grasso requested, and got, leave because he could not face the prisoners but Malvi's reaction was anticipated by no one. Though he sent Hudspeth to the cooler for two weeks, a punishment none considered excessive, he took no mass reprisals and, on the contrary, restored the privileges withdrawn after Hudspeth's disappearance.

It was thought he was so delighted to find his perfect record still intact that it more than compensated for the ignominy of being made to look foolish. It was, however, some days before he reduced the frequency of surprise searches. He knew that Hudspeth could only have hidden in a tunnel and was determined to find it. When at last the tunnel which Grasso had suspected was discovered, the number and intensity of searches returned to normal.

It was now late March. Lang, Byrd and Moran had been prisoners for three months. Byrd received a letter from his wife, their first direct communication from the world outside. Flora had been in touch with Lang's parents and Moran's father. They were all known to be safe, and parcels and more mail were on the way. And they had all been awarded the Air Medal and Distinguished Flying Cross for combat hours flown before their last mission. Later, when Lang let it slip to PO Perkins his DFC was for two hundred combat hours and not some individual feat of daring, Perkins made rude comments. Perkins's own DFC was for shooting down six enemy aircraft and destroying two others on the ground. He had no idea how many combat hours he had flown.

At first they were tremendously stimulated at having at last established a link with home but their elation was transient. Until the letter came, home had been an abstraction, the place where prisoners went when they slept. Now it became too distressingly real. They could feel its tantalizing existence in Flora's letter, tantalizing because the letter was a piece of home they could hold in their hands but not enough of home to satisfy any craving.

And Lang resented the fact Byrd had received a letter before he did. Probably because Jaybird was a captain and a pilot, he thought. Moran was resentful, too, though his resentment was not directed at Byrd. Flora had sent the letter airmail and the older prisoners now told them airmail letters normally came more quickly than regular mail.

"Why the hell didn't one of you bastards tell us that before?" Moran demanded.

"They should have known it at home, like Flora did," Lang said, turning his anger against his parents. "Anybody ought to know airmail is faster."

"My old man's probably too busy chasing the babes to think about anything as simple as that," Moran said.

137

There was a querulous note in Moran's voice Lang had never heard before and he welcomed it. The two of them immediately wrote postcards home urging their parents to write airmail.

Reaction set in more slowly with Byrd but it was stronger when it came. The letter pierced his defenses as nothing else had been able to and for a time he found the privations of P.G. 203 as galling as Moran did.

Lang was the first to recover. He had no Flora waiting for him, he had his trading and he discovered a new outlet, reading. Moran, who had read voraciously before capture despite the fact he had little patience with inaction, was responsible. Seeing Lang scowling at the book which had cost him so much of his capital, Moran picked it up and began leafing idly through it. He turned back to the first page and began reading it, standing by Lang's bunk. He chuckled. Then, holding the open book in one hand, he vaulted into his own bunk and lay there, engrossed. Lang waited impatiently for Moran to give it back and when Moran did not he stood up and cleared his throat.

"You gonna keep my book all day?" he demanded.

Moran looked at him, annoyed, marking his place with a finger.

"You weren't reading it," he said. "How about letting me?"

"Okay," Lang said reluctantly. "But read it fast, will you?"

He had just been reaching a decision to lend the book for a five-cigarette fee and was anxious to begin operations. He felt Moran had somehow tricked him.

Moran spent the rest of the day reading in his bunk. When the poker game started after supper he did not take his customary seat. He read until lights out, then went into the latrine with his stool and a blanket and read until the chill sent him back to his bunk. He returned to the book after breakfast and finished by evening parade.

138

It was an uneasy period for Lang. He was anxious to put *Dombey and Son* to work and kept a constant, though surreptitious check on Moran's progress. He was impressed by Moran's complete immersion in the book and by his changing expressions. Moran who did not have the patience to slice a loaf thinly but hacked at it with his knife, who in a poker game impatiently cried, "Deal the tickets," when the cards did not fall fast enough, who sometimes stared helplessly around the bay and hit a bunkpost with his fist.

He envied Moran as he watched him. It was as if Moran had escaped from P.G. 203 for the moment and left him behind.

"Damn, that was good," Moran said when he returned the book. "I never really gave a rat's ass for Dickens before. Too long-winded. Damon Runyon was my boy."

Bertram had been a Runyon fan, too, and Lang had sometimes been jealous of Moran and Bertram when he heard the two of them laughing and speaking Runyonese together. It had made him feel even more left out than usual.

"I'm gonna charge five cigarettes to let guys read it," Lang said. "Think they'll pay that much?"

"Hell, yes."

"I guess I'll get started then."

"You mean you ain't going to read it yourself?"

"I got most of my cigarettes tied up in it," Lang said. "I got to start getting 'em back."

"Of all the clowns," Moran said with disgust. "You ain't read a book since you been here and you pass up one like this. I'll tell you what, Blubber," he added thoughtfully, "I'll give you five cigarettes to read it."

"I wasn't going to charge you," Lang protested, hoping Moran would insist anyhow.

"I don't mean for me to read it, for Christ's sake. I mean for you to read it."

"How come?" Lang demanded, suspecting a joke of some kind.

"Because you're so damn fatheaded it chaps my ass," Moran said. "Because when I like something I want to talk about it to somebody. So read the damn book and we can talk about it."

"Like you and Bertram used to talk about Damon Runyon?"

"You remember that?" Moran said, surprised.

Lang did not expect to enjoy the book as much as Moran had but if it would help make Moran like him as much as he had liked Bertram he was determined to read it and, if necessary, pretend he liked it. He did not have to pretend. He found the book as engrossing as Moran had and laughed aloud while reading it. Nothing like that had occurred when he read *Oliver Twist* in school. Maybe it was because he understood the characters better now, he thought, having lived among the English for months, or because he was more bored than he had realized, or was so anxious to please Moran.

When he finished the book he and Moran sat up for more than an hour after lights out talking about it and for that period of time Lang felt Moran liked him as much as he had liked Bertram. He found himself being glad Bertram was dead. If Bertram had not been killed the bombardier, not he, would be sitting on Moran's bunk, legs dangling, filled with laughter and excitement. Lang fell into guilty silence.

"What's the matter, Blubber?" Moran asked.

"I was thinking about Bertram," Lang said.

"What a guy," Moran said.

"Yeah," Lang agreed, feeling hypocritical because of the reason he had remembered Bertram.

He dreamed of Bertram that night. In the dream, he was back in the quarantine prison, sleeping. Something, a sound or a presence, awakened him and, looking toward the window, he saw it blocked by a shadowy outline. He rose on one elbow and when his eyes grew accustomed to the darkness he saw it was Bertram standing at the window looking out, his back to the room. Bertram wore his flying suit, still wet from the sea. It was the sound of water dripping on the floor that had awakened him, Lang realized.

"Bertram?" he called quietly, so as not to awaken Moran, asleep in the next bed.

He was not frightened, for it did not seem threatening for Bertram to be in the room, only strange.

"Yeah," the shape answered without turning.

"I thought you were dead," Lang said.

"No," said Bertram matter-of-factly, still not turning around, "I got out."

Lang felt a great wash of relief. Bertram was not dead and he was absolved of guilt for all the unkind thoughts he had had of the bombardier.

When Lang awakened in his bunk at P.G. 203 and knew it had been a dream and Bertram was dead, his eyes filled with tears and because he now cried for Bertram he felt truly absolved. He did not tell Byrd and Moran of his dream.

It was midmorning before Lang was himself again, thinking of the trades that should be made, of his pleasure in *Dombey and Son* and through it of his pleasure in Moran, and of the other book belonging to Pilot Officer Perkins, *Pendennis*. At lunch he asked Perkins if he might borrow it.

"I've rather a long waiting list, Distinguished Flier," Perkins said.

"Will you put me on it?" Lang said, ignoring Perkins's sly reference to his medal.

"I should hope we'll not be in the bag that long. And I get three cigarettes for the loan of it."

"I'll give four," Lang said recklessly.

"Done," said Perkins. "If you have it back in forty-eight hours."

"Forty-eight hours? A book that long?"

"Thackeray is rather a wordy chap," Perkins conceded. "Three days, then."

Lang began reading *Pendennis* at once, stopping only for meals. He finished it in one full day and half an uncomfortable night on a stool in the latrine. Then he let Moran read it for four cigarettes on condition it be finished in two days. Lang did not feel he was taking advantage of Moran. He had made no profit on the transaction and Moran would not have otherwise had an opportunity to read the book.

There were other books in camp, he discovered, which the owners would lend for cigarettes or in exchange for the loan of another book. Instead of renting out *Dombey* he loaned it for other books except when he had an urgent need of cigarettes for trading. When he was able to finish a book in less than the allotted time he would let Moran read it for a small fee. Moran was satisfied with the arrangement and it continued until a small library was organized from books sent in by the Red Cross and the YMCA, augmented by donations from the prisoners themselves. Book owners were encouraged to contribute by receiving in exchange for their books a special library card entitling them to first choice every morning when the library opened. Lang's first reaction was to retain his book and rent it out, contenting himself with the leavings of those who had preferred cards, but when he found no one would pay to borrow a book when they could be had free at the library he turned it in.

Though he had been a teacher, Byrd did not read as much as Lang and Moran, being greatly occupied with his camp duties. When he did read he preferred nonfiction. Lang liked novels best. Moran would read anything. When the three of them talked together it was not about books but most often about home or, with Byrd guiding the conversation, about the war and escape. Byrd talked often of escape, most urgently after letters from Flora. Moran was anxious as he to get out of P.G. 203 but had no patience for planning. Moran worked in the American tunnel but with no real hope of ever seeing it to completion because the clay was like stone. Lang knew he should be just as anxious as either of them to get out of the camp but could not work up genuine enthusiasm, though on occasion he would simulate it to please Byrd.

There was first of all the danger. A man could get shot trying to escape and if caught in the outer compound would certainly be severely beaten. And if they did get out, where could they go, Lang thought. They were the enemy and in a strange land. Byrd had learned some Italian but certainly could not pose as an Italian. There was an element of futility even in planning escape. No one had escaped yet. During the months Lang had been in P.G. 203 not one man had even gotten beyond the outer compound though there had been half a dozen attempts. Most of them had been detected attempting to scale the wall and one had been caught trying to march out with a search detail one night wearing the Italian uniform they had held back. How could they hope to make it, Lang thought, when the British, who were better at such things than Americans, had all failed.

And, as weeks passed, he was growing more content with things as they were. It was as if he had known no other life. He was often hungry, though seldom ravenous, but because of his trades ate better than most other prisoners. Knowing this gave him a kind of nourishment of its own. The weather was becoming milder and he was not cold any more. He had begun getting letters from home flattering in their expressions of concern and telling him of food and book parcels on the way. He wanted to be there when they came. Though he was aware he could have all the things being sent him and far more if he were free, he knew also they would not have the same drama and the value outside the prison camp. He had waited too long for the things that were coming and thought about them too often and too vividly to be denied them.

And he had more friends here than ever he had outside and far more status. Everyone knew Steven Lang, even the SBO and Rosie Ribolla. Pellini told him things no one else in the camp knew. Gorsely said he was indispensable to the ORs and there was always someone ready to discuss a trade or a book or ask his advice in preparing a dish for the cookhouse.

More Americans were coming into P.G. 203 now that

143

North African operations were stepping up again and, although they eventually learned his nickname was Blubberbutt and began calling him that, to them he was a seasoned airman and prisoner and one who cut a figure in camp life. Lang liked the company of new prisoners. They came in bewildered and were absurdly grateful for small favors. He had a certain arrogance with them which amused Moran but alienated few of the newcomers because they accepted it with his favors and his position in the camp.

And because of all these things, though he missed his parents and the good things of the free life and wanted girls, he was willing to wait for them not too impatiently. The Allies were on the move in North Africa and eventually they would come to liberate him. He would be happy when they came but until then he would take no chances.

He realized just how accustomed he had become to P.G. 203 when Pellini told him fifty English officers were to be transferred to another camp to make room for Americans and his first reaction was one of relief that he was not among those being sent among strangers. The reaction of many of the British officers selected for transfer eased Lang's feeling of unworthiness for accepting life in P.G. 203 so readily. They did not want to be transferred, either. They did not want to leave their friends or interrupt the flow of mail and parcels, and despite the excitement of change in their monotonous lives they were gripped by the inertia which came to men relieved of the need to make decisions. It was this inertia more than fear of danger, though Lang did not know it, which had limited the number of men working actively on escape plans.

There were other officers, however, who saw in the transfer a chance to escape. Among them was Byrd. He invited Lang and Moran to walk with him around the compound and brought up the subject with uncharacteristic reticence.

"Would you care if I tried to escape without you?" he said, as if asking forgiveness.

144

"If you get a chance to go, take it," Moran said. "But what's the deal?"

Lang was glad Moran had spoken first. He had felt an obligation to protest so Byrd would not think him a coward.

"Yeah," he said. "You're married and we're not."

"There's an officer on the list about my size and build," Byrd said. "He said he'd trade places with me if I wanted to. If I can jump off the train I'd try to get to an airfield and fly to Switzerland or Malta. One of the RAF officers taught me the SOP for taking off a Macchi. I don't think more than one man would have a chance," he added apologetically.

"If anybody can make it, you can," Moran said.

"That's right," Lang agreed, but he did not really believe that even Jaybird could pull it off.

Even if he got a chance to jump off the train he could get hurt when he landed, and what chance would he have of getting on an airfield, the way they were guarded, or have time to get a plane engine warmed up enough to take off if he did get on? He remembered how they had had to turn the props through by hand before starting the engines of their bomber when they had no energizer, and if Italian fighters had to be started the same way Jaybird was in trouble. But he assumed Jaybird knew all about that. Jaybird always seemed to know anything he had to.

"I feel like I'm running out on you two," Byrd said unhappily.

"Don't feel that way," Lang said. "We'd do the same if we had the chance."

Byrd presented his plan to Colonel Waterfield and Colonel Townes-Baker and it was approved by both. He was supplied with maps and Italian money, the latter obtained through Gorsely by Lang, whose connections with the ORs had gradually acquired tacit, semiofficial approval. Major Hudspeth was to become head of the escape committee again. Surprisingly, he was not on the list to be transferred. Pellini told Lang it was because Colonel Malvi did not want the major boasting of his exploit in another camp.

The night before Byrd was to leave the three of them sat on Moran's bunk and talked until late in much the same vein as they had at the quarantine prison on Christmas Eve except that now the nostalgia had an undertone of excitement. In the morning Byrd dyed his red hair and sandy eyebrows black with ink and exchanged his tin captain's bars for the shoulder pips of an English lieutenant.

"If I make it I'll go see your folks first thing," he told them.

"Good luck, you redheaded bastard," Moran said, moved at the prospect of not seeing Byrd again. "Be careful or I'll kick your ass."

It was the first time Lang had ever heard Moran talk roughly to Jaybird. He had always been more respectful to their pilot than to anyone else, regardless of rank.

"So long, Jaybird," Lang said. "I hope you make it."

They shook hands and Byrd left for his substitute's bay taking with him the Red Cross parcel box containing everything he owned. They did not speak to each other again. With the rest of the prisoners, Lang and Moran assembled at the camp street to see the fifty prisoners leave. Jock Guthrie was among those leaving. He waved at Lang as they moved out.

When the gate closed behind Byrd, Lang felt deserted, envious and sad. He wished he had had the guts to do what Byrd was doing.

For a day or so after Byrd left Lang felt lonely and adrift despite the fact he had not spent much time with his pilot for many weeks and was much closer to Moran. It was not Colonel Townes-Baker or Colonel Waterfield to whom he had looked for authority but to Jaybird, he realized. And though he had friends now, Jaybird had been the first to treat him decently.

Moran missed Byrd, too, but it took the form of a rag-

146

ing restlessness that would not permit him to read or play poker.

"Why the hell didn't I go, too?" he said angrily as they walked side by side on the street. "I could be shacked up somewhere with an Eyetie family right now."

"You know Jaybird hasn't got a chance," Lang said, trying to comfort him.

Moran stopped and gripped Lang's arm, his face hard and threatening.

"You say that again and I'll knock you on your ass!" he said viciously.

"Cut it out, Moran," Lang begged. "I didn't mean anything."

Moran looked away and blew out a loud breath like a fighter clearing his lungs.

"I'm sorry, Blubber," he said. "I don't know what the hell's wrong with me."

A few evenings after Byrd's departure Lang persuaded Moran to go to the theater with him.

"It's *Of Mice and Men* with an all-limey cast," he coaxed. "The accents'll kill you."

George's accent was Oxfordian and Lennie's pure Yorkshire but once the novelty had worn off both Lang and Moran became engrossed. The performance ended during the second act, however, when a power failure shut off all lights in the camp. A bugle blew in the outer compound and the roving guards within the prisoners' compound and the sentries in the boxes on the wall began calling to each other apprehensively. The Italian officer of the day came into the prisoners' compound with the extra guards summoned by the bugle call and in a strained voice ordered the prisoners to return at once to their own bays. Lang and Moran passed near him as he was making his announcement and Moran, who had extraordinary night vision, plucked off the officer's cap. The officer gasped and whirled around but Moran was already yards away, dragging the frightened Lang behind him.

"What'd you do?" Lang panted as they ran.

"I just wanted to give the bastard a thrill," Moran said, choking with laughter.

He stopped and sailed the cap on top of a bungalow.

There was an edge of panic in the shouts of the guards now. Those inside the prison compound had flashlights which they kept on for only seconds at a time, as if afraid they would be attacked by the prisoners if they betrayed their positions.

"Jesus, what a chance to escape," Moran said.

"How?" Lang demanded.

"Hell," Moran said with sudden resolution. "Let's go over the wall, Blubber."

"You crazy?" Lang demanded. "What about the concertina wire and the fence?"

"We can clear the wire if we jump out far enough," Moran said excitedly, hustling Lang toward the wall. "And climb the fence."

Before he could protest, Lang was over the tripwire and standing at the wall, bitten by fear. What if the lights came on now, he thought. You could get shot just for crossing the tripwire.

"Come on," Moran whispered urgently, "give me a boost."

Dumbly, Lang clasped his hands in a stirrup for Moran's foot and raised him high enough to reach up to the top of the wall. Moran pulled himself up with apelike agility and reached down for Lang. Lang did not move.

"Come on, Blubber, we ain't got all night," he whispered.

"No," Lang said, finding his will at last. "We'll get caught."

"I'm going whether you come or not. You coming?"

"Don't," Lang begged.

"So long, Blubber," said Moran.

There was the sound of boots scraping on the top of the wall, a body landing, a rattle of wire and Moran's suppressed cursing. Lang took one panic-stricken step toward safety, then forced himself to stop.

"Moran?" he called.

"I'm caught in the wire," came Moran's low, urgent reply. "Beat it, Blubber."

Lang hesitated. A voice called out a challenge from the nearest guardbox. He froze. Another challenge, and then a spurt of fire and the crack of a shot fired into the air. Lang ran. He blundered blindly through the darkness, gasping, crashing into other prisoners who were running now, stumbling, avoiding the shouting inner guards and their probing flashlights. He did not stop until he was inside his own bungalow. He groped his way along the noisy corridor to his bay. He could see the shapes of men crowded around the window calling out questions.

"Colonel Waterfield," he cried.

A figure detached itself and shuffled toward him in the darkness.

"That you, Lang?" it asked.

"Yes, sir," Lang gasped. "Moran's out there. He's caught in the wire."

"That damn fool!" Colonel Waterfield cried angrily.

There was more shooting outside now from all around the wall, and running footsteps and frantic shouting in Italian.

"Get down!" Colonel Waterfield yelled. "They're shooting wild."

Lang dropped down with the others, his heart pounding against the tiles.

I hope Moran's all right, he thought. If anything happens to him . . .

From outside the wall came a shout of surprise, fear and anger, and then Moran cursing and crying out, "You little son of a bitch!"

Then more cries outside the wall, excited and growing almost festive, and Moran grunting and cursing.

149

"They're beating him up," Colonel Waterfield said. "Thank God they didn't shoot him."

Lang shriveled inside, glad it was not he outside in the wire but feeling almost as much terror as if it were, afraid for Moran but just as afraid for himself though he was safe inside the bungalow.

The lights came on then, and the shouting and the shots and the running stopped. Everyone got up off the floor and began talking at the same time, asking Lang for his story. In a few minutes Captain Ribolla hurried in, looking grim, to summon Captain Stagno.

"A foolish venture," he told Waterfield.

"How is he?" Lang demanded.

"Unrepentant," Ribolla said curtly.

Lang thought he saw a fleeting smile cross the Italian's grim face but he was not sure.

He waited up with Colonel Waterfield until Stagno returned.

"They've got him in the cooler," Stagno said. "They gave him a working over but nothing's broken. He may be in serious trouble, though."

"Why?" said Waterfield.

"He broke a guard's nose."

"The crazy galoot," Waterfield said.

There was admiration in his voice, not anger. Lang was jealous. He wished he had gone over the wall, too.

CHAPTER 9

Moran was not tried for assaulting the guard. Townes-Baker, working through Dr. Stagno and his Italian medical colleague, made a deal with Colonel Malvi not to report Moran's beating to the Protecting Power, the Swiss representative who made periodic inspections of P.G. 203, if Malvi did not file charges against the American. Moran got only the customary two weeks in the cooler.

With both Byrd and Moran gone Lang felt as if he had lost some of his identity, yet there was a sense of liberation as well, for now there was no one around with personal knowledge of his past faults and failures.

He was glad, though, when Byrd returned to P.G. 203 in the first week of Moran's absence. The English officer Byrd replaced had been identified some days before and was now occupying the solitary confinement cell next to Moran's.

"I never got a chance to jump," Byrd said. "Jock Guthrie made a break as soon as we pulled out of the station and after that they watched us like hawks."

"Did he make it?" Lang asked.

Byrd gave him a strange look.

"Didn't Malvi announce it?" he asked. "Jock bought it."

"Oh, hell," Lang groaned, saddened but feeling he somehow shared the Scot's daring and tragedy because he had known Jock and been accepted by him as a friend. He felt heroic, as when he survived the crash of the *High Flying Flora* and others had not.

Byrd blamed himself for Moran's misadventure.

"If I'd been here I'd never have let him do it," he said. "Next time nobody's going out unless we all go out together. Okay, Steve?"

"Okay," Lang said. "I told him not to but he wouldn't listen."

Moran came out of the cooler on a Wednesday. In preparation for the occasion Lang made rissoles from two whole OR loaves and the three of them had a tea party in celebration of their reunion. Moran had a scab over one eyebrow and scratches on his hands like Wog Simpson's.

"Those little bastards are rough as a cob," he said, almost admiringly. "They kicked the living crap outta me. But I got me one of 'em. Right in the snoot."

"We heard about it," Lang said.

"It was almost worth it to pop one of 'em," Moran said, smiling reminiscently. "But I tell you one thing, don't let 'em catch you outside the wall. It really chaps 'em. They act like you'd hopped their mother or something."

Lang's skin prickled. He hoped Byrd was not intending to involve him in any scheme which might expose him to that risk.

As days went by and Byrd did not bring up the subject

of escape again Lang forgot about it. Life became easier as the weather grew warmer. The isolated little trees in the prisoners' compound burst into leaf and some days it was warm enough to bask against the bungalow wall out of the wind. Even the nights were comfortable. The first week in May the camp went on full parcels and there was more to eat for everyone. Lang traded more for recreation than for actual need.

The first American Red Cross parcels arrived and at last there were American cigarettes in camp, but not brands with which any of the older prisoners were familiar.

"What the hell is this?" Moran demanded indignantly when he opened his first American parcel. "They making special brands for prisoners of war?"

Lang was also dissatisfied with the American parcels. They were neither as nourishing as the Canadian nor as varied as the British. There was an orange drink powder in it which Dr. Stagno said would prevent scurvy and instead of condensed milk or Klim there was a tin of evaporated milk which was useless except in brews and which soured if not used the first few days. There was coffee in the parcels, however, which almost made up for the shortcomings. The British officers, who had professed to prefer tea and who still received British parcels, clamored for it. Because of this, Waterfield was able to make a deal with Townes-Baker to issue British parcels to the Americans who preferred them.

The camp grew more restless as newly arrived American captives brought news of an invasion buildup in Tunisia. Lang did not share this restlessness. He carried his straw mattress out into the courtyard between the wings of his bungalow and spent hours sunbathing and reading. At other times he would visit bays where new American prisoners lived and tell them about the old days of operations out of Palestine and Egypt, and of the hardships of half parcels and frigid weather in the Italian winter at P.G. 203. There was always a new and receptive audience and, more talkative than he had ever been

153

in his life, he reveled in the attention. Lang talked to let them know he was an important person; he talked to make up for the years in which no one would listen.

Sometimes he was awakened in the night by the song of nightingales outside the wall and in the moment before full awareness thought they were mockingbirds singing outside his window at home but the ensuing nostalgia was more voluptuous than aching.

Now that he was well fed and warm his night thoughts turned with increasing urgency to girls but he was not nearly so frustrated in this as Moran, for even outside the prison camp his successes with girls had been hardly less imaginary than inside.

Life was good for Lang that Italian spring.

Until Byrd announced it was time to start thinking about escape.

"The Allies will be invading Italy any day and we'll have some place to go," he said. "We're in good shape now and we'll be able to live off the land until we get to our own lines."

"What lines?" Lang demanded. "They haven't got here yet."

"They will have by the time we get out," Byrd said.

"If they make a landing maybe we won't have to escape," Lang protested. "If we just stay put they'll liberate us. Why take a chance on getting killed if we don't have to?"

"It might take months to reach us. The Italians might move us up north. Anything could happen. The tunnel will be past the wire in two or three months and when it gets there we're going out."

"But, Jaybrid!"

"I thought you'd be tickled pink," Byrd said. "Colonel Waterfield didn't want to include you in the escape party because you didn't do any work but I told him I wouldn't go without you."

"Thanks," Lang said ungraciously.

He was relieved when, a week or so later, Rosie Ribolla

154

discovered the tunnel. The Italians had never suspected a tunnel in a latrine because the light was kept on all night but one morning the American cleanup detail was careless and an Italian soldier found a smear of fresh clay on the floor. Ribolla came into the compound late at night and after a vigil outside the latrine saw a shift change through a crack in the blackout shutter. It was a crushing blow to all except Lang. He felt he could now wait for the Allies in peace.

But Byrd would not be discouraged. He began a methodical study of the compound, looking for weak points and, standing on a top bunk, he looked over the seven-foot inner wall into the outer compound for hours on end. He made a scale drawing of the inner compound and what he could see of the outer, plotting the lines of sight from all the guardboxes. At night he checked the orbits of the searchlights and plotted and timed the movements of the roving guards from vantage points in both wings of the bungalow.

Lang observed this with a foreboding which increased when, after the fall of the islands of Pantelleria and Lampedusa in June, Byrd stained his bedsheet with dirt and began crawling around the compound after curfew. Some nights he was gone for hours. In this way he obtained more information about the movement of guards in the prison compound. Discovering he could climb on the inner wall where it joined the camp wall and lie there out of the field of the searchlights and the view of wall sentries and roving guards, he learned when the troops went to bed and when they arose, when the guard changed and where it formed to march into the prison compound. He also deduced when all the off-duty troops could be expected to be sleeping. There would be no singing.

The off-duty troops always sang when they were awake, sometimes singly, sometimes in groups. They had guitars and accordions on which they accompanied themselves. On Saturday nights or feast days when they had extra wine they sang and played late into the evening and many prisoners found them more entertaining than the theater.

155

From these activities Byrd developed a plan which was approved by Colonel Townes-Baker, Colonel Waterfield and the escape committee. He called Lang and Moran together and explained it to them. They would scale the wall to the outer compound and, hidden by camouflaged bedsheets, creep along the camp wall past the rear of the troop barracks to the angle of the front and side walls. There, concealed from the view of anyone in the outer compound by the troop barracks, and from the view of the wall sentry by his own guardbox, they would scale the wall.

"The guardbox is up on posts," Byrd explained. "There's an eighteen- or twenty-inch space between the top of the wall and the floor of the box. If we don't make any noise we can crawl under it and drop down outside the camp."

"Molto benny," said Moran. "When do we leave?"

"The first air alert blackout after the invasion," Byrd said.

Lang said nothing. Moran looked at him thoughtfully.

"If you're gonna crawl under that guardbox you got to reduce, Blubber," he said. "Since we went on full parcels your ass got big again."

"You think you're so funny," Lang said.

It was like old times.

Byrd had them camouflage their bedsheets and start saving chocolate for escape rations. Lang thought Jaybird's order to save chocolate a gross abuse of authority. Chocolate bars gave him some of his best moments. He ate them in his bunk after lights out, a small bite at a time, letting the chocolate melt in his mouth.

Byrd insisted he practice crawling around outside in his bedsheet after curfew to prepare himself for the assault on the outer compound. Byrd had him practice in the courtyard between the wings after lights out and watched him from the window.

"You carry your tail too high," Byrd said after his first attempt. "Keep down. Like a snake."

"Act like you're trying to plow with your joint," Moran said. "That keeps your butt down." He added regretfully, "I could sure as hell plow with mine. It gets so hard a cat couldn't scratch it."

Lang was far more disturbed by the new escape plan than he had been by the prospect of leaving through the tunnel. The thought of being caught in the outer compound terrified him. He lay awake nights worrying. He tried to think positively of escape, of easily eluding the guards, of helpful civilians and secret agents, of a timely landing, a waiting submarine or airplane, of returning to an awed Serena the Butterfly Girl and a hero's welcome at home. But he could conjure up only a savage beating or a bullet in the back.

He revealed none of this to Byrd or Moran. Jaybird was his pilot and he always did what Jaybird told him to. And Moran would not be his friend any more if Moran knew he was such a coward.

Lang found temporary relief when the Allies invaded Sicily instead of the mainland in July but Byrd quickly adapted his strategy to the situation.

"We'll head south," he said. "That way we'll be okay whether they push across the Strait of Messina to the toe or make another landing higher up."

Five days after the invasion of Sicily, Byrd awakened Lang at two in the morning.

"We're taking off," he whispered. "Get your stuff together."

Something clawed to get out of Lang's stomach and he felt nauseated.

"I think I'm sick," he said.

"You'll be all right once we start moving," Byrd said. "I'm nervous, too."

"Come on," Moran whispered. "The blackout ain't gonna last all night."

Lang rose and made his preparations reluctantly, his will and limbs as unresponsive as if in a nightmare.

157

The three of them pulled socks provided by the escape committee over their shoes to muffle the sound of their feet and shook hands with Colonel Waterfield, who went to the back door to see them off and wish them luck. He held the door open and they slipped out one by one draped in their bedsheets, first Moran, then Lang, then Byrd.

They had ideal conditions for the attempt. The alert had come when the off-duty guards were sleeping and the night was foggy and moonless. They stepped across the trip-wire and moved quickly along the base of the wall. They had waited at the back door for the roving guard to pass so there was no need to crawl. Moran went to the wall between the compounds. Lang followed and made a stirrup for him. Moran pulled him to the top of the wall and eased him over to the other side. Lang was witless with fear.

He was in the outer compound.

He lay down against the perimeter wall and covered himself with his sheet as Byrd had instructed him. He could hear the faint sounds of Moran helping Byrd over and was sure they must be echoing through the troop barracks. Moran came crawling past wearing his sheet. After a few moments Byrd touched Lang's foot in a signal to follow Moran.

Lang was frightened but he felt silly crawling through the night in a dirty bedsheet. His arms ached with the effort of pulling himself across the ground and sharp pebbles dug into his elbows and knees. Dirt worked its way under his belt and trickled down to his crotch, where it tickled annoyingly. He felt a touch on his ankle and he froze.

It was Byrd. Byrd pulled himself alongside and put his lips close to Lang's ear.

"Don't breathe so loud," he whispered. "I can hear you ten feet back."

"I can't help it," Lang said.

"Concentrate. We're about to pass the troop barracks."

Lang forced himself to breathe shallowly. He had reached a point midway behind the troop barracks when a dim square of light appeared in the darkness. A back door had opened. Lang shrank against the wall. He heard dragging footsteps, a yawn, and then a patter like rain. He thought of Moran urinating out of the window at the quarantine prison. He wondered why the soldier had come outside instead of using the latrine. Maybe it was a trick. He stopped breathing entirely. He could hear the Italian scratching himself and humming. Then a sigh, and retreating footsteps. The square of light vanished. Lang crawled on.

Moran was waiting for him at the front wall. Lang made another stirrup and boosted him up. Moran was quiet as an animal. Lying on his stomach he reached down for Lang. Lang's muffled feet scrabbled at the wall. Moran stopped pulling and they listened, Lang dangling by his arms in Moran's crushing grip. The guard was singing to himself in a low voice. He obviously had heard nothing. Moran pulled Lang to the top of the wall. They lay flat beneath the guardbox catching their breath. The floor creaked above them as the guard moved restlessly about. Moran crawled to the edge of the wall and hung by his fingers a moment before dropping to the ground outside. Lang waited. Byrd waited at the wall below him. The plan was to give Moran time to cross the road to the field on the other side.

Lang reached down into the darkness and groped for Byrd's upraised arms. He found them and they grasped wrists. Lang was not as strong as Moran and Byrd had to use the leverage of his knees and elbows against the wall. There was movement at the window of the guardbox. The beam of a flashlight played over the ground below them. They were shielded from the light by the overhanging floor of the box. With a desperate heave Lang pulled Byrd to the top of the wall. The guard was flashing his light along the top of the wall now, and leaning out the window to probe the ground at its base. He called out something in Italian.

Byrd put his lips against Lang's ear.

"He's calling for help," he whispered. "Get going."

159

Lang started crawling toward the edge. A door slammed, feet pounded, a voice cried out. A nail protruding from the floor dug into Lang's buttock and he could go no farther. Byrd was at his heels, pushing. The nail dug deeper into Lang's flesh and he wanted desperately to cry out to Byrd. The guard and the man on the ground were shouting at each other now and there were more running feet and cries and flashlights waving erratically in the darkness.

"Jump!" Byrd whispered urgently.

"I'm caught," Lang whispered back.

A shot cracked above them and Byrd gave him a mighty shove. Arms flailing, Lang toppled off the wall, not into the open street in front but into the concertina wire along the side. He landed on his back, the breath driven from his body by the impact. Everyone was shooting now. He scarcely heard them for the blood singing in his ears.

The shots stopped but men were still running and shouting in the outer compound and on the road. They're after Jaybird, Lang thought. He got away. Everybody got away but me. He had not wanted to come and he was the one tangled in the wire where they would catch him and beat him, or even kill him. There was anger in his fear.

He lay very still, the barbs biting his flesh. Maybe they were all chasing Jaybird and would not think to look around the corner in the wire. Light struck his face, as palpable as ice water, and a voice cried out. Lang closed his eyes. This was it. Feet came running, voices babbled. The play of flashlights pierced his clenched lids. Not moving, he opened them a chink and peered out at ominous lights and shapes. Something hard banged into his ribs and he grunted. Someone laughed excitedly.

A guard took off his belt, made a loop of it and tried to lasso him. It slipped off his hunched shoulders. Another try hooked under his chin. The guard pulled. Lang tore an arm free from the wire and thrust it through the loop to keep from being strangled. The soldier could not pull him from his nest of wire and others took hold. Lang steeled himself for the agony of barbed wire pulling at his flesh, hoping he would faint and feel nothing. When the pain came, fierce though it was, it was not as terrible as he had anticipated. It was like being scratched by a cat, he thought, a big cat. A tiger.

"Ow!" he yelled.

The soldiers laughed and kept pulling.

The humiliation was as deep as the pain. To be dragged at the end of a belt. This was no way to treat an officer. And they were ruining his uniform.

Then he was out of the wire and on his feet. The soldiers began cuffing him, the blows of mischievous schoolboys tormenting another. Lang put his chin on his chest and crossed his arms over his face. The blows grew harder. Mingled with his fear was astonished pride. He could take it. It was not so terrible to be beaten after all. If he had only known that when Dogass bullied him.

Someone tried to pull his arms away from his face but he kept them firmly crossed. A pain exploded between his legs and he collapsed. He fouled me, Lang thought indignantly in a blur of nausea. Captain Ribolla's voice sounded above him, high-pitched and furious.

Hands helped him up.

"You are badly injured?" Ribolla's voice asked, worried. "These barbarians have made damage?"

He was safe! Rosie Ribolla had saved him.

"Naw," Lang said hoarsely.

He'd show the little bastards he had as much guts as Moran. If they didn't watch out he might break a nose himself.

But he did not. He let himself be led submissively to the administration building and locked in a cell. He collapsed on the iron camp bed but leaped up with a cry. He could not sit on the buttock the nail had torn. He lowered himself gingerly on his stomach. Despite the pain, the bruises and the cuts he was pleased with himself. He had not escaped but he had tried.

He had done a daring thing. He had gone into the outer compound and come out again. He wished everybody in his bay, and in the bomb group, and his parents and Serena the Butterfly Girl and everybody back home could see him now, know what he had been through and how he had stood up to it. He was sorry now he had not hit a guard, the way Moran had.

He wondered where Moran was, and Jaybird. Moran had gotten away but they had probably caught Jaybird. He was glad he was not with Moran. He felt guilty for that but it was true. Moran was still in danger, and so was Jaybird if they had not caught him at the wall. But he could wait now until he was liberated and nobody could say anything because he had made his try and taken his lumps.

The cell door opened and Dr. Stagno came in carrying a cloth bag. They looked at each other solemnly.

"You look like hell," Stagno said.

That pleased Lang.

"It was pretty rough, Doc," he admitted casually.

"Get undressed," Stagno said. "They sent me in to patch you up."

Lang bit back his groans as he gingerly took off his clothes. He wanted Doc Stagno to take back a good report of his behavior under pain.

"Nothing too bad except this wound in your ass," Stagno said. "Bayonet?"

"Yeah," said Lang.

That's what he'd tell everybody. He was glad Doc Stagno gave him the idea.

"This will hurt," Stagno said.

The cut felt as if Stagno had put a blowtorch to it and Lang yelped.

"That's just the disinfectant," Stagno said.

Lang bit a fold of his blanket and kept biting while Stagno took four stitches in his buttock. He did not cry out again although he could not suppress a groan now and then.

162

"What about Jaybird and Moran?" he asked when he could speak.

"You'll have a scar but it shouldn't handicap you socially."

"Did Jaybird get away?"

"They gave you a good going-over, didn't they?" said Stagno. He pushed a thumb in Lang's side. "This hurt?"

"Ouch!" Lang cried.

"It hurts," Stagno said dryly. "Just a bruise."

Lang sat up, favoring his wound.

"Something's happened," he said.

"Don't get excited," Stagno said. "You've had a rough time."

Lang grabbed Stagno's arm and dug his fingers in.

"Is Jaybird all right?" he said harshly.

Stagno stared at him a moment without reply. Then he sighed.

"Captain Byrd is dead," he said.

CHAPTER 10

Lang cried.

It was his fault Byrd was dead. If he had not been so clumsy on the wall Jaybird would have had time to jump.

During his two weeks in the cooler he thought constantly of Byrd and how Byrd would still be alive if he had moved faster. But it was Jaybird's fault he was there in the first place. He had not wanted to go. Jaybird had made him. He hoped everybody knew that. Colonel Waterfield and everybody couldn't blame him for what happened.

Lang did not know which thoughts made him more miserable, those blaming himself for Byrd's death or those trying to excuse himself at Byrd's expense.

He wondered about Moran, hoping he would get away

and hoping he would not, feeling disloyal and depraved for wishing Moran ill yet unable not to because it would be unfair if Moran got away and he did not when they had come in together. And if Moran got away it would prove it was possible to escape and show how cowardly he was to think it was not possible and not even want to try.

He did not have long to speculate. Moran was recaptured less than twenty-four hours later only a few miles from camp. Pellini came to visit Lang in his cell and told him about it.

"I don't know why you guys tried it," Pellini said. "When all you got to do is sit it out."

"It's the first duty of a prisoner," Lang said solemnly, wishing he were not so pleased with the news of Moran's recapture.

"He was all broke up about Captain Byrd," Pellini said. "I told him what they did to you and he said tell you he hoped you were okay."

"Tell him it's a piece of cake." He paused. "I mean tell him I'm getting well fast. I'll probably be all right."

"He's sure sore at Colonel Malvi," Pellini said.

"Malvi isn't going to get away with it," Lang said, feeling he had to match Moran. "Don't think he is."

"It wasn't the colonel's fault," Pellini protested. "He tells his men to teach anybody they catch a lesson, but not kill 'em, for Christ's sake. He was as shook up as anybody."

"I'll bet," Lang said bitterly

"Anyway, you guys knew it wasn't no game goin' into the outer compound."

Lang had to agree with that.

Pellini came to see him often during the two weeks, bringing him little extras and exchanging messages with Moran although it was prohibited. Colonel Malvi himself visited him once and asked about his wound. He said he had not authorized the use of bayonets except in self-defense and that he was very sorry about Capitano Byrd but anyone foolhardy and ungrateful enough to go over the wall took his life in his hands.

One day Lang heard cheering among both the prisoners and the Italians and that night there was singing and the music of accordions and stringed instruments. Next day Pellini told him they had been celebrating Mussolini's fall.

"The Fascists kicked him out and put in Marshal Badoglio," Pellini said. "It ain't gonna be long now, Lieutenant. When this thing is over you won't forget who your buddy was, will you?"

Lang was nervous when they let him out of the cooler. He did not know what kind of reception to expect. They might blame him for Jaybird's death. He always got the blame. He asked Pellini what they were saying about him in the camp but Pellini did not know.

He limped a little, favoring the healing buttock, and when the gate to the inner compound swung open he exaggerated the limp so there would be no doubt of the gravity of his wound. There was a welcoming committee waiting for him and a cheer went up when he entered. He had never been cheered before. His eyes filled with tears of relief and pride and mourning for Byrd.

Colonel Waterfield put an arm around his shoulders and said, "Don't be ashamed, son. We all feel that way about Jim."

Harbold shook his hand and for a moment Lang did not hate him. A crowd of men escorted him to his bay. He limped badly but bravely refused all assistance.

When Moran came out of the cooler the next day Lang had a favored position between the two colonels in the welcoming committee and Moran crushed him in a bear hug. He's really glad to see me, Lang thought, wondering if he would be so glad if he knew what happened on the wall. As soon as they were alone he told Moran, unable to contain his guilt and hoping for absolution.

"Hell, it wasn't your fault you got hung up," Moran said. "It could of happened to anybody."

Lang was greatly relieved.

"Hey, Moran," he said, studying the floor, "don't tell anybody it was a nail, huh? They all think it was a bayonet."

Moran laughed.

"You know something, Blubber?" he said. "You're a funny son of a bitch."

But he did not tell anyone it was a nail.

A parcel had come for Byrd while they were in the cooler and Waterfield turned it over to them. It was a marvelous parcel, with almond Hershey bars, powdered eggs, oatmeal and Gillette Blue Blades. Lang wondered if Flora knew Bryd was dead. When the war was over he would go see her and tell her what a great guy Jaybird had been. He had written her the day he got out of the cooler but that was not the same as telling.

They shared the parcel as if sharing guilt until, as they sat eating powdered eggs, Moran hit Lang on the arm half in anger, half in play and cried, "God damn it, Blubber, will you stop looking so low-down? You're spoiling my appetite."

They grinned at each other sheepishly and no longer felt guilty eating the food Flora had sent Jaybird. She would rather they had it than strangers.

As days went by Lang found it difficult to hang on to thoughts of Byrd though he believed it important that he do so. It was as if it had all happened a long time ago, and inevitably. He mentioned this hesitantly to Moran and was relieved to discover Moran felt the same. They were ashamed of it, but it was true.

A few days later a personal parcel arrived for Lang. It was not as well chosen as Byrd's and after his first flush of pleasure Lang was disappointed and irritated with his parents.

"Who the hell needs vegetable bouillon cubes?" he said angrily. "And tea, for God's sake!"

"What the hell you complaining about?" Moran snapped. "At least you got a friggin' parcel. What the hell's keeping mine? If my old man ever sent one."

Lang did not share his parcel with Moran nor did it occur to either of them that he might. No one shared personal parcels.

Byrd's bunk remained unassigned until the end of August when a dazed second lieutenant came in without having first passed through the quarantine prison. He was a B-26 co-pilot, the only survivor of his plane's skip-bombing attack on enemy shipping.

He was young and had not yet fully grasped the fact that he was alive though he was traumatically aware that all his friends were dead. His helplessness made Lang feel immensely superior. Lang helped him get settled and, since it was almost teatime, gave him bread, butter and jam.

"Thank you, sir," said the newcomer with flattering humility.

"That's okay, kid," said Lang, who was perhaps a year older. "I try to take care of you new guys."

"Jesus," said Moran.

"Well, I do," Lang said.

To show Moran, and because the new man was so abjectly grateful for any favor, Lang did look after him the first few days, giving him bread, showing him how to wash his bloody shirt with a dhobi stick and offering pointers on getting along in P.G. 203. When the lieutenant found friends from his own bomb group and began spending time with them Lang felt betrayed and ended his largesse.

Had it not been for Byrd's death, Lang would have found the days after his release from the cooler almost idyllic. His attempted escape added to his stature among the old prisoners as well as the new, and to the new ones particularly he was a hero. He kept his limp long after it was necessary and began a mustache. He looked at it often in the washroom mirror, studying his features and wishing the nail scar was on his face like Colonel Townes-Baker's instead of where no one could see it.

There was fresh fruit in the mess now, figs, cherries, tangerines, grapes and something the Italians called *mespoli,*

168

which reminded Lang of his childhood because they had grown in his own yard in Houston. They were called Japanese plums in Houston and his mother had told him they would make him sick if he ate them. When he got home he intended telling her she had been wrong.

The weather was hot and the sun burned each day like a lens but Lang vastly preferred it to the cold and wet of winter. It was like being on the beach at Galveston. He did not even mind the swarming flies too much. He enjoyed lying on his mattress in the sun, reading or talking to Moran or telling stories to the new men.

Sometimes he watched the softball game with Perkins or Moran in the hard-baked yard between the settori. The British had first shunned the game when the YMCA sent the equipment but were now devoted to it to the point of giving up cricket. Cricket had never been really satisfactory at P.G. 203 because the playing area was too small. When Moran could be persuaded to play he was an outstanding pitcher and batter but more often than not he refused. Games were for schoolboys, he said. Lang envied him both his skill and his nonchalant rejection of an opportunity to display it.

Perkins had been appalled by the way the Americans shouted insults at the umpire and profane encouragement to the team of their choice. The British politely applauded a well-hit ball and suffered questionable decisions in silence. Soon, however, the British were as noisy as the Americans and Perkins became one of the most vociferous spectators.

"I say, old boy," he shouted once after a close call at home plate, "I'll have your bloody liver for that," and, turning to Lang with a look of utter happiness, added, "Lovely match, what?"

The time Lang liked best was in the evening just before curfew. There was a public address system in camp now and every night there was music from Radio Rome on the loudspeaker. When Radio Rome began signing off each night with "Lili Marlene," the favorite song of Rommel's Afrika Korps and Montgomery's Eighth Army, Colonel Malvi acceded to Colonel Townes-Baker's request to extend curfew half an hour so the prisoners could sit outside and listen to it.

Perkins told Lang the real name of the song was *"Lied Eines Jungen Wachtposten,"* "The Song of the Young Sentry," and translated the words for him.

Every evening Lang would sit on the front steps with Moran, the lights of Settore I dim and yellow across the way like a shoreline viewed from high in the air, listening in the blue gauze night to the seductive woman's voice singing of the young sentry and the girl who had waited for him outside the barracks before he went off to war. No sweetheart had ever waited for Lang anywhere, but every night for a few moments he was the young sentry longing for a distant lover, and when the song ended with its muffled drumbeat he would sigh and go to his bunk to think about girls. It was often Serena the Butterfly Girl. Both he and Moran would be very quiet after the song.

One day about the time the young lieutenant took Byrd's bunk Lang lost interest in trading as abruptly as if a switch had been thrown. He was feeling guilty, lolling in the sun with a book while bulletin boards went unread and Gorsely unrepresented, when he realized with astonishment he was not hungry and had not been for weeks, nor was there any food available in the camp he wanted more than that already at his disposal. He felt an enormous sense of relief, as if he had dropped a burden he had not known he bore. When he quit calling on Gorsely and Gorsely sent an inquiry by the bay orderly, Lang referred him to Harbold.

He regretted it immediately. He did not want to do any favors for Harbold. Dogass flawed his serenity. Though he was friendly enough now, Lang could not forget how Harbold had humiliated him and wondered if others did not also remember it. He pretended to be friends with Harbold but when he could avoided him.

With the invasion of the mainland early in September the mood of P.G. 203 became giddy. The prisoners stopped all escape activities and started betting pools on the arrival of Allied troops. The guards went about their duties apologetically and some of the prisoners taunted them until ordered not to do so by Townes-Baker. Ribolla carried on as if all were serene, Grasso was doggedly antagonistic and Malvi surprised everyone by being cheerful. He came into the inner compound more often than had been his custom and smiled benignly at the prisoners. It was thought he was trying to curry favor.

Lang and the others stayed outside all day watching for planes and listening to the increasingly heavy traffic on the road outside the wall. Waterfield thought it was the Germans pulling back but Hudspeth believed that on the contrary the Germans were moving toward the Allied beachhead on the Strait of Messina. Major Hudspeth's analysis was not very popular in P.G. 203.

Shortly after the invasion Pellini came into the compound and asked for a word with Lang. Lang agreed grudgingly, aware of the disagreeable looks he was getting but risking displeasure because no one could say any longer Pellini might be fishing for secrets. There was little need for secrets any more.

Pellini was very nervous.

"Look, Lieutenant," he said, "will you do me a favor?"

"That all depends," Lang said cautiously.

"I want you to ask Colonel Waterfield something for me."

"Why don't you do it yourself?"

"He hates me. You know that. He's got me all wrong. Everybody in this dump has but you."

Lang was flattered.

"What you want me to ask him?"

Pellini hesitated for a long time. He looked at his boots, at Lang's chest, at the mountains over the north wall.

"This is gonna sound kind of crazy," he said at last. "When they come to get you guys, will you ask him if I can go with you?"

"Man, that is crazy!" Lang said. "What you better do is hide."

"Maybe if you told 'em how I'd helped you guys they'd give me a break."

"An American who joined the Eyeties?"

"I'll level with you, Lieutenant. If you promise not to tell anybody." He continued without waiting for Lang's assurance. "I ain't exactly American. I got double citizenship on account I was born in the U.S. But I didn't stay. My folks brought me back here when I wasn't much more'n a kid. And that's God's own truth."

"Don't that make you an Italian?"

Pellini shook his head vigorously.

"I don't feel like no Italian. I don't like it here. Look, if I can just get back to the States I don't care if they treat me like a P.G. once I get there. It's gonna be bad here, Lieutenant. How about it?"

He was desperate now, and pleading.

"Okay," Lang said reluctantly. "I'll ask him."

"You're aces, Lieutenant," Pellini said fervently. "I won't forget it."

Lang was afraid to ask Colonel Waterfield. He knew what the answer would be and he did not intend doing anything to hurt the position he had achieved by risking his life in the outer compound. He told the crestfallen Pellini that Colonel Waterfield had said no.

Lang was caught up in the general ferment. He no longer thought life in P.G. 203 idyllic now that liberation seemed more than a wistful dream. He saw his existence inside the walls for what it was, constrained, Spartan and temporary. He was no longer satisfied to lie in the sun with a book, nor did he find OR loaves and fresh fruit an adequate substitute for the

172

meals he would have when he got back home. Nor his vague and hopeless fantasies of Serena the Butterfly Girl as exciting as prospects of the real thing.

He was impatient to be free but Moran was feverish.

"Jesus," Moran cried, hitting his mattress with his fist, "what are they waiting on? When's somebody gonna get us out of here?"

"They're coming," Lang said soothingly.

"Then why ain't they here? They must be stopping to pick up souvenirs."

A few days after the invasion of the mainland Townes-Baker was summoned to the outer compound obviously on a matter of importance. By the time he returned everyone had turned out in the wide space between the settori waiting for him. He looked a little dazed.

Someone shouted, "Is it over?" and hundreds of other voices repeated the question.

"We're to wait for an announcement," Townes-Baker replied.

The prisoners began shouting and milling around.

"Wait for the bloody announcement," Townes-Baker cried. "It's not official yet."

He walked aside and spoke quietly with Waterfield and Hudspeth.

Shortly thereafter the roll-call bugle blew and they formed the customary lines on either side of the street. The Italians came in but instead of proceeding with the count they remained in formation in the street. Other troops could be heard assembling in the outer compound. The public address system crackled and came on. Colonel Malvi spoke, with Pellini translating as usual.

"My brave Italian soldiers, Allied officers and Other Ranks. Your attention please for an announcement of gravest importance. We tune to Radio Roma."

There was a minute or two of strained, restless silence,

then an old, tired and infinitely sad voice spoke. Major Hudspeth translated. The speaker was Marshal Badoglio. He announced Italy's unconditional surrender.

A roar drowned out the end of his speech. Surprisingly, there were cheers and rifle shots from the outer compound. Captain Ribolla and Lieutenant Grasso wept, the latter noisily.

Lang and Moran quit yelling for a moment and shook hands solemnly, then began shouting again. Townes-Baker's commands for order were ignored. The public address system crackled and Malvi's voice implored silence. With the help of Townes-Baker and Waterfield he got it.

"Congratulations, gentlemen," Pellini's voice translated. "It is with great pleasure I now turn over the administration of P.G. 203 to your senior officer, Colonel Townes-Baker. Colonel Townes-Baker, I await your orders."

Malvi's voice had sounded cheerful and self-satisfied. The prisoners cheered him.

"He's not such a bad son of a bitch after all," Moran said.

Townes-Baker and Waterfield hurried to the outer compound. All the Italians left the inner compound and the prisoners collected in small groups to speculate about the machinery of repatriation and tell each other rapturously what they intended doing when they were free.

"Come on, Moran," Lang said, turning toward the bungalow. "Let's celebrate. Let's scoff everything."

"Always thinking about your stomach," Moran said, but he went with him.

They got out their boxes and sat on Moran's bunk eating methodically. Moran stopped eating and sighed.

"I wish Jaybird was here," he said.

"Yeah," Lang said.

"Hell," said Moran.

Lang felt guilty because Moran had thought about Byrd and he had not. He wished Byrd was there too, and going home with them, but Byrd was not and it was not their fault. Peo-

174

ple got killed in wars. It made him feel tough to think that. It was better to feel tough than to destroy this mood of elation by feeling sad.

"Snap out of it," he said with determined cheerfulness. "We're going home."

Moran brightened.

"We sure as hell are, ain't we?" he cried.

They began eating again and talking about home, and going to see Flora and Bertram's parents.

"We'll stay good friends, won't we?" Lang said.

Moran looked at him quizzically.

"Sure," he said. "Why wouldn't we?"

"I don't know," Lang said.

The thought had struck him that once they got out of the prison camp Moran wouldn't like him any more, the way it had been before they were captured.

When Waterfield returned from the outer compound he was smoking a poisonous black Italian cigar. He announced that Colonel Malvi was calling in a company of Alpine troops to protect the prisoners from dissident Fascists or passing Germans who might want to make trouble.

"Not that we expect any," he added. "The Jerries seem to be pulling back north of us and even if they wanted to take us with them they haven't got the transport."

Meanwhile they were to remain safely inside the camp until friendly troops came for them.

"We don't want to draw any more attention to ourselves than we have to," Waterfield explained.

A little later Pellini came to call on Lang, looking about fearfully as if expecting the prisoners to fall upon him. Except for a few offhand jeers, he was ignored. Italians no longer mattered to them.

"Remember what I asked you?" Pellini said in a low voice. "How about asking him again?"

"I told you he said no," Lang said angrily.

He wished Pellini would leave him alone. Now that the

Italians were not in charge any more Pellini was no longer useful or important. He was just a nuisance.

"But it's different now," Pellini said hopefully. "Nobody's mad at nobody no more."

Lang shook his head. Pellini left, disconsolate.

That night the Italian troops celebrated as if they, not the prisoners, had been liberated. They drank wine, played and sang, and had their womenfolk in. Moran took his stool outside and stood on tiptoe watching enviously over the dividing wall.

"Look at 'em," he said to Lang, whom he had persuaded to join him. "It always did chap my ass not to get invited when they threw a party next door."

Lang was not so affected. He had been too often uninvited to feel any slight.

The lights remained on until midnight so the prisoners could celebrate, with everyone cautioned to keep the blackout shutters closed to avoid attracting the attention of passing German troops or Allied aircraft. Lang lay awake after the bay at last settled down for the night. He could hear Moran squirming above him. He was glad he was not that impatient. But when he thought about home he felt as if bubbles were bursting just beneath his skin. Tomorrow or the next day someone would come for them and they would get in planes and go home. His picture would be in the paper, wearing his medals, and he would be a hero. His dad would take him to lunch downtown and show him off to everybody and the girls would not make lame excuses when he asked them for dates.

In the morning he sat on the steps with Moran waiting for the first sight of their deliverers. No one came for them. The prisoners and their former guards mingled freely but no Allied soldiers appeared. Lang traded for souvenirs but he did so desultorily, wanting merely to while away the hours before he left. The Italians bid spiritedly for soap and tea. They offered their equipment, bits of uniforms, craftwork and their tobacco ration. Lang got canteens and knapsacks for himself and Moran,

176

a sheath knife with a handworked hilt and a carbine without ammunition. Waterfield made him return the carbine.

Colonel Malvi walked through the compound beaming and shaking hands, his eyes merry behind the spectacles. Losing the war did not appear to have disturbed him. He had come through it with a perfect record. Not one prisoner had escaped from P.G. 203 and he was content. Pellini came, too, and whenever Lang looked his way he found the sergeant's mournful, accusing gaze on him.

That night a number of prisoners, Moran among them, said they were going to leave if someone did not come for them soon and Townes-Baker sent around orders no one was allowed out the front gate without his written permission.

Next day Radio Rome, to which the public address system was tuned, abruptly went off the air. Minutes later it came back on. In German. The prisoners ran out into the street and clustered around the speakers. Those who knew German translated for the others. Rome had been occupied by German troops. The German High Command was calling on the Italians to refuse to accept the surrender forced upon them by false leaders and fight side by side with them against the traitors and invaders.

There was consternation in both compounds. The prisoners angrily asked explanations of each other, demanding to know why the Germans had done this thing and how it would affect them, as if enough anger and enough insistence would force answers. In the outer compound a nervous, laughing voice cried, "Tutti è casa."

"Everybody go home," someone translated.

"That ain't a bad idea at all," Moran said.

He looked grim.

"It don't sound to me like the Jerries are about to pull out," he said. "Where does that leave us?"

"Colonel Townes-Baker says they haven't got the transport," Lang said hopefully.

177

"He better be right. If they were to move us outta here after being this close . . ."

Moran did not finish. He could not express the enormity of such a possibility.

Townes-Baker hurried out to confer with Malvi and came back furious.

"Washed his hands of the whole bloody mess," he said angrily. "I'd throttle the smarmy bugger if it helped matters."

The Alpini had never arrived and the guards were preparing to leave. Malvi had said he could do nothing to stop them. There were so few of them and so many *tedeschi*, he said, that it would be worse than useless, criminal in fact, if he ordered them to oppose the Germans should they attempt to take over P.G. 203. But most likely it would not happen, he had told Townes-Baker. The *tedeschi* were too busy fighting for their lives to bother with a few prisoners of war. His advice was to stay inside the camp until friendly troops came.

"His advice!" Townes-Baker raged. "The bloody bastard. He's not wasting any time getting out. Said he was leaving to join the resistance. Bloody likely."

He called a staff meeting at which it was decided to wait until dark and send men out to see what they could learn about the local military situation and form some opinion of German intentions and the proximity of Allied troops.

"If Jerry's in full retreat we'll stay put," Waterfield told his bay. "If not, we'll go over the back wall and scatter."

"Just point me south and stand clear," Moran said, delighted with the prospect of action.

Lang was not so pleased. It was one thing to be liberated by friendly troops and sent home with bands playing but something else again to be alone and helpless in a hostile country aswarm with bloodthirsty Germans.

As soon as it was dark Major Hudspeth and another English officer slipped out the front gate. Italian troops came into the inner compound with ladders to scale the back wall, as far from the road and its German traffic as they could get.

The prisoners turned out to watch in a mood both festive and disconcerted. It was amusing to watch their erstwhile guards escaping but the implications were unsettling.

"Hey, Blubber, let's go with 'em," Moran said suddenly.

"You crazy?" Lang demanded. "What if everybody stays here and goes home and we get caught out there?"

"Yeah," said Moran. "Maybe you're right."

Ribolla came in to tell Waterfield good-bye and wish him luck. He was leaving, too, but by the front gate.

Pellini stood with Lang watching the Italian soldiers go over the wall.

"Aren't you going?" Lang asked.

Pellini shook his head.

"Maybe if I stay Colonel Waterfield'll change his mind," he said.

Hudspeth and the other officer returned before midnight with little information except that the Germans were not in rout. Military traffic was moving in both directions on the road and there was nothing to indicate Allied troops were within striking distance. Townes-Baker decided to leave.

Moran was ecstatic, Lang apprehensive. He did not doubt that if he left the safety of the camp he would be killed or sent to Germany.

"That was sharp, getting us knapsacks and canteens, Blubber," Moran said. "They're gonna come in handy."

Lang did not answer. He resented Moran's cheerfulness.

The storerooms were thrown open and ORs set to distributing Red Cross parcels to whoever wanted food for the road. In the midst of the preparations to leave a German medium tank nosed through the front gate and illuminated the scene with a searchlight. The prisoners scattered, the major portion running for the ladders against the back wall. A burst of machine-gun fire overhead stopped many but others continued running. Moran was one of them. Lang ran after him, not wanting to but not wanting to be separated from him. He felt hideously vulnerable in the relentless beam of the searchlight playing over the inner wall. The all-illuminating light revived a forgotten terror. On a night raid over Tobruk the *High Flying Flora* had been caught in a cone of light and held there for minutes. The nose had been illuminated bright as day, revealing a terror in Bertram's face equal to his own. Both knew that anti-aircraft batteries worked in concert with the searchlights and that the cone of light pinpointed the bomber's position. Even Byrd had been frightened and wracked the ponderous aircraft about in desperate evasive action. Somehow the flak batteries had failed to find the range and Byrd at last wrenched the bomber free of the telltale lights. Now Lang wished he were back in the *High Flying Flora*, or anywhere but here.

A searchlight came on outside the back wall, then others on the two sides. P.G. 203 was surrounded.

Moran cursed with bitter vehemence. He cursed the Italians, he cursed the Germans, he cursed the Allies who had not come and most of all he cursed himself for not leaving with the guards. Lang said nothing. He, too, was bitterly disappointed but he was more accustomed than Moran to disappointment. It had been his experience that if things could go badly for him they almost always did. And if he had his choice of trying to escape through the German lines or being safe here, he preferred being safe here.

Just because the Germans were taking over the camp did not mean they would be sent to Germany. Everybody said the Germans did not have the transport. What would the Germans want with them anyhow? They probably just didn't want a lot of Allied prisoners running around loose behind their lines. He tried to explain that to Moran.

He thought for a moment Moran was going to hit him.

CHAPTER 11

There were thirty in each boxcar.

The Germans had kept them in P.G. 203 for two days while they accumulated enough transport to evacuate the camp. All the Italians left before the takeover except Pellini, who had found himself a khaki uniform and moved in with the ORs. He told Lang he had inserted a forged record in the office files establishing himself as a staff sergeant in the United States Army.

"You mean you're going to let 'em take you to Germany when you don't have to?" Lang demanded.

"I'd rather be an American P.G. in Germany than an Eyetie in Italy," Pellini said. "It's gonna be rough. The Jerries are gonna want 'em fightin' the Allies and the Allies are gonna want 'em fightin' the Jerries and what the hell."

The last Lang saw of him he was climbing into a boxcar with the ORs. He grinned over his shoulder at Lang and held up his thumb in greeting and farewell. He was the only smiling man in the more than one thousand boarding the cars.

The Germans had distributed all the Red Cross stores and heavy Italian Air Force blankets so Lang and Moran were heavily laden when they climbed into their boxcar. They each had an Italian knapsack, an Italian canteen, two Red Cross parcels tied together with rope and a blanket roll containing a sweater and winter uniform. They were in the second truckload to enter their car. The first group had spread out over the floor and was lounging among its possessions. There was no place for the second to sit.

"How about a little room, you guys?" Moran said.

"Tough shit," somebody answered.

Moran scowled.

"Well, now," he said.

He began picking up people, parcels, blanket rolls and knapsacks and piling them in the middle of the car. The earlier arrivals scrambled to their feet and under Moran's direction all hard baggage was stacked neatly in the exact center of the car. Each half was carefully paced off. Fifteen men got on each side of the stack with their soft baggage. There was room for everyone to sit now if they kept their legs tucked up. Lang sat on his knapsack and blanket roll with his back against the side of the car, wedged between Moran and Petitclerq, the RCAF pilot. He did not think they were giving him his fair share of wall space. And Harbold, sitting in front of him, was too close. He pressed his knees into Harbold's shoulder blades.

Harbold turned around and said, "You want all the room?"

"Go to hell," Lang said.

Harbold pushed back against his legs and there was a shoving match until Moran said, "You guys cut that out, for Christ's sake."

They stopped. Everyone had accepted Moran as the officer in charge when he began stacking men and baggage. Lang glowered. He thought Moran should have taken his side.

The train did not move for several hours, during which they all grew increasingly stiff, hot, thirsty and irritable. Lang drank all his water. Several men who had not brought canteens or water bottles looked at him fixedly each time he put the canteen to his lips but he did not offer a drink to any of them.

A German soldier in a cloth cap thrust his head and shoulders inside the car, saw the Red Cross parcels stacked in the middle, murmured, "So viel," and slid the door shut. It was immediately darker and hotter in the car.

Someone gave a long, fervent, quivering sigh.

Little was said in the car during the next forty-five minutes in which it remained motionless. There were brief arguments about leg room, snatches of conversation, a labored nervous joke or two. But brooding silence prevailed. The sealing of the car door had a finality even the most optimistic could not surmount. Lang was thirsty. Sweat soaked his crotch and armpits and his khaki shirt seemed to soak up heat. He wondered if Moran would give him a drink but did not ask.

The train heaved and moved a few creaking inches. Everyone sat very still. A man stopped talking in mid-sentence. The train moved again, and then again. It gained speed with cruel inexorability. It rattled and swayed on the tracks faster than Lang thought freight trains could move. It went as swiftly as the first-class coach which had taken them from Naples to Rome. He wished he was in a first-class car, cool, with room to stretch out, sitting across from a bella ragazza. He would smile at her and she would be impressed by his uniform and mustache.

He closed his eyes and leaned back against the side of the boxcar. The rail joints clicked like crickets chirping. She would pass him a note, in English, with an address on it where he could hide until the underground could pass him through to Allied lines. When it was dark he would ask the guard to let him go to the *gabinetto*. The train swayed and clicked as he crouched in the window of the toilet, poised to jump.

"Jesus, we're really moving," said Moran.

Lang opened his eyes.

"Yeah," he said.

"If it don't go any slower than this we can't jump," Moran said.

"Jump?"

"You gonna let 'em haul your ass to Germany?"

Lang did not say anything. They were locked in. How did Moran intend to get out?

Men began grumbling. There was no water. It was hot. There was no room. They bickered among themselves as they moved restlessly to ease cramped limbs. The train raced and swayed, slowing in small towns, sometimes stopping a few minutes. At every stop the prisoners would bang on the sides of the car and demand water. The Germans would bang on the outside and shout back at them. Once the door slid open to admit boxes of Italian hardtack and corned beef but no water.

There was a relief can by the door. When a man used it two others had to steady him against the pitching of the train.

High up in the car was a window covered with steel mesh. Soon after the train gathered speed Moran had put a parcel box under it despite the protests of the men he had to disturb doing so and he stood looking out at the fleeting countryside. After the ration stop he called Lang over. Lang stood beside him on the parcel box. It was cooler there and he could stretch.

"Hey, Moran," he said. "How about a drink?"

"What happened to your water?"

"I drank it."

"You dumb bastard."

But Moran gave him a drink. Another man asked for a

drink and Moran was about to give it to him when others crowded around. Moran screwed the cap back on his canteen.

"If it gets real rough I'll give you some," he said.

Someone cursed him.

"Tough shit," said Moran. He turned to Lang and whispered, "I been casing things. We'll go out tonight when we slow up for a town."

"They got us locked in," Lang protested.

"I'll fix that next time they open up," Moran said.

Moran went back and sat by the door after a brief discussion with the man occupying the space. Lang remained on the box, looking out. He had been enjoying the scenery but now it lost its charm. Trees, fields, telegraph poles whizzed by, promising broken bones. He did not want to jump. Moran was as bad as Byrd, he thought, telling him to do things he did not want to. Moran did not have that right, not the way Byrd did. He wished Jaybird was there. Jaybird would want to escape, but he was sensible.

They were allowed to fill their canteens and water bottles at the next stop. Guards with machine pistols took them to a water tap in the small station. Italian civilians watched with guarded sympathy. Moran gave Lang his canteen to fill and remained in the car. When Lang returned he whispered, "I fixed the lock." Lang's heart sank.

"When I was hopping freights I never knew it was gonna come in so handy," Moran said.

Lang knew about the summer Moran had hoboed from Los Angeles to Aberdeen, Washington. In the long months at P.G. 203 they had told each other everything about themselves, though Lang had given a judiciously altered account of his past.

Late in the afternoon Moran said, "We better eat something," and fetched hardtack and tinned corned beef from the boxes the Germans had put in the car. The hardtack was flinty and tasteless and the corned beef greasy. Lang choked some of the meat down and regretted it at once. His stomach was tight with apprehension and held the greasy beef in an indigestible wad. He wanted to vomit.

Dusk came. The thought of leaping into the darkness from a moving train terrified him. Moran had him open his blanket roll and put on all his extra clothing, including his greatcoat.

"Pad you when you hit," Moran said.

He put their loose food in one knapsack and discarded the other. Lang had hidden his souvenir sheath knife in his knapsack. Moran instructed him to slide it down inside his sock. He gave Lang both canteens, showing him how to hang them down from his shoulders and clutch them against his sides with his elbows.

"So they won't choke you to death when you start rolling," he said.

Moran put the knapsack on backward and clutched it to his chest.

They stood by the door and waited for the train to slow. Lang sweated in his khakis, sweater, greatcoat and fear. It had become cooler with darkness. He could catch a cold sweating like that, Lang thought. His mother always said that was the worst way to catch a cold. Never go out in the night air until you cooled off. He felt silly thinking of that, worrying about catching a cold when he might be jumping to his death, or shot by a guard hiding on the roof or between the cars.

He wanted desperately not to jump. It was not the risk alone that deterred him. When he jumped he would leave behind the painstaking accumulation of nine months of captivity, his books, his letters from home, the desert shorts that cost fifty cigarettes, the pencil sketch Perkins had done of him, his notebooks, his drinking cup, an olivewood box Pellini had given him, everything. The others would stay behind and divide it up among them. Dogass might even get some of his things. When he was recaptured, as he surely would be if he were fortunate enough not to be killed, he would be as destitute as the day he was fished dripping from the Mediterranean. He would have to start all over again.

To leave his possessions was like leaving home. In the bag home was what you owned and could carry with you.

Yet he could not refuse to do as Moran wanted. Moran would call him a coward. If Moran jumped, he would jump. In a way, Moran was home, too. He could always accumulate more possessions but he doubted very much if he could find another friend like Moran.

The train slowed. Moran slid the door open.

"Right after me," he said. "But not on top. Keep your elbows in and your knees bent. Roll with it when you hit."

The wheels grated on the tracks.

"Must be a town," Moran said. "Quick."

He jumped.

Lang tucked in his elbows and followed though it seemed to him the train was still moving at terrifying speed. The instant he was in space he regretted jumping. Damn Moran.

The darkness solidified into an enormous fist and smashed the air from his body. Gasping, he rolled across rough ground, bouncing like a ball. One of the canteens, dislodged, flailed at the end of its carrying strap beating him as he rolled. He would never stop. He would roll to the edge of a precipice and fall to the bottom, he would smash into a stone wall. Damn Moran to hell.

And then he stopped rolling. He lay still, panting, scratched, disheveled but alive. The train was stopping a few hundred yards up the tracks. He could hear metal grinding against metal. He moved his arms and legs. Everything functioned. He should get up and run but the night pressed down on him like stones. He felt a curious elation. He had actually jumped and he was alive.

But where was Moran?

He struggled to his knees, his ears ringing, and peered around him. He was in a shallow ditch. Up ahead, where the train was, he saw lights and heard voices and ominous shouts.

He began crawling away from the lights and the voices. If anything had happened to Moran he would be all alone. He was no longer elated.

The canteens bumped on the stony ditch bottom. The greatcoat, the sweater and the battle dress swathed him in his own body heat and he ran with sweat.

"Blubber?" a strained voice whispered from the shadows.

"Yeah," Lang said.

"I banged hell outta my knee."

"That's all we need," Lang said bitterly.

Moran was supposed to be the one who knew how to jump off a train. Now that they had a chance to get away he'd gone and ruined it.

"Let's crawl along the ditch," Moran said. "But go slow. I got to take it easy."

"Great," Lang said spitefully.

"What the hell's eatin' you?" Moran demanded.

"Nothing," Lang said.

They were always getting him in trouble. Like Jaybird at the wall. Jaybird. He wished Byrd was not dead and was with them now. He would know what to do. Moran was crawling ahead of him, cursing softly. Moran turned over on his back to take the weight off his knee and moved on his elbows and one heel. The knapsack made a mound on his chest and he looked like an enormous crippled spider. He stopped suddenly and Lang bumped into him.

"Son of a bitch!" Moran groaned. "Listen," he said.

The guards were shouting back in the station and the prisoners were hooting.

"They must know somebody jumped," he said. "The stupid bastards in our car are needling 'em. Let's get moving."

He could not see ahead, crawling backward, and Lang took the lead. They inched along, panting. Behind them someone shouted orders in German.

"They're gonna catch us," Lang said, his voice shrill.

"Shut up and keep moving."

188

Up ahead the ditch stopped at a dusty gleam of road. Lang raised his head cautiously. Where the road crossed the tracks he could make out the dark shape of a helmeted figure. He edged back to Moran and put his lips to Moran's ear as Byrd had once done to his.

"There's a German up there," he said. "What we gonna do?"

"I don't know," Moran said.

Lang felt utterly lost. Someone was always supposed to know what to do. When they were shot down Byrd knew how to ditch and Moran knew to take down the escape hatch. And Byrd had made the other decisions and now Moran was supposed to. It had been his idea to jump.

"It's all your fault," he whispered on the verge of panic.

"Shut up," Moran whispered back.

Far behind them they could hear two loud German voices.

"They must be working this way," Moran said. "If we could just get past that bastard on the road."

"How?" Lang demanded.

"We got your knife," Moran said.

"Are you crazy?" Lang said.

"Give it to me," Moran said.

"I ain't gonna do it. You want to get us killed?"

"You want to go to Germany?"

"Let's just lie still. Maybe they won't look this far."

"Of all the guys I could of jumped with."

That infuriated Lang. It had not been his idea to jump. Moran had made him do it. And if Moran had not hurt his knee they would have been out of the ditch and into the fields before the Germans began looking for them. And now Moran was blaming him.

"I guess I'm the one can't run," he said.

Moran did not answer.

They lay still. The two soldiers drew closer, but leisurely. The sentry was whistling "Lili Marlene." Lang wished he was back in P.G. 203 sitting on the steps in the soft night. The sentry stopped whistling.

"Was ist los?" he called.

Lang stiffened and felt Moran do the same. Had the sentry seen them?

"Wir haben zwei Englander vom Zug verloren," a voice shouted from the darkness behind them. "Haben Sie etwas gesehen?"

"Ich sehe nie etwas in diesem Gottverlassenen Ort," the crossing guard yelled back.

The soldiers approaching from the train laughed. They joked with the crossing guard as they approached.

We've had it, Lang thought. We've really had it. He wondered if he should stand up and surrender or just lie still until the soldiers found them.

The sentry left his post and walked toward the soldiers. He passed so close to Lang on the lip of the ditch that pebbles trickled down upon him. The sentry kept walking until he reached the soldiers from the train. Moran stirred behind Lang.

"They're lighting cigarettes," he whispered. "Let's get across the road before he comes back."

Lang could not move. He wanted to stay exactly where he was just as he had done when he was caught in the wire outside P.G. 203.

"Get goin', God damn it," Moran grated.

Lang moved.

They crawled to the end of the ditch and across the road into a field. They kept crawling until they could no longer hear the soldiers, then lay panting, gathering strength.

"Jesus, Blubber," Moran said. "We got it made."

He did not sound mad any more and Lang suddenly was no longer angry at him. We got away, he thought exultantly. He had left everything behind but it no longer mattered.

"How's your knee?" he asked.

"Hurts like hell."

190

Moran stood up. He cursed once when he put weight on the leg.

"I can walk if I favor it," he said.

"Lean on me," Lang said, picking up the knapsack.

He had stopped sweating and felt strong and reckless. He began whistling "Lili Marlene" through his teeth.

"Shut up, you nut," Moran said, laughing.

Lang took the sheath knife out of his sock and thrust it in his waistband. Next time they ran into a Jerry he would know what to do with it. He wondered how he could have been so frightened back in the ditch. When a man was escaping there were certain chances he had to take.

They crossed the field and found a narrow, rutted dirt road. They walked along it, Moran cursing when he stumbled on the uneven surface.

"Jesus," he said after a while. "I need a smoke."

He thrust his face in Lang's unbuttoned greatcoat to hide the flare of the match. He inhaled with such a sigh of contentment that Lang had a yearning to try. He had not smoked since he was a child. It had made him vomit. He might like it now, he thought. He was a grown man. And he wanted to do something unusual to celebrate.

"You got another one?" he asked.

"What?" said Moran, surprised. "Sure."

The cigarette gave Lang no pleasure.

"You got to inhale," Moran said.

Lang inhaled. The smoke strangled him and he coughed violently. He threw the cigarette away. He would have to find some other way to celebrate.

They reached a huddle of low, silent houses. No light showed anywhere.

"What do you think, Blubber?" Moran said.

"I don't know."

"My knee's killing me. This looks like as good a place as any."

"Yeah," Lang said.

Moran was right. This was as good a place as any. The Italians were on their side now. Maybe they could get a hot meal and a place to hide out until they decided what to do next.

Moran knocked on a door. Lang took the knife from his waistband, still in its sheath, and held it ready. He did not know why. It just seemed that this was what a man would do who would stop at nothing. When there was no answer Moran knocked again.

"Maybe nobody lives here," Lang said.

"Let's bust in," Moran said.

"We'll get in trouble."

Moran laughed. Lang did, too. That was a stupid thing to say, he thought. There was a shuttered window at the side of the house. Moran pulled at the shutter until something snapped and it came open. There was no glass in the window. Moran crawled inside, grunting with pain. Lang followed. They stood side by side in the darkness. Moran's fingers dug into Lang's arm. There was someone in the room with them, breathing heavily. The someone moved stealthily toward the door. Moran hopped toward the sound on his one good leg. There was a squeal of fear, and Moran cried, "Got you, you son of a bitch."

"Who is it?" Lang cried.

"Turn on a light," Moran said.

"I don't know where it is," Lang said. "Ask him."

An Italian voice babbled.

"Simmer down," Moran said. "We ain't gonna hurt you. We're friends. Americans."

The babbling stopped.

"Americani?" the voice said.

"American," Moran said. "Amigos."

"Americani," the voice said. "Molto bene."

Lang knew what that meant. Whoever it was liked Americans. He put the knife, still in its sheath, back in his waistband.

"How about a light, Tony?" Moran said. "Electrico? Capish?"

Lang wished he had not dropped his Italian class.

"Si, si," the man said anxiously.

Moran kept his fingers hooked in the Italian's belt as the man groped through the darkness. A match flared and a lamp was lit. The Italian studied them furtively, his expression frightened and ingratiating. He was a wiry little man with large hairy hands protruding from his nightshirt. His hair stuck up in tufts and his mustache was more Hitlerian than Italian.

The floor was stone and scabbed with dirt. The only furniture was a wooden table, three straight chairs and a tall wooden cabinet. A doorway without a door led to a back room. On one wall was a large photograph of Mussolini, badly hand-tinted. Moran looked at it, caught Lang's eye and nodded toward it. The Italian saw the gesture.

"Finito Benito," he said, spitting on the floor contemptuously.

"Why don't you take his picture down then?" Moran asked.

The Italian did not understand.

"You help us?" Moran said. "We go American lines. Capish?"

He did not understand that either.

Moran and Lang made signs. They pointed, pantomimed and used the few Italian words they knew. He understood at last.

"Si, si," he said, bobbing his head up and down.

He started for the back room and Moran grabbed his arm.

"Where you goin'?" he demanded.

The Italian made reassuring signs.

"Go with him, Blubber," Moran said. "I don't trust him."

Lang took the lamp and followed him into the back

193

room. It was smaller than the other room, and windowless. The Italian took a pair of baggy-kneed trousers from a nail and slipped them on over his nightshirt, shrugging into the suspenders. He folded soiled cloths around his feet, pulled on broken shoes and put on a ragged coat smelling of manure.

When they returned to the larger room Moran was sitting on a chair with his right leg out straight and his pants pulled up past the knee. The knee was pink and white and swollen. The Italian clucked his tongue sympathetically.

"Is it busted?" Lang asked.

Moran shook his head.

"If I had something to use for a crutch I could walk," he said.

The Italian said something and started for the door.

"Hey!" Moran cried.

The Italian gestured that he would return and continued toward the door. Lang did not like his eyes. When the man looked at him they had seemed to slide away.

"You stay here," Lang said. "We all go together."

He caught at the man's arm. The man shook his head and pulled away. Lang took the sheathed knife from his waistband. That would show he meant business. The little man stared at it and backed away. He turned suddenly and sprang for the door.

"Get him!" Moran yelled, jumping up and falling in a heap.

Lang lunged after the man. The sheath fell to the floor and the blade shone nakedly. The Italian had shown fear when Lang sprang after him but, strangely, he seemed to lose it at the sight of the knife. He faced Lang, his knees flexed, and reached into his coat pocket.

"Watch out!" Moran shouted as the Italian's hand darted from his pocket.

Lang drove at the Italian, the knife thrust straight ahead at arm's length. It was a purely reflex action. The blade touched the ragged coat, grated on a rib and slid in up to the guard. It made a thumping sound. The Italian's mouth flew

194

open as if he were going to scream but no sound came out. He looked down and saw the hilt of the knife protruding from his chest and his eyes went wide with astonishment. He stared incredulously at Lang and dropped suddenly to the floor as if boneless.

Lang stared down at him in disbelief.

"I didn't mean to," he cried.

And why did he flop around and twitch like that? In the movies a man crumpled slowly and lay quietly.

"Jesus," Moran said softly.

He hobbled to the man's side and knelt awkwardly, holding his bad knee away from the floor. The Italian rolled over on his back, gave a final twitch and was still. Lang could not move. He could only stare at the open mouth, the knife hilt planted in a growing stain.

"He's had it," Moran said.

"Oh, my God," Lang whispered.

It was the first dead man he had ever seen. He had helped kill many men, navigating the *High Flying Flora* over enemy harbors, shipping, fortifications. But he had not seen them, only the blossoming flash and billow of bombs far below, too far below to be heard above the roar of engines and throb of propellers.

Moran picked up an object which had fallen from the Italian's hand. It was a horn-handled clasp knife. He opened it and held it up. The blade was worn and deadly looking.

Lang began shaking.

"I killed him," he said.

Moran came to him and put an arm around his shoulders.

"You saved our ass, Steve," he said.

There was something in his voice Lang had never heard before. He called me Steve, he thought, not Blubberbutt. Lang took a long breath and stopped shaking.

"We better make tracks," Moran said. "If we get caught here . . ."

He tore a board from the tall cabinet, broke it to size

and padded an end with a piece of blanket. He tucked it under his armpit and took an experimental step. He blew out the lamp.

"Come on, Steve," he said.

They went back out into the night. They walked with desperate haste, Moran hopping nimbly on his crutch. They walked with their heads down, not looking at one another, not speaking. They lost their way in the blankness of the night and walked toward the station instead of away from it. They did not realize their error until they blundered into a detail of German soldiers returning to the train with a kettle of soup for the troops.

They were hustled back to the train and locked in a boxcar with thirty British officers, who protested they were already overcrowded.

Lang was not sorry they had been recaptured. It was the first time he had felt safe since he killed the Italian.

CHAPTER 12

Moran sat against the wall with his bad leg thrust straight out. In any other position the knee stiffened and throbbed agonizingly. He swore when anyone moved against it. The floor was solid with entwined bodies and he swore frequently.

Lang burrowed among the arms and legs and tried to sleep. Hands and feet were over him and under him, in his back, his face and his crotch. When he grew cramped in a position and shifted, the tangle in which he was imbedded protested sleepily, as he did when someone else turned over. Lang could not forget the look on the Italian's face when he saw the knife hilt in his chest, or the way he had twitched on the floor like a catfish with a broken back, and most of all the way he lay without moving at all. When he fell asleep he killed the Italian again in a dream, and just as the knife went in the face changed to Jaybird's. He awakened with a scream choked in his throat and did not try to sleep again.

The train went north all day. It stopped sometimes for minutes, sometimes for almost an hour. It stopped on sidings in the open countryside and in busy stations. Sometimes the guards would open the door to empty the relief can or let the prisoners out to stretch their legs and sometimes they would not. When the men protested loudly enough the guards would take them to fill their canteens.

Italian civilians assembled to cheer departing Italian prisoners of the Germans greeted them in the larger stations. When the guards slid the doors open, as they did occasionally, pretty girls came forward to distribute the fruit and steaming artificial coffee intended for their own countrymen.

"And we had to pick a Fascist bastard," Moran said when he saw Italians looking at them with sympathy and friendship. "Anybody else and we'd had it made."

All the same, Lang wished he had not killed the Italian. He had committed murder. But if it was not murder to kill with a five-hundred-pound bomb it was not murder to kill with a knife. It was wartime and he was a soldier and he had done it to save himself and Moran. If I hadn't got him he'd of got me, Lang thought. He felt a perverse desire to tell everyone about it, an excuse and a boast. But he remained silent. He and Moran had agreed it must be kept secret.

A night and a day went by, and part of another day. It seemed they had been locked in for an eternity and Lang longed for nothing more than mere room to stretch out full length with no knees or elbows burrowing into him, remembering how penned up and uncomfortable he had felt in the chair car to San Antonio when he went into the army and thinking how luxurious the accommodations would seem to him now.

198

On the third day they entered Bologna. A German officer came and told them in English they would be in the station for some time and could get out of the cars a few at a time but must remain close by them.

"If you mingle with the people you will be shot and they will be shot," he said.

No one had eaten the Italian hardtack and someone tossed it out of the car. A guard shoved it out on the platform and instantly well-dressed civilians began scrambling for it shamefacedly, tucking it into their clothes and walking quickly away.

"Would you believe it?" Moran said. "They're worse off for chow than we are."

"Let's see if they'll let us go back to our own boxcar," Lang said. "We got stuff back there."

He had been thinking about that for two days, wondering if anyone had been at his things.

"Why ask?" Moran said. "Let's just go."

Lang helped him down and they edged along the line of cars. A German guard gave them an intimidating look and shifted his machine pistol. Moran grinned and said, "Just visiting buddies, old buddy," and pulled Lang after him. The guard did not understand but, disarmed by Moran's nonchalance, did not stop them. They looked in the open boxcar doors until they found their own.

"It's Moran and Blubberbutt!" someone cried.

The others began shouting questions and a soldier came ιο look inside the door. Everyone got quiet until he left.

"I thought you guys got away or bought it or something," Harbold said. "What happened?"

Lang looked at Moran.

"We ran into a Jerry patrol," Moran said. "Anybody else make it?"

"No," said Harbold. "When you guys jumped we were too close to the station."

Lang was glad no one else from the car had jumped.

It showed he and Moran had more guts than they did. He found his possessions intact.

So many prisoners wanted to use the station toilets that the guards, unable to supervise them, conducted groups to the side of the boxcars away from the platform. While Lang was squatting by a boxcar with a long row of fellow prisoners a passenger train drew into the station and stopped alongside them. Civilians stared out their car windows at the squatting men, amused, repelled, shocked. Lang stared back at them, unembarrassed. It was not like him not to be embarrassed. As a child he had been shy about his bodily functions and even after he was older, until he entered the military service, he craved utter privacy.

But he did not feel he belonged to the same world as the Italians in the passenger cars. Not because they were Italians but because they were not prisoners of war. His world was other prisoners. He felt he belonged with them and with no one else, even Harbold, whom he still disliked though Harbold had appeared glad to see him.

And so he was no more disturbed by the staring Italians than if they had been horses or stones.

He thought about that when he was back in the boxcar. It made him feel enigmatic and hardened and a little tragic. And he wondered if he would feel that way with people he had known all his life when he got home again.

It grew colder as the train continued its northern progress. The air in the boxcar was comfortable. The scenery changed outside. Lang looked out at long sloping meadows, vividly green, and streams, and distant mountains, some mantled with snow. He had seen snow rarely, and never snowclad mountains, and the sight inspired in him a sense of anticipation and adventure.

He hardly thought now of the man he had killed. The farther he drew geographically from anything the farther away it seemed in time. The crash of the *High Flying Flora* was ancient history, Byrd a memory, P.G. 203 an incident, the dead Italian a bad dream. Only the boxcar had time and place, the boxcar and the train and the swaying, and what could be seen through the steel mesh of the window.

On the afternoon of the fourth day the train crept over a broad river and into a marshaling yard.

"Bolzano," someone said. "We're getting near the Brenner Pass."

The boxcars were shunted to a siding and the prisoners waited for the guards to open the doors. A hospital train drew in across the yard and as Lang watched from the window German soldiers in bandages and casts got out and walked about.

In the distance a siren moaned. The Germans stopped walking and listened. The locomotive pulling the hospital train began blowing its whistle in sharp, short bursts and the wounded men scrambled back aboard.

"Hey, Moran," Lang said, "something's going on over there."

More sirens joined the first as Moran limped to the window. The locomotive across the way snorted a long plume of steam and began moving.

"Sounds like an air raid somewhere," Harbold said carelessly.

"Shut up!" Moran cried abruptly. "Listen."

There was no sound in the boxcar except heavy breathing and restless movement of bodies. From outside came only the sound of the departing hospital train and sirens in the middle distance. Then they were ringed with the rising and falling shriek of sirens. Germans called to each other. A German troop train labored by, its locomotive chuffing steam. Soldiers hung out the windows looking into the sky.

Bees hummed.

"Listen," said Lang, holding up his hand for silence in the silent car.

Not bees, planes. The hum swelled into a drone, into a heavy throbbing. Germans ran across the marshaling yard, shouting.

"Oh, God!" someone shrieked in the car. "They're gonna bomb us!"

Lang was angry. Why did the guy have to yell like that and scare everybody? Nobody was going to bomb them. They were prisoners of war.

Flak batteries opened fire. The throb of many engines filled the air. Lang and Moran dropped to the floor. Outside men were running and yelling and more batteries joined the barrage. The car shook and shrapnel pattered on the roof. And then the bombs began falling.

At first Lang did not know they were bombs. He thought bombs whistled or screamed as they fell. These slanted through the air with a ponderous clatter and rattle like an immense load of gravel sliding over a corrugated tin roof. The boxcar shook with concussion. More men were running past now and there were rifle shots. Lang burrowed under the pile of men on the floor, aching physically with terror. There was fury in his terror. It was not fair. He had not swum out of the *High Flying Flora* and spent nine months in a prison camp and killed a man for this, to be killed by his own planes. And as he groveled he remembered the one time his crew had bombed troops. They had not found the tanker convoy reported in the Mediterranean and were returning over the desert with their bombs. Bertram had seen a retreating column of German vehicles and directed Byrd to the attack. The trucks turned off the road and little figures scurried from them as the plane made its bombing run. High in their shining cage of Plexiglass Lang and Bertram had laughed at their curious antics.

"Just like sandfleas!" Lang had shouted.

Now the terrified men stampeding past his boxcar must look that way to the bomber crews above them. He wished he had not made fun of the Afrika Korps men scrambling in the desert, wondering if this was retribution, and wishing with fanatical intensity he was outside and running, too, and hoping the men on top of him were big men who would absorb the blast if bombs burst near the boxcar.

202

Moran was the first man in the car to conquer his terror. He hobbled to the door over the sprawling bodies and tore at it vainly, then beat it with his fists.

"Open up, you bastards!" he yelled. "Let us out!"

With an intolerable effort of will and muscles Lang wrenched himself from the supine mass of bodies and stumbled to the window. Prisoners and guards ran by together, united in their fear.

"Open the door!" he screamed. "We're locked in!"

He was ignored. He mixed his pleas with curses and kicked and beat the wall. Others joined him at the window, shouting for help, and somewhere in the car a man shrieked hysterically. In a tiny corner of his consciousness Lang was embarrassed. The Germans would hear the screaming and think prisoners were yellow. He was as frightened as anyone but you did not let down other prisoners in front of outsiders.

Perkins loped into view, his expression less perturbed than earnest, his round eyes looking up into the thunderous sky with a tourist's interest while other men raced past him, heads down.

"Perkins!" Lang cried, trying not to sound panicky. "We're locked in!"

Perkins stopped and looked along the cars.

"In here!" Lang yelled. "It's me, Lang. Open our door!"

"Oh, there you are," Perkins said. "Half a mo'."

He scrambled over the coupling and came around to flip back the bolt and throw open the door.

"Andiamo, Distinguished Flier," he said, trotting off.

Men poured out of the boxcar and ran across the yard. Bombs were still falling. Though they sounded as if they were coming directly into the marshaling yard none had yet landed there. Moran had jumped ahead of Lang. He ran with an awkward hopping gait, cursing each time his bad leg touched the ground. Lang passed him without an acknowledging glance. He felt extraordinarily vulnerable in the open where jagged metal was falling from the sky and guards still at their posts might decide to open fire.

Once across the yard, Lang stopped, panting, and waited for Moran to catch up. They saw men running into an apartment building and followed them to a basement crowded with prisoners and Italian civilians. Among them was a German soldier, looking as if he felt out of place. An old woman moaned and worried a rosary. A prisoner, shirtless, kneeled on the floor sobbing and clutching the legs of a companion. The building shook above them and dust sifted down from the ceiling.

The last bomb fell and the sound of engines faded in the distance. The German soldier left.

"Let's try to get away," Moran said.

"How about your knee?" Lang demanded.

"It's better. Didn't you see me making knots across those tracks?"

"We're too far north," Lang protested.

"Maybe somebody'll help us get to Switzerland. We ain't gonna get another chance like this one."

Outside, the prisoners were streaming back toward the boxcars with little prompting from scattered German soldiers. The long, cramped ride and the shock of the bombing had made them docile.

Smoke was billowing to the south. The bombers had attacked the bridge, not the marshaling yard.

Lang and Moran walked against the stream of prisoners, looking for a break in the solid front of buildings. They saw a German soldier up ahead and ducked into a doorway. They were in a dark hall with doors on either side. Moran knocked on all of them one after the other without an answer. They went down into the basement and found a window opening on the rear. They scrambled through it and ran at a crouch across the walled courtyard. Moran limped badly but did not complain. They helped each other to the top of the wall and dropped to the paved street. An old man came out of a house carrying a shotgun.

"Halt!" he shouted, his accent German.

He pointed the gun at them, not carelessly from the hip but like a hunter, cheek against stock, finger on trigger. His eyes burned like those of a revivalist preacher Lang had once seen at a tent service to which neighbors had taken him in childhood. Lang was as frightened now as he had been then.

Lang and Moran put up their hands.

"The old bastard looks like he's dying to scrag us," Moran whispered.

"Schweig!" the old man screamed.

He had on baggy knickers and a tweed jacket with leather patches on the elbows. A cloth band on his arm bore the initials SOD.

"Marchieren!" he cried, waving them on with the shotgun held to his shoulder.

On the way back to the marshaling yard he apprehended three more prisoners, all English.

"Decent of the old sod to label himself," one of them said.

They learned later that SOD were the initials of a civilian auxiliary comprising overage German and Austrian civilians.

Back at the boxcars British officers were building small fires among the tracks and brewing tea. Few of the prisoners had escaped during the bombing. Civilians had been afraid to hide them in their houses and the streets had been cordoned off by military patrols and SODs.

The prisoners were sent into the cars for their belongings and marched through the town to a brick-paved courtyard behind a warren of flats. Lang had been unable to find his canteen in the boxcar and now he went looking for it, accosting every prisoner with an Italian canteen and asking to inspect it. There were only a few such canteens and by good fortune he found his in the crowded courtyard.

"This is mine," he said without preamble.

"Who says so?" the possessor demanded belligerently.

Lang breathed deeply. This guy was trying to back him down. He was not going to back down. Not this time. He had jumped from a moving train and killed a man in hand-to-hand combat and been bombed and a man all that had happened to was not going to be intimidated. And also his opponent was not very big.

"I said so. You going to give it to me or do I have to take it away from you?"

"You and who else, Blubberbutt?"

Lang stepped closer to the man, his face hard and determined. The man stepped back involuntarily.

"Just me," Lang said. "And don't call me Blubberbutt."

"How you know it's yours?" the man said, less belligerently.

Lang pointed to his initials on the cover.

"Somebody gave it to me," the man said, handing it over. "I didn't know it was yours."

"I ought to bust you one," Lang said.

Moran, seeing the encounter, hobbled over to them.

"What's the problem?" he asked.

"No problem," Lang said.

The man turned as if to walk away.

"Hold it," Lang said.

"You got your canteen back," the man said. "What more you want?"

"A piece of your butt," said Lang.

Lang shoved him. He felt hard and powerful. When the man did not retaliate he shoved him again.

"You yellow?" he demanded.

"Come off it, Steve," Moran said.

He turned to Lang's opponent.

"Beat it, Mac," he said.

The man left quickly.

"He was asking for it," Lang protested.

"No, he wasn't," said Moran. "Let me tell you something. When a man don't want to fight, don't push him."

206

"I should have busted him one," Lang said doggedly.

Moran looked at him almost fondly.

"Man, you've sure got ironass all of a sudden, ain't you?" he said.

They bedded down early for the night. The courtyard bricks were cold but there was room to stretch out full length. Lang and Moran spread one of their heavy blankets on the bricks and pulled the others and their greatcoats over them. They lay for a long time looking up into the star-flecked night, talking and listening for the sound of engines, apprehensive about night bombers. At last they slept.

They were kept in the courtyard until midmorning. With other prisoners they amused themselves throwing their German army bread rations to the civilians who lived in the flats. The Italians had been ordered to remain indoors and from behind drawn curtains they looked out at the prisoners and the bread falling on the balconies.

"I bet it's just full of bella ragatsas," Moran said longingly.

A young German soldier who looked as if he had not yet begun shaving spoke disapprovingly to Lang in halting English.

"Why you give them?"

Lang did not answer. He had seen how mean the Germans were to the Italians in the stations when they tried to be nice to the prisoners. Even if the Italians had killed Byrd he liked them better than the Germans.

Back in the boxcars, the prisoners did not feel safe until the train left the marshaling yard, and when it halted after a few miles listened in strained silence for the sound of engines. A single plane flew over but they knew it was not an American bomber. The Americans synchronized their engines and the Germans did not. German multiengine planes had a characteristic drone instead of the smooth throb of a B-17.

The door opened and a German officer looked in.

"You have entered the German Reich," he announced. "Escape is now forbidden on penalty of death. If a prisoner of war should escape from this wagon five of you will be shot."

"Screw you," said Moran.

Lang wished Moran would keep his mouth shut. He was going to get them all in trouble. To Lang's relief the officer did not understand the idiom.

"Use your noodle and do not attempt to escape," the German said.

Someone snickered at his attempt at American slang.

"You think they really would?" Lang asked Moran when the door was locked again.

"Hell, no," said Moran.

"Let's don't take the chance," Lang said.

"I couldn't jump with this knee even if I wanted to," Moran said.

Lang was glad.

He stood at the window much of the way through the Brenner Pass, staring at the postcard shimmer of green valleys and snowy peaks. There were signs in German along the right-of-way, the first he had seen in the language. It was at once thrilling and depressing. He was in a new country but he did not much like being there.

The snow on the mountains was the color of pineapple sherbet. It had snowed in Houston only three or four times in Lang's memory and, looking at the white-clad peaks he recalled how once his mother had filled a bowl with newly fallen snow and mixed in sugar, milk and vanilla extract. If he was on a mountain now he could mix Klim and sugar with the snow and have ice cream like his mother had made.

Late in the day the train halted in an isolated snowfield and the prisoners were allowed to get out of the cars. They ran out into the snow to stretch and relieve themselves, then began shouting and throwing snowballs. One of the younger guards put down his rifle and joined the horseplay. Moran hit him in back of the head with a hard-packed snowball and was roughhousing innocently with Lang when he whirled around in anger. Moran laughed until tears ran down his cheeks. Lang was frightened and did not dare laugh until he saw the guard did not know who had hit him.

Whistles blew. Guards shouted "Einsteigen" and motioned everyone back into the boxcars. On the way Lang scooped up a double handful of snow and scrambled aboard awkwardly cupping it in his palms.

"What the hell you gonna do with that?" Moran demanded.

"I'm going to eat it," Lang said.

"Eat it? You must be crackin' up."

Lang mixed the snow with Klim and sugar. He wished he had kept the orange powder in American parcels that was supposed to prevent scurvy.

"I wish I had me some vanilla extract," he said wistfully.

"Christ," said Moran.

But he ate a share of Lang's ice cream and admitted he liked it.

They reached Innsbruck after dark and were allowed outside to fill their canteens and receive hot soup. When he could write letters again Lang intended telling his parents he had seen the Brenner Pass and the Alps and Innsbruck. They had never been to Europe.

Later he slept, not awakening until the cars were shunted onto a siding. When no one came to open the door he fell asleep again. He was awakened at first light by shuffling feet and a babble of voices. He went to the window and looked out. A band of unkempt men in stained British and American uniforms walked a muddy road beside the tracks, ORs and enlisted men on their way to work details.

"Where are we?" Lang called.

"It bloody well ain't Piccadilly Circus," a Cockney voice replied.

CHAPTER 13

Stalag VIIA was a sprawling complex of barbed-wire enclosures containing long stucco buildings dirtier and more crowded than those at P.G. 203. They were to be there only a short time and Lang found the camp tolerable once he had been assured by its permanent inmates there was no chance of being bombed. Munich, kilometers distant, was the nearest military target anyone knew about. VIIA was an enlisted men's camp, crammed with prisoners of many nationalities fenced into separate compounds. Each compound had its own guard but Lang soon learned the guards were corrupt and let a man leave his compound for two cigarettes.

He took advantage of this to visit a thriving black market in an open courtyard behind the central cookhouse where

Russian, French, English, Yugoslav, and American prisoners circulated with ritual solemnity displaying what they had to trade — cigarette lighters, pocket knives, Swiss watches, gold wedding rings, Red Cross food, clothing, medals, writing paper, toilet articles, handicrafts. The *Hundfuehrers*, guards who patrolled with dogs, occasionally would unleash their animals into the throng to amuse themselves and the prisoners would scatter in panic, though the dogs never actually attacked anyone.

For two packages of American cigarettes Lang bought a Swiss knife with a cutting blade, punch, can opener, screwdriver and corkscrew. Knives had been prohibited at P.G. 203. On the advice of a prisoner who had been through a German winter he bought wooden shoes for himself and Moran from a Russian prisoner who worked in the camp cobbler's shop. Despite the thriving commerce of Stalag VIIA he made no other purchases except, at Moran's instructions, a bottle of beer from their compound guard, who smuggled it in under his cape.

In his new-found belligerence Lang had two fistfights, winning one and not feeling particularly humiliated when he lost the other because Moran stopped it before he was too badly beaten. He was gaining experience to fight Harbold but before he thought himself ready Harbold and the other American ground officers were shipped out to a Wehrmacht prisoner of war camp in Poland. The flying officers left two days later.

Lang was afraid his pocket knife would be confiscated despite the assurances of the seller at the time of the sale that they were permitted in German camps. He hid it inside his trousers on a string dangling from a fly button. It was found and confiscated when the prisoners had to drop their trousers during a personal search. Lang had seen other pocket knives go by unchallenged.

"How come you took mine and not theirs?" he demanded.

"Shut up!" Moran ordered. "You want to louse things up for everybody else?"

211

"You should not try to make me the fool," said the soldier who had found the knife. "I teach you lesson."

Moran took a cigarette out of his pack and let two others spill out at the soldier's feet. He looked at the German. The soldier stooped to pick them up. When he straightened, the cigarettes were gone and the knife was on the ground in their place.

"Hey, you dropped . . ." Lang began.

Moran stopped him with an elbow in the ribs.

"Pick it up, you dumb bastard," he whispered.

Lang did.

The two-day trip to Upper Silesia was considerably more agreeable than the journey from Italy. The car had been fitted with a toilet and rows of straight-backed wooden benches and the two guards riding inside with the prisoners allowed them to keep the sliding doors open during daylight hours except in cities. The prisoners would be silent then, listening for air-raid sirens.

They walked from a railway siding to their new camp through a pine woods. The air was cool and scented with resin, the ground carpeted with resilient pine needles. Lang took great breaths of the pungent air and thought of home on brisk spring mornings when his mother opened all the windows and sponged the bathroom tiles with Pine-o-Pine, and of walks in the woods with his father, and shooting at pine cones with the twenty-two rifle his father had bought him for his twelfth birthday over his mother's objections.

In the Vorlager, the German administrative compound, they were searched, photographed and given forms to fill out. Lang boldly laid out his pocket knife with the contents of his pockets. His cheap Italian fountain pen was confiscated, and a receipt given to him for it, but the knife was returned without comment. The blue-clad Luftwaffe guards and clerks appeared alert and well disciplined and Lang did not think he would be able to move from compound to compound for two cigarettes.

"You will find life quite pleasant in Stalag Luft 9," a German officer said in excellent English. "Concerts, sports in season and as much leisure as one could wish for. I envy you, gentlemen."

"Give me fifteen minutes' start and I'll trade uniforms with you," said Moran.

American and British prisoners were assigned to different compounds. Lang had hoped to find Perkins but had not been allowed to leave the processing line. He had not seen him since Perkins opened the boxcar at Bolzano.

The prison camp was in a great clearing in the pine woods, surrounded by a tall double fence of barbed wire with coils and tangles of concertina wire in the eight-foot space between the fences. In each of the two adjoining compounds were rows of long narrow wooden buildings painted green, and large open spaces. After P.G. 203's wall and Stalag VIIA's crowds Stalag Luft 9 looked spacious and inviting to Lang.

They entered the South Lager through a swinging gate of wood and wire. The guard saluted the sergeant escorting the prisoners. Another guard looked down from a watchtower mounting a machine gun.

When the prisoners approached the gate someone inside had bellowed, "Purge in! Purge in!" and now men came tumbling out of the wooden buildings and racing toward them. The crowd grew as men arrived from the more distant barracks. They looked well fed, almost clean and adequately clothed in American uniforms.

"Very rich Americans," said Moran.

Hundreds of prisoners massed at the gate. The German sergeant pushed and threatened as he cleared a path through them.

Someone yelled, "Bernie Moran!" and elbowed his way through the crowd.

He was a strikingly handsome second lieutenant, tall, with wavy dark hair, a lock of which dangled over one eye.

"Hartman, you old bastard!" Moran cried, shaking his hand. "What the hell you doing here?"

"Where'd they get you?" Hartman demanded.

"We been in Italy," Moran replied. "This is my navigator, Steve Lang. Blubber, this is Eddie Hartman. We were classmates at advanced."

Lang shook hands with Hartman, wishing Moran had not called him Blubber. This was a new place and now that he was not so fat maybe he could lose the nickname. As soon as they were alone he would have to ask Moran not to call him that any more.

"You made first," Hartman said accusingly, looking at the tin bar on Moran's shoulder.

"Class tells," said Moran.

"We've got empty bunks in our room," Hartman said. "I'll get you in with me."

He turned to the sergeant.

"Hey, Froehlich," he said ingratiatingly, "how about putting these two in with me? Room 3, Block 2B. We've got empty bunks."

Froehlich was blond, with the face of a prematurely aged high school senior. His wheaten hair was parted on the side and looked as if he had just washed and combed it. His eyes were blue and unwavering. He smiled. It was not a warm smile.

"You people act as if you were privileged guests," he said. "But, as you wish."

His accent was upper-class British.

"You're a pal," Hartman said.

Froehlich grimaced.

He was not at all like Pellini, Lang thought. He found himself missing Pellini. It was useful to have a contact in the administrative office. Froehlich did not seem like a man you could cultivate. Lang wondered what had happened to Pellini. He had not seen the sergeant again after they were locked in the boxcars at P.G. 203. Maybe he had changed his mind about going to Germany and jumped off the train.

214

A clutter of men followed them into the room asking questions about the war and Italy. Lang was disappointed when Hartman shooed them outside. He liked telling about his adventures.

Block 2B was the second barracks in the second row of buildings. Room 3 was twelve by twenty feet with two four-paned casement windows framed in wood. Three double-deck wooden bunks, more strongly made than those at P.G. 203, were ranged against the walls. There were three tall wooden lockers against the fourth wall and another turned on its side. In one corner was a brick stove and in the center of the room a wooden table with a bench on each of the long sides. The furnishings also included two comfortable-looking armchairs made of Red Cross parcel crates on which the stenciling still showed.

"They got a country club here," Lang said to Moran.

"Oh, yeah?" said one of his new roommates. "It's rough here. Rough as a cob."

He was a couple of inches shorter than Lang, all bone and angles. His shoulders extended from his slender neck in a straight line, as if there was a stick across them under his Eisenhower jacket. His eyes were pale blue and his face thin and discontented. He wore navigator wings. Real ones. Lang had made his own of tin.

"Phil Augustine," Hartman said, introducing him. "He doesn't like it here."

"Steve Lang," Lang said quickly before Moran could call him Blubberbutt. "They call me Tex. Sometimes."

He looked imploringly at Moran, who grinned and said nothing.

"Crumb Crumbacker," Hartman said, nodding at the other roommate. "My bombardier."

Crumbacker was Moran's height, round-headed and round-shouldered. His eyes were brown and glittered as if set in the center with small diamonds. He was spectacularly dirty and unkempt.

"Raunchiest man in South Camp," Hartman added.

"In Stalag Luft 9," Crumbacker said proudly.

"Why stop there?" Augustine demanded. "Why not the whole world? When you going to take a bath? You smell like the abort."

"Abort?" said Moran.

"Latrine," Hartman explained. "The Goons call it the abort."

"Goons?" said Lang.

"Germans," Augustine said.

Their belongings arrived in a horse-drawn wagon which also brought bedding, bedboards and eating utensils. Crumbacker left them to follow the wagon with a cardboard box and wooden spatula.

"He's got a garden," Hartman explained.

Hartman and Augustine helped them bring in their bundles and pile them on the table.

"Look at all that," Hartman said reverently. "What kind of deal did you guys have in Italy, anyway?"

"You couldn't pile up that kind of chow here in a million years," Augustine said.

Lang could tell he was not going to like Augustine.

"We didn't get it until they moved us out," he said testily. "And we picked up a lot of stuff from guys who weren't man enough to carry it. We were on half parcels all winter."

"Would you look at the blankets?" Augustine said, stroking a blanket roll enviously.

"We didn't get those till we left, either," Lang said. "The ones we had all winter were thinner than yours. And we didn't have a stove in our room like you guys."

"What are you trying to prove?" Augustine demanded.

"Nothing. You just don't know what rough is, is all."

"Okay," Hartman said briskly. "Let's put the stuff away."

"Put it away?" Lang said. "What you mean?"

216

"We pool all the Red Cross stuff except sugar, chocolate and cigarettes," Hartman said.

"You expect us to give you our stuff after we lugged it all the way from Italy?" Lang demanded indignantly.

"Yeah, Eddie," Moran said. "You trying to put the big pants on us?"

"That'll be the day," said Hartman. "When anybody can gyp Bernard Joseph Moran."

He explained that the men in each room pooled their food and ate together, with dinner cooked on a communal stove in the block.

"That's different," Lang said, welcoming the prospect of special dishes every day instead of only for Tuesday's tea. "But I don't see why we have to put in everything. Look how much more we got than you guys."

"Yeah?" Augustine said. "Look at this."

He opened the locker turned on its side. One side was filled with potatoes.

"Jesus!" Moran whispered reverently.

Lang was speechless.

Potatoes had been a delicacy at P.G. 203, and a rare one.

"They're the main Goon issue," Hartman said. "We saved them up last summer."

"You didn't have to carry 'em all the way from Italy like we did our stuff," Lang said, adding grudgingly, "but I guess it's even."

Crumbacker thrust his grinning face in a window.

"He dropped a load," he announced. "We're gonna have a good garden next summer. If we're still here."

"You kidding?" said Augustine. "This war's going to last a hundred years."

"Bitter, bitter, bitter," Hartman said.

For lunch they had a thin slice of dark army bread with cheese from a small paper-wrapped block and a heavy potato soup ladled from a dixie brought around by two American enlisted men.

217

"Room service," said Moran. "Can you get me a babe, Sarge?"

"Will a clean old man do, Lieutenant?" the sergeant replied.

"I ain't been in the bag that long," Moran said. "Try me tomorrow."

They ate at the table. In Italy, when they ate in the bay, they stood or sat on the edge of a bunk. Lang liked eating together at the table. It was like a family.

"Bono minestrone," Moran said after his first mouthful of soup.

"Multi bono," Lang said, adding, "that means very good in Eyetie."

"Molto buono," said Augustine.

"What?" Lang said.

"It's molto buono, not multi bono."

"Who says so?"

"An Eyetie named Augustine, that's who."

Augustine stressed the Eyetie.

Crumbacker, who had been digging the horse droppings into the ground with a sharpened stick, climbed in the window and sat next to Augustine with his soup. Augustine got up and moved several feet away.

"What's wrong, Phil?" Crumbacker asked innocently, wiping soup from his chin with the back of a dirty hand.

"Don't you even wash your hands after picking up horse manure?" Augustine demanded.

"I didn't pick it up with my hands. I used my paddle."

Lang was the only one who laughed. Crumbacker did smell of manure.

"If you won't take a bath you could at least wash your hands," Hartman said.

"And give myself a manicure, like you do, Wings?" Crumbacker said impishly.

"It wouldn't hurt you to clean your nails once in a

218

while," Hartman said without rancor, as if this were a friendly argument of long standing.

His hands were strong and graceful, the nails trimmed and clean.

"He used to get free manicures at advanced," Moran said. "This babe in the barbershop had the hots for him. Till I shot him out of the saddle."

"I never could understand what she saw in a sawed-off runt like you," Hartman said.

"I ain't sawed off all over," Moran said.

There was coffee with lunch, brewed with Nescafé and hot water fetched from the cookhouse in a large blue jug by Augustine.

"This is living, ain't it, uh, Tex?" Moran said, chuckling as if he had said something very funny.

Lang glowered.

"Well," said Augustine when they finished eating, "we might as well get the there-I-wuz stories over with."

"We got a house rule," Hartman explained. "New guys get to tell how they were shot down just one time."

"New guys?" Lang demanded, insulted. "Who you calling new guys? Which one of y'all's been in the longest?"

"Me," said Crumbacker. "Right at six months. April 14. We were coming off the target when these sixteen ME-109s . . ."

"He just asked you how long," Hartman interrupted.

"Six months," Lang said disdainfully. "I bet me and Moran got more prison camp time than you got overseas time."

"How were the English to live with?" Hartman asked.

"Swell," said Lang.

"So were English women," Hartman said with a reminiscent smile.

"You lucky bastard," said Moran. "All we had in our theater was camels."

Hartman, Augustine and Crumbacker each had a top bunk and a wooden locker. They odd-manned to see who

219

would not have to share his locker with the new men and Hartman won. Moran elected to share with Augustine, for which Lang was grateful, even more so when he discovered Crumbacker's locker was not as unkempt as Crumbacker. His sparse wardrobe was clean and his other possessions neatly arranged. Augustine's things, on the contrary, had to be refolded, rehung and rearranged to make room for Moran's.

Men from other rooms visited while they were getting settled, asking about Italy. Moran tired of answering the same questions but Lang enjoyed being the center of attention. He introduced himself to everyone as Tex.

Later Hartman took them on a tour of the block and the compound. Block 2B, like the other twenty-three in the South Camp, was a prefabricated building of wood and beaverboard set just high enough off the sandy ground for a man to crawl under inspecting for tunnels. At each end were doors connected by a hall dividing the block the long way. On each side of the hall were rooms for from two to eight men. The block had its own kitchen, a narrow room containing an iron stove and a heap of pressed coal briquettes; a cement-floored washroom and a lavatory just large enough to contain its single commode.

"Look," Moran cried when he saw the commode. "You can sit down. Does it flush?"

Hartman nodded.

"But we can't use it except after lockup," he said. "We have to use the outside aborts."

"Do they flush?" Moran asked.

"No, but you can sit down."

"You can't have everything," Moran said.

The abort was like the privy of a prosperous farmer with an enormous family. The abort, the cookhouse and the theater, the last built by the prisoners themselves, were the most sturdily constructed buildings in the compound. The cookhouse was cleaner and better equipped than that in P.G.

203. American enlisted men worked in it under the supervision of Germans. The cookhouse had a paved veranda to the roof of which was fixed a louspeaker playing Wagner. A number of prisoners stood around listening.

"They ever play anything good?" Moran asked.

"Oh, yeah," Hartman said. "They've got some American records out in the Vorlager. And they broadcast the daily communiqué and the *Luftlage Meldung*. The air situation report."

"What's an air situation report?" Lang asked, feeling a gnaw of apprehension.

"Enemy aircraft. But there's never been any around here. Nearest target's Berlin. Must be ninety miles."

"That's near enough," said Moran.

The kitchen building housed a dispensary well stocked with first-aid equipment, a storeroom for sports equipment and a swap shop.

"We call it the PX," Hartman said. "Everything's priced in cigarettes. If you want to, you can turn stuff in and open a charge account."

The English had not been nearly so well organized at P.G. 203, Lang thought. These guys were really operators. Well, if he wanted to, he could show them a thing or two. They didn't know what it was like to have to really scramble. They had it easy. But that meant he was going to have it easy, too.

Though the earth was almost as trampled as that at P.G. 203, it was sandy instead of claylike and not as hard on the feet. The entire area had been hacked out of a pine and birch forest and a few of the pines had been left standing. The stumps of hundreds of others dotted the compound.

From time to time in their walk they encountered German guards with slung rifles and men in blue coveralls carrying flashlights in their pockets and long screwdrivers in their hands, like the searchers in Italy.

"Ferrets," said Hartman. "Sometimes they crawl under the blocks and listen, so be careful what you say. The Hund-fuehrers come in at night."

A bugle blew.

"Appell," said Hartman. "Roll call."

They joined the hundreds of other men streaming toward the parade ground. Lang and Moran stood with the other men of their block in hollow square formation in an area large enough to contain the whole of P.G. 203. Far across a double barbed-wire fence the blue-uniformed RAF prisoners were also in formation. Lang looked for PO Perkins but the formations were much too far apart to distinguish individuals.

The roll was taken quickly, supervised by a German captain who chatted easily with the Senior American Officer in the center of the parade ground while his men counted the rows of prisoners. It was the first time Lang had seen the SAO. He was a colonel with command pilot wings, a burly man in his mid-thirties with a thick neck, the face of a friendly traffic cop, thinning hair the color of Jaybird's cut short and a slightly cauliflowered left ear.

"Colonel Ozmozius," Hartman whispered. "Rugged but right."

Moran and Lang laughed. They had remembered Pellini's description of Colonel Malvi.

When the formation was dismissed the men broke ranks and sauntered away. Lang missed the snappy British right turn and salute before breaking formation. There were some things they did better than Americans. He remembered how the British cadets at preflight always won the daily parade award for best formation, and how smartly they did close-order drill. "Square bashing," they called it.

It was Hartman's week to cook and he hurried back to the block. Lang watched his preparation of the evening meal with rapt attention. It made his own efforts at P.G. 203 seem primitive. The room had a pot and other cooking utensils made

222

of strips of tin cans skillfully joined together with tightly pounded seams.

Lang wanted to watch him cook the meal but there was a rule prohibiting anyone except room cooks and their helpers from being in the kitchen during the cooking period, and then only during the time reserved for their rooms. Augustine was the stooge, or helper, that week. He peeled the potatoes, set the table and brought hot water from the kitchen in the blue jug.

In honor of the occasion Hartman prepared a special meal of fried Spam, boiled potatoes and a dessert of Klim, water and jam beaten vigorously to the consistency of heavy whipped cream. Lang, his mouth full of fried Spam, looked at Moran. They grinned at each other.

If he had not killed the Italian and Jaybird were alive, everything would be perfect, Lang thought.

CHAPTER 14

After a few days, when the newness wore off, the enormity of having been moved from Italy beset Moran again.

"If we'd had any kind of break we'd be home now," he said.

"Yeah," said Lang, "but it could be worse."

"You know something, Steve?" Moran said thoughtfully. He would not call Lang Tex as some of the other men did but he had stopped calling him Blubberbutt. "I almost think you like it here."

"You must be around the bend," Lang protested.

But it was true, he thought. He did like it here. There was more to eat here than P.G. 203, and more variety in its preparation. The library was bigger and better, the theater seats more comfortable. With no wall and so much open space, life seemed almost unconfined. He could walk about the camp without seeing a German uniform, except in the guardboxes. If he wanted to he could sit under a pine tree with a book, or look across the wire at the pine woods.

Here he had more status than at P.G. 203. That was the most important thing of all. In P.G. 203 nearly all the other prisoners had been in captivity longer. Here, he and Moran were among the most senior prisoners. Seniority carried both prestige and privilege in Stalag Luft 9. Older prisoners were automatically included in the circle of such notables as the camp interpreter, favorite performers in theatricals, the head of the escape committee, the mail officer and an authority on the preparation of kriegie brew, a concoction distilled from fermented dried fruit. Kriegie was the name the prisoners had given themselves from the German word for prisoner of war, *Kriegsgefangenen.*

In any group only the senior prisoner present could complain without fear of ridicule of the long wait between letters, the monotony of Lager life or the frustrations of celibacy. Senior prisoners were first on the list for new uniforms, shoes, long underwear and other luxuries which reached Stalag Luft 9 in insufficient quantities to go around.

And Lang had a reputation of his own even among the senior prisoners. Only the handful who had come up from Italy knew of his early days when he was fat and timid and greedy and called Blubberbutt. Now he was called Steve, or Lang, or Tex, which he preferred. His roommates had repeated the stories he and Moran had told of Italy, how they had gone over the wall and Jaybird had been killed, and how they had jumped from the speeding train, and he was considered one of the more daring men in the South Camp. Lang sometimes wondered if Moran still remembered how he had begged for help in the water when the *High Flying Flora* broke up. Moran had never referred to it.

If they had not been shot down he did not think Moran

would ever have become his friend. It was almost worth being shot down to have a friend like Moran, a man everybody liked but who liked him better than he did any of the others. Maybe some day people would like him the way they liked Moran.

For almost three weeks Lang read, ate, told his stories to anyone who would listen, groomed his mustache and was content. In the third week, during his tenure as room stooge, he was in the cookhouse line with a tall metal pitcher called a *Keintrinkwasser* to draw wash water for the lunchtime soup bowls. The man behind him trod on his heels and pushed a Keintrinkwasser into his back. Irritated but accustomed to being jostled in the interminable lines which were a prisoner's lot, Lang said nothing and moved closer to the man in front. The man behind continued crowding him. Lang whirled angrily, fists clenched. The heated words on his lips went unspoken. The man behind Lang towered over him and his shoulders seemed to block the sky. It was not his size alone which made him so formidable. There was something implacable in his gaunt hungry face and his tawny eyes had a feral gleam like those of a revivalist preacher or a bloodthirsty SOD staring over the barrel of a shotgun.

"Something wrong, pal?" he asked in a hard, deep voice.

"How about a little room?" Lang said mildly. "You're stepping all over me."

"If you'd get your finger outta your ass and move along I wouldn't," the man said.

"Listen," Lang snapped, immediately regretting his belligerent tone.

"I'm listening," the man said.

"Nothing," Lang said meekly.

The men behind them provided a welcome excuse by yelling at them to move along. Lang hurried to close the gap that had opened during the confrontation. The big man bumped him again with his Kein. Lang tightened his jaw and said nothing.

226

"I thought you were supposed to be salty, Blubber-butt," the man said in his ear.

Lang looked over his shoulder.

"Don't call me that," he said.

"Ain't that what they called you in Italy?" the tall man said.

Lang wondered who had told him. If he ever found out who was telling people his old nickname he'd knock him on his butt.

"Who said so?" he demanded.

"I guessed it from the size of your ass, Blubberbutt."

"I said don't call me that," Lang said grimly.

"I just did. What you gonna do about it?"

"That's all right what I'll do."

How do I get out of this? he wondered. The line had not moved. Everyone was watching and listening. No one could blame him for avoiding trouble with someone this big but, on the other hand, he had a reputation now for being tough and did not want to lose it. Nor be called Blubberbutt again.

"Show me," the tall man said, stepping out of line and putting his Kein on the ground.

"Show him, Tex," someone said encouragingly.

"Show me," the tall man said again, facing Lang with his long, sinewy hands dangling loosely at his sides.

Maybe if I swing on him they'll stop the fight before it really gets started, Lang thought. They're all on my side. He remembered how Moran had broken up the fight he was losing at Stalag VIIA and wished Moran were around now. Moran would know how to get him out of it. But Moran wasn't there. He was on his own. Moran said always get in the first lick. That was his only chance. He dropped his Kein in the dirt and swung a long right at his opponent.

The tall man stepped back without changing expression and let the blow go by harmlessly. Lang hesitated, not know-

227

ing what to do next. The spectators formed themselves into a circle around the pair.

"Fight, fight!" someone cried in the distance.

Lang wondered angrily who it was. And these men around him. He thought they were his friends. Why didn't they try to stop it instead of watching in rapt anticipation?

The tall man reached out suddenly and slapped his face, not hard but contemptuously. Lang forgot all fear and caution. He sprang at his tormentor in fury, lashing out blindly with both fists. A low rumbling sound rose from the growing circle of spectators. The tall man turned his gaunt face to wink at the crowd and one of Lang's punches smashed against his cheekbone.

His face grew wrathful and he clipped Lang precisely on the chin. Though the blow appeared deliberately casual Lang found himself suddenly on the ground. He felt no pain and little shock and was surprised to find himself off his feet.

This isn't as bad as I thought it would be, he thought. Maybe I am tough. He scrambled to his feet and was knocked down again though the tall man was still pulling his punches, as if he wanted to prolong and savor the encounter. Lang got up again, a bit more slowly.

Don't swing again and maybe he'll stop, Lang thought. Maybe Moran will come, or a guard. He's put me down twice and I got up both times and nobody can say I don't have guts. The tall man jabbed him in the nose, drawing blood and driving him to renewed fury. Lang rushed him, not caring what happened if only he could drive his fist into the contemptuous face before him. The tall man had grown careless. When he slipped Lang's wild right-hand punch a left hook caught him. Now his nose was bleeding, too. Oddly, his eyes lost their fanatic's gleam and his expression grew almost benign. He hit Lang on the side of the head. He was not playing now. It was as if he were showing respect for Lang by taking him seriously.

Lang dropped to his knees, dazed, propped on his hands and staring into the dirt. He heard murmurs and shouts, as from a distance. A drop of blood oozed from his nose and fell to the ground between his hands. He looked at the small dark smear and beyond it at the scuffed toes of two enormous GI shoes. Dimly, he recalled a saying about going down for the third time. When you went down for the third time you never came up again. But that was swimming, not fighting. He struggled to his feet and faced the tall man, swaying.

"That's enough, Killer," someone cried and Lang loved him for it.

"Shut up!" the tall man said. "It's not over yet."

Lang waited helplessly. He could not lift his hands. He was not sure he wanted to.

"Colonel Osmosis!" someone yelled.

Feet pounded and the men with the Keins quickly reformed the wash-water line, leaving Lang and his opponent isolated. Colonel Ozmozius was hurrying toward them, his policeman's face stern. He stared grimly at the tall man.

"At it again, O'Meara?" he grated.

"We were just sparring around and I guess I accidentally let one go," the tall man said.

"Is that a fact?"

He stared at Lang. Lang said nothing.

"What's your name?" the colonel said.

"Lang. Sir."

"You accidentally let one go, too?"

"Sir?"

"You two men wipe the blood off your stupid faces and report to my quarters. On the double."

"Yes, sir," said Lang and his opponent in unison.

O'Meara led the way. As soon as they were out of the colonel's sight he stopped double-timing and put his long arm across Lang's shoulders.

"You're a pretty rugged boy," he said conversationally.

Lang did not know what to say. He was intensely relieved to find the tall man was no longer pugnacious.

"What's your name?" O'Meara said. "Your first name."
"Steve."

He wiped his nose. The bleeding had stopped and except for a numbness on one side of his face he felt recovered. "They call me Tex," he added tentatively.

"They call me Killer," O'Meara said. "Killer O'Meara. The Goons, too. Der Töter. How about that?"

"Swell," said Lang.

"They're scared of me, just like everybody else in here. Except you. You know Froehlich? He won't come near me without a guard." He chuckled mirthlessly deep in his chest. "One time I acted like I was gonna jump him and he nearly peed in his rompers."

"Is that right?" Lang said warily.

He felt smothered by O'Meara's heavy arm. He wondered how he had ever had the nerve to swing at him. But he was glad he had done so now that he had come out of it uninjured and O'Meara wasn't mad any more. Except that he was in trouble with the SAO.

"Anybody calls you Blubberbutt I'll prang 'em personally. Okay, Tex?"

"Okay."

"I'll take care of the punk from Italy told me they called you that. Unless you want to."

"You can if you want to," Lang said magnanimously.

He did not have a great deal of interest in fighting at the moment.

"Hey. I called you because he said you liked to go. You're not sore, are you?"

"No," Lang said. "I'm not sore."

"We pals now?"

"Sure."

"Shake on it?"

They shook hands. His grip was like Moran's but the hand was twice as large.

Colonel Ozmozius's quarters were in a six-by-ten two-

230

man room at the end of his block. He occupied the room alone. He was the only man in the South Camp with a room to himself. He was, therefore, the only man in the South Camp who had any privacy. There was no other place in the entire compound where a man could be alone. He had an iron camp bed and a locker to himself. Except for these things, he had no more comforts than his subordinates.

O'Meara made himself at home on the colonel's cot. Lang leaned against the wall. He was weary. He noticed for the first time that O'Meara had brought his Kein along. Lang had forgotten his and left it at the cookhouse. He hoped nobody had taken it. He was supposed to be back at the room washing the soup bowls. Moran and the others were probably sore at him.

"You pranged me a couple good ones," O'Meara said. "I think I'd of had to really prang you good to keep you down. Maybe hurt you bad. I'm almost glad Colonel Osmosis broke it up."

"I'm almost glad, too," said Lang.

O'Meara threw back his head and laughed. There was no trace left of the malicious bully.

"That's a good one," he said.

His laughter was infectious and Lang joined him. Colonel Ozmozius caught them unaware.

"What's the joke?" he demanded.

They stopped laughing immediately. O'Meara scrambled to his feet.

"Don't you men pop to for your commanding officer?" the colonel snapped.

They came to attention.

"Tough guys," Colonel Ozmozius said sarcastically.

The colonel's censure did not chasten Lang. He liked it. Colonel Osmosis was comparing him with Killer O'Meara. Killer Lang.

"Wipe that silly grin off your puss, Lieutenant," the colonel said. "You're in trouble."

"Yes, sir," said Lang.

The colonel turned his attention to O'Meara.

"What did I tell you about making trouble?" he said.

Lang relaxed.

"Who gave you at ease?" Colonel Ozmozius said without turning his head.

Lang snapped back to attention.

"If it happens again, O'Meara, I'm going to charge you with insubordination, conduct unbecoming an officer and anything else I can think of. And I guarandamntee you'll be court-martialed when we get back to the States. Got that?"

"Yes, sir," said O'Meara.

"Meanwhile you're confined to quarters until further notice. And don't think that lets you out of room details. When you're stooging you can go to the cookhouse and the bread slicer. Double time both ways. Got it?"

"Yes, sir."

"Dismissed."

O'Meara started for the door. Lang followed him.

"Not you, damn it!" said the colonel.

Colonel Ozmozius eyed him speculatively when O'Meara had gone.

"At ease," he said at last. You're one of the Italy bunch, aren't you?"

"Yes, sir."

"You a troublemaker there, too?"

"No, sir," Lang said, flattered that Colonel Ozmozius should think so.

"You must have more guts than brains, fighting a man like Killer O'Meara. Don't you know he's poison? Maybe you think you are, too."

"No, sir."

"Then why the fight?"

"No excuse, sir."

"Oh, for God's sake, don't hand me any of that cadet nonsense," Colonel Ozmozius said impatiently.

232

"He was pushing me around and he called me . . ." Lang stopped himself before he said the hated nickname. "It was a personal matter."

"There aren't any personal matters in here, Lang. You're still in the army. I don't know how it was in Italy but that's the way it is here. Got that?"

"Yes, sir."

"I've had my share of fights," Colonel Ozmozius said, absently touching his cauliflower ear, "but I won't tolerate fighting in here. How you think it looks to the Goons? I'm going to let you off this time. There's not a doubt in my mind O'Meara started it. Nobody in his right mind would pick a fight with him. And I don't want any more trouble between you and O'Meara. Got that?"

"Don't worry, sir," Lang said earnestly.

Colonel Ozmozius smiled.

"You can depend on it, Lieutenant," he said. "Dismissed."

Lang's hand was on the doorknob when the colonel said, "Just one more thing, Lang."

"Sir?"

"O'Meara's nose looked like a tomato. Congratulations."

Lang ran all the way back to his block to tell Moran everything. Moran had already heard about it from Crumbacker, who had been in the crowd watching the fight.

"I thought you'd look worse," he said, "the way Crumb told it."

"If Colonel Osmosis hadn't showed up he'd of killed you," Crumbacker said, his eyes sparkling. "The way you kept getting up."

"I don't know," Lang said sharply, "I landed some pretty good ones."

"Yeah," Crumbacker agreed, admiringly. "Right on the nose. Pow."

Even Augustine was impressed.

"Nobody fools with the Killer," he said. "He's crazy.

233

He chased Froehlich once and it's a wonder he didn't get shot. Froehlich yelled at a guard to but too many guys were in the way."

"You should of had more sense than to tangle with a guy like that," Moran said.

"He was pushing me around," said Lang. "Nobody pushes me around."

He thought of Harbold. He wished Harbold were here now and tried something.

"You better keep out of his way from now on," Moran said. "Next time Colonel Osmosis might not be so handy."

"We're friends now," Lang said. "He's not such a bad guy when you get to know him."

"Don't kid yourself. He's nothing but grief."

"You don't even know him."

"I know the type."

Next day O'Meara sent one of his roommates to fetch Lang.

"I told you we were friends," Lang said to Moran.

"Can I go with you?" Crumbacker asked.

"You weren't invited," Lang said.

Augustine looked at Crumbacker incredulously.

"What do you want with Killer O'Meara?" he demanded.

"He's the toughest guy in the South Camp, that's what," said Crumbacker. "Him and Tex."

Confinement was already chafing O'Meara.

"My roommates are a bunch of tea sippers," he said, in the presence of two of them who pretended not to hear. "I like to talk to a real man once in a while. That's why I asked you to come see me."

"Any time, Killer," said Lang.

O'Meara did not seem in the least ominous to Lang. He was merely a restless, starved-looking giant. Moran was wrong about him. People just didn't know how to get along with the Killer the way he did.

234

"When Osmosis lifts my confinement we'll have us some fun," O'Meara promised.

Lang visited O'Meara every day during his confinement to quarters, during which period he exchanged few words with the Killer's roommates. There seemed to be a deep estrangement which extended to any friend of O'Meara's. O'Meara did most of the talking. Lang was surprised to discover he had a degree in mechanical engineering. O'Meara had seemed so mindless when they fought. The Killer did not talk about engineering, however, but the quantities of whiskey he had consumed and the brawls he had had when drunk.

"Before I got shot down I never fought except when I was drunk. I'd get mean. Mean. But there's nothing else to do in here. You know how it is."

"Sure," said Lang.

"I get mean when I'm hungry, too. And I'm hungry all the time. A man my size needs more than the average guy."

"Sure, Killer," said Lang.

O'Meara showed a flattering interest in Lang's exploits. Lang told him about his attempted escape at P.G. 203, appropriating for himself Moran's earlier feat of slugging a guard, and about jumping off the train. He resisted a strong temptation to tell him about killing the Italian.

Moran objected to his growing friendship with O'Meara, Crumbacker envied it and Augustine made fun of it. Hartman made little comment, as if fearing to become involved with O'Meara in any way.

The day his confinement ended, O'Meara came for Lang and took him for a walk around the camp perimeter.

"Watch this," he said as they approached a guard tower. "I'm gonna twist the Goon's tail."

The guard towers, called goonboxes by the prisoners, were larger and more sturdily built than those at P.G. 203 and set high on heavy timbers the size of telephone poles just outside the wire. Each mounted a machine gun and had a telephone. The guards checked their areas periodically with powerful binoculars. The guard they were approaching now was resting his arms on the chest-high side of the box and watching the prisoners with an air of boredom. O'Meara looked at him until he caught the German's attention. Then he folded his arms and stared fixedly at the guard. The German looked away, momentarily disconcerted. Lang felt uncomfortable. The guard stole a glance at O'Meara and saw him still staring. He leaned out of the box.

"Was ist los?" he demanded.

O'Meara said nothing.

"Geh' weg," the guard said angrily, waving them on.

Lang moved a step.

"Stay put," O'Meara whispered. "The fun's just starting."

His eyes had the feral gleam Lang had seen when they fought.

Other perimeter walkers had stopped to watch from a safe distance. The guard swiveled his machine gun on its mount and pointed it down at O'Meara, who did not budge. Lang felt a familiar contraction in his belly. The machine gun was pointed his way, too.

"Hey," he whispered.

"He won't shoot," O'Meara whispered. "They never do."

There's always a first time, Lang thought.

"Zum letzten mal," the guard cried.

His eyes locked with O'Meara's over the gun barrel. Lang edged away, but only a foot or so, afraid to reveal his fear to O'Meara. The deadlock continued for half a minute.

"Zum Teufel!" the guard cried, turning away in defeat.

O'Meara winked at Lang.

"I told you we'd have some fun," he said.

Lang winked back. He felt brave and reckless. O'Meara was like a lion, fearing nothing, and if O'Meara was a lion so, in a way, was he because he was the lion's chosen companion.

"Come on, Tex," said O'Meara. "Let's get up a sweat."

He began jogging. Lang jogged after him. Soon he was puffing.

"Hey, Killer," he panted. "Let's rest a minute."

O'Meara slowed to a walk and looked at him disapprovingly.

"You got a gut on you like a thirty-year-old man," he said. "How'd you let yourself get out of shape so bad?"

Lang did not think it expedient to tell O'Meara he was in the best condition of his life.

"It was rough in Italy," he said. "Mostly soup. It bloats you. And you know how hard it is to keep in shape in the bag."

"I'm in the bag, ain't I?" O'Meara said. "Look at the shape I'm in."

He tightened his stomach.

"Hit me in the gut," he said.

"Aw, Killer," said Lang.

"Go ahead," O'Meara said sharply, his face suddenly ominous.

Lang hit him, but carefully.

"You can hit harder than that. Come on, give me your best shot."

Lang hit him as hard as he could. It was like hitting a washboard.

"That's the way you ought to be," O'Meara said. "Come on."

He led Lang to the cookhouse where a room had been fitted out as a gymnasium with a bag of sand hanging on a rope, a five-foot pole cemented into jam tins at each end, a chinning bar and a slanted board for sit-ups. O'Meara was astonished to find Lang could chin himself only three times. Lang did not tell him before his capture he could not do it even once. O'Meara did fifteen.

"I could do twenty-five if I wasn't so weak from hunger," he said apologetically.

He conducted Lang through a routine of calisthenics, weight lifting and bag punching. Lang was sweaty, sore and stumbling with fatigue when O'Meara at last announced the session was over.

"Don't you worry, Tex," O'Meara said. "I'll get you back in shape. Tomorrow we'll really get with it."

Lang crept back to his room, relieved to be free of O'Meara at last. The mere tension of O'Meara's changing moods had been exhausting even without the grueling workout. When he opened the door his four roommates were waiting for him.

"Where the hell you been?" Moran demanded. "You forget we got the stump puller this afternoon?"

The stump puller was a ponderous device of timber and iron which, when straddling one of the pine stumps dotting the compound, could pull it from the earth like a monstrous tooth. The prisoners were allowed to use it in turn to augment the small issue of pressed coal briquettes to be burned in the room stoves when the weather turned cold. With it went two shovels and an ax for digging around the stumps and cutting the more accessible roots. The mere act of moving the device from stump to stump was backbreaking. Lang groaned.

"I was working out in the gym," he apologized.

"I'll give you all the workout you want," Moran said. "Let's get with it."

Moran took charge of the work detail, driving his roommates relentlessly and doing more work himself than any of them, digging, chopping roots and pulling on the thick twelve-foot wooden lever that drew the stumps from the ground when worked like a jack handle. Lang moved in a daze.

"Come on, come on," Moran kept urging.

"How about a five-minute break?" Lang said at last.

"Yeah," said Crumbacker, "you trying to kill us?"

Augustine and Hartman mumbled agreement.

"You got all night to rest," said Moran. "It's gonna be a cold winter and we ain't gonna stand short."

Lang's hands blistered and the blisters broke. Sparks danced before his eyes and his muscles shrieked. The Appell bugle was like a song of angels. They had pulled eleven stumps, which Moran thought might be a record for the time they had worked. Lang could scarcely keep his balance during Appell and when it was over dragged himself back to the block, stripped off his sweat-soaked uniform and collapsed in his bunk without supper. He ached and burned worse than after his adventure in the concertina wire at P.G. 203 and knew he would never be whole and rested again.

And O'Meara had said tomorrow they'd really get with it.

CHAPTER 15

Lang begged off when O'Meara came for him next morning.

"Stump puller," he said, showing his torn hands.

"Can't lift weights with those," O'Meara agreed. "Today we'll just do roadwork."

Lang was afraid to refuse. The warning light in O'Meara's eyes turned on too easily.

O'Meara made him trot with him around the perimeter until breathing was agony and next day, though Lang's hands were still unhealed, took him to the gym for calisthenics. As soon as Lang's hands permitted, O'Meara launched him on an intensive program of chins, lifts, bag punching and complicated and difficult exercises of his own invention. After the

240

gym came roadwork. Lang tried without success to convince him this might be the reason he was always so hungry.

At first Lang detested all of it. He tried hiding but O'Meara always found him. He complained of illness but O'Meara said the best thing for a headache or upset stomach was to work it off. At night he fell aching into bed. In the morning he awakened stiff and sore. He was constantly ravenous and when he was not scheming to avoid O'Meara he was thinking about food.

But after two weeks, when he could chin himself seven times and trot the three-quarter-mile perimeter without wanting to vomit, he began enjoying it. He read little now but was never bored. He slept deeply at night and seldom dreamed of home or Serena the Butterfly Girl.

There was a mirror in the block washroom and when Hartman had finished his nightly prolonged brushing of his beautiful wavy hair, which he feared might grow thin if not cared for properly, Lang would strip to wooden shoes and long drawers in the deserted washroom and look at his emerging muscles. With his muscles, his leanness and his mustache they would hardly recognize him at home, he thought. When he got into his blouse and pinks, with his wings and ribbons on, including the Purple Heart for his bayonet wound, they'd all know he was somebody.

Moran came into the washroom one night and surprised him as he was admiring a side view of his expanded chest and flexed biceps.

"What the hell you doing?" Moran demanded.

"I was just, you know, checking," Lang said, embarrassed.

"You were looking at your chest like there were tits on it."

"I was just checking," Lang protested. "I been working out with the Killer every day."

"You spend too much time with that clown. He's bad news."

"Not if you know how to handle him," Lang said.

And he knew how. Being O'Meara's friend was demanding, but it was exciting, too, like riding a roller coaster. When the Killer twisted a Goon's tail or bullied someone he shared O'Meara's strength and power. That sense of strength and power was worth guarding every word and action and gauging O'Meara's moods. What did he care if everyone except Crumbacker left the room when O'Meara came to visit and if he was no longer popular around the compound? He was feared now almost as much as the Killer and fear meant respect. Respect was something he had never had enough of before.

"Nobody knows how to handle a guy like that," Moran said. "If you keep hanging around him you're gonna find out the hard way."

Lang did not want to argue with Moran even though Moran had it all wrong. Moran was his best friend. Maybe his only friend, now, except for the Killer and Crumbacker, who often shadowed them at a safe distance when there were no horse-drawn wagons to follow. But at times lately Moran did not seem as close as he had been.

"Hey, Moran," Lang said ingratiatingly. "I can press the weight eleven times now. Remember how out of shape I was?"

"Yeah, you are looking better," Moran said grudgingly. "But you're starting to act just like that clown O'Meara."

Augustine also saw him making muscles at the mirror one night, though Lang did not know it until he returned to the room and Augustine gravely removed his shirt, threw out his skinny chest and displayed a bicep the size of a golf ball.

"Look at this, Wings," he said to Hartman. "Mr. America."

"You think you're so damn funny," Lang growled in his best imitation of O'Meara.

Augustine looked at him in feigned astonishment.

"What's eating you, Tex?" he asked.

Lang stole a glance at Moran. Moran was grinning.

242

It snowed a week before Christmas. They treated themselves to a fire in the room stove the entire day of the snow instead of only in the evening as had been their practice. Lang loved the snow. He ran out into it in his wooden shoes and romped with Crumbacker when none of his other roommates would come out.

The snow gave the South Camp misleading beauty. The blocks, so drab inside and chilly, were roofed with fluffy white and the barren earth around them was a smooth, dazzling plain broken only by muddy paths. The scattering of pines which had been left standing within the compound thrust out of the snow like green candles on a vast frosted cake and the woods separating the compound from the Vorlager were heaped with tufts of cotton. Ice transformed the barbed wire into ropes of diamonds which sparkled in the sun. To Lang, the compound no longer looked like a prison camp. For the first few days of the snow, until he became accustomed to it, he spent much of his time out of doors.

Moran and O'Meara hated the snow, O'Meara because it interfered with roadwork and Moran because it was cold and damp.

"You wear your GI shoes, you freeze your feet," he said. "You wear your wooden shoes, it's like walking with weights on."

"I think it's keen," Lang said.

"Why don't you shove some up your ass?" Moran said irritably. "If it's that good it can't hurt you."

The Germans shared Moran's antipathy for snow. The soldiers in the goonboxes stamped their numb feet on the frosty planks and wiped the snow from their machine guns with oily rags. Twisting the Goons' tail became more perilous and even O'Meara was careful not to goad them too far. The ferrets, the men with blue coveralls, searched the warm cookhouse with great diligence except when Froehlich was on hand to see that they made their regular rounds of the blocks. After dark the Hundfuehrers would stand outside the blocks with their backs against the warm walls of the kitchens and send their dogs to range the compound unaccompanied. The prisoners would tease the dogs from the windows, growling or mewing like kittens. One night Moran threw a Keintrinkwasser of cold water on one of them. The dog bared his long white teeth in a silent snarl and reared up on his hind legs, his front paws caked with snow and the hair of his belly matted with it.

"Oh, you'd like to get me, wouldn't you, you Goon dog you," Moran crooned.

"How come you did that?" Lang demanded. "That poor dog."

"You around the bend?" Moran said. "That's a Goon dog."

The approach of Christmas brought holiday Red Cross parcels and a special issue of food from the Argentine and Turkish Red Cross. There was not enough of everything to go around in the special issue and drawings were held in each block to establish the order in which each room would make its choice of the limited items. Moran insisted that Lang represent their room for the distribution of the Christmas extras.

"Steve never stands short," he said when Augustine proposed that Hartman do it.

Lang returned with sharp Argentine cheese, canned pork sausage, nuts, dates and pork and beans. Even Augustine was satisfied with his selections.

Christmas also brought an invitation for a limited number of Americans to attend a performance of *Twelfth Night* in the British compound. Colonel Ozmozius selected the attendees on the basis of seniority and Lang and Moran were among those to go.

"Personally I don't give a kiss of my ass for Shakespeare but to get outta this place I'd sit through a Chinese ceremonial goose stuffing," said Moran.

"What's a Chinese ceremonial goose stuffing?" Hartman asked.

244

"If you was a Chinese goose you'd know," Moran said.

"It's not right," Augustine complained. "You guys just got in and you get to visit the British compound instead of guys who've been here practically since the camp started."

"Ha-ard luck," Lang said, making two syllables of the adjective.

O'Meara also objected to Lang's forthcoming excursion.

"Why you want to fool around with a bunch of limeys?" he demanded.

"I got friends over there," Lang said placatingly.

"I'm the only friend you need."

"You're just sore 'cause you didn't rate going," Lang said incautiously.

"You getting salty?" O'Meara said.

O'Meara did not seem on the brink of violence. The usual warning signs were not up. Lang decided to take a chance. He was the only friend the Killer had in the camp and the Killer knew it.

"I've been salty," he said.

"Maybe you could give me a halfway decent fight now," O'Meara said. "Want to?"

It was an invitation, not a threat.

"Fight you?" Lang said. "You think I'm around the bend?"

O'Meara laughed.

"You're okay, Tex," he said.

Lang hid his relief. Peace with honor. He wished Moran had been there to see how he had handled O'Meara. Moran would change his mind about him not knowing how to. You had to stand up to the Killer but not enough to make him really sore. The trick was knowing how far to go.

Christmas Eve they had a hand-cranked phonograph and a dozen American records for an hour. They took turns winding it. There was "We'll Meet Again," which reminded Lang more of P.G. 203 than of earlier days, and "You Are Always in My Heart," and Dinah Shore's "Mad About Him Sad About Him How Can I Be Glad Without Him Blues" that they'd had at Ramat Jonas, "Joseph, Joseph" which he had last heard at the Mimosa Club in Beirut on leave with Bertram, which was also the third and last time he'd had a woman, and a new record called "Cow Cow Boogie."

He and Moran sat on Moran's bunk listening. They had turned out the light in the room so they could listen in the dark. Lang and Moran talked of old times while the music played, of the quarantine prison and P.G. 203, of Jaybird and Bertram and before they were shot down. It was strange and marvelously fulfilling how Moran talked of the days before they were shot down as if they had not disliked each other then and he had not ever been called Blubberbutt. It was as if Moran had declared Lang's transformation and their friendship retroactive.

Christmas Day was the best Lang could remember, even better than those of his childhood when he borrowed a stocking from an enormously fat woman next door and Santa Claus had filled it with fruit and nuts and candy and small gifts and under the tree left a Daisy air rifle and a tricycle and an Indian suit with a feathered headdress. What he missed most this day, knowing it was a strange thing to miss and not blurting it out to Moran as he once might have done, was the orange in the toe of the stocking.

The fire of pine roots and coal briquettes burned in the room all day and the resinous odor evoked memories of the fires the neighborhood children would sometimes build in a vacant lot on summer nights, when he would hang back out of the light, on the outer limits of the circle, wanting to be a part of the circle but hoping he would not be noticed and therefore not teased or picked on. He was part of the circle now and he longed to be able to turn back time and be part of that circle, too.

Augustine was the cook that week and he prepared a sumptuous meal. It was the first time since Lang and Moran had been in the room that the one cooked meal of the day was not based on potatoes, boiled, mashed, with cheese or, on Saturday nights, fried. Augustine had eliminated potatoes from the menu deliberately to mark the occasion of their first Christmas in the bag, a commemoration marred slightly when Lang pointed out it was his and Moran's second but quickly put to rights when Lang acknowledged how much superior this one was to their first, and for the moment their antagonism was forgotten.

After dinner Lang and Moran shaved and put on their most presentable uniforms for the afternoon's visit to the North Camp and *Twelfth Night*.

The soldiers escorting the American guests of the British wore sprigs of mistletoe in their greatcoat buttonholes. Sergeant Frochlich, disgruntled, was in charge of the detail.

"This is a bit thick," he said, "giving up one's Christmas Day so you people can enjoy an outing."

"I didn't know you went for Christmas that much," Moran said. "Seeing's how it's a Jew's birthday."

The prisoners laughed and Froehlich's thin lips whitened.

"Very droll," he said frostily. "Obviously you do not know Weihnacht is an ancient German custom. Only later was it merged with the Christian celebration."

"Ain't you a Christian?" Moran asked.

"Of course," Froehlich snapped. "Are you?"

"Knock it off, Moran," said a prisoner named Lefkowitz. "He'll be asking me next."

There had been no evidence of discrimination against Jewish officers in Stalag Luft 9 but they had once seen a work party of emaciated concentration camp inmates in striped uniforms outside the wire and Lefkowitz had called out in Yiddish, "I am a Jew. We will bury the Nazis."

Moran did not answer Froehlich.

There being no direct passage between the British and American compounds, the party walked through the Vorlager to a path skirting the outer perimeter of Stalag Luft 9. Here and there in the surrounding pine woods snow had fallen from the birches, uncovering patches of flaming color. Smoke rose straight up into the limpid air from scores of chimneys inside the camp and a white world glistened in the winter sun. As he looked upon this scene Lang was not sorry he was a prisoner.

If he were not here he would not have seen all this. He would not be going to the British compound to see a play, one of a select few men. He would not have killed a man and saved himself and Moran, for this is what he had come to believe, or stood up to the Killer and impressed a thousand men with his courage. He would not have lost his bulging stomach and hardened his muscles. Moran and everyone else would still be calling him Blubberbutt.

Moran put snow down the collar of the man in front of him and soon the men were romping like schoolboys.

"If you do not conduct yourselves as officers and gentlemen I shall be forced to return you to quarters," Froehlich shouted. "I warn you, I have full authority to do so at my discretion."

They fell silent except for laughter and the surreptitious flinging of snowballs hastily scooped up from the path.

A number of British officers were waiting at the North Camp gate to greet the Americans. Among them were many who had come up from P.G. 203. These quickly gathered around Moran and Lang. Lang hoped the other Americans noted the enthusiasm of their reception.

Pilot Officer Perkins, resplendent in his service ribbons and a new uniform, called out above the babble, "Distinguished Flier," and rushed to shake Lang's hand.

"Never fancied I'd miss you ruddy Yanks," he said. "What news from the Colonies?"

Moran pumped his hand.

"I never had a chance to thank you for letting us out," he said.

Perkins retrieved his hand, laughing.

"Breaking my fingers is no way to show gratitude," he said. "Lost a good bit of weight, haven't you?" he added, addressing Lang. "Those bloody American parcels I expect."

"Oh, no," Lang said. "They've changed 'em. They're great now." He was tempted to add that the new-style American Red Cross parcels were superior to the British but refrained. "I've been exercising to keep in shape."

"It becomes you, D.F." Perkins said. "Come along, you chaps. I'll walk you to the theater."

They followed the others through the snow.

"Are you still keen on Dickens?" Perkins asked.

"What?" said Lang. "Oh, yeah. Only I haven't had much time to read lately."

He felt guilty about that. He did not think Perkins would be pleased if Perkins knew he had stopped reading and he was certain Perkins would not approve of Killer O'Meara.

"You'll come for tea after the performance, I hope," Perkins said. "We're laying on a wizard bash."

He gave Lang and Moran directions for reaching his room and left them at the theater. The theater was much like that in the South Camp but the scenery of papier-mâché and Red Cross packing crates was more skillfully done. The acting was better, too, particularly in the female roles. The Americans did not have the experience of the British in all-male school theatricals and were more self-conscious playing women. Though the Olivia was fetchingly padded and costumed, however, her make-up could not conceal the fact she was somewhat in need of a shave.

Lang was bored. He had seen productions of Shakespeare in high school and college, and once when the Lunts brought *The Taming of the Shrew* to Houston his parents had taken him. He had been bored then, too.

Moran shifted restlessly beside him.

"Maybe it wouldn't be so bad if they had real babes," he whispered to Lang.

After the first act they exchanged questioning looks. "It's okay with me," Lang said.

They often knew what the other was thinking without having to be told. They trudged through the snow to Perkins's block. Outside it was like their own, but inside the doors had been painted in various colors and on each was neatly lettered the name and rank of the senior man. Perkins was surprised to see them so early.

"Surely the play isn't over," he said. "Did Jerry find the radio?"

"What radio?" Lang asked.

"For the BBC communiqué," Perkins said. "It's hidden in the dressing room."

"No," said Moran. "The play was putting us to sleep."

"Barbarians, you colonials," Perkins said. "Most popular show of the season."

"What I'd like to see is Gypsy Rose Lee," said Moran.

"Who?"

"She's a striptease dancer," Lang explained.

"I'd fancy that myself," said Perkins.

Perkins's seven roommates rose and shook hands formally when he introduced them. Two had come up from Italy, the others were German captives of long standing. One of these, a Flight Lieutenant Cresswell, had been captured early in the war and spoke fluent German.

"The room swot," Perkins said. "Studying for his master of arts at London University. By post, of course."

"Naturally I'd prefer Oxford," said Cresswell. "But Jerry doesn't give one much choice."

There were curtains of English material on the windows and a colorful rag rug on the floor. The naked bulb in the ceiling had been equipped with a handsome reflector made of woven strips of tin and the bunks were all hand-rubbed to a rich finish. On several of them were ornamental pillows, one crudely embroidered with the legend, "Brighton, 1937," and the others with leering cherubs. There were wall shelves, an

250

open cupboard for food and utensils, a bookcase and a framed oil painting of a Hurricane shooting a Junkers 88 down in flames.

When Lang was small, he had been taken by his parents to visit a wealthy acquaintance of his father's at the Warwick in Houston, an apartment hotel on Main Street across from the Sunken Garden. He was impressed now by his surroundings much as he had been then. When they got back to the South Camp he and Moran were going to have to do something to make their room look better, he resolved.

Perkins and his roommates had been receiving personal parcels regularly from England and had spent days preparing Christmas tea. A pudding made with ground English ration biscuits and sultana raisins was boiling on the stove in a cloth bag. The table was spread with a white sheet painstakingly appliquéd with an intricate design. On it were tin salvers decorated with nail-hole designs and filled with nuts, dried fruits, cookies and candies. Cans decorated with similar designs held Players, State Express, Capstan and other cigarettes. In the center of the table was a cut-glass decanter filled with kriegie brew.

When Lang saw the spread he was hungry again. It was the first time in his year of captivity that he had dined out or sat down to a meal for which he had not contributed his share. He and Moran ate sparingly at first, knowing intuitively this was prison camp etiquette, but when Perkins and his roommates pressed food upon them and themselves ate heartily, they devoured everything before them as if they had not eaten the largest meal of their captivity only hours before.

The pudding came last. The officer who had prepared it, an observer with a fierce mustache which Lang envied, served. He carefully removed the cloth bag, deposited it tenderly on a tin salver on which the rondel of the Royal Air Force was punched and, after pouring over it the contents of a pan of kriegie brew warmed on the stove, ignited the pudding and set it flaming in the center of the table. His room-mates pounded their tea mugs on the table in admiration.

After acknowledging the applause with suitable modesty he sliced the pudding meticulously into ten equal portions and spooned over each a sauce of margarine, sugar, Klim and kriegie brew.

"Who says the English are lousy cooks?" Moran demanded after his first bite.

"The English," said Perkins.

"This is better than my mother's pineapple upside-down cake," Lang said earnestly.

He was pleased when everyone laughed though he had not intended it as a joke.

When the last morsel was eaten, Cresswell poured each man a portion of kriegie brew from the decanter and lifted his cup. Everyone rose. They raised their cups.

"Gentlemen," said Cresswell. "The King."

They drank.

Lang choked on his. The brew was raw and fiery. He looked at Moran, who was not discomfited.

"Rugged but right," Moran said.

Perkins rolled a sip on his tongue, swallowed, looked reflective and said, "Birnberg, forty-three?"

"Bang on!" cried the observer. "Perkie, you've a wizard palate."

"Some of us are blessed," Perkins said.

Birnberg was a small town a mile or so from Stalag Luft 9. It was not known to distill spirits though it was reputed in the South Camp to have a brewery and to be overrun with buxom German girls whose husbands and sweethearts were all away on the Russian front and who believed American fliers were sexy. In the British compound they were reputed to believe British fliers were sexy.

"I seem to have neglected something," said Cresswell, refilling the cups. "Gentlemen, the President of the United States."

252

They drank.

"Another toast," said Perkins.

Cresswell refilled the cups.

"Strafe Deutschland," said Perkins.

"Hear, hear," everyone shouted.

They sat down and Cresswell brought a flat wooden box from his locker.

"I thought you were saving them for your graduation," Perkins said.

"Pray God I'll be home for it," Cresswell said.

"As scarce in England as here, I'm told," said the observer.

Cresswell opened the box. In it were a dozen dark, dry cigars. He offered it first to the guests. Moran took one. Lang hesitated, wondering if it would be bad taste to take one for Moran. It would be, he decided. Cresswell's roommates also declined.

"Don't any of you guys smoke cigars?" Moran asked suspiciously.

No one answered.

"You're not gonna smoke one either?" he asked Cresswell.

"Actually, I had mine last night after dinner," Cresswell said.

"Look," said Moran, embarrassed. "If they're that short . . ."

He tried to return the cigar but Cresswell insisted he smoke it.

"It's only proper," Perkins said. "It was the Colonies who gave us tobacco."

Moran bit off the end of the cigar. Cresswell winced at the barbarism.

"I wish I'd known they were that scarce over here," Lang said. "We get 'em in tobacco parcels all the time. They've got some for sale in the South Camp PX. Next time I come over . . ."

He stopped abruptly. There would be no next time. He might not be seeing Perkins again until the end of the war. He felt sad.

"Perkie, do Mr. Pickwick's Christmas," someone said.

"You surely shouldn't like hearing it again," Perkins said modestly.

Everyone rapped their tea mugs on the table. Pleased, Perkins fetched *The Pickwick Papers* and began reading aloud. He was familiar with the passage and referred to the text infrequently. He read eloquently. Lang was entranced. He had forgotten the pleasures of reading since his involvement with O'Meara. He would have to get back to it.

Everyone applauded when Perkins finished.

"That sure beat *Twelfth Night*," Lang said.

"There's no accounting for tastes, Distinguished Flier," said Perkins, but he was pleased.

They had more kriegie brew, Lang abstaining, and when the bugle blew summoning the Americans to the gate everyone groaned in protest.

Perkins walked to the gate with Lang and just before the Americans left tucked his copy of *The Pickwick Papers* under Lang's arm.

"I couldn't," Lang protested.

"I'd like you to have it," Perkins said. "You fancied it so just now. There's another in the block."

The Americans were quiet on the way back, even Moran, who was a little tipsy.

"I wish we lived in the British compound," Lang said.

"You think they eat like that every day?" said Moran.

"It's not that," Lang replied.

When they got back to the South Camp O'Meara was waiting. For an instant Lang felt as if he had walked into an ambush. He had forgotten all about the Killer while he was in the North Camp.

CHAPTER 16

Lang tried to avoid O'Meara after Christmas but the Killer was inescapable. He even came into the abort two days after the party in Perkins's room searching for Lang and found him engrossed in *The Pickwick Papers*, oblivious to the cold.

"Augustine told me you were here," O'Meara said.

I'll kill the little bastard, Lang thought.

"What the hell you doin'?" O'Meara demanded.

"What does it look like I'm doing? Taking a crap."

"You're reading," O'Meara said accusingly.

"What's wrong with that?"

"That's all you been doing the past two days. Let's go for a walk."

Lang sighed.

"Okay," he said.

The snow around the perimeter had been trodden into icy ruts and they found it easier to walk in the ankle-deep blanket bordering the path.

"All you been doing is reading," O'Meara said. "You getting soft on me?"

"Like hell," Lang said.

He stopped and faced O'Meara squarely.

"I'll show you who's getting soft," he said. "Hit me in the stomach. Go ahead."

"Sure," said O'Meara.

Lang tightened his stomach muscles and O'Meara hit him. The world became black and airless. Lang rolled in the snow, fully conscious but unable to breathe or utter a sound, even a groan. It was minutes before he could breathe normally though he felt no aftereffects.

"You hit pretty hard," he said.

"I don't read books," O'Meara replied pointedly.

New Year's Eve, O'Meara invited him over for kriegie brew. Lang did not like the harsh distillate, he remembered what the Killer had said about getting mean when he drank and he wanted to spend New Year's Eve with Moran but in the bag, as outside, it was an affront to refuse to drink with a friend.

"I hope you don't bring him back here," Augustine said. "We don't want that nut ruining our New Year's Eve."

"What do you mean, we?" Lang demanded.

He looked around the room. Hartman looked away, avoiding taking sides as he usually did when O'Meara was involved.

"I'm with Phil," Moran said flatly. "I can't take the clown."

"You're just jealous because I'm having kriegie brew," Lang said, feeling Moran had let him down.

"I ain't saying I wouldn't jump at the chance for a few

belts," said Moran. "But not with Killer O'Meara. I wouldn't drink with him if he had Vat 69."

"I wish you would bring him back here," Crumbacker said.

"Looks like you're the only pal I got in this room," Lang said with a meaningful look at Moran.

"Oh, Christ!" Moran said angrily.

They drank alone in O'Meara's room. Though O'Meara's roommates had joined him in weeks of saving dried fruit and sugar from Red Cross parcels to go into the brew, they did not care to drink it with him. They had taken their share to other rooms.

Lang and O'Meara sat at the table hunched over mugs. Lang had expected something to eat with the kriegie brew but O'Meara had brought out only two white coffee mugs and an oleomargarine tin full of the drink. O'Meara tossed his down, lifting his chin and displaying the tendons in his stringy, powerful throat. Lang sipped his cautiously but even the small quantities he swallowed trickled fire down into his stomach.

O'Meara divided the brew with scrupulous care and, since he drank so much more quickly than Lang, urged him to hurry between drinks. Except for this, he was at first morose and silent, sitting with both hands clutching his mug, his enormous shoulders hunched, his eyes dull.

"Last New Year's Eve I was in New York," he said with uncharacteristic poignance. "I had fourteen Scotches in two hours and fifteen minutes by the clock. Didn't cost me a thing. It was in this bar and everybody was setting me up because I was going overseas."

He smiled reminiscently.

"I whipped four guys at the same time. The cops told me one of 'em had to go to the hospital."

The smile brightened.

"When they found out I was heading overseas they turned me loose. One of the cops gave me a drink out of his own bottle. He was a good cop. But his whiskey was lousy."

He sighed.

"Better than this rotgut, though. I never thought I'd be in a place like this the next New Year's Eve."

"What you bitching about?" said Lang, who was beginning to find kriegie brew a little less vile and O'Meara's company a little less depressing. "Last New Year's Eve I was already in the bag."

"I know you were. You talk about it enough. Hell, it doesn't take any brains to get shot down."

"You can say that again, Killer. 'Cause you're in here."

O'Meara looked up hopefully.

"You getting salty with me, Tex?"

Lang shook his head.

"Trouble with you, you got no sense of humor," he said.

O'Meara tore open his shirt collar.

"It's hot in here," he complained.

"Yeah," said Lang. "Let's open the windows."

"Let's go outside."

In celebration of the New Year, the German authorities had delayed lockup time until 1 A.M. to permit the prisoners to visit between blocks. The Hundfuehrers kept their dogs leashed and most of them were in the aborts, out of the cold wind.

O'Meara divided the last of the kriegie brew and they took their cups out into the snowy night. The air had a bracing sting, like strong after-shave lotion. Lang had become giddy in the heated room but now he felt unusually perceptive and carefree. There were other prisoners out of doors, singing and throwing snowballs. The night was intensely black except for glimmers of light around blackout shutters and the occasional sweep of a goonbox searchlight.

"Let's bust out," O'Meara said.

"Right now?"

"I don't mean next year."

258

"Even if we got out we wouldn't have a chance. In this weather."

"You yellow?" O'Meara demanded.

"That ain't a nice thing to say and you know it," Lang replied, aggrieved.

They waded through the snow, sipping from their cups. Far across the wire, in the British compound, Lang heard men shouting drunkenly in the night.

"I wish we were over there," he said.

"Over where?"

"North Camp."

"With those limeys?"

"One of 'em let us out of the boxcar at Bolzano. When we got bombed. I got a present for him. Cigars."

Lang sipped his drink. It seemed to have mellowed in the cup and went down like velvet.

"This sure is smooth stuff," Lang said. "When you get out I bet you could get rich selling it."

"Trouble is you always get sick the next day."

"Too bad," said Lang.

"Want to take 'em over to him?" O'Meara said.

"Take what to who?"

"The cigars to the limey let you out, stupid."

"How?"

"Through the wire."

"Okay," said Lang.

He wondered why he had not thought of that before. There was nothing between him and Perkins but a couple of fences and a little concertina wire. He could not imagine why he had thought them such an insurmountable barrier.

"Let's go get my present," he said.

"Let's meet back here," O'Meara replied. "I got to get something, too."

Moran and the others were playing bridge. Because of the length of the table they had to sit two to a side with each set of partners facing each other diagonally across it. Crumbacker, who was cook that week, had baked a ground hardtack cake. When Lang entered the room they were eating it with coffee and joking about the last hand.

"There were a thousand ways to make it if you hadn't played it like a tart," Moran said.

Moran sounded as if he was enjoying himself and Lang felt resentful and excluded. Lang went to his locker without speaking and got the cigars which he had bought at the PX for an exorbitant price in cigarettes.

"How about your piece of cake, Steve?" Moran said.

"Haven't got time."

"All you got is time."

If Moran knew where he was going he wouldn't act so smart, Lang thought. He thought he was so smart sitting there playing bridge and eating Crumbacker's crummy cake when some people were going through the wire to the British compound. If he knew that's what some people were doing he wouldn't think he was so smart.

"What the hell are you giggling about?" Moran demanded. "You're drunk, for Christ's sake."

"I may have been drinking but I'm not drunk," Lang said with dignity.

"How would you know?" Moran said, laughing. "You never been drunk before."

"Oh, yeah? How about that time back at Ramat Jonas when I drank all that camel hockey?"

Camel hockey was Carmel Hock, a Palestinian wine with which Lang had experimented disastrously in the officers' mess.

"I wasn't there," Moran said.

"Okay, then," Lang said triumphantly.

O'Meara was waiting for him.

"Look what I got," O'Meara said, holding out his hand.

Lang could see nothing in the darkness.

"What?" he said irritably.

260

"You blind?" O'Meara demanded. "Wire cutters."

The wire cutters belonged to the escape committee, of which one of O'Meara's roommates was a member. They had been purchased from a Polish ferret for five hundred cigarettes. O'Meara had seen his roommate hide the tool.

"That's nice," Lang said, unimpressed.

It seemed natural that a pair of wire cutters should be available when needed.

"Grab hold of that," O'Meara said, indicating a bulky object on the snow at his feet.

It was a mattress.

"We going to sleep over there?" Lang said.

"Dope. Just bring it like I said."

They walked to the wire making no attempt at silence. Lang began softly humming "Lili Marlene." He thought about P.G. 203 and Jaybird, and then about Serena the Butterfly Girl waiting for him beneath the lamppost.

"Shut up!" O'Meara ordered.

"Don't you like 'Lili Marlene'?"

"You want the Goons to hear us?"

Lang was astonished. The Killer afraid of a few Germans?

"You yellow?" he said.

They lay on their backs in the snow while O'Meara clipped the bottom strand of the first fence. O'Meara threw the mattress atop the concertina wire and crawled across it to the second fence where he again snipped the bottom strand. Lang followed, thinking O'Meara was smart to bring the mattress. The Killer was smarter than Moran gave him credit for. In a few moments they were standing unchallenged in the North Lager.

"Get the mattress."

"How come?"

"You want the Goons to see it?"

"Who cares?" Lang said blithely.

"You salty bastard," O'Meara said affectionately. "Get it before I knock you on your ass."

Lang dragged the mattress across the unsullied whiteness of the parade ground. He began singing "Lili Marlene." Perkins had taught him the German words.

"Vor der Kaserne, dum de dum de dum, stand eine Laterne und steht Sie da di da."

Suddenly a Hundfuehrer and his dog materialized. O'Meara halted abruptly. Lang blundered into him, still singing.

"Mit dir, Lili Marlene."

"Sehr schoen," said the Hundfuehrer, who could not see they were Americans in the darkness.

"I'll take him," O'Meara whispered. "You get the dog."

Lang stopped singing.

"I wouldn't hurt a dog," Lang said. "I like dogs."

The Hundfuehrer sang a verse of "Lili Marlene" himself.

"Sehr schoen," said Lang. "Happy New Year, Goon."

"Danke," said the Hundfuehrer.

"You salty bastard," said O'Meara.

They blundered from block to block, seeking Perkins, leaving confusion and merriment behind them.

When at last they found the door bearing Cresswell's name, Lang knocked politely.

"That's no way to knock on a door," O'Meara said, pushing him aside.

He beat it with his fists.

Doors popped open the length of the hall and inquiring faces stared out. Cresswell's door opened and Cresswell himself appeared in it, wearing a nightcap with a tassel on it.

"What the bloody . . ." he cried. "Why, it's Leftenant Lang. Whatever are you doing here, dear boy?"

"Dear boy," O'Meara mimicked.

"I brought Perkins his Christmas present," Lang said matter-of-factly.

262

Cresswell's seven roommates crowded behind him.

"My word," said Perkins.

"Come in, come in," Cresswell said. "We're just having a spot of tea before turning in."

"Tea," said O'Meara.

"Laced with kriegie brew," Cresswell said.

"Wizard," said Lang.

They all sat down around the table. The English officers looked at Lang and O'Meara politely but quizzically over their cups.

"Distinguished Flier," Perkins said at last, "how the devil did you get here?"

"Through the fence," said Lang, surprised a man as bright as Perkins had to ask.

"My word," Perkins murmured. "And that?" he said, indicating the mattress.

"His," said Lang, nodding at O'Meara.

"I see," said Perkins doubtfully.

Lang began fishing cigars, some of them intact, from inside his jacket. He lined them up on the table.

"I brought you your Christmas present, Perkie," he said.

Perkins was touched.

None of his roommates would accept a whole cigar but there were enough smokable lengths of damaged cigars for everyone. O'Meara had not said a word since entering the room. Now he sat chewing a cigar and looking from face to face with an expression Lang remembered from his first encounter with O'Meara.

"I hate limeys," he said suddenly.

Lang was mortified. The English officers, however, after the briefest expression of surprise, ignored O'Meara's remark and continued to chat easily.

"Hear what I said?" O'Meara demanded. "I hate limeys."

"Bad show," Cresswell said calmly.

"What you gonna do about it?" said O'Meara.

263

"Shut up," Lang said. "I wouldn't have brought you if I'd known you were gonna act like this."

"Who you tellin' to shut up?" O'Meara snapped, getting to his feet. "You shut up."

He stared challengingly at the Englishmen.

"I can lick any three men in the room," he said.

"Sit down, for pity's sake," Cresswell said wearily.

"You wanna be first?" O'Meara demanded.

Lang stood up, swaying. He felt very light, as if he might float to the ceiling if he were not careful. It was like the time the ME-109s had come in when the *High Flying Flora* bombed Navarino Bay and Jaybird put the nose down, leaving Lang hanging in the air above his navigation table.

"Killer, you quit trying to start trouble with my friends," he said severely.

"You wanna be first?" O'Meara demanded.

"This is becoming a frightful bore," said Perkins.

"It is, rather," said Cresswell.

He walked behind O'Meara to the cupboard, brought out a section of peeled birch limb which served as a rolling pin and wrapped it carefully in a dishcloth made of sacking. Neither Lang nor O'Meara paid him any attention. They were facing each other, two feet apart, both swaying. Cresswell hit O'Meara on the back of the head with the rolling pin. He misjudged the thickness of O'Meara's hair and skull and the Killer merely blinked. Cresswell hit him again, harder. O'Meara fell to the floor with a crash and lay motionless.

Everyone regarded him for a while in silence.

Then Lang said, casually, "Is he dead?"

"You can't kill that sort with a stick," Cresswell said. "Worse luck."

"Next time I won't bring him," Lang said.

"Next time?" said Perkins. "Dear me, I'd quite forgot your situation. However will you get back?"

"Same's I got in," said Lang. "Through the wire."

"That's very well for you, Damon," Perkins said, "but what about Pythias here?"

He looked down at O'Meara, who was now snoring peacefully on the floor, his arms flung wide and a smile on his lips.

"Or do you intend making us a gift of the bloody great lump?" Perkins continued.

"He's not so bad when you get to know him," Lang said.

"I dare say," said Cresswell. "In any case, you can't leave. It's after lockup. There's nothing for it but to tuck the pair of you in for the night. We'll discuss ways and means in the morning."

Lang covered O'Meara with borrowed greatcoats and lay down on the mattress. The room fishtailed gently, as if airborne, and Lang had the illusion he was flying.

O'Meara's snores filled the room.

"This is a bit much," Cresswell said. "Perkie, lend us a hand, will you?"

Each grasped a foot and dragged O'Meara out in the hallway where they tucked him tenderly into the greatcoats again.

"Good night, gang," Lang said drowsily.

He was floating now. Jaybird had the nose down and they were sinking, sinking. Crete rose toward them, spiny with mountains, and then the shining sea, flat and streaked with color like a sheet of tin over a flame.

Next morning Lang was ill and apprehensive. He wondered how they would get back to the South Camp and what the Germans would do if they caught them here, and what Colonel Ozmozius would say when he found out. The previous night had been a terrible mistake and he would never again drink kriegie brew.

O'Meara was ill, too.

"First time in my life I ever passed out drinking," he said. "I went out like a light."

He touched his head gingerly.

"I hit my head last night?" he asked. "I got a bump as big as a turkey egg."

"I shouldn't be surprised, Leftenant," said Perkins.

"We've got to sort things out before Appell," Cresswell said. "Else Jerry'll be in a frightful flap."

He went off to find the Senior British Officer and came back with instructions for O'Meara to leave the wire cutters so they would not be found if he was searched and for the pair of them to go to the gate, alone, and turn themselves in.

"You're to say nothing about how you got in or with whom you were visiting," Cresswell said. "They'll find out how you entered soon enough."

There was consternation at the gate when they presented themselves dragging the mattress. When the gate guard realized they were Americans he began shouting. A ferret came running, then a soldier with a rifle. None spoke English. The gate guard called headquarters on his field telephone and in ten minutes Froehlich arrived, furious, with two soldiers armed with machine pistols.

Froehlich escorted them to headquarters, scolding them all the way but keeping a soldier between himself and O'Meara. He need not have bothered. O'Meara walked with his head down, neither cowed nor contrite but nursing a hangover. Lang kept his head down, too, nausea and apprehension fighting a battle for his attention. At headquarters they were questioned sharply about their method of entry. They said they were too drunk to remember. Since the cut strands had not been discovered, the Germans assumed they had thrown the mattress between the fences to protect themselves from the concertina wire and then climbed after it. The commandant, more amused than angered by the escapade, permitted them to return to their own compound after a warning.

Colonel Ozmozius did not let them off so easy. When both O'Meara and the wire cutters were discovered missing it was obvious he had taken them, a grave offense. He summoned them to his room and paced back and forth in the confined space before them as they stood at attention.

"You're really in deep trouble now, O'Meara," he said in barely controlled fury. "When you get out of here . . . if you get out of here, I'll see you're court-martialed."

He whirled on Lang.

"Why'd you let him do it?" he demanded. "You've got more sense than that."

"I didn't . . ." Lang began sheepishly.

He caught himself. That was the old Lang, Blubberbutt. Tex wouldn't run out on a pal.

"No excuse, sir."

"What did I tell you about that cadet nonsense? All right. I can figure it out for myself. You're in trouble, too, but it's nothing like you'll find yourself in if you keep fooling around with this eight ball."

Colonel Ozmozius ought not to talk about O'Meara like that in front of people, Lang thought. It was embarrassing.

"He's heading for a dishonorable discharge, if he doesn't get himself killed first," Ozmozius said. "You want that, too?"

The colonel and Moran ought to get together, Lang thought. They were both always preaching about O'Meara.

"Both you apes are confined to quarters for two weeks except for Appell and room duties. Now get out of here. I can't stand the sight of either of you."

O'Meara winked at Lang as they left the room. Lang did not wink back. It had suddenly occurred to him that possibly Colonel Ozmozius and Moran were right.

His two-week confinement was at first more reprieve than punishment. He missed the weekly entertainment at the theater and the records played over the cookhouse speaker, his walks in the snow, the strenuous pleasures of the little gymnasium. But he did not miss O'Meara. O'Meara had got him in trouble, as Moran always said he would, and had insulted his friends.

267

Now that he had time and O'Meara was not there to disapprove, he read voraciously. He quickly finished *The Pickwick Papers* and turned to the books his roommates checked out of the library. His own borrowing privileges had been suspended with his confinement. Moran got a book for him occasionally but Augustine and Hartman borrowed to please their own tastes. Crumbacker never went near the library.

Lang particularly disliked Augustine's taste but read his books because it annoyed Augustine so.

He was in Augustine's bunk one afternoon reading a mystery when Augustine returned from the cookhouse with brew water.

"Why don't you read in your own sack?" Augustine demanded, his thin body tense with outrage.

"Don't you ever read anything but detective stories?" Lang said. "Didn't you ever hear of Thackeray or Dickens?"

"I know 'em better than you do," Augustine said. "Read in your own sack. And I want my book."

"After a while," Lang said, turning a page.

"Get out of my sack!" Augustine said tightly.

"Take off," Lang said, his eyes still on the book.

"I said get out of my sack!"

Augustine was pale now and his voice trembled. Lang looked at him coolly, imitating O'Meara's contemptuous nonchalance.

"You gonna make me?" he said.

Their roommates were watching. Moran was silent but disapproving, Hartman wary and Crumbacker twittery with anticipation.

Augustine grabbed the blue jug from the table, spilling hot water.

"You get out of my sack or I'll crown you!" he cried.

"Careful, Phil," Hartman said. "You'll spill the brew water."

Lang marked his place with insolent care, put the book down and dropped to the floor. He looked down at Augustine.

268

"Go ahead," he said.

"You think I won't?" Augustine demanded, clenching and unclenching his free hand.

"I know you won't," Lang said. "You're all hot air."

Augustine put the jug down and faced him. He was shaking but his fists were clenched defiantly.

"Go ahead and hit me," Lang said.

Augustine did not move.

"I won't hit you back," Lang said. "I'm too much man for you. I'll just put you across my knee and fan your little butt."

Augustine's eyes glistened with tears of rage and humiliation. It was obvious he wanted to hit Lang but was afraid. Lang waited, with insolent patience.

"Knock it off, both of you," Moran said suddenly. "The brew water's getting cold."

Augustine looked at him gratefully. Lang swaggered a little when he took his cup to the table. Augustine did not take coffee. He crawled into his bunk and lay there with his back to the room. Lang sneaked a glance at Augustine over the rim of his cup, remembering how he had fled to his own bunk at P.G. 203 when Dogass humiliated him. He felt a rush of sympathy for Augustine but the impulse was transient. Augustine had it coming. Augustine was always needling him. Now maybe he'd cut it out. It was not at all the same as it had been with him and Dogass.

Later, when they had a moment alone in the room, Moran said to Lang, "You were a real horse's ass a while ago."

"Like hell I was," Lang said, insulted. "He was going to hit me with that jug."

"You know damn well he wasn't. You wanted an excuse to cream him."

"He was asking for it."

"The hell he was. You know something, big buddy? You've turned into a real shit since you started running around with O'Meara."

269

Lang was appalled. Moran was supposed to be his best friend.

"Oh, yeah?" he said.

"Yeah," said Moran sadly.

There was a coolness in the room after that. Augustine acted as if Lang did not exist and Moran stopped getting special books for him. Occasionally Hartman would horseplay with him but with transparent reluctance. Only Crumbacker welcomed his attention but this was in itself a humiliation. Crumbacker's trousers were grimy at the knees and his woolen underwear showed through a rent in the seat. He still bathed only when his roommates insisted and if a horse-drawn wagon came into the camp he would drop whatever he was doing to seize his cardboard box and spatula to trail it.

Bored with books, Lang studied German. If he knew German he could translate the communiqué broadcast over the speaker and not have to wait for it to be posted on the cookhouse bulletin board. He could read the newspapers and *Der Adler* and other magazines circulated in the block. If he had known Italian he might not have been obliged to kill a man.

Hartman had a grammar which he gladly loaned to Lang. When Lang was bored he wanted to trade blows on the arm or engage in similar horseplay and Hartman was the only one available. If Lang was occupied with the grammar he would have less time for that.

Strenuous exercise had become a habit with Lang and he continued doing it in the room until Moran insisted he use the shower room. After every workout he would scrub himself with a washrag dipped in cold water and return to the room glowing with complacent health.

His studies and exercise did not prevent boredom or compensate for Moran's coolness and when O'Meara came for him at the end of their confinement he at first welcomed the Killer's company. It was better to have a friend like O'Meara than no friend at all.

The feeling did not persist. The theft of the wire cut-

270

ters was known to everyone and they were avoided wherever they went. Despite Colonel Ozmozius's warning, O'Meara reacted to this ostracism with increasing pugnacity toward the other prisoners and the goonbox guards. The tension of O'Meara's company grew increasingly unbearable but Lang could not escape him.

If he walked alone, O'Meara joined him. If he sought other companions O'Meara almost always appeared and the others would drift away, leaving the two of them alone. O'Meara pursued him even in dreams, displacing home, Serena the Butterfly Girl and the man he killed. It was as if O'Meara owned him. Lang wanted desperately to end the relationship but did not know how. He considered asking Moran's advice but was afraid Moran would only say I told you so. Simply asking O'Meara to leave him alone was out of the question. Lang knew how O'Meara would react to that.

Weeks passed without bringing a solution to Lang's dilemma. In mid-February he was walking with O'Meara with Crumbacker at their heels, as the little ragamuffin so often was, when Crumbacker trod on O'Meara's foot in his eagerness to overhear their conversation. O'Meara whirled angrily.

"Watch that, you little squirt!" he cried.

"Sorry, Killer," Crumbacker said in his serenely impudent way.

"You get on my nerves, always hanging around," O'Meara said. "Beat it."

"Sure, Killer."

But he dropped back only a few yards and continued following them.

"I said quit following us," O'Meara said, stopping.

"Why don't you leave him alone?" said Lang, who would have preferred even Crumbacker's companionship to O'Meara's. "He's not bothering anybody."

"He bothers me," O'Meara said.

"He doesn't bother me," Lang replied.

"You arguing with me?" O'Meara said, ominously calm.

271

"No," Lang said. "I just don't see anything wrong with Crumb walking with us."

"Yeah? Well, I do, and if he keeps tagging along I'm going back to my room."

Lang felt a chill deeper than the February cold. If he gave in now O'Meara would truly own him.

"Okay," he said. "Go ahead."

O'Meara stared at him, dumfounded, his face filled with hurt and fury. Lang thought the Killer was going to hit him but instead he said, "So Crumb's your big buddy now."

Crumbacker had edged close again, fascinated by the argument of which he was himself the subject. With a sudden movement O'Meara reached out and grabbed him. Crumbacker squealed in terror and surprise. O'Meara twisted his arm behind his back.

"You're hurting me," Crumbacker moaned.

"Don't, Killer," Lang said.

"Shut up!" said O'Meara.

He gave Crumbacker's arm a twist and tears rolled down the youngster's cheeks.

"You going to leave us alone, you raunchy little runt?" O'Meara demanded.

"I will, I will," Crumbacker cried desperately.

"Let go of him, Killer," Lang said. "You're hurting him."

"You gonna make me?" O'Meara said, not releasing his hold.

Lang felt sick, not because of Crumbacker's pain but because he knew what he must do. He seized O'Meara's arm and tried to pull him away but the Killer was too strong. O'Meara jerked free and shoved Crumbacker sprawling in the snow. He turned to face Lang. In his eyes was the feral gleam which Lang knew and feared.

"You asking for it?" O'Meara said.

Lang shook his head dumbly.

"You crawling?"

Lang wanted to say yes, to end this perilous confrontation, but he knew it would be the end of Tex Lang forever, in the South Camp and everywhere. And even if he said yes it would not be over. The Killer would forget neither his opposition nor surrender and O'Meara's contempt was no less dangerous than his fury. He let out a breath which was close to a sigh.

"No," he said. "I'm not crawling."

"I'm going to beat your brains out," O'Meara said quietly.

A handful of men had gathered around them and more were approaching. Despite his trepidation Lang was glad he had not backed down in front of so many witnesses. He waited, watchfully. O'Meara stood with his long arms dangling, no hint of threat in his posture. Maybe O'Meara was just testing him again, Lang thought. He licked his lips. And then he knew that O'Meara had meant what he said, that the Killer was drinking in his fear, savoring it, and he felt a moment of the same paralyzing terror as in the boxcar at Bolzano.

The crowd around them was growing. O'Meara looked around the circle and wiped his hands on his trousers.

"Here I come, Tex," he said conversationally.

Lang could not have answered even if he wished. His throat was constricted as much in dread of showing fear as in fear itself.

O'Meara pawed lazily with his outstretched left hand. Lang avoided it easily, stepping back with his fists poised in defense. O'Meara pawed at him again and again Lang evaded the blow. Maybe the Killer had slowed down, he thought, or he had become faster. Maybe he had a chance after all.

O'Meara, with a lurch, hit him on the cheek with his right hand. The blow hurt but it did not stun. It filled Lang with wild and reckless anger. He sprang at O'Meara punching furiously. Some of his blows landed. He had become faster than the Killer and O'Meara was taken by surprise. Lang drove him back a few feet before O'Meara retaliated, ignoring Lang's

273

blows and battering down Lang's defenses with sheer strength. He knocked Lang down. Lang got up and fought more cautiously. But O'Meara was also more cautious. He would feint, then throw a flurry of punches. In each exchange Lang would land heavy blows of his own but in the end be staggered or knocked to the snow. He kept getting up, each time more slowly than the last. Both of them were bloody now. Lang was no longer faster than the Killer and O'Meara could have ended the fight if he wished, but he did not wish. Lang's resistance increased his pleasure. It was like rape.

There was a great crowd around them now, surging back and forth with the movements of the combatants. The prisoners were festive. Two hated men were beating one another and there was little enough entertainment to be had at Stalag Luft 9.

Lang yearned for unconsciousness. He knew he could not beat O'Meara but pride would not let him stay down so long as he was able to struggle to his feet. In his pain and dullness he could hear voices in the crowd cheering him on. It's almost worth it, he thought. They're on my side.

And then, on his face in the snow, he found he could not rise. He got to his knees but could go no farther. O'Meara reached down and pulled him to his feet. Smiling, dripping blood, O'Meara held him up with a hand wound in his jacket and poised the other for a final, crushing blow. Lang waited dully, beyond pain or fear. I hope he doesn't knock out any teeth, he thought.

"Don't do that," said Moran's voice.

Lang and O'Meara turned to look. Moran was pushing himself through the crowd.

"You gonna stop me?" O'Meara said, still holding Lang erect.

"Yeah," said Moran. "I'm gonna stop you."

O'Meara threw back his head and laughed, flinging droplets of blood into the sunlight.

274

"You sawed-off little bastard," he said. "Let me see you try."

"There you are and here I am," Moran said. "Come get me."

O'Meara released Lang, who would have fallen if Crumbacker had not darted out of the crowd to support him. O'Meara moved toward Moran, breathing heavily and weaving a little. He was tired from beating Lang. Moran crouched slightly, his fists chest high and close to his body. O'Meara pawed at his face, as he had first done with Lang. Instead of stepping back, Moran ducked beneath the outstretched arm and, shifting, drove his left fist into O'Meara's body, leaning into the blow from his firmly planted right foot. O'Meara's mouth flew open and more droplets glistened in the sunlight. Pivoting to face O'Meara squarely, Moran hit him again and again in the place the first blow had landed, his fists flashing.

O'Meara sagged. Moran stepped back, straightening. He hit him three swift blows to the jaw, two with his left hand and one with his right, the last as O'Meara was falling. O'Meara fell ponderously, like a great tree, slowly at first, then gaining momentum to crash in the snow. He seemed to bounce, and then he lay still.

The crowd cheered. Moran whirled to face them.

"You dirty bastards!" he said. "Why didn't you stop it?"

He went quickly to Lang, who could now stand without Crumbacker's assistance.

"You okay, Steve?" he said gently.

Lang tried to smile, tasting blood in his mouth.

"I'll live," he said.

Moran draped Lang's arm across his shoulders and supported him with an arm around his waist.

"Let's go home," he said.

275

CHAPTER 17

When Colonel Ozmozius summoned Lang to his quarters it was with Moran, not O'Meara. Lang expected a dressing down and restriction to quarters but their reception was cordial.

"I understand I missed a hell of a scrap," the colonel said, adding quickly, "not that I approve of brawling."

He looked at Moran with obvious respect.

"They tell me you put O'Meara down without him laying a hand on you," he said.

"Didn't take much, Colonel," Moran said. "Lang ran him outta gas for me."

"I told this to O'Meara and I'm telling the block commanders to pass it down," said Ozmozius. "It goes for you,

276

too, Lieutenant. Nobody's to take him on alone. If he starts making trouble, everybody in sight gangs up on him. Fists, feet, sticks, whatever it takes. Got it?"

"Yes, sir," Moran said reluctantly.

"You can go," said Ozmozius. "Lieutenant Lang, you stick around."

Moran left, neglecting to salute, an oversight which the colonel ignored. He studied Lang's face. Lang had cuts above both eyes, another under his left eye, a split lip and a livid cheekbone.

"I don't suppose I have to order you not to try taking on the Killer by yourself again," he said dryly.

"No, sir!" Lang said, knowing bravado would not impress the colonel.

"And I don't suppose I have to tell you to quit palling around with him."

"No, sir."

"They tell me it started when you tried to stop O'Meara from hazing Lieutenant Crumbacker."

"Yes, sir."

"I misjudged you, Lang. You're all right."

It was difficult for Lang not to show how flattered he was. He admired Colonel Ozmozius. Colonel Ozmozius was a real soldier.

"Who's senior man in your room?" Ozmozius said.

"I guess I am, sir," Lang said, puzzled.

Hartman, Augustine and Crumbacker were second lieutenants and he had been promoted to first a week before Moran.

"Tell Crumbacker to burn those raunchy pants and wear the ones I had him issued last month."

"Yes, sir," said Lang, surprised that the colonel had noticed a little thing like Crumbacker's pants with all the men there were in the camp.

"And you might try being a little more military yourself, Lieutenant. You're pretty raunchy."

That wasn't fair, Lang thought. His uniform was no dirtier than anyone else's and he shaved twice a week just like most of the others. And he kept the flared ends of his mustache neat. Moran even kidded him about it. First Colonel Osmosis praised him and now he was down on him. Lang knew he was looking sullen but he could not help it.

"It's easy to let yourself go in the bag," Ozmozius said. "The leaders have to set the example."

The leaders!

Lang looked at Colonel Ozmozius sharply. The colonel's expression was noncommittal. Did the colonel really think he was a leader or was he just kidding?

"Dismissed," said Ozmozius. "And keep your nose clean."

Moran was waiting outside.

"He rack you back?" Moran asked.

Lang shook his head.

"He said I was a leader," Lang said wonderingly.

"You're kidding," said Moran.

Lang shook his head again.

"Hey," he said. "That was swell what you told him. About me running the Killer out of gas for you."

"You did," Moran said. "Maybe I could have whipped him anyhow because he don't really know how to fight. He's so big he never had to learn. But it would of been tough. You used him up pretty good, Steve."

"I did get him some good ones," Lang said. "I bet I could whip Dogass easy now."

Moran looked at him speculatively.

"You still think about that?" he said.

"No," Lang lied.

Back in the room, Lang told Crumbacker to get rid of his filthy pants. When Crumbacker protested, Lang took them off forcibly. If Colonel Osmosis thought he was a leader he intended acting like a leader. Augustine called him a bully. Hartman helped him catch Crumbacker.

278

"Now let's take him in the washroom and scrub him up," Hartman urged, his handsome face gleeful.

"It's too cold!" Crumbacker shrieked piteously.

"No," said Lang.

Colonel Osmosis hadn't said anything about that, only about the pants.

It was weeks before Lang lost his sense of foreboding and omission. It would nag him, vague at first and annoying, and then he would realize he was waiting for Killer O'Meara to come for him. When he understood this was the source of his uneasiness he would feel afresh a sense of freedom and deliverance because O'Meara would not be coming for him any more. The first few days he was never fully at ease out of doors, apprehensive about coming unexpectedly upon O'Meara. He no longer feared the Killer, no one did now that Colonel Ozmozius had made it clear they must protect each other from him, but he knew it would be embarrassing because he had been O'Meara's only friend and now O'Meara was friendless. And he understood friendlessness. When he saw O'Meara he would turn and walk the other way or duck into the most convenient block to visit friends. For he had friends again.

He was not sure he need bother to avoid O'Meara, for in the rare brief moments when their eyes met there was no belligerence in the Killer's face, only a kind of entreaty, and Lang felt sorry for him. Maybe O'Meara really wasn't so terrible when you understood him. Yet he never spoke to O'Meara again, nor O'Meara to him.

Day followed orderly day but time was curiously imbalanced, measured not by clock and calendar but by event. The length of morning was the span between first Appell and the distribution of mail, and its minutes did not move. Lang and Moran often deliberately remained away from the room at mailtime to mitigate the daily agony of anticipation. Mail made the balance of the day pass swiftly, no mail made time congeal. Sleep was the measure of night. Waking hours were interminable and tantalizing, those spent in sleep too quickly fled. Weeks did not pass from Sunday to Sunday but from parcel day to parcel day and would not be hurried. Months crept like glaciers but, once over, seemed to have passed in a twinkling.

Time to Moran was a relentless tyrant but Lang found increasing ways to make it his servant.

He went to the gym and he walked the perimeter regularly, with Moran when Moran could be persuaded to leave the room and with new friends when he could not be. He cropped his RAF mustache to an imitation of Colonel Ozmozius's military brush and devoted much time to its care. He tended his uniform with equal care, teaching himself to sew and darn. Despite the fact he was not by nature orderly, he learned to be slow and meticulous about it for the double benefit of a job neatly done and time consumed. In his notebook he kept records of letters sent and received, of the contents of personal parcels and future needs, of pay accrued, of his turn as stooge, of his turn as cook, of his winnings and losses of cigarettes at poker, which Moran was teaching him to play, of the books he read, of the plays and the occasional movies he saw in the theater, the nights he heard the RAF pounding Berlin, ninety miles away, the dates the Russian Army recaptured cities or made significant advances — he loved the Russian Army, as did all the prisoners in the South Camp, and resented the inactivity of the Anglo-American forces — and the addresses of fellow prisoners he intended looking up after the war. Augustine accused him of also recording his bowel movements but this was not true.

He learned many kinds of solitaire, preferring the longer types, and played them with profound deliberation. He particularly liked a kind of double solitaire called Russian Bank. Moran would not play it with him because Lang played so slowly. When his cards became speckled with dirt and grease, Lang would scrape them clean with a table knife, one card at a time.

He studied German every day, poring over the

Voelkische Beobachter, Der Adler and other newspapers and magazines with Hartman's grammar at his side. He joined the daily throng around the cookhouse loudspeaker in the afternoon at military communiqué time and made lists of the words he did not understand. He learned to translate the communiqué more quickly than the periodicals. The language was deliberately simple and restricted to military terms with the same words and phrases occurring day after day. Colonel Ozmozius had a translation of the communiqué posted on the cookhouse bulletin board every day but often it was not ready until after second Appell and most prisoners were too impatient to wait. There was in the camp an appetite for war news second only to that for food and women. Though the Russian offensive, followed in scores of rooms on hand-drawn maps, was still far from Stalag Luft 9 it held promise, however remote, of some day reaching them. Few of the prisoners assembling around the speaker at communiqué time could translate for themselves and those who knew German were besieged for translations while the report was being broadcast. Lang acquired a clique of followers who assembled around him daily. He translated the report for them with an air of princely condescension.

And Lang read prodigiously. Mysteries, Dickens, Thackeray, modern novels, biography, Dante, Thoreau. He did not enjoy everything he read but never failed to finish every book he began. Language acquired an extraordinary vividness not necessarily related to subject matter. The most simple words often and unexpectedly evoked complete and sharply detailed images or fantasies.

Lunch. A table covered with linen, set with silver and crowded with the things Lang liked best to eat.

Ankle. Not merely an ankle but the entire girl, often naked and always unusually endowed. Bosom evoked stronger visions even when used to describe the location of a wound.

Carpet. Bare feet in thick rugs, whole rooms luxuriously furnished, fireplaces, soft armchairs, bookcases, phonographs with racks of records, beds with real mattresses.

Trip. Trains, buses, streetcars, automobiles. Long vistas of green valleys, woods, snowy peaks, rivers, seashore, little country towns. Freedom.

Hero. Tex Lang, erect, mustached, beribboned, coming home to bands, parades, tears of joy, hot passionate kisses. But part of him grave and unreachable, the part with sad and manly memories of Bertram and Jaybird, secret remorse for the Italian he killed, the part which listened with a secret ear to "The Song of the Young Sentry" which meant to him things civilians would never understand — the nights on the bungalow steps at P.G. 203, beatings in the wire, Jaybird dead, the Italian killed, the Killer fought, someone waiting for him in the lamplight. It would be his theme song. Girls would ask him why he hummed it so sadly but he would not tell them. Or perhaps he would. It depended.

Early in March, Lang stood outside with Moran listening to the first American air raid on Berlin. It was the first time they had heard bombs exploding by day. They had heard them often during winter nights when the RAF attacked Berlin. The distant explosions would rattle windows and they would open the blackout shutters and look toward the tormented city, exulting. When there was an overcast they could even see a distant glow, changing in intensity as they watched.

"Listen," Lang said. "We're really pranging 'em."

"I guess it's better than nothing," Moran said.

"What do you mean, better than nothing?" Lang demanded. "This must be the most important day raid yet."

"Why the hell don't they get off their butts like the Russians and try some hand to hand?" Moran said angrily.

He had grown increasingly restless and morose in the months of boredom and inactivity.

They fell silent, listening to the muted thump of distant bombs. Moran sighed. There was fury and impatience and helplessness in the sigh. The fury and impatience had grown familiar to Lang in the long winter but the helplessness was new.

"What's the matter, Bernie?" Lang asked.

282

"What's the matter, he says!" Moran cried. "This God damn place is the matter! Don't you know we're wasting the best years of our lives in this hole?"

That's what they all said, Lang thought, that they were wasting the best years of their lives in the bag. It didn't matter if they were kids barely old enough to join the cadets or the forty-one-year-old intelligence officer in the next block, the oldest man in the South Camp. But it really wasn't all that bad. In some ways Stalag Luft 9 even had it over the outside. Where else would a man have that much time to read and study and build up his muscles and have so many people think he was somebody? Where else was he Tex Lang, a tough smart cookie who had never been fat or helpless or backed down to Dogass Harbold? Nobody had a past here. You were measured by your accomplishments within the wire. It was as if they had all been born here.

Daytime raids deep within Germany became frequent though the prisoners seldom heard exploding bombs again. Lang followed the air war closely in the German newspapers and the hourly Luftlage Meldung, air situation report, on the camp speaker. He tried without success to cheer Moran with this evidence of Allied activity.

When the early warning sirens sounded in the area of Stalag Luft 9 the prisoners were required to remain indoors. The official German explanation was that the prisoners' antics during air raids angered the guards and they were kept inside for their own safety. It was Colonel Ozmozius's opinion that it was to guard against the possibility of weapons being dropped to the prisoners. This disturbed Lang. He had no desire to fight his way out of captivity. He wished to be called for.

Despite his fear of being bombed, Lang was undisturbed by the sirens or distant explosions. There were no military targets near Stalag Luft 9 as far as anyone knew. One crisp April day, however, a formation of B-17s flew directly over the camp after attacking a target many miles away. The chips of silver swimming leisurely in the blue filled Lang with an irrational fear and he dived under the table, with Moran close behind him.

"Jesus," said Moran, "I thought that was one thing we didn't have to worry about."

When they crawled from beneath the table they found Hartman, Crumbacker and Augustine grinning at them.

"If one of you bastards says a word I'll knock him on his ass," Moran said. "If you'd ever been bombed you wouldn't think it was so funny."

Lang was not ashamed of having shown his fear. Moran had been scared, too. It showed how much more they knew about war than their roommates. Lang never again enjoyed an air raid no matter how distant it was reported to be on the Luftlage Meldung.

The guards, once almost indifferent to the prisoners, grew openly antagonistic and increasingly touchy with the stepped-up air offensive. Their families wrote them disturbing letters from target areas and the newspapers they read were filled with scathing attacks on American Luftgangsters. Some of the prisoners, Lang and Moran not among them, added to the tension by walking the perimeter after the all clear to grin impudently at the goonboxes. Colonel Ozmozius issued orders against it but the practice did not end until mid-May when a prisoner discovered a barracks door unlocked and stepped outside during an alert. He was shot dead by a guard patrolling the wire a hundred yards away.

May was a good month for Lang. He received eleven letters, a book parcel, a tobacco parcel and a food parcel. There was a brief argument with Hartman and Augustine about which items of the food parcel should go into the communal larder but it was settled to Lang's satisfaction when Moran and Crumbacker supported him. He shared the personal items with Moran.

The few parcels which Moran received from his father were hopelessly impractical and Moran would curse him with helpless affection.

"Now what does my old man expect me to do with

284

smoked oysters?" he said. "Don't he know oysters make
you horny? And if there's one thing I don't need . . ."

In May, Lang became more skillful in translating newspaper articles, which lacked the simple clarity and directness of
the war communiqué, adding to his reputation as a military and
political theorist, and in May, Crumbacker's garden sprouted
a promise of lettuce, tomatoes, onions and new potatoes. The
seeds for all but the potatoes had come from the International
Red Cross in Switzerland and Crumbacker's garden was the
only one in camp doing well. The soil of Stalag Luft 9 was acid
and unproductive but his indefatigable pursuit of the horse-
drawn trash and cesspool wagons had provided fertilizer.

And in May the coupling of two dogs which had strayed
into the compound provided the most exciting entertainment
the prisoners had known since Lang's fight with O'Meara. Lang
and Moran joined the hundreds of prisoners milling around
the panting animals and following them across the parade
ground during the courtship and culmination.

"Would you look at this?" Moran said unbelievingly as
his eyes wandered from the dogs to the jostling, cheering,
laughing throng. "If we could charge admission we'd be rich."

The first week in June, Lang went to the cookhouse, as
was his custom, to await the morning Luftlage Meldung. He
was alone there except for a Polish ferret listening to an opera
being broadcast on the German radio network. Though prisoners not specifically authorized to do so were forbidden to
speak with their captors, Lang exchanged polite, noncommittal greetings with the ferret. When there were no witnesses
he liked to practice speaking German. The music stopped
abruptly and an excited announcer broke in with a special bulletin. After a few words this, too, was cut off abruptly and the
speaker went dead. Lang and the ferret stared at each other.

"Invasion!" Lang shouted.

An American enlisted man thrust his head out of the
window through which hot water was dispensed and cried,
"What did you say, Lieutenant?"

Others within earshot turned and ran toward the cookhouse but Lang was already sprinting across the compound to Colonel Ozmozius's quarters. The SAO should be told first.

Though Lang was accustomed to jogging around the perimeter, excitement made breathing difficult and he was panting heavily when he knocked on the colonel's door and burst into the room without waiting for permission. Colonel Ozmozius looked up annoyed from the can of cold corned beef he was eating with a spoon.

"It's started!" Lang cried. "The invasion."

Ozmozius leaped to his feet.

"When? Where? How do you know?"

"This morning, sir," Lang said, leaning against the wall for support. "I don't know where. They cut the radio off in the Vorlager right away."

"Let's get over to the cookhouse," Ozmozius said. "Maybe they'll turn it on again."

Men were popping out of doors and windows and running to the cookhouse. The crowd around the silent loudspeaker made a place for Lang and the colonel. Men plucked at Lang's sleeves, wanting confirmation of the news from his own lips. He shook them off impatiently. Couldn't they see he was with the SAO? When Moran pushed his way to his side Lang whispered what he had heard. Moran was visibly disappointed at the lack of detail.

"Bet it's just a false alarm," he said.

Ferrets and guards joined the throng at the cookhouse. In the North Camp the British were throwing their caps in the air on the parade ground. Outside the wire German soldiers were calling to each other for news. The crowd grew restive. Some men left. The speaker crackled. The crowd fell silent. Muffled German voices, conversational and unintelligible, were heard. Then music, a recording of "Stars Fell on Alabama" from the Vorlager library of American records.

The air was filled with curses and groans and the crowd dispersed. Colonel Ozmozius turned to Lang.

"Lang, how well do you know German?" he demanded.

"Pretty good, sir," Lang said. "Military German. Sometimes I have trouble with the newspaper. . . ."

"I'm going to the gate to see if I can get a call through to Colonel Bruckmann," Ozmozius said, cutting him short. Bruckmann was Stalag Luft 9 Commandant. "You stay here and monitor the radio. I'll have you relieved in an hour."

"Yes, sir!" said Lang.

He glowed to the roots of his hair. Colonel Ozmozius was making him his right-hand man, like Jaybird with Colonel Waterfield.

Ozmozius returned with word the radio would not be turned on again until the regular daily communiqué and, to Lang's keen disappointment, released him from monitor duty without further instructions. But at communiqué time, when the entire compound assembled around the speaker in a throng spilling back between the blocks, Ozmozius summoned him to the fore with the camp staff.

When the speaker came on there was utter silence except for the surflike shuffle of feet edging closer. Despite the claim of German successes, it was quickly obvious that the Normandy landings were a full-scale invasion in force, not another disappointing Dieppe raid. The rest of the communiqué was drowned out in a shattering roar from the assembled prisoners.

The tempo and spirit of the South Lager changed abruptly. Time was measured not by mail or parcels but by the progress of Allied arms in Normandy. Boredom and frustration gave way to boundless optimism. Impatience mounted, but an invigorating kind of impatience.

To Lang and Moran the excitement of the times was greater and the prospects more enthralling than in P.G. 203 after the invasion of the Italian mainland. In Italy, it now seemed in retrospect, the specter of being moved to Germany had shadowed their hopes. Now there was no such specter. And the forces pressing Germany on two fronts were far greater than those in Italy and moving more rapidly.

Moran's winter depression and spring cynicism lifted with the invasion, though he evaded complete surrender to optimism.

"They never got off their butts until they ran outta beer and babes in England," he said. "Let's see how long it takes 'em to run outta wine and women in France. Because they ain't coming for us until they do."

But he said it cheerfully.

Oberst Bruckmann permitted the radio to be on continuously upon receiving assurance from Colonel Ozmozius there would be no disorders stemming from war news and the cookhouse speaker was monitored from breakfast until lockup. There were news reports and bulletins throughout the day. Lang was one of those assigned to monitor the cookhouse speaker by Colonel Ozmozius and every day relieved another translator at 10 A.M. for his hour's duty. He was never far from the speaker the rest of the day. He was relieved from room stooge duties by unanimous vote of his roommates to permit this, even Augustine submerging his animosity in his thirst for news. It was warm now, and except for his official hour at the speaker Lang wore only shorts in the hip pocket of which he had always his pencil and paper for writing down place names. He took down reports verbatim during his official hour of duty and, wearing his shirt, shoes and socks, delivered the translation directly to Colonel Ozmozius as did the other monitors.

In the first days of the invasion hundreds of prisoners assembled at the speaker and remained there for hours. Others came running when shouts and cheers announced a news report. The reports also drew ferrets and guards, and often Sergeant Froehlich, who endured the taunts of the prisoners in annoyed silence. Sometimes Lang found himself exchanging bits of information with a German when the noise of the crowd interfered with reception, but never with Froehlich. When Froehlich came, the other Germans left.

Lang took his position as monitor seriously. He not only

dressed for it but also refused to give translations to the men besieging him for them.

"Colonel Osmosis gets it first," he said. "You guys'll have to wait."

A group of prisoners always followed him to the colonel's quarters and waited outside for him.

"What's this gang that follows you around?" Ozmozius asked one day. "An honor guard?"

"No, sir," Lang said, embarrassed that the colonel had noticed. He'd have to tell them to cut that out. He was getting fed up with them, anyhow. After every news report everyone pestered him for individual summaries and he was tired of repeating himself. "They're waiting for the news."

"Waiting for the news?" Colonel Ozmozius demanded. "Don't they get it at the cookhouse?"

"Oh, no, sir. I don't give anybody the news before you get it."

The corners of the colonel's mouth and eyes twitched.

"You're a real eager beaver, aren't you, Lieutenant?" he said.

"No, sir," Lang said with what he hoped was humility. "I just got a job to do."

"I see," Colonel Ozmozius said gravely. "Well, keep up the good work."

Lang looked forward to his daily visit with the SAO. He thought perhaps Colonel Ozmozius liked him now. The colonel often smiled at things he said and it had been weeks since the colonel had felt obliged to point out he was raunchy. When he saw the colonel out walking Lang would contrive to cross his path, drawing himself up in a military manner, because the colonel always acknowledged his presence with a word or a smile. And sometimes the colonel would keep him in his room for several minutes, questioning him about things he had read in the newspapers.

In some things Colonel Ozmozius reminded him of Jaybird. He believed in military discipline, as had Jaybird, though not so humorlessly. And he knew all about the obligations and responsibilities of leadership, like Jaybird. Lang remembered how he had often resented these qualities in Jaybird because they made difficulties for him. He wished he could apologize to Jaybird for that, and that Jaybird could see how he had come to believe in the same things. Sometimes after a visit with Ozmozius Lang thought of Jaybird with great poignance, feeling he had not truly known or understood him until now.

He was impressed with the colonel's neatness of person and quarters. Ozmozius's room was always swept and his bunk always made tautly, with square corners, like the bed of a cadet. There was never a garment thrown carelessly across it and the little shelf that held his toilet articles and other small possessions was always neatly arranged. There was nothing fussy about the colonel's neatness. To Lang it signified an orderly mind and a sense of security.

He even admired the way Colonel Ozmozius smoked a pipe, remembering how Colonel Waterfield had sucked on his pipe in frustration when it was empty and when it was not had worried it with tamping and relighting and inspection. Colonel Ozmozius usually smoked cigarettes but when he smoked a pipe he did it with an unawareness of the awkward mechanics of filling and lighting and drawing. Clenched between Colonel Ozmozius's teeth, a pipe looked military as well as manly, not scoutmasterish.

Lang began making his bunk tautly, with square corners. He did not lie on it during the day and when he took off his shirt he hung it on a nail instead of dropping it carelessly on the bed. He swept around and under his bunk every morning despite Augustine's complaint that it raised dust. He bought a pipe for a carton of cigarettes and traded more cigarettes for a tin of Player's tobacco. Though he practiced when unobserved, he was unable to fill and light it with the colonel's casual ease. And sometimes it made him sick.

When he remembered, he walked erect with his shoulders back, as the colonel did. It made him feel more than a first lieutenant, and taller.

290

CHAPTER 18

A new wave of anticipation swept the camp in July with the attempt on Hitler's life. It was thought that German military resistance might collapse at any time and that liberation might be only days or weeks away. Lang scoured the newspapers for indications. It was his theory, freely expressed, that Hitler had been killed in the explosion and an impostor substituted. Many prisoners and some of the ferrets thought the same. Lang accepted the proof of photographs and a radio speech by Hitler only reluctantly.

To Moran, who had been ecstatic at the first report of the attempted assassination, its failure was a personal affront.

"These damn Goons," he raged. "Why the hell couldn't they show some of their friggin' efficiency knocking him off instead of saving it all for the friggin' war?"

The Russians pushed in the east and the Anglo-Americans in the west and no one in the South Camp was pessimistic for long, even Moran. The air war mounted in fury as well and new prisoners poured into the compound. Lang's room, which was intended for six men, was brought up to strength.

The new man was Riley Jackson, a Negro fighter pilot shot down escorting bombers out of Italy. He was Augustine's height, five-nine or so, but more muscular, with large hands and feet. A second lieutenant, he was at twenty-seven the oldest man in the room. Moran was a few months younger, Hartman was twenty-four, as was Lang, who had celebrated two birthdays in captivity. Augustine was now twenty-three and Crumbacker twenty-two. Crumbacker was no longer one of the youngest officers in the South Camp. Some of the new prisoners, pilots, were no more than twenty.

Jackson acknowledged introductions warily and did not relax until he saw the climate of the room was friendly. Lang had never met a Negro socially before and was overly cordial. The new man betrayed a hint of truculence when he heard Lang's accent but made no comment. Within a few days the strangeness vanished and it was with a jolt of surprise Lang sometimes noticed Jackson's face was black. It was like the sound of propellers on a long bombing mission. After an hour or so in the air Lang had stopped hearing them and when, on occasion, the noise intruded, he would think Jaybird had changed the prop pitch or throttle settings.

Lang and his roommates did, however, resent the Red Cross capture kit which Jackson brought with him. A fiber suitcase given to him at the German interrogation center, it contained such luxuries as pajamas and toilet articles. The older prisoners thought it unfair a new man should be issued things they were not.

In August, when an Allied victory appeared possible before the year was out, Colonel Ozmozius organized the South Camp into a clandestine military unit and Lang was given three assignments. He was appointed interpreter for the block squadron, commander of the room flight and officer in charge

292

of the enlisted men working in the cookhouse. There were a dozen enlisted men, chiefly corporals and buck sergeants, headed by a master sergeant. They had moved to what had once been a storeroom in Lang's block when the camp began filling up. The master sergeant supervised their work and Lang was charged only with their discipline and welfare.

After dinner the day he was placed in charge of the enlisted men, Lang shaved, put on a complete uniform and went to inspect his new command. The room was more crowded than his own and clothes were strewn about carelessly. The master sergeant called the men to attention when he entered and Lang was delighted with the assurance with which he was able to give the master sergeant and his men a command of "At ease."

"I'm Lieutenant Lang, your new CO," he said, wondering if he should offer to shake hands with the master sergeant. You did it with officers but he was not sure about enlisted men, not when it was an official visit. He had never been a CO before and could not remember what he had been taught at preflight.

The master sergeant solved the problem for him by maintaining a respectful distance.

"Glad to meet the lieutenant, sir," he said. "Master Sergeant Boyd Tomlove, sir, NCOIC." Seeing Lang's puzzled expression, he added, "Noncommissioned officer in charge."

Lang felt he had already made a mistake, letting the sergeant see he did not know what NCOIC meant. Well, Tomlove better not take that as a sign he did not know how to command. He walked around the room, poking at bedding and running his finger over the window ledges looking for dirt the way the tactical officer had done at inspections in preflight. He found it. Lang held up his begrimed finger for all to see.

"I don't like this, men," he said. "I don't like this at all."

He looked around for something on which to wipe his finger. Expressionless, Sergeant Tomlove handed him an undershirt. The other enlisted men looked at one another, some grinning insubordinately, Lang thought — others resentful.

"I want these quarters policed up and kept policed up," Lang said. "And when you take clothes off, hang 'em up or put 'em out of sight. Got it?"

"Yes, sir, Lieutenant," said Sergeant Tomlove, still without expression.

Sergeant Tomlove was an army regular and, at thirty-six, the second oldest man in the South Camp. He was Lang's height, and thicker in body. His face was marked by long years of sun, wind, fists and celebrations.

"If you got any problems, I'm here to help you," Lang said, tempering his severity and letting them know that while he was a stickler for order and discipline he also intended looking out for his enlisted men. "Any questions?"

"No, sir," said Sergeant Tomlove.

"Carry on," Lang said.

He returned Tomlove's salute and left the room. When he turned to shut the door behind him he found it blocked by Sergeant Tomlove's broad figure. The sergeant stepped out in the hall and shut the door behind him.

"Sergeant Tomlove requests permission to talk to the lieutenant," he said formally.

"Say on," said Lang.

Tomlove's tone became less formal, almost confidential.

"Lieutenant," he said, "we put in long hours in that kitchen and when we finish up we're wore out. We don't hardly have time to police up the billet once a week, much less every day."

Lang opened his mouth to object.

"Excuse me, sir," said Tomlove. "I ain't finished yet. If we was in garrison I'd be all for this spit and polish and snap crap stuff. I been soldiering long enough to know that's how it's got to be. But we ain't in garrison, sir. Not by some. We don't intend to give the lieutenant no crap and we'd sure appreciate it if the lieutenant don't give us none. That way everybody'll be happy. Okay, Lieutenant?"

294

Lang was taken aback, then indignant. This was no way for an enlisted man to address an officer. Lance Corporal Gorsely would not have dreamed of talking to him like this. But Master Sergeant Tomlove was not Lance Corporal Gorsely. Lang did not think he was ready to test his authority against the sergeant's shrewdness and experience. And besides, on more than one occasion he had seen Colonel Ozmozius talking and laughing with Sergeant Tomlove in a friendly, easy way. Maybe it was all right for a sergeant to talk to a lieutenant the way he had. Lang decided to wait until Tomlove really stepped out of line before showing him who was in charge.

It never happened. Lang found that if he gave the enlisted men no trouble, they gave him none, just as Sergeant Tomlove had promised. They became friendly and, though he was hardly aware of it, Lang dropped the condescending manner he assumed when dealing with enlisted men. Despite the friendship, Tomlove seldom let Lang forget he was an officer and the sergeant an enlisted man. It was a habit of twenty years which nothing could break. He stopped addressing him in the third person but continued to rise when Lang entered the enlisted men's quarters and had his men remain at attention until Lang gave them at ease. Lang sometimes visited Sergeant Tomlove for the practice it gave him in commanding enlisted men and the pleasure he got from seeing twelve men leap to attention at his entry.

In his own room the role of commander was not so plainly defined or so easily performed. They were all officers and there was little need for a commander. The senior man drew bulk issues of GI soap and toilet paper and checked the room at Appell to make sure everyone had left for the parade ground. Finding these duties unchallenging, Lang argued for better seats in the theater, for a better cooking period on the block stove and for more records when they had the phonograph. He had everyone sweep around his own bunk after morning Appell and the sweepings taken out to the incinerator by the day's stooge.

"Tell it to the chaplain," Lang said when Augustine objected to the daily chore.

"You can't make me sweep if I don't want to," said Augustine, whose only true objection to the arrangement was that it had been ordered by Lang.

"You want me to report you for insubordination?" Lang said.

"I ought to know you'd go running to the SAO," said Augustine. "You're always brown-nosing him."

"I could make you do it by whipping your little butt," Lang said, controlling his anger as he thought a good commander should, "but that's not the military way."

He was determined to do things the military way.

Lang insisted clothing be hung up and cigarette butts be put in cans instead of thrown on the floor. Moran was the worst offender with butts. Lang did not know how to handle the situation. Moran was his best friend but a rule was a rule. He nailed a can on Moran's bunkpost but though Moran took the hint he sometimes forgot to use it. Lang took him aside and asked him earnestly to try harder. Moran promised he would but at night, after lights out, breaking a camp rule of much more importance than Lang's, he smoked in bed and sometimes dreamily let a butt drop to the floor to burn itself out and fill the room with acrid fumes. Unable to convince Moran of the gravity of this offense, Lang thought Moran was taking unfair advantage of their friendship.

To make the situation even more difficult, Augustine sometimes lit a cigarette in the hall after lights out and slipped back into the room to flip it under Lang's bunk. He knew Lang would blame Moran. Lang soon realized Augustine was the culprit but never managed to catch him in the act. He began climbing out of bed when he smelled a burning cigarette and quietly stubbing it out. Each time he did so he had a dismal sense of failure as a commander.

The summer was the busiest period of Lang's life, busier even than his most active days in P.G. 203, filled with the duties of command, following a war on two fronts, listening to the news on the speaker and reading it in the newspapers, shaping up his roommates, looking after his enlisted men, keeping his uniforms neat, and trotting the perimeter and working out in the gym. He gave up reading for pleasure and fell asleep quickly at night when thoughts of the next day's duties did not intrude. He thought more often of the next day's duties than of home or girls and in his reveries before falling asleep he saw a map on which was clearly marked the most recent Russian and Anglo-American advances more often than he saw the tender outlines of Serena the Butterfly Girl waving her gauzy wings in a bath of colored lights.

He snatched time to write home only out of habit, sharing the belief of most of his fellow prisoners that the war might well be over before they reached home. Many of the men in the South Camp had, in fact, stopped writing.

Moran stopped writing home, but not out of assurance the war would be ending. He was too restless to write. His impatience mounted with each Allied success and neither the Russians nor the Anglo-Americans moved swiftly enough to satisfy him.

"God damn it," he said to Lang one night when he was too agitated to sleep and had invited him out into the hall to talk, "it was bad enough when they were dragging their ass but this is murder. It's like every day maybe it'll be over. But then it ain't and we got another day to get through."

"They're driving on both fronts," Lang said soothingly. "Maybe it won't be but another couple months."

"Another couple months!" Moran said. "I don't think I can take another couple days of this."

But he was not always so agitated and sometimes he would walk the perimeter with Lang talking seriously of the future. He intended getting out of the service at the earliest opportunity and returning to Los Angeles to sell cars. He wanted Lang to go with him.

"With what you and me'll have coming in back pay we

can go in business for ourselves," he said. "Everybody's gonna be wild for a car and my old man's got the connections to get 'em. We'll clean up."

Lang was flattered by the offer but evaded committing himself. He intended being Moran's friend forever but he was not ready to make a decision about the future. He would not decide what to do until he was out of the bag. There were too many choices outside the wire for a man to commit himself to any one of them before he was used to being free again. He might want to make a career of the Army Air Force, or homestead in Alaska, or buy five acres and live off them as he had read in a book in the library, or get his master's degree at Oxford or the Sorbonne, or just travel around for a while, meeting girls. Because now, of course, he would know what to do with them. He was not fat and shy any more and looked good in a uniform. Especially since he had grown the mustache.

It was Sergeant Tomlove's opinion as much as anything which made him consider a military career.

"Lieutenant," Tomlove said one day when they were sitting over coffee as Lang had once sat over tea with Gorsely, "you're regular, ain't you?"

"No," Lang said. "Reserve."

"Then you must of taken the ROTC."

"No, I went into the cadets right out of civilian."

"I could of swore you had more military than that. I guess some are natural officers and some ain't."

Lang was flattered by Tomlove's praise as he had been by Colonel Ozmozius's. At both preflight and advanced navigation school he had been considered notoriously poor officer material.

He was somewhat less naïve now than he had been with Gorsely but felt that Tomlove had grounds on which to base his judgment. A good officer took care of his enlisted men and Lang had been doing that. When Tomlove complained enlisted men's letters and parcels did not come as promptly as officers',

298

he had gone to the SAO about it and Oberst Bruckmann himself had ordered an investigation. He saw they got good seats at the theater and had a regular turn with the record player. The enlisted men were always short of cigarettes and when Lang visited them he passed around a pack. When he received a tobacco parcel containing Webster cigars he gave Tomlove five and his men one each.

It was Tomlove's first cigar in captivity. For this and other favors Tomlove sometimes reciprocated by giving Lang a slice of cake baked illicitly in the kitchen despite the supervision of a German noncommissioned officer. Lang would have liked to share with Moran but Tomlove asked him to eat it in the enlisted men's quarters.

"And brush the crumbs off your shirt before you leave, Lieutenant," he said. "What goes on in the kitchen behind the Goons' backs ain't nobody's business but yours."

Summer ended.

The days continued warm but the nights cooled and smelled of autumn. Day and night clouds of ducks and geese flew south over the camp in wavering vees. Their cries filled the prisoners with restless longings. The Allies advanced on the Western front but not with the dramatic lunges of early summer and there was growing concern the war would last another winter. Prisoners stopped gathering around the cookhouse speaker for the communiqué and began writing home again.

The prospect of another winter in Stalag Luft 9 dismayed Lang but did not appall him. He would have his studies, his exercises and his enlisted men, who would need him more than ever. Moran was not so complacent. His moods were keyed directly to Allied successes and he became morose again with the slackening of the advance on the Western front. He resented Lang's optimism and took a perverse, savage joy in indications the war was going less well than everyone had predicted. A letter from his father distracted him briefly from his preoccupation with the progress of the war.

"What kind of name is Opal?" he demanded.

"What?" said Lang.

"My old man's going with some babe named Opal."

"So what?"

"Don't that sound like some cheap kid to you?"

"No," Lang said.

They'd had a twice a week maid once named Opal. Over forty, dour and very black. Sometimes when his mother was away all afternoon Opal would bake herself a cake on the sly to take home to her family. She baked a little one for him not to tell. Just the way Sergeant Tomlove did. Lang grinned.

"What the hell you grinning about?" Moran demanded. "This is serious. With all the young guys gone, the babes are probably after the old guys."

"You jealous? Just because you're in the bag don't mean he ought to crawl off in a hole somewhere."

"That ain't it at all. She's got to be playing him for a sucker. He makes damn good money."

"It's his money, not yours."

"He sounds sweet on her, for Christ's sake. He always was a sucker for women, ever since my mother died. If it wasn't for the babes he'd be in the chips now, with his own lot instead of working for somebody else. But at least he always knew it was his money they were after. The way he talks now, he's serious about this Opal."

"You want him to stay single the rest of his life?"

"I just don't want no little tramp young enough to be his daughter making a sucker out of him. He's damn near fifty years old."

"How you know she's a tramp just because her name's Opal? And isn't he old enough to take care of himself?"

Moran snorted.

"You don't know my old man where the babes are concerned," he said. "Who you think I take after?"

Moran sat down and wrote his father for the first time in weeks, asking for a picture of Opal.

300

"But I can already tell what she looks like," he told Lang darkly. "I know how his mind runs."

The RAF and the United States Army Air Force lashed at Germany with continued fury and the relationship between the prisoners and their captors grew ever more strained. Sergeant Froehlich, unexpectedly, seemed unmoved. He sometimes listened to the communiqué with the translators and hinted confidently at secret weapons and dramatic changes in the tides of war. Lang and his friends scoffed at Froehlich and were not swayed from their optimism even when reports came of the V-1 and V-2 *Vergeltungswaffen*, the retaliation weapons of which he had hinted. They saw a V-1 occasionally, stubby-winged shapes mounted piggyback on bombers flying over the camp.

Once a strange aircraft without a propeller flew over the camp, roaring and whistling, but they ridiculed Froehlich's boasts that such a plane would soon drive the B-17 from the skies.

"Maybe he knows something," Moran said when Lang told him of Froehlich's latest prediction. "The way we keep sitting on our butts no telling what the Goons will come up with."

"Germany's whipped," Lang said. "It's just a matter of time."

"I wish somebody'd tell the Goons that. They sure as hell don't act like they know it."

"How come you always believe the bad news instead of the good news?" Lang demanded, exasperated.

The air war disrupted communications and cut the flow of Red Cross supplies. Stalag Luft 9 went on half parcels. Moran was bitterly triumphant.

"What did I tell you?" he said. "I knew things would get worse instead of better."

"You're looking at it the wrong way," Lang protested. "It shows how much the Goons are hurting for transport."

301

"My aching back," Moran groaned helplessly. "We go on starvation rations and he thinks it's great."

Things would be more difficult, Lang knew, but they would not starve. They had not starved on half parcels in Italy and in Italy there had been no potatoes. Hartman, Augustine and Crumbacker, who had never been on half parcels, shared Moran's concern. The usually taciturn Jackson was amused by their distress.

"They won't let us starve to death," he said gravely. "Look at all the guards it would throw out of work."

The days turned colder. They were always hungry but no one actually suffered though Hartman maintained the limited diet made his hair brittle and wrote home for vitamin pills. The birches among the pines flamed with color. In the mornings, after rains, the puddles would be edged with ice. Hartman and Augustine demanded they be allowed to resign in the midst of their two-week duty as cook and stooge.

"All you guys do is bitch about my cooking," Hartman said. "Let's see one of you do any better on half parcels."

"You just want more time for your hair," Lang said.

Hartman thought he detected signs of impending baldness and had begun spending an hour or more daily kneading his scalp and vigorously brushing his lustrous hair.

"You should have seen what Steve did on half parcels in Italy," Moran said. "And we didn't even have our own stove."

"If he's so great why doesn't he cook?" said Augustine.

"With everything he's got to do?" Crumbacker said loyally.

"You mean the enlisted men?" Augustine demanded. "All he does is go in there and drink real coffee."

Real coffee was that brewed from the ground bean instead of soluble powder and hot water.

"You're just jealous of Tex," said Crumbacker.

"Okay, I'll cook," Lang said, ending the argument. "Who wants to stooge for me?"

302

It was true he had many responsibilities but in times of need a commander had to take over. And he had no doubt he could do better than any of the others.

"I will," Crumbacker said.

"No, thanks," said Lang.

At Lang's insistence Crumbacker had become neater but he was still casual about washing his hands and his shirt was often flecked with dandruff.

"I've got nothing better to do," Jackson said. "And I'm an expert."

"Thanks," Lang said.

He had hoped Moran would volunteer. In his impatience Moran often ruined bread at the slicer and cut potato peelings too thick but Lang thought stooge duties might help take his mind off the war.

Jackson was indeed expert at all household chores.

"I was the oldest of five kids," he said. "All boys."

Lang was glad Moran had not volunteered.

He took his duties as room cook as seriously as he did his camp jobs. He stretched the parcel food with millet, barley, kohlrabi and turnips from the German issue and invented variations on the dishes which could be prepared from his limited ingredients. He divided the portions with scrupulous accuracy. Firm foods like salmon loaf, which could be sliced, he measured with a ruler. Soft foods like mashed potatoes he measured by spoonfuls. He did not take the cook's prerogative of licking the dessert bowl and instead let his roommates share the privilege by roster.

"Maybe we could open a café," said Jackson, who had become less reserved with Lang after working with him. "How are you on Texas fried chicken?"

Even Augustine could find no fault with the way Lang was managing the rations.

CHAPTER 19

The first snow of late fall plunged Moran into the blackest mood Lang had seen since the German seizure of P.G. 203.

"I told you we'd spend another winter here," he said bitterly. "We ain't ever gonna get out of the bag."

The thought of his father being in the clutches of a young harpy preyed on his mind, too, until he received a letter with a picture of Opal. She was a comfortably middle-aged woman with a sweet face and Lang was grateful there was at least one thing which would no longer trouble Moran.

"I told you not to worry about it," he said.

Moran scowled.

"Look at her," he said, flicking the picture disdainfully with his finger. "Some old bag looking for a meal ticket."

"She looks real nice to me," Lang said.

"It ain't your old man she's after. I'll bet she's got a houseful of kids. Anyway, she's too old for my old man."

"Oh, my back!" Lang cried. "First she was too young and now she's too old. What the hell do you want?"

Ten days before Christmas, when the German counteroffensive smashed deep into Belgium, most of Stalag Luft 9 shared Moran's pessimism though few shared his perverse pride in vindicated judgment.

"See," he said triumphantly to Lang, "I told you we weren't ever gonna get out of here."

"It's going to shorten the war," Lang answered, unperturbed. "The Goons have finally come out of their holes where we can clobber 'em."

Moran was so enraged by Lang's calm optimism he did not speak to him the remainder of the day. He apologized for it that night but still insisted Lang was being unrealistic.

Despite the snow and freezing temperatures, prisoners began gathering at the cookhouse speaker again to follow the war news. Colonel Ozmozius, anticipating a breakdown in transportation, ordered every man in the South Camp to save an emergency ration of chocolate bars and ration biscuits.

Though Lang and his roommates normally retained their Red Cross chocolate bars for personal use they had pooled some of them for desserts during the days of comparative plenty and under Lang's management still had several in the room larder. Hartman wanted to share them out to help meet Colonel Ozmozius's minimums. Lang refused.

"How do you expect us to save anything out of the little bit we get now?" Hartman demanded. "It's easy for you. You've already got some saved up."

"You could have saved, too," Lang said, "instead of always bashing your D bar as soon as you got it. I'm not the only one with chocolate. Moran's got some, too."

He knew Augustine also had a hoard but could not bring himself to cite Augustine as an example.

"That chocolate in the larder belongs to the whole room and we're not going to divide it with guys who've been bashing while the others been saving," he continued.

Jackson looked uncomfortable.

"I wasn't in the room when you guys saved it," he said. "If you divide it up I don't expect any."

Lang realized Jackson thought this was what had influenced his decision.

"That's got nothing to do with it," he said. "We divide up, some of the guys will bash it right away and still won't have their emergency ration."

"I think we ought to divide them up," Augustine said suddenly.

Lang knew Augustine was doing it merely to oppose him. Augustine had the smallest appetite in the room.

"Who asked you?" Lang said.

"Let's take a vote," said Augustine.

"No," Lang replied.

"You afraid to?"

"Steve's right," Moran said.

"You keep out of this, Moran!" Lang said angrily, surprising himself as much as his roommates.

But he did not need Moran's help and Moran had no right to interfere. He was room commander, not Moran, and could handle it without anybody's help.

"You just like to throw your weight around," Augustine said.

"I'm not throwing any weight around," Lang replied, furious.

"You think you're such a wheel," Augustine said. "Always telling everybody what to do and blowing off about the war and acting like such a big shot."

"You look here, you long-nosed son of a bitch!" Lang cried, taking a step toward Augustine.

Augustine flinched, then defiantly stood his ground. Lang sensed the tension and embarrassment flooding the room. This is not the way a commander should act, he told himself. He should not lose his temper and he should not have to threaten to command obedience. He waited until he regained control of himself before continuing.

"I'm flight leader of this room and I've got a job to do," he said quietly. "If parcels get cut off completely we're going to need every drop of food in the larder so every man has got to save his own emergency ration. You can argue all you want but that's how it is. And no vote. You get out of the service you can vote. But not in here. In here you just take orders. I take 'em, too, just like everybody else."

"Hear, hear," said Jackson.

Augustine looked chastened.

But later Lang wondered if he had been so adamant because he had to be or because he liked throwing his weight around, as Augustine said. He asked Moran's opinion at the first opportunity. The others were out of the room and Moran was idly watching him grate a D bar for gedoing pudding.

"Do I act the way Augustine said?" Lang asked hesitantly. "Like I think I'm such a big shot?"

"You are a big shot," Moran said uncomfortably.

"That's not what I asked you. Do you think I act like one?"

"You don't exactly sell yourself short," Moran said after a moment's hesitation.

"You do think so, don't you?" Lang demanded, hurt.

He felt his underlip creeping out. He tried to hold it in, but too late. He knew he looked petulant.

"Okay," he said. "I'll quit acting like a big shot. And next time somebody wants the communiqué translated or something they can just ask somebody else."

"Jesus Christ, Steve," Moran said, "you're acting like a child. You know your trouble? You're always trying to prove something."

307

"Like what?" Lang said.

"Forget it," said Moran.

He refused to discuss the matter further. Lang wondered what he meant. Lang fell asleep that night wondering.

By the end of the month, when the Battle of the Bulge ended in a German defeat, Moran grudgingly acknowledged Lang had been right about the fate of the enemy counteroffensive but continued to be no less pessimistic about an early end to the war. Even when the Russian Army began smashing across Poland toward Upper Silesia and Stalag Luft 9 he refused to share the mounting excitement of the South Camp.

"We'll be gone by the time they get here," he said. "The Goons'll move us if they get close."

Everyone except Lang laughed at Moran's gloomy prediction.

Lang did not think the Germans had the will or the means to move them but he did not contradict Moran. The memory of Italy lingered.

The Russians drew closer. Every day planes flew low over the camp from the East in a curious variety; little Fieseller Storch observation planes, the clumsy six-engine Messerschmitt Gigant, almost everything in between them in the inventory of the Luftwaffe and Wehrmacht. The stream of planes continued at night and Lang and Moran lay awake in fear lest they be Russians hunting targets.

The crowd around the cookhouse speaker grew into hundreds. Froehlich stayed away except when duty demanded his presence and the Poles among the ferrets began trying to make friends. Colonel Ozmozius's request for slit trenches was denied but a number of roofs were marked with white crosses. Moran said they would make fine aiming points for Russian bombardiers. Prisoners marked the backs of their jackets and greatcoats with hand-drawn American flags and Colonel Ozmozius circulated copies of the Russian words for United States to be lettered beneath them. He instructed block commanders not to discount the possibility the camp would be evacuated ahead of the Russian advance and to have their men ready to move out without notice.

Most of the prisoners refused to take the instructions seriously. The optimism and excitement sweeping the camp exceeded that of the first days of the invasion. Everyone stopped writing home again and in every block there were betting pools to pick the exact time of the Russians' arrival.

Lang was as optimistic and excited as anyone but the specter of Italy continued to haunt him. When other rooms began devouring their emergency rations and food saved during the summer he would not permit his roommates to do the same and instead stopped the traditional Sunday breakfast of oatmeal.

"It's easy to carry," he said curtly when Hartman and Augustine protested.

Augustine did not ask for a vote.

Lang tried without success to trade for knapsacks and canteens as he had in Italy. He improvised a knapsack from a khaki shirt, sewing it across the bottom and stitching the cuffs to the sides to make straps. He made carrying bags from the legs of his summer trousers. When he instructed the others to do the same, Hartman and Augustine objected, as usual. Instead of commanding compliance, he tried persuasion.

"Even if the Russians liberate us we'll still be moving out," he said. "You'll have something to carry your stuff in."

"What's to carry?" Hartman said blithely.

Augustine made a knapsack and bags from Lang's design but grudgingly and surreptitiously.

Jackson had no summer uniform and Lang found khaki pants and trousers for him to work with. Moran botched his carrying gear, being too impatient to sew properly, and Lang redid the work for him.

After a struggle with his conscience, Lang broke a camp rule by trading with a ferret for a handful of nails and built a sled of bedboards. They had been saving the bedboards for kindling after slinging their mattresses with rope salvaged

309

from the bindings of Red Cross parcels. He put tin strips on the runners.

"You going to play in the snow?" Augustine asked, grinning. "We'll build you a little hill to coast down."

"I'll slide down that long nose you're always sticking in my business," Lang said grimly.

He almost wished they would be moved out ahead of the Russians just to wipe the complacent amusement from Augustine's face.

When the Russians drew less than a hundred kilometers from Stalag Luft 9 Oberst Bruckmann discontinued the daily broadcast of the German communiqué. Though rumors proliferated, sweeping the camp within minutes after they began, Colonel Ozmozius began withholding details of the BBC communiqué on the compound's clandestine radio. He did not trust the reliability of the reports from the Russian front and feared the prisoners, sensing imminent liberation, might react rashly and prematurely. Nevertheless, when the Russians established a bridgehead over the Bober River within forty kilometers of the camp, the news spread quickly, brought in by a guard.

Now the prisoners became wildly happy and insolent to their guards, as Colonel Ozmozius had anticipated. The Germans, however, swallowed their resentment.

Lang and his roommates were awakened one night by the distant roll of artillery and Crumbacker cried out, "They're here!"

Everyone tumbled out of bed and ran to the window. They could see nothing out of the ordinary.

"You damn fool!" Moran said angrily, "they could be fifty miles away. Don't you know how sound travels at night?"

Soon they were hearing explosions by day as well as by night, though they never saw a Russian plane or heard small-arms fire, and Lang's roommates wanted to celebrate by feasting. Lang was adamant.

"If we stick to our regular ration we've got enough for

maybe two, three weeks. Four or five days if we bash. What if the drive stalls and we don't get any parcels?"

"You're always going out of your way looking for things to worry about," Hartman said.

"You'll be glad he did when they move your butt out of here," Moran said.

"How could they?" Hartman demanded. "They haven't got the transportation to pull out their own troops, much less a bunch of kriegies."

"That's what we thought in Italy," Moran said. "You're wearing all the transportation the Goons'll need if they want to move you out."

"Bernie's right," Lang said. "I don't want you guys getting in a flap but we could be walking out of here."

"You can walk if you want to," said Augustine. "Me, I'm riding in a Russian truck."

"I hope you do," Lang said. "I just hope you don't trip over that long nose of yours climbing onto it and break your neck."

"Why are you always making fun of my nose?" Augustine demanded angrily.

Lang looked at him coldly. It was a look he had been practicing since he decided a commander should not lose his temper with a subordinate.

"Because it looks like it was just put there to be busted," he said.

Everyone except Augustine laughed and there was no further opposition to husbanding the rations. Lang was pleased.

The roll of artillery came appreciably closer but there still was no sound of small-arms fire. There were frequent explosions in the near distance and billows of smoke beyond the surrounding forest but the excitement caused by this dwindled quickly when the guards said they were demolitions to hinder the Russian advance if they broke out of the Bober bridgehead.

It was the last week in January. It had snowed intermittently during the day but had stopped now. Lang and his roommates sat around the table drinking a late brew in celebration of Crumbacker's twenty-third birthday. There was a fire in the stove and they had eaten a special treat of prunes boiled with Klim, made at dinnertime and cooled on a beam above the plywood ceiling under the roof. They spoke of liberation, when it would come and what would happen after, as Lang and Moran had once spoken at P.G. 203.

"Maybe they'll take us out through Russia," Hartman said. "I hear Russian women are as friendly as English women."

"The German papers say the Russians have women soldiers," Lang said. "Fighting right with the men."

"That's what's holding 'em up," Moran said. "They're humping each other instead of fighting the Goons. Hey, Wings, how'd you like to be liberated by a bunch of babes? Not that we're gonna be liberated," he added quickly, knocking on wood.

The lights went out.

"What the hell?" he said.

Everyone began talking at once.

"Shut up!" Lang cried. "Maybe it's an air raid."

They listened for the sound of sirens and engines. Men called to each other in the block. Someone shouted far across the camp and in the distance Russian artillery boomed monotonously. But there were no sirens, no ominous roar of aircraft.

The lights came on again.

"Power failure," Moran said, relieved.

There was movement outside the block now, shouts and feet crunching in the icy snow. Lang looked at his wristwatch.

"It's too early for the theater to be out," he said.

"Maybe somebody stole the trombone again," Moran said.

A concert had once been canceled when someone took the trombone to use the slide as a coil in distilling kriegie brew.

312

There was yelling in the front rooms. Footsteps thudded in the hall. The door flew open and the block commander's agitated face appeared in the opening.

"We're moving out!" he cried in a high-pitched voice. "Everybody load up and stand by to fall out when the whistle blows."

The door slammed shut before Lang recovered presence of mind to ask for details. No one spoke. They could only stare at each other in stunned silence. There was a puddle of coffee by Hartman's hand where he had jarred his mug at the block commander's announcement. Hartman dabbled at it with a dirty handkerchief, biting his lip. Lang started to protest. Hartman was wiping the table they ate from with a handkerchief he'd used to blow his nose. But they would not be eating from the table any more. There was a faint smile on Moran's lips, humorless and vindictive. Crumbacker's eyes were round and staring.

Then they were all on their feet, their voices loud. The block vibrated with blind movement as everyone in other rooms did the same. Panic held Lang fast, like the coils of a great snake. He could not think or act, now or ever again.

"Tex!" Crumbacker cried, close to hysteria. "What do we do?"

The great snake eased its coils. He was in command here, Lang told himself. Though he had never really believed they would be moved he had prepared for it and tried to prepare his men. Now, except for Moran, they were running around like chickens with their heads cut off. He had seen them, chickens with their heads cut off. Opal, the twice a week maid, did it in the back yard under the fig tree with a Boy Scout hatchet. They staggered jerkily, wings flapping, and their blood glistened in the Bermuda grass like dew. The image gave him needed detachment.

"Simmer down!" he ordered, his voice controlled.

They continued shouting and pawing at their belongings.

"I said simmer down!" he shouted.

The authority in his voice reached them. They gathered around him, white-faced and eager to be led.

"No use getting in a flap," Lang said, keeping his voice normal with great effort. "They're not going to leave without us."

"You can bet your happy ass on that," Moran said.

No one moved. They were waiting to be told what to do and expecting Lang to tell them. Lang felt confidence growing in him.

"That's better," he said. "Okay. First of all, lay everything out on your sack. Hold out what you're going to wear and pack everything else. Make bedrolls with your blankets. Bernie, you pass out the rope. Wear everything you can. It's easier to wear it than carry it. And it's gonna be cold out there. Don't take anything you can't eat or wear."

"Or smoke," said Moran.

"Right," Lang said.

Cigarettes were like money wherever they might be going.

Crumbacker and Hartman began scrambling among their possessions, strewing their bunks and the floor around them. Augustine stood by his bunk looking with bewildered eyes at a shirt dangling from his hand as if he did not know how it came there or what to do with it. Lang touched his shoulder.

"Snap out of it, Augustine," Lang said.

Augustine nodded and began packing. Lang went to Crumbacker, who was cramming everything within reach into a pantleg bag.

"Not your sweater, damn it!" he said. "Wear that. Just your extra clothes and emergency rations. Wings, why aren't you packing?"

"I didn't make a bag," Hartman said apologetically.

"I'll give you one of mine," Lang said. "Next time listen to what I tell you."

When everyone was usefully employed Lang began his own packing. It was quickly done. His emergency rations were already stowed in a pants leg and he had only to go through his clothing. He put his notebooks and letters with his emergency rations. They weighed little and he could throw them away on the road if they became burdensome. He pulled on three pairs of socks, two pairs of pants, two shirts, a turtleneck sweater his mother had knit for him and his British battle dress jacket. On his bunk he laid out leather-palmed GI gloves, knit mittens and scarf from home and a British Army overseas cap, the sides of which could be let down to form earflaps. He made a bedroll of his best blankets, putting his pantleg bag and towel inside and tying it neatly with the Red Cross rope Moran had distributed. He lay the bedroll on his bunk with the shirt knapsack and the outer garments he intended donning later. Hartman and Crumbacker were still fumbling with bedrolls.

"Bernie," Lang said, "how about you and Jackson clearing out the larder and stowing everything on the sled? I got to help these guys."

"Roger," said Jackson.

"You talk like a flier," said Moran. "Were you in the war?"

Lang showed Crumbacker and Hartman how to roll and tie their blanket rolls. Everyone was packed now. Men were still cursing, yelling and scrambling in other rooms. Lang was pleased with his men.

"How about this open can of Klim?" Moran asked.

"I'll make some milk," Lang said.

They were all hot and thirsty. It would help.

He brought a pitcher of water from the kitchen and began mixing it with milk powder. Suddenly he was filled with shame. He had forgotten all about his enlisted men. A good officer always took care of his enlisted men before himself.

"Stir this, will you, Wings?" he said. "I got to run next door a minute."

315

Sergeant Tomlove and his men were packed and patiently waiting. They had two sleds, both of them larger and more expertly made than Lang's, the loads piled high and lashed down snugly under blankets. A huge pot of coffee steamed on the stove and they sat around the table drinking it with slices of bread thickly covered with jam. Sergeant Tomlove was not eating. He sat calmly, his jaws working. He was chewing Brown's Mule. The plug of tobacco had come in a personal parcel and he kept it for special occasions. For the first time he did not call attention when Lang came into the room.

"You guys okay?" Lang asked, his voice trailing away when he realized how needless it was to ask.

"Fine, Lieutenant," Tomlove said conversationally. "Just fine. I was wondering. We're used to walking but how you think you flyboys gonna make out?"

"Okay, I hope," Lang said candidly. "You all set for emergency rations? I got a little extra."

Tomlove's eyes strayed to the loaded sleds.

"I expect we can make out," he said. "But I thank you. How about a cup of coffee? Plenty on the fire."

"I better get back to my room," Lang said. "Some of 'em are pretty nervous."

"Wouldn't be a bit surprised," Tomlove said. "Take the coffeepot with you. We had ours."

"I couldn't do that, Sarge," Lang protested.

"Just go to waste."

"Well, thanks, then."

Someone handed Lang the pot and Tomlove walked to the door with him. He patted Lang on the back. It was the first time he had ever touched Lang except to shake hands.

"I ain't worried none about you, Lieutenant," he said. "You'll do. But if you need some help with your flyboy friends on the road, look me up."

Lang was both chastened and flattered.

He took the coffee back to the room and mixed it with the milk, stirring in sugar.

316

"Everybody drink up," he said. "Give you energy."

Everyone had trouble getting it down. Their stomachs were knotted with tension. Hartman retched after a few swallows.

"Take it easy," Lang cautioned. "Everybody take it easy."

Easy to say, he thought. Harder to do. And suddenly he was as calm as he had ever been in his life. The packs were filled, the bedrolls made, the sled loaded. They were as ready as they would ever be. He made a last check of the room and his roommates. The floor was strewn with papers, bits of clothing. Crumbacker was bareheaded.

"Where's your ditty cap, Crumb?" he asked. "You want to freeze your ears off?"

"I don't know," Crumbacker said helplessly. "I must of lost it."

Lang found it for him in the litter on the floor and put it on his head.

Calmed by his quiet efficiency, the others put on gloves, scarves, balaclavas and greatcoats and sat down to wait. Outside voices called, shrill against the distant rumble of cannon. It was hot in the room. Lang wanted to open the windows but the lights were on and the guards fired into rooms if the blackout shutters were opened.

The whistle blew.

Everyone rose.

Feet scraped in the hall. Doors slammed. Lang looked quizzically at Moran.

"Here we go again, Bernie," he said.

⛓⛓⛓⛓⛓⛓⛓ *CHAPTER 20*

There was no glimmer in the night sky. Somehow, he did not know why, Lang had hoped for stars. He stood between Moran and Jackson as they waited in front of the block to be counted. The prisoners, muffled to the eyes, bulky with layers of clothing, spoke in whispers or not at all. Their shoes squeaked on the crusty snow like mice trampled underfoot. Some of the other rooms had sleds, one of them merely a bench turned seat down with bedboards nailed on the sides for runners. Some men had shirt packs like Lang's, some flimsy German suitcases or fiber capture kit boxes. Lang had advised Jackson to leave his capture kit behind. A knapsack was less awkward for a man on foot. No one was better prepared for the march than his men, Lang thought.

318

After the count they moved toward the gate, joined by other blocks, rivers of men with faces hidden against the cold, swollen in greatcoats over jackets, sweaters, extra shirts, burdened with knapsacks, bedrolls, summer trousers stuffed with clothing, suitcases, cloth bags, dragging sleds, urged on by nervous guards, most of them as heavily laden as the prisoners under field packs, weapons and extra ammunition. At the gate Colonel Ozmozius called for quiet, his voice robust and undismayed in the frosty air.

"Men," he cried, "I don't know where we're going yet but as soon as I do I'll let you know. Stay together and take it slow and easy. And remember this. The Germans have to march as far as we do. Let's walk 'em into the ground."

There was a spattering of applause, a self-conscious cry of "Hear, hear." They moved through the gate, flanked by guards. Outside the Vorlager they were counted again on a snowy road, standing in columns of five, shuffling in place against the cold. They waited. The cold pressed in more insistently. The prisoners grew restless, muttering complaints.

"Ain't we got no numbers they like?" Moran said jovially when they were counted a second time.

Something in him seemed to have loosened and the morose bitterness of past months had vanished.

"They've got to balance the books," Lang said. "If they can't balance the books they got to call the whole thing off."

"They won't get me back in there," Moran said. "Not the shape we left it in."

"How can you guys joke?" Hartman demanded. "My feet are hurting already."

Far up the road, a thousand men away, a voice cried, "Vorwaerts!" The cry came back on the lips of guards spaced along the column in the heavier snow on either side of the road. There was a great stirring and heaving, boots slithered and squeaked, and they were moving at last.

Lang felt a kind of intoxication. Tension, doubt, apprehension fell away. He was outside of Stalag Luft 9 at last, outside forever, not free but with freedom sounding at his heels in a thunder of cannon. Immobility and routine had given way to movement, flux, change. He did not know where he was going but he was going. And this was not exactly real. It was like a moving picture in which he had a leading role.

A similar intoxication swept the long column as if the mere act of moving had ended a drugged slumber. Loud excited voices and bursts of laughter rose above the creak and slither. Lang, at the right of his rank of five, and Moran, next to him, pulled the sled together. Jackson was next to Moran and next to him Augustine and Crumbacker. Hartman was behind Lang. To Lang's right, wading in the soft, deep snow, a small German soldier labored under a huge pack, a heavy metal ammunition canister in his hand, his rifle slung and dangling down his back. He had a long nose. Like Augustine's, Lang thought.

As he walked, Lang looked about him at the unfamiliar spectacle of open country. There was little to see but the night and the backs of the men in front. Snow gleamed faintly close at hand, feathering into darkness a few paces beyond the road. Snowflakes materialized out of the blackness overhead and brushed his cheek.

"That's all we need," Hartman said behind him. "More snow."

The laughter and the loud talk died away. Snow clung to eyebrows and dusted greatcoats. Lang's head came down. It was easier marching that way. He walked steadily, his eyes on trampled snow, bootheels, crusted trouser cuffs. He looked around regularly to check his men and the German soldier. It amused him to see the guard floundering in the snow.

The pace of the column was even and brisk the first minutes, settling later into plodding monotony. Lang's group was well back and they stumbled over the trodden snow. The sled bumped clumsily over ruts. At the first halt, an hour from the camp, they smoked and chatted. The guard sat down heavily in the snow, leaning against his pack, the ammunition can-

320

ister in his lap like an infant. The end of his nose was white. "Watch that guy, Bernie," Lang said, remembering the night in the depot office outside P.G. 203. "I think he's going to make a break for it."

"I got my eye on him," Moran said. "Don't worry."

They moved on. Lang passed the sled to Jackson and Augustine. It was easier walking now. The soldier's back was bending under the weight of his huge pack. His long nose edged toward the snow. He shifted the ammunition canister from hand to hand with increasing frequency. After a while he looked around furtively and threw it into a snowdrift. He saw Lang watching and smiled apologetically.

"You're going to miss that if the Russians catch up with us," Lang said in English.

The guard stared at him, breathing heavily. He's old, Lang thought, forty or more. It's not right for an old guy like that to be out in the snow on a night like this. He should be back in the barracks, or home with his kids. Lang wondered if the guards were sore about having to walk all night with a mob of Luftgangsters instead of being cozy in the *Kaserne. Kaserne.* Barracks. He'd learned that word in Italy, sitting on the steps at P.G. 203 in the soft night listening to "Lili Marlene." He was a long way from P.G. 203 and soft nights now. But there would be soft nights again. He hummed softly to himself.

"Vor der Kaserne, vor dem grossen Tor."

She waited under the lamppost outside the barracks and the big gate. But the young sentry was far away.

The soldier was bent almost double now, his nose inches from the snow. His pack, indistinguishable from his greatcoat in its blanket of white, was like a hump. Lang nudged Moran. Only Moran's eyes showed, dark beneath brows whitened with snowflakes. Yet Lang knew Moran was grinning.

"Why don't you give him a hand?" Lang said.

"We've done enough for him already," said Moran. "If it wasn't for us he'd be back there fighting Russians."

They rested ten minutes every hour. They no longer stood smoking and chatting but dropped to the ground keeping their packs on to avoid having to struggle into them again. Lang and his roommates sat back to back in two rows of three supporting one another, their legs stretched out. At one stop Jackson sat between Lang and Moran.

"Hey, Jackson," Lang said. "Where'd you get the name Riley?"

"You'll laugh," said Jackson.

"No, I won't," Lang promised.

"It's James Whitcomb Riley," Jackson said.

Lang laughed.

"I knew you would," said Jackson.

Discarded food, clothing, even cigarettes littered the line of march. When they could do so without breaking stride, Lang, Moran and Jackson bent to pick up canned goods and cigarettes, stuffing them into their greatcoats until there was a halt and putting them under the blankets on the sled.

They moved along empty back roads between white fields and snow-laden clumps of trees. Once a huge owl flew out of a tree in a shower of loosened snow and swooped low over the column. A man stumbled and fell in panic and others fell over him. When the pile untangled itself the back of the column scrambled to catch up with the front.

Word came back that Colonel Ozmozius had refused to ride in a staff car and was marching at the head of the column. It cheered the prisoners briefly. At stops there were rumors of lightning thrusts by Russian spearheads cutting off the evacuation route but few believed them.

Motorcycles with guards in sidecars patrolled the line of march. When they passed, the prisoners would stand aside to make room, staring at them dumbly and welcoming the brief respite from walking. Moran held out his thumb once, as if he were hitchhiking, and only Lang smiled.

There was no laughter now, and no conversation, only

heavy breathing, the creak of wood and shoulder straps, the crunch of feet on trampled snow.

Lang and his roommates passed the sled from hand to hand at every stop but it grew heavier by the hour with the added food and diminishing strength of the men dragging it.

The night stretched on interminably. Lang wondered if anyone, even the Germans, knew where they were going or if they were only walking aimlessly and would continue to do so until they could walk no farther. Sometimes he stumbled against Moran or Moran stumbled against him, or Hartman bumped him from behind. They had long since stopped muttering apologies. Except for such contacts Lang felt alone.

A half-hour rest was announced. The prisoners sprawled where they stood. Lang and his roommates slipped out of their packs and sat with their backs against the sled. A horse-drawn wagon creaked along the column and German soldiers handed down lumps of bread and margarine. Lang's group struggled to their feet to receive the ration. The margarine was frozen solid. Lang bit into his as if it were an apple, alternating with bites from the frigid chunk of bread. The margarine was tasteless until it thawed in his mouth. Then it was delicious.

Hartman munched a D bar.

"Don't do that," Lang said. "You'll need it later. Eat your bread and marge. Then you won't have to carry it."

Hartman put the chocolate away and began eating his German ration. Augustine was not eating anything. Lang knew he should urge him to eat but said nothing. Let the smart aleck look out for himself. Hartman began unlacing his shoes.

"What the hell you doing?" Lang demanded.

"My feet hurt."

"You take your shoes off you'll never get 'em back on," Lang said.

He dragged up a bedroll, propped Hartman's feet on it and wiped the crusted snow off his shoes with the sleeve of his greatcoat.

"Keep 'em off the ground for a while," he said.

Froehlich came by in a sidecar followed by a wagon. He shouted as he inched along the column.

"Those unable to continue may enter the wagon. All weaklings may ride. Had we known there were so many we would have arranged more wagons."

Three sheepish prisoners looked over the side of the wagon at their sprawling comrades.

Hartman and Crumbacker looked longingly at the wagon.

"Let's stick together as long as we can," Lang said. "Don't anybody drop out unless he has to."

"If you think I'm leaving my share of the groceries you're nuts," Crumbacker said with a touch of bravado.

"Aufstehen!" the guards cried. "Vorwaerts!"

The prisoners struggled to their feet, cursing and groaning, pulling on packs and bedrolls, leaving the snow strewn with abandoned possessions.

Dawn came. The ragged column plodded through a gray and white morning. Snow fell, swirling in an icy wind. Lang could taste the cold through the scarf covering his mouth. Cold tasted like wool. Ice crystals formed on the hairs in his nostrils when he breathed in, vanishing when he exhaled. He kept his eyes half closed against the wind-driven snow. When, at rare intervals, he lifted his head, he saw the same snowy fields, the same trees of previous hours. Maybe they were lost, he thought, and marching in circles. At any moment the pines and barbed wire of Stalag Luft 9 would loom out of the swirling snow. He thought of the room they had left, the fire in the stove, the snug sleeping bag he had made of his Italian blanket quilted with German newspapers, of taking his shoes off and massaging his cramped feet. He yearned for rest, warmth, pause. And yet he would rather be here, plodding over rutted snow in an icy wind, than back in the camp.

The little German had long since discarded his pack and he staggered through the heavy snow as if off balance, each breath a groan. Hartman was groaning, too, behind Lang, but with less urgency than the German.

Late in the morning they stopped at a huddle of farm buildings and word came back they would rest here. Faint cheers flickered along the column.

"It's about time," Hartman sighed. "I couldn't go another step."

I could have, Lang thought. I could have kept on going. He was surprised, and pleased, to discover he was not as tired as he had thought only minutes ago when the march appeared endless.

His section of the column was marched to a barn at the back of a farmyard. The line moved slowly as Froehlich counted the men creeping wearily through the door.

"These God damn Goons," Moran said. "Do they think anybody's gonna be crazy enough to take off in this friggin' snowstorm?"

Moran's eyes were bright, his voice strong. Throughout the march he had not complained of the weight of the sled. Lang wondered where he got the stamina. Moran had not tried to keep in shape in all the months at Stalag Luft 9 and yet of all their group, not excluding Lang himself, he seemed the least affected by the grueling march.

The line stopped moving.

"No more room below," Froehlich said.

Protests filled the air.

"You should be grateful merely to break the march," Froehlich said. "German soldiers march happily night and day."

Lang thought about the soldier who had floundered beside him.

"I notice you had your ass in that sidecar all night," Moran said.

"I advise you to watch your tongue," Froehlich said. "The war is not yet over."

Two old men smelling of manure brought a wooden

325

ladder and set it against the side of the barn under an opening. Prisoners pulled themselves up it painfully, groaning and complaining. It embarrassed Lang that they should do this in front of Froehlich.

"What did you guys expect?" Lang demanded. "Elevators?"

Hartman, Crumbacker and Augustine were too exhausted to climb the ladder with their knapsacks and Lang had them leave the packs with the sled. It took all his strength to climb the shaky ladder with his own possessions but when he put his pack and bedroll down he joined Moran at the entrance of the loft to assist the others. When Augustine saw him reaching down, Augustine jerked back his own outstretched hand and pulled himself up the last step unaided.

The floor of the loft was covered with deep straw. With the help of Moran and Jackson, Lang wedged out a space large enough for the six men in his group to stretch out. Under his direction they undid bedrolls and made a pallet. He was glad he had made them make bags to hold the things rolled in their blankets. On the trip from Italy everything got scattered when he opened his bedroll.

"Before you go to sleep take off your shoes and socks and rub your feet," he said. "We've got to keep 'em in shape."

Hartman groaned when he removed his shoes. His feet were red and swollen.

"I'll never get my shoes back on," he said.

Colonel Ozmozius's voice rang in the farmyard.

"There's hot water for anybody who wants it."

"Jesus," said Moran. "Could I use a cup of hot coffee."

"Those lucky bastards downstairs," Hartman said.

Lang looked into the faces of his roommates. On the march he had not been able to see them behind their masks of scarf and balaclava. The faces, except for Moran's, were lined and apathetic. They need something hot, he thought. He felt responsible for them. He was the flight leader.

"Come on, Bernie," he said. "Let's get some."

326

They climbed wearily down the ladder and joined a line stretching to a farmhouse door. Inside the kitchen enormous kettles were heating on a wood-burning stove tended by women who ladled the hot water into the prisoners' cups. The presence of the women tapped a hidden source of vitality in Moran.

"How do you offer a babe into the sack in Goon?" he asked Lang.

"They're foreign workers, not Germans," Lang said.

He had heard them talking together in a language he did not understand.

"I'll bet they know the Goon for sack," Moran said.

He smiled at one of the younger and less repellent women and said, "Bella ragatsa."

"My friend says you are very pretty," Lang said in German.

She looked away, then smiled at Moran, shyly coquettish.

"Ask her if she has a room of her own," Moran said.

"My friend asks if you have a bucket for the water," Lang said.

She nodded vigorous assent.

"Jesus," Moran said, "what do I do now? I'm so tired I couldn't even unbutton my fly."

"I asked her to lend us a bucket," Lang said.

Moran shoved him.

"Swinehoont," he said.

They inched up the ladder with the steaming bucket. Jackson went down to the sled for bread, margarine and jam while Lang assembled cups and made thick, heavily sugared cocoa. Their less enterprising neighbors watched enviously as they ate and drank. No one's appetite was affected by this watchful audience. Their enjoyment was, in fact, enhanced. It was good to function better than the next man, have more. I take good care of my men, Lang thought.

"Oh, this is great," Hartman said dreamily. "Isn't it, Phil?"

Augustine glanced briefly at Lang.

"It's okay," he said.

The bastard, Lang thought. He wished he didn't have to take care of Augustine with the others.

"Hey, Wings," Moran said. "You know I had something going with a farmer's daughter down there? I didn't know I still had it in me."

"You kidding?" Lang said, warm now, loose and drowsy. "Two days after you're dead they'll have to nail it down with a silver spike to keep it from poking out of the coffin."

There was hot water left and though his neighbors eyed it covetously Lang had his roommates dip their feet in it and dry them vigorously with spare clothing.

"God, that feels good," Hartman said, sighing luxuriously. "I think I'll live after all."

They lay close together on the pallet and pulled blankets over them. They were warm and snug, as in a nest, but deep sleep evaded all but Hartman, who snored. He had never snored in the room. Lang floated in easy warmth but when he was on the verge of drifting down into sleep vagrant thoughts and a residual tension pulled him back. When he dozed he saw trampled snow, boots, men's backs and thought he was on the road again. Awake, he could not curb his thoughts. Where were the Russians? How long the march? To where? The girl in the kitchen, was her smile for him or Moran? Could they hide here under the hay and wait for the Russians to come?

Of the six hours they spent in the barn he slept no more than two, and that in snatches.

They left the barn late in the afternoon to assemble on the road. Though they had slept badly, they were rested now and cheerful.

"Hey, Jackson," Moran said. "You all right?"

"Yeah. Why?"

"You look pale," Moran said gravely.

"You better get in the wagon next time it comes by," Jackson said, equally grave. "You've gone snow blind."

They were counted and, after a wait, counted again. It grew appreciably colder. A wind rose, piercing boots, greatcoats, mittens, scarves, knit caps. The prisoners lost their good humor. They stamped their numbing feet and cursed all Germans and were counted a third time. It was almost dark when they marched away at last, stiff with cold and inactivity and as tired as when they began their six-hour rest. German efficiency, Lang thought angrily. If he ever heard anybody brag about German efficiency again he was going to bust him in the mouth.

The cold deepened with the departing light. Darkness engulfed the column. It lost all cohesion, stringing out and bunching again erratically. Lang, like all around him, walked briskly at times and then, without being aware of it, would gradually diminish the pace until, with a start, he saw there were no longer boots and snowy legs ahead of him and hurry, painfully, to catch up.

The air grew colder, the night bleaker, the hours longer. The erratic pace was more fatiguing than the plodding monotony of the previous night. Falter, fall behind, stumble ahead to close the gap. Repeated endlessly. The sled a willful beast passed from hand to hand, balking at ruts, pulling back perversely on its rope.

Hartman could no longer take his turn pulling the sled. He walked with his eyes closed, his mouth open. Lang could not keep his own eyes open. It was not so much fatigue that pulled his lids down as it was the need, somehow, in any way at all, to break the monotony of plod and stumble, boots, backs, packed snow.

The road seemed slowly to be tilting, for each step was more difficult than the one before. Lang's steps became slower and shorter. Walking was as much effort of will as of joint and muscle. To lift a foot and place it ahead of the other took intense concentration.

Men blundered into each other, eyes closed. Hartman was groaning. Augustine fell to his knees and Jackson pulled him to his feet. Lang felt he should say something to encourage his men but words evaded him. He could form them in his mind but not on his lips.

Froehlich drove along the column in his sidecar at long intervals looking less composed each time, and older, exhorting the prisoners to close ranks. Those with enough energy cursed him and demanded to know when the march would end.

"Not far, not far," he shouted. "What are you made of, not to be able to make a little march?"

The cold was arid and parching. Lang's throat ached with it. He did not dare break stride to dip his hand into the snow but when he stumbled would reach down into drifts beside the road and fill his mouth. The melting snow dissolved to nothingness and did not slake his thirst. He wondered dully why. Snow was frozen water.

He dozed, walking. His knees, relaxed in sleep, buckled and he awakened falling. He caught himself at the last moment before plunging face down into the snow, thinking he was back in the nose of the *High Flying Flora* over the South Atlantic bound for Accra on the Gold Coast. They had taken off from Natal on the bulge of Brazil and he had been up all night shooting the stars. He dared not sit on his navigator's table because he would sleep and miss the hourly three-star fix, so he had remained standing throughout the long flight, falling asleep on his feet, startled to wakefulness when his knees buckled and he felt himself falling. But now he was not in the nose of a B-24 but in the grip of cold and darkness in a snowy ocean without guiding stars or destination, with nothing ahead but the next step.

Word came back along the column. The vanguard had entered a town. They would halt there for what was left of the night. Lang opened his eyes and lifted his head, quickening his stride and lengthening his pace with the others.

"If it's not the straight poop I'll lay right down and die," Hartman croaked.

Augustine stumbled forward blindly, as if he had not heard the news. He looked worse than Hartman, Lang thought, but had not once complained. Augustine had guts, he thought grudgingly. Lang did not hate Augustine any longer because nothing between them was important now. Soon they would stop walking and that was the only thing important. To stop walking and lie down in a warm place and sleep. Only that was important. To reach the town and stop walking.

To reach the town.

He could think of nothing else.

A sullen murmur pierced with angry cries swept back along the column. The vanguard had passed through the village without stopping. Lang and his companions stumbled between dark buildings, adding their curses to the swelling tide of anger and despair. The dirty bastards, Lang thought. Promising them rest and then not stopping. All he had cared about was reaching the town. Only thoughts of reaching it had kept him going. Now they had taken that away from him. He did not know how much longer he could stay on his feet. Maybe if they abandoned the sled . . .

"No!" he said aloud.

"What did you say?" Moran demanded.

"Nothing," said Lang.

Motorcycle patrols were rounding up men who had refused to walk farther or could not, shouting some of them back into the column, lifting others into crowded wagons.

"Maybe we ought to put Phil in a wagon," Moran said.

Augustine shook his head doggedly. His eyes were glazed beneath the snow-crusted bill of his ditty cap.

A cry came back from the front of the column.

"We're turning off!"

They left the main road for a lesser one, toward a smudge of buildings. The front ranks halted and those behind continued moving forward blindly and mechanically. The column telescoped to half its former length, crushing men together. They disentangled themselves, spiritlessly cursing each other and the Germans. Lang leaned gratefully against the man ahead of him before regaining his balance. The man grunted and twitched his shoulders but did not turn around.

Augustine suddenly pitched forward, bounced off the man in front of him and staggered off balance out of the column. Lang, not knowing where he got the will or the strength, reached out for him and propped Augustine's body on his hip, planting his feet wide to keep them both from toppling into the snow. Augustine bent forward, retching. Lang supported him with a hand under his forehead. He remembered all the times they had argued and he had ridiculed Augustine, how only hours before he had begrudged him the cocoa he drank, and was ashamed.

Moran supported Augustine on the other side and they held him until he finished vomiting. Only when he straightened, wiping his lips on the back of a snowy mitten, did Augustine see who it was had held his head.

"Lang," he murmured incredulously.

His surprise and disbelief were stronger than an insult. What a bastard he must think I am, Lang thought. And maybe I have been.

"Just hang on to me, Phil," he said. "We'll get you inside as soon as we can."

Augustine's lips moved. Lang had to bend to hear him.

"I'm sorry about the sled," Augustine whispered.

"What?" said Lang.

Augustine must be delirious.

"Made fun of the sled," Augustine said weakly.

With Moran's help he slipped off Augustine's pack. His own felt like a malignant growth, an intolerable burden but nevertheless part of his body. He knew if he took it off he would never be able to lift it again.

They moved toward a low building. Light streamed from its open door with infinite promise. The door was

332

blocked with groaning, cursing, whining men pressing without strength against a wall of backs. Lang, still supporting Augustine, was pinned against them by those behind. He welcomed the warmth and support of the packed bodies, fearing only that Augustine would be trampled underfoot if he released him.

He could hear Colonel Ozmozius shouting inside, his voice weary but brutal with authority.

"You men! Up and back! Off the floor. Up and back! Make room. Get up. Move back. On your feet!"

The rear of the column kept pressing forward blindly, wedging the men in the door more tightly together. Augustine weighed heavily on Lang's hip, groaning now. Lang did not know how much longer he could support Augustine and did not trust the pressure of the mob to keep him from collapsing beneath their feet.

"Bernie," he cried. "We've got to get Phil inside."

"Follow me," said Moran.

Putting his thick shoulder into the mass he forced a passage. Lang followed closely, dragging Augustine, before the bodies flowed together again. Once through the press Lang was drowned in heat. It made him giddy. He would have fallen over the prostrate bodies blocking the door if Moran had not steadied him. It was these bodies which had caused the jam. Dozens of men had collapsed with fatigue, with simple cessation of will to stand, as soon as they found themselves within the warmth and shelter of the building.

Colonel Ozmozius was standing on a platform girding a brick furnace, exhorting the fallen men to clear the door and move to the rear. Flames danced in the open door of the furnace.

Lang and Moran lifted Augustine over the carpet of bodies.

"What's going on, Lang?" Colonel Ozmozius called.

"We got a sick man, sir. We got to lay him down somewhere."

"We have a lot of sick men," Colonel Ozmozius said. "Get him settled in the rear."

They made a space for Augustine against a back wall and stretched him out full length among the supine bodies of sleeping men. Lang put his pack beneath Augustine's head, removed his cap and scarf for him and unbuttoned his greatcoat and jacket. Augustine's eyes opened.

"You're going to be okay," Lang said. "Just get some sleep."

"Steve," Augustine said. "Steve, I'm sorry I . . ."

He fell asleep in mid-sentence and Lang did not know if he was apologizing for his weakness or for past differences.

Moran had removed his pack and stretched out beside Augustine. He, too, was asleep at once, drugged by the heat. Lang shook his head to clear it, resisting overpowering lethargy, knowing if he remained motionless another moment he would collapse. His men were outside in the cold. His place was with them. Colonel Ozmozius would not like that when he found out. Colonel Ozmozius would not respect him any more.

He tottered toward the door, picking his way among the bodies, treading on some of them. Even those upon whom he walked most heavily made no outcry beyond a whimper.

"Where the devil you think you're going?" Ozmozius shouted.

His voice is so strong, Lang thought. How can his voice be so strong?

"My men," Lang said, the words so wraithlike he felt them floating out of his mouth toward the ceiling.

How would they ever reach Colonel Ozmosis's ears if they drifted to the ceiling?

"I left them in the cold."

"Are you out of your . . . Get back where you were."

Colonel Osmosis did not understand. He had pushed in out of turn, and he had left his men behind.

"They're outside in the cold," he explained groggily.

"There're a lot of men outside in the cold," said the colonel. "If you're that eager clear that door for me."

Lang's stupor vanished. Strength flowed back into his limbs. Colonel Osmosis had given him an order. He plunged among the prostrate men, yelling at them as he had heard Ozmozius yell. Some rose to their feet and crept dumbly toward the rear. Others he seized bodily and dragged backward over the carpet of bodies, scarcely aware the lumpy softness in which he planted his feet was human flesh.

The jam broke. Men stumbled inside, halting as if stunned when the heat lashed them. Lang shunted them on before they could sink to the floor. From the furnace platform Ozmozius urged them on unremittingly.

"Move back! Keep moving! Move back!"

Lang's arms soon lost their vigor. He shoved the passive bodies without strength but needed none. The merest pressure was enough to start men blindly forward, not to stop until they met the resistance of other bodies.

Hartman entered, supported by Jackson. His face was gray and puffy, no longer handsome. Crumbacker was behind them looking like a wizened little old man. He tried to smile.

"Hi, Tex," he said through parched lips.

"Bernie and Phil are all the way back," Lang said. "See if you can find 'em."

They moved on. Lang was relieved. His men were out of the cold now and he no longer felt he had abandoned them. He wanted to go with them but the colonel had not dismissed him.

"Hold it, Lang!" Ozmozius said minutes later. "No more in here. We're full up."

Lang spread his arms across the doorway. A wall of men pushed against him, but without force, making small, querulous sounds. Colonel Ozmozius picked his way over the bodies to join Lang.

"You men go to the next building," he ordered. "This one's full up."

335

An anguished, high-pitched wail started at the door and ran its way along the column.

"Knock that off!" Ozmozius bawled.

He turned to Lang and said quietly, as if sharing a confidence, "Poor bastards."

Raising his voice again, "Follow me."

He went outside and led the men away.

Lang stared after him in adoration.

The snow between the buildings was pocked and pitted, strewn with sleds, packs, bedrolls, bits of clothing and food and stained with frozen splatters of urine. The cold was bracing at first, then biting. Lang went back inside and quickly shut the door behind him. For the first time since he had entered the building he could look about him.

It was a factory of some kind. The furnace was against a wall. Two sets of narrow steps led to the platform on which men stood to tend the furnace but there were no workmen here now. A conveyor belt system circled the room two or three feet above the floor, crossed at intervals by steps, like country stiles.

The floor, the conveyor belt system, every inch of flat space was thickly covered with tangles of men from which protruded heads, arms and legs as if thrusting from a sea of sodden olive drab wool. The factory seethed and pulsated with their convulsive slumber, and over all swelled a deep insistent drone. When Lang listened carefully the drone sorted itself into sighs, sobs, groans, whimpers, labored breathing, incoherent muttering.

Movement caught his eye across the sea of bodies. A small cabinet stood against a wall and on its top, four feet long and a foot wide, a man lay sleeping in a cruelly ludicrous position. He lay half kneeling, his head pillowed on a knapsack, his buttocks in the air. Another man was pawing at the knapsack to pull it down. The sleeper clutched it dumbly in a mute tug of war. Suddenly he lifted his head and stared down blindly at the other man, his eyes wide but blank. With a final heave, the man on the floor pulled the pack from the cabinet top. It fell on the men below, who stirred and muttered but did not waken. The man on the cabinet stared at his tormenter a long moment, unseeing, then his hands, still clutching the spot where the pack had lain, grew limp and his head sank slowly to the hard wood. No sound had been uttered. Lang did not find that strange. He picked his way over the thickly entwined bodies and found Moran and the others. He burrowed among them.

And slept at last.

✇✇✇✇✇✇✇✇ CHAPTER 21

They rested in the glass factory for thirty-six hours.

The German lieutenant colonel in charge had wanted to move out early the first afternoon but Colonel Ozmozius refused to transmit the order to his men. Lang, who remained within calling distance of the colonel should he be needed, heard them arguing.

"We won't move without a full night's rest," Ozmozius said, adding as if in afterthought, "and I demand my men be fed a hot meal."

"You know that is impossible," the German said stiffly.

"Don't tell me your troubles, Colonel," said Ozmozius.

"I have my orders," the German said. "The prisoners are to prepare to leave at fifteen hundred hours."

"Not a chance," said Ozmozius.

The German had a plump, solemn face and reminded Lang of the teller in the savings department of his bank in Houston. He did not look as if he had rested any more than the prisoners though his uniform was tidy and his face cleanshaven. Colonel Ozmozius, though rumpled, looked far more soldierly to Lang.

"I shall use whatever degree of force necessary," the German said.

"What'll you do?" Ozmozius demanded angrily. "Shoot us? Would you care to begin with me?"

The German became angry, too. His cheeks reddened and his fists clenched in their fur-lined gloves. Lang was impressed by the colonel's defiance, but apprehensive.

When the German answered his lips scarcely moved.

"Very well, my dear Oberst," he said, his voice cold and filled with irony. "Please inform me when it is your pleasure to resume the march."

He bowed slightly, knocked his newly polished boots together in a studied parody of deference and stalked away.

Lang's awe at Ozmozius's victory showed plainly in his face.

"I had him by the short hairs," the colonel said deprecatingly. "He's undermanned and his troops are as bad off as we are. He could send for help but he's not about to admit he can't control us himself."

"If he started shooting he could," Lang said. "That's what I was scared of."

"With the war lost and all the witnesses?" said Ozmozius. "I'll tell you something, just between us. If I'd thought there was a chance of that we'd have been out of here so fast it would make your head swim."

He gave Lang a paternal smile, sensing his disillusion.

"There are times to be tough and times to roll over and play dead," he explained. "Just be damned sure you know which is which."

When they left the next afternoon Lang and his roommates had almost fully recovered from their ordeal, even Augustine. The first morning Lang had borrowed an iron kettle and made oatmeal over an open fire in the factory yard. Few of the other prisoners had managed a hot meal.

"Steve," Augustine said sheepishly, "I'm sorry I raised so much hell when you cut out oatmeal breakfasts."

"That's okay," Lang said, embarrassed. "I'm sorry about the way I did it."

"When you guys getting married?" Moran said, nudging Hartman.

There was unlimited hot water from a tap at one of the factory buildings and glassware to fetch it in. Lang made frequent hot brews for the group and had all wash their feet and socks. Hartman's sore feet responded quickly to this and treatment from a German first-aid kit and he regained his good looks and much of his optimism.

Lang shaved and washed his upper body at the outdoor tap after seeing Colonel Ozmozius do so, though the air was freezing despite the reappearance of bright sunshine. It helped his morale greatly.

They resumed the march cheerfully. Ozmozius had announced it would be made in easy stages, with no walking after dark. The Germans tried to count them before starting out but gave up the attempt when the prisoners, encouraged by the colonel's earlier victory, refused to wait about in the cold.

The column, walking in leisurely disorder, left the back roads for a broad autobahn choked with refugee traffic through which from time to time came staff cars and motorcycles with tired, impatient drivers. The sun was bright, the air bracing, and Lang felt as if he were out for an afternoon stroll. He looked eagerly at everything, knowing at the end of the march, wherever that might be, he would be again behind barbed wire.

The column shared the autobahn with an endless pa-

340

rade of great wagons drawn by oxen and piled high with furniture, bedding, stoves, mirrors, clocks, hay, crates of stupefied
fowl and large families of weary, anxious pink-cheeked Germans. The *Ostdeutsche* were returning to the homeland from
the eastern territories. Children stared out of the creaking
wagons as they inched along the column and those of the
adults not stunned by their calamity sometimes smiled tentatively at the prisoners. Lang felt little compassion except for
the children. They had lived as conquerors and now it was
over. And they were triply alien to him. They were civilian,
German and not prisoners.

The children's eyes and mouths flew open when they
saw Jackson's black face and their expressions did not change
when he smiled and called to them in broken German.

"When I first got picked up one little kid ran up and
tried to see if it rubbed off," he told Lang.

Small boys and old men drilled with ancient weapons
in the snowy fields along the autobahn or crept toward junked
trucks carrying *Panzerfaust* antitank weapons in simulated attacks.

"Der Fuehrer's Volksturm," Lang said derisively to
Moran when they passed a ragged group crawling self-consciously along a ditch.

"If that's what the Goons are down to I wouldn't mind
doing a piece of hand to hand myself," said Moran. "I think I
could whip that old joskin with the beard."

In the villages civilians came out of doors to cheer the
column on, not knowing who or what they were except that
they were soldiers and promised no threat.

In one of them, as Lang's group strolled past smoking
cigarettes and talking in loud, confident voices, an elderly
civilian in a leather coat cried out to a German guard asking
who they were. Froehlich, who chanced to be passing in his
sidecar, answered that they were Russian prisoners and that
German troops had won a great victory on the Eastern front.
The Germans, who had poured out of their houses at the ap-

341

proach of the column, began cheering and waving handkerchiefs.

"What a liar," Lang shouted in German. "We're
American prisoners of war from Stalag Luft 9. We're all running from the Russians together."

The Germans stopped celebrating the victory and
Froehlich looked at Lang long and hard. Lang grinned at him
unabashed, remembering what Colonel Ozmozius had said the
day before. This was not one of those occasions when it was
wiser to roll over and play dead.

They spent the night in a hay-filled barn. The farmer
came around imploring everyone not to smoke in the hay and
announced they could come into the kitchen a few at a time
for hot water. His wife heated the water on a big stove and the
farmer gratefully accepted donations of cigarettes though he
demanded none. He had a luxuriant untended gray mustache
and a weathered, deeply lined face. He was short and wiry with
dung on his shoes. Put him in Levi's and a workshirt and cow-
boy boots, leaving him the same sheepskin coat he had on,
and you wouldn't be able to tell him from a West Texas
rancher, Lang thought.

In the morning when the old man came out in the farmyard to bid them good-bye Lang impulsively gave him a cigar
and was embarrassed when the farmer wept and tried to kiss
his hand.

"Why'd you do that?" Moran demanded as they joined
the column. "Giving that Goon a cigar?"

"They gave us hot water last night," Lang said apologetically, ashamed he could not dislike this old man even if
he was a German, nor the rosy-cheeked old woman ladling
out hot water and clucking in sympathy for all the young
men so far from their mothers.

The day's march was shorter than the previous one.
They spent the night in military shops at a Wehrmacht transport center. Lang was concerned that it might be a tempting
target for night bombers but said nothing to anyone except

342

Moran, who had similar apprehensions. Lang slept well nonetheless.

Next day they were fed hot soup and marched to a marshaling yard where they were loaded into boxcars, fifty men to each. They did not leave the cars, except for brief sanitation stops, for four nights and three days. Lang had thought the crowding intolerable when they had been brought from Italy thirty to a boxcar. That would be luxury now. He could not move without the cooperation of those around him and to reach the urine can by the door was an arduous undertaking. He slept sitting or sometimes burrowed among bodies as he had the first night in the glass factory. He longed for the sunlight and airy space of the march's final days, thinking as he did so how strange it was he should long for this and not true freedom. That was too much to hope for and would come when it would come.

They were given soup, bread, margarine and canned meat at irregular intervals, never much and always scrupulously shared out by the fifty men in the boxcar. For the three days of the interminable journey Lang and his roommates ate only this and D-ration chocolate bars.

"I'm glad you made us save 'em," said Crumbacker. "We'd be hurtin' now if you hadn't."

"What I like about you is your size, Crumb," Lang said. "I wish I had forty-nine like you in here with me."

"I resent that," said Jackson. "You could never tell I weighed one seventy-five when I scrunch up."

"Then why have I been wearin' that big ass of yours in my face the last two days?" Moran demanded.

Lang was proud of his friends. Crammed together though they were, they had not bickered and jockeyed for space among themselves as most of the others had done, though they had jealously guarded their small portion of the floor, nor questioned their share of the rations. Sometimes, as now, they were even able to joke.

This should be horrible, Lang thought, but it isn't. It's

just uncomfortable and boring. He wondered if he could have endured the discomforts and privations with such equanimity a year earlier, knowing he could not. You never knew what you could stand until you had to, he thought, remembering the second night of the march, the concertina wire at P.G. 203, the fights with O'Meara and, for the first time in weeks, the killing of the Italian civilian. It seemed so unnecessary now to have killed him. He was so much bigger than the Italian. If he had not been such a coward then he could have grabbed him or knocked him down.

He was still afraid of some things, he acknowledged to himself, a pointed gun and, when they stopped too long in a marshaling yard, the sound of sirens, but it did not disturb him to admit this. Colonel Ozmozius himself had said it was sometimes better to roll over and play dead than to act tough. And Colonel Ozmozius was the toughest man he had ever known.

The journey ended at Stalag VIIA.

They crept out of the boxcars, stiff and blinking in the early morning light. The lane from the siding was rutted and muddy with thawing snow.

"I never thought I'd be glad to see this place again," said Lang as they picked their way through the slush.

"I wonder if they saved our rooms?" Moran said.

"What's it like here?" Augustine asked.

"They don't even heat the chains," Lang replied gravely.

Augustine smiled. He knew Lang was not making fun of him. Lang had not said a cruel word to him since the night they left Stalag Luft 9.

They marched past the main gate to a desolate barbed-wire enclosure containing only two long empty sheds where they were assigned floor space and given sodden excelsior on which to spread their blankets. They had all expected something better and stood in wretched apathy until Lang, the first to overcome his disappointment, set them to opening their bedrolls to make a pallet in the small space assigned them. When that was done he built a fire of bits of wood he had gathered on entering the enclosure and gave them breakfast of coffee and ration biscuits. The wood he did not burn he stacked beside their pallet, refusing those who demanded to share it. He had seen it first and this was no time for philan-throphy.

They called the enclosure the Snake Pit and spent four days there with little to do but complain of mud, cold and crowding and speculate about the war. Both fronts seemed re-mote now and the end of the war farther away than when they had set out on their journey.

On the fourth day they were transferred out of the Snake Pit in small groups. Lang's group was not processed until after midnight. They were first carefully searched and then permitted to soak as long as they wished in the shower room while their clothing was fumigated.

They finished their processing refreshed and high-spir-ited but the raw predawn darkness hung with misty rain into which they emerged stilled their laughter. Sullen guards led them down the silent, wire-girt main street of the camp and left them in a long peeling stucco barracks in a narrow com-pound. There were puddles on the floor where the roof had leaked. Twelve-man bunks, three high, two long, two wide, were hung with sagging wire netting. The walls were streaked and the windows scaly with dirt. Two naked bulbs in the ceiling shed a feeble light.

"This ain't the way I remember it," Moran said.

"Well, it's better than the Snake Pit," Lang replied without conviction.

A middle-aged soldier in a shapeless uniform, face sour and manner grumpy, limping badly but with an indifference to it bespeaking an old infirmity, unlocked a door at the end of the building and wordlessly passed out bowls and spoons. His silence, the hour, the feeble light and the utter squalor of the long room had a cheerless unreality which plunged them all, even Lang, into gloom.

The German kicked a pile of moldy blankets, indicating they were to take two each, and nodded his head curtly at a heap of stained and lumpy paillasses in the center aisle between the rows of twelve-man bunks.

"You're a cheerful bastard, ain't you?" said Moran.

The German gave no indication he understood or had even heard.

"Reminds me of a landlady me and my old man had once," Moran said to Lang. "Only she was taller."

"When do we get morning brew?" Lang asked the soldier in German. "If we get any?"

The German shrugged and limped heavily out the door.

"I think that was my landlady," said Moran.

The prisoners were so dispirited even their curses and complaints had no conviction. There was a brief resurgence of energy when they scrambled to lay claim to the less decrepit bunks but it quickly died away.

Lang could not sleep.

He stared at Moran's paillasse sagging inches from his stomach through a hole in the wire netting above him, breathed the dank, musty air, aware again of smells now that he was himself clean from the long shower; listened to the mutter, groan and whimper of prisoners sleeping, and could no longer resist despair.

This was so much worse than he had expected. Stalag VIIA had been dirty and crowded before, but not cheerless. To have endured the march, four incredible nights in the boxcar, the barren Snake Pit and in the end reached not a haven but this, and without the consolation of impermanence. For this was the end of the road. He would be here the rest of the war. If he was lucky and they were not marched out again some frantic night split with the sounds of artillery.

But it's almost always like this in a new place, he thought. You expect something better at the end of the trip, a place where you can find respite and a kind of compensation

346

for the privations you endured on the way, and if you do not you are doubly and triply disappointed. But then you learn to live with it and find it is not really so bad as you first thought. Even the glass factory, the boxcar and the Snake Pit had become endurable when he learned to adjust to them. He would always adjust. He should know that by now and not surrender to disappointments experience had shown were transient.

Don't just lay there, Blubberbutt, he thought, disturbed and yet amused he should call himself that when he had not even thought of the despised nickname in so many months.

He crawled out of his bunk and slipped on his clammy shoes. He had gone to bed wearing everything except shoes and greatcoat.

It was growing light in the compound but he saw no sign of life, not even a guard. The barracks were silent in the compounds on either side and Lang did not know if they were empty or filled with sleeping men. Silence hung over the vast camp and for an eerie moment Lang felt he was alone in it, tiny and lost in a maze of barbed wire and empty buildings, and that if he were to walk the main street to the gate he could leave unchallenged.

There were two barracks in the compound and a foul abort of brick and crumbling plaster. Behind his barracks was a pile of rubble. He went to it. Rubbish heaps, he had learned in his months as a prisoner, sometimes contained treasures for a man who knew how to improvise. As he poked among the broken boards, bits of cloth, brick, plaster, paper and tin cans he smelled charred and sodden wood, and was plunged into vivid recollection of a long-forgotten incident of his childhood. Walking to school one morning, was it the first or second grade, he had passed a little shop that had burned in the night. There had been treasures in the ruins, still sodden from the firehoses. Cracked and soot-blackened bottles, drawer pulls, charred ledgers, a fruit jar containing thumbtacks, paper clips, six pennies and a dime. He had reached the school late and filthy and was sent home by the teacher to clean up. He had been spanked for it but later his mother had shined the coins for him with Old Dutch Cleanser.

It had been more than two years now since he had seen a penny or a dime or any kind of money except the camp lira at P.G. 203. He wondered what it would be like to have money in his pocket again and things to buy with it. But he did not need money at the moment. The rubbish heap was his store and he could have whatever he wanted for the taking.

He found a long three-quarter-inch bolt with a rusted nut on the end and began pounding nails out of boards. He grew conscious of a presence and looked over his shoulder. A guard, arms up to the elbows in the pockets of his ankle-length greatcoat, was watching him.

"How goes it?" Lang asked in German without stopping his labors.

"Not good," the German replied. "This is a terrible place."

"I know," said Lang. "But better than the Russian front, is it not true?"

The German took his mittened hands from his pockets and held them aloft for emphasis.

"God in Heaven, I should say so! You have come from there, yes?"

"We could hear their artillery," Lang said.

"Animals, those Russians. I am hoping to be captured by Americans. You are American, yes?"

Lang nodded.

"When do you expect this to happen?" Lang said. "Soon?"

The German shook his head in disgust.

"They continue fighting, the damned fools. If it were me . . ."

He stopped abruptly as if he feared he had said too much.

"You speak German," he said. "You are a Jew?"

"No," Lang said. "Why?"

"Many Jews who are Americans speak German."

He smiled, showing ugly teeth.

"Glauber cannot sleep at night because he can do nothing to them. Glauber is my sergeant."

Lang turned to face him.

"How about you?" he said. "Does it bother you?"

The soldier laughed.

"Jews mean nothing to me. But Glauber. I cannot sleep at night because I can do nothing to him."

Lang laughed, too. Privates were the same in every army.

"If you see Glauber you will say nothing of this?" the guard said. "You will know him at once. He has the face of a donkey."

"No," Lang said.

He gave the soldier a cigarette from the pack he always carried for making trades.

"Thank you," the soldier said. "I should have known you were no Jew."

Lang wished he had not given him a cigarette.

The German went away and Lang continued his scavenging. He left the rubbish heap in revived spirits with the bolt, a double handful of nails, a dozen feet of rusty wire in short lengths and an armload of boards. The misty rain still hung in the air but he no longer found it oppressive, nor the sodden compound or peeling barracks.

Moran awakened while he was patching the holes in the wire netting of his bunk and peered sleepily down at him.

"What the hell you think you're doing?" Moran said.

Lang stopped whistling and grinned up at Moran.

"Redecorating," he said cheerfully.

Moran scowled.

"You son of a bitch," he said. "Don't anything ever get you down?"

☗☗☗☗☗☗☗☗ CHAPTER 22

Later in the morning Lang helped the others repair the rents in their bunk netting, make shelves and pound in nails on which to hang things. In the next weeks they learned to make only temporary improvements in their accommodations, for they were moved to another compound a few days later and after that shifted and regrouped continually as prisoners of all nationalities poured into the already crowded camp from areas threatened by Allied advances. For one period they lived in tents, which Lang found stimulating because the air of impermanence seemed to presage an imminent end to the war.

Whatever the compound, the barracks were the same. Teeming, deteriorating, verminous and fusty. At night the bedbugs came out of cracks and seams and bit Lang's wrists and ankles. He found them no more bothersome than the mosquitoes and chiggers of his youth but Moran got up at night to hunt them with precious matches and Hartman, whose skin was tender, developed great itchy welts.

Because of the cold and their diet they rose often in the night to relieve themselves, having to grope their way through total blackness to a metal drum at the rear of the barracks. When it was full, as it always was if they visited it in the predawn hours, they were obliged to trudge outside through the mud and climb the crumbling steps of the noisome abort. When Lang awakened in the night he would try to convince himself he could wait until morning, hating to leave his warm nest for the tortuous, obstacle-strewn journey in inky darkness, but invariably the need was irresistible. When he waited beyond the limits of endurance he would blunder the last yards in panic-stricken haste. Once when he miscounted his steps on the return trip he discovered his error only when he had one leg in an occupied bunk. He fled through the dark, laughing and embarrassed, to indignant cries.

In his third week at Stalag VIIA he took a bath at an inside tap. His body clean, he found the smell of his underwear unbearable and washed it. It was three days before the underwear dried, a period during which he was wretchedly cold. He did not take a full bath again until warmer weather though his knees grew speckled with blackheads from the grease and grime of his wool trousers.

The camp was on half parcels, the German ration was meager and there were no personal cooking facilities except a wood-burning stove in the kitchens separating the long barracks in the middle. The stoves were constantly crowded and there was never enough fuel. The prisoners devised a tiny cooking stove made of two tin cans wired one atop the other which worked efficiently on a handful of wood shavings fed into it a few at a time. They filled the barracks with choking smoke and burned rings on the wooden floors until their use was limited to the cement-floored kitchens and washrooms

351

and out of doors. Lang made a stove and within a few days the fingers with which he fed it were blackened, horny and almost impervious to heat.

Because of the scarcity of food and lack of facilities Lang's roommates could no longer prepare meals as a group. Most of the other prisoners split up into two-man combines sharing the weekly parcel but Lang and his roommates, though they prepared the one scanty hot meal of the day separately, ate together. When they moved, as they did frequently, they got adjacent bunks, taking their nails, wire and shelving with them. It was Lang who kept them together, not through any demands of his own but because they fared better than most of the other prisoners through his efforts. He had learned how to exist amid shortages and now he traded as indefatigably as he had during his winter in Italy. Now, however, he traded for his combine instead of only Moran and himself. At Augustine's suggestion the six of them pooled half their cigarette ration each week and turned them over to Lang to trade for extra bread. Once, when Hartman thought he had not received as much bread as his cigarettes should buy and demanded an accounting, he was shouted down by the other members of the combine, Lang abstaining, and threatened with a punch in the nose by Augustine. Lang was unruffled by Hartman's accusation and amused that the fiery little Augustine, who had once hated him so, should appoint himself as his defender.

When a member of the combine wanted to make a personal trade it was always entrusted to Lang. The prisoners were no longer confined to their own compounds and Lang prowled the main body of the camp freely. He acquired contacts among Russians, Yugoslavs, Frenchmen, American enlisted men, German guards, British officers and Other Ranks. He traded in English, German and sign language. The Russians were not allowed out of their compounds, squalid even in comparison with others at VIIA, except on work details and Lang bartered with them over barbed-wire fences, throwing the items of trade back and forth.

On one of his expeditions among the ORs, he found Lance Corporal Gorsely from P.G. 203, who did not immediately recognize him.

"You've that changed, sir," Gorsely said apologetically when Lang made himself known.

"Just lost my baby fat."

Gorsely eyed his hard, lean face.

"That you 'ave, sir," he said with more genuine respect than he had ever shown at P.G. 203 and no longer affecting a cultivated accent.

He had somehow acquired sergeant's stripes.

"You've changed yourself . . . Sergeant," Lang said, grinning.

"Oh, that, sir. When I got to bloody Germany I thought I'd give myself a bit of promotion. They'd lost my records, you know. I hope you'll not . . ."

"If anybody asks me I'll swear you're a sergeant major," said Lang. "Is Pellini here?"

"Oo? Oh, the colonnello's bumboy. 'Aven't seen 'ide nor 'air of 'im since the bloody train."

Gorsely, who had lost none of his enterprise, became as helpful as before in the role of go-between.

When the North Camp arrived from Stalag Luft 9 Lang had gone looking for Pilot Officer Perkins now, legitimately, Flying Officer Perkins, and helped him get settled. Every week they exchanged invitations to tea, the guest always supplying his own sugar and slice of bread, and they set up a tea and coffee exchange between the British and Americans by which they both profited.

Despite Lang's efforts, the final weeks of winter were difficult for his combine, particularly one bleak period when Stalag VIIA ran out of Red Cross parcels, but spring came earlier in Bavaria than Upper Silesia and with warm weather life grew easier. United States Army trucks transferred to Swiss control and driven by prisoners of war on parole came directly into the camp from Switzerland, and Stalag VIIA went on full parcels. German control deteriorated with the military situation and the prisoners had increasing freedom within the camp. Prisoners took over the unloading and distribution of supplies, roll calls and many of the administrative duties. Tight security was maintained only on the outer perimeter of Stalag VIIA and the German command more often submitted requests than issued orders.

But the carefree, ever more hopeful vagabond existence within the wire was marred by the increasing frequency of bomber formations overhead and the brooding menace of another move ahead of advancing Allied forces. Though the German Army was falling back on both fronts, there were persistent rumors that Hitler had given orders VIIA was not to be permitted to fall into Allied hands. Prisoners were to be marched to the final redoubt at Berchtesgaden and held as hostages or, if need be, shot. There was talk of resisting such a move and overwhelming the dispirited and undermanned guard force with sheer numbers, but Lang and others knew that one man with a machine pistol could control hundreds of unarmed men. He acquired maps of the area and told his combine if they were moved they would escape from the column at the first opportunity and hide out until liberated.

When it became evident the bomber formations, sometimes a thousand strong, were using the camp as a checkpoint and therefore must know its function, the fear of bombing or strafing by friendly aircraft abated. Lang began actually enjoying the spectacle of the enormous formations throbbing endlessly above the camp. The camp had no warning system and at the report of approaching aircraft the control section would send out soldiers on bicycles to ride about alerting the guards with hand-cranked sirens. At the feeble sound the prisoners would pour out of the barracks to search the skies.

When a guard brought in an air-dropped leaflet warning of heavy reprisals if prisoners were harmed or moved they at long last surrendered fully to impatient optimism. Lang no longer required his combine to withhold food for emergencies and instead, the day before parcel issue, they would eat everything left from the previous week. Having a bash, they called it.

Lang was shaving in the washroom which with the kitchen divided his barracks one balmy afternoon when Moran came running in to him.

"The guys from Poland are coming in," he said. "All the ground grippers from P.G. 203. They been on the road for weeks."

"You see Dogass?" Lang asked, wondering immediately why he had done so.

There were so many others from P.G. 203 he was more interested in seeing. Colonel Waterfield, Doc Stagno, Sergeant Pellini. He had never stopped wondering if Pellini's masquerade had succeeded. Why should he care about Dogass Harbold? It no longer mattered that Harbold had once humiliated him and he no longer thirsted for revenge. Too many things had happened since then. And yet the thought of Harbold's contempt annoyed him. Harbold was no match for him now and he had no desire to demonstrate that fact to him. But Harbold was carrying a wrong impression of him. There was a need to correct that impression, small but nagging. If Harbold could see him as he was now it would be finished at last.

"No," Moran had answered while this coursed through Lang's mind. "I heard some of 'em went somewhere else. Grandma Waterfield and a bunch of others."

Lang wiped the soap off his face and went to the last fence before the outer compound, in which prisoners still were not permitted. The column of men from the east was still filing in. They looked tanned and fit, as if the march had not been difficult. Most of them had unopened Red Cross parcels and many had heaps of possessions which they trundled in wheelbarrows, toy wagons and baby carriages. They exchanged shouted greetings and information with the welcoming throng.

Lang saw Harbold among them, thinner than he remembered and without the sly menacing expression he had always pictured. Harbold was pulling a heavily laden toy wagon. Lang started to speak but did not when Harbold passed without acknowledging his presence. So Harbold had not forgotten their differences, Lang thought. The sorry bastard. But if that was the way he wanted it, fine. Harbold dropped the handle of his wagon and came running back.

"Blubberbutt, you old hoss!" he cried, seizing Lang's hand and pumping it. "I didn't recognize you at first."

Lang winced at the nickname, not offended but disappointed in himself to find it could still annoy him.

He returned Harbold's handshake warmly.

"Dogass! Great to see you."

Harbold stepped back and studied him.

"You lost your gut," he said.

Was it condescending, Lang thought, or was he only imagining so. He had never dreamed he would be so touchy. It was childish of him.

"You lost yours, too," he said.

"Yeah. I've been getting all that healthy exercise. But we ate pretty good on the road. Trading with the civilians and everything. How's the chow situation here?"

"Not bad," said Lang. "We're on full parcels. The Goon ration's not much."

"Had any real eggs?"

"We haven't even had powdered eggs here."

"Man, we had nothing but eggs on the road. Chickens, too. I still got about a dozen left. Eggs."

"A dozen real eggs?"

Lang could not keep the envy from his voice. Fresh eggs were one of the things he and Moran had talked about when they were hungry and dissatisfied with the unvarying menu of Red Cross food. Moran had even dreamed about them one night and tantalized Lang with an exact description of the crisp brown edges and unbroken yolk.

356

"Straight from the hen's butt," said Harbold. "Want some?"

Lang was instantly wary. Harbold was setting him up for a deal. He remembered the kind of deals Harbold made.

"What you asking?" he asked casually.

"What you take me for?" Harbold demanded, insulted.

"Nothing."

"That wouldn't be right," Lang said, ashamed of his doubts. "I bet you could get a pack of cigarettes for an egg in here."

"English or American?" Harbold said instinctively, then resolutely, "Hell, no! They're not for sale. I'm gonna give you some no matter what they're worth."

"That's sure nice of you," said Lang, adding hesitantly, "You think maybe you could sell me a couple for Moran?"

"Moran? Oh, the short joker with all the muscles. He still with you?"

"Yeah. We've stuck together the whole time."

Strange, Lang thought, how people forgot each other. Gorsely hadn't remembered Pellini immediately either.

"I'll give you enough for him, too. Tell you what. When I get squared away in my barracks I'll bring 'em over. You got something to cook on?"

Lang nodded.

"I'll bring 'em over and we'll bash the whole damn dozen," Harbold said.

Lang told Harbold how to find him and Harbold came over at suppertime. Lang cooked the eggs out of doors on his tin-can stove. Everyone cooked outside now that it was warm and the Germans no longer protested that the tiny flames would attract bombers. Word spread quickly that Lang was frying fresh eggs and he soon had an audience of scores. They melted away politely when the eggs were ready for eating. With Harbold's permission Lang gave each man in his combine a bite of egg and they, too, left. Lang, Moran and Harbold

357

ate the dozen eggs and a can of fried Spam, potatoes and a Klim tin of prune whip provided by the hosts.

While they were eating Lang put Canadian coffee on to boil, stoking the fire with shavings between bites, and when they finished they sat cross-legged on the ground drinking it. The night was pungent with smoke from the myriad cooking fires around them and the crowded stars flared in the sky like strong lights reflected on India ink. Lang whistled softly to himself, drugged with food and contentment. On nights like this, he thought, all the young sentries must be thinking of girls waiting in the lamplight and perhaps somewhere one waited for him, someone he did not even know yet and who did not know for whom she was waiting, and he closed his eyes and Serena the Butterfly Girl fluttered her wings of gauze.

"Hey, Blubber," said Harbold. "Remember how we used to sit on the steps at P.G. 203 and listen to that every night?"

The tune died on Lang's lips and he tumbled out of reverie into a cage reeking with woodsmoke and thick with prisoners.

"Doug," he said casually. "Will you do me a favor?"

"Sure," said Harbold.

"Don't call me Blubber, huh?"

He tried not to sound annoyed or angry or threatening. It took great care.

"Sure," said Harbold. "It don't exactly fit you now anyway. What you want me to call you?"

Moran snickered.

"Tex," Moran said.

"You bastard," Lang said, leaning forward suddenly and shoving Moran on his back.

Moran lay there, laughing.

"My, my," he said.

"Steve," said Lang.

"Okay, Steve," Harbold said.

And suddenly it was as if Harbold had always been a friend, not just now but even back at P.G. 203 and Lang knew how foolish he had been to carry a grudge all those months, no matter how deeply buried, and that what had been to him a scarifying humiliation had been to Harbold and the others an incident not worth remembering. And he knew that all those months he had been judging Harbold wrongly, just as he had judged Augustine wrongly, because it had been something in himself that made them hateful to him, not something in them, and whatever it was in him that had caused that was gone now.

There was no curfew now and they sat up late talking about the old days at P.G. 203 as if they were old grads at a reunion. That night Lang dreamed that Jaybird came into the camp wearing flight coveralls and earphones, tall, spotless and clean-shaven. He looked startled when Lang rushed to hug him, crying, "I thought you were dead!"

"I got away," Byrd said. "Don't you remember? Come on, the plane's waiting."

"I've forgotten how to navigate," Lang cried in panic.

"Yes sir, no sir and no excuse, sir," Byrd said sternly.

"But what about Moran?"

"I can't wait."

"I can't go without Moran. And Augustine and everybody."

Then Jaybird was gone and a B-24, painted desert pink, was thundering along the center road, its four thrashing propellers rattling windows in the barracks, and he was running after it bawling, "Wait, Jaybird, wait!"

Lang awakened disconsolate and angry with Jaybird until he remembered Byrd was dead.

The East and West fronts drove closer together. The German guards grew silent and uncertain except for those who seemed to look forward to final defeat as to liberation, like the prisoners. The camp fell into a kind of festive anarchy. The senior officers issued orders against escape but there was no need for it. No one had tried for weeks.

Everyone remained out of doors except when it rained, watching the bombers and fighter planes, listening for the sounds which would signal the approach of friendly troops. Amid the feeble protests of their guards they tore down the interior fences and fed the posts into their cooking fires sliver by sliver. They took the wooden partitions in the aborts, the blackout shutters, the subflooring of the barracks. One night when Lang was with a group tearing down partitions in an abort they were surprised by a Hundfuehrer and fled into the darkness. He called them back and, holding his dog in check, said wistfully to Lang, "Why must you do this now? In one-quarter hour my duty ends. Please wait."

When Lang translated what he had said the others agreed and remained outside until the Hundfuehrer left the compound.

As anything which would burn disappeared into the little tin-can stoves splinter by splinter the German commandant, in an attempt to save the buildings themselves from destruction, authorized forage parties outside the wire. Small parties, selected by seniority, were permitted to leave the camp on parole with a single guard to gather firewood on the countryside. Half of what they gathered was to be allotted for use in the communal kitchen stoves, the rest for personal use.

Lang and Moran were prepared to await their turn to go out with a forage party without particular impatience until the first such group returned with potatoes and eggs. The ration potatoes were issued already boiled, soggy and a little sour from long winter storage under straw. Lang's combine had looked back with longing on the fresh potatoes of Stalag Luft 9 even though they had eaten them every day there for more than a year.

Having discovered they could trade on the outside, Lang and Moran haunted the compound bulletin board until

360

their names were posted for a wood walk, the third to be made. They rose earlier than was necessary the morning they were to go, shaved, washed faces, arms and necks and put on their most presentable uniforms. They folded a barracks bag they had been issued recently as small as possible and filled their pockets and shirts with coffee, D bars, tea, cigarettes and soap. Lang had been told German housewives were particularly avid for soap, of which there was a surplus among the prisoners, who did not bathe as often as the Red Cross apparently assumed they did. Some of the valuables belonged to Augustine, Crumbacker, Jackson and Hartman, who had little prospect of getting on a wood walk because they lacked seniority.

The foragers were counted desultorily at the inner gate and again at the outer one. They were led away by a soldier who kept his rifle slung and scarcely gave them a glance. The prisoners were impatient to reach their destination, whatever it might be, but he refused to be hurried. He led them to a clearing in the woods, sat down with his back against a tree, crossed his legs and lit a cigarette one of the prisoners had given him.

"Return at four o'clock," he said carelessly in German.

Lang translated for the others.

"You mean we just take off?" Moran said.

"You complaining?" Lang said.

The prisoners scattered in all directions. Lang and Moran hurried back along the path by which they had reached the clearing. When they were out of sight of everyone Moran ran a few steps and leaped into the air, knocking his heels together.

"Hooray!" he shouted.

He gave Lang a sheepish look.

"I just couldn't help it," he said.

He began running again and Lang ran after him. Every few steps they would leap into the air like frolicking schoolboys. They raced through the woods, yelling and laughing, plucking at grasses and leafing twigs, unable to contain their exuberance.

361

It was like being free, Lang thought. For the next two hours they could go where they wanted and do what they wanted.

They settled down to a decorous walk when they reached a road. They continued along it to a bridge over a broad river guarded by a German soldier with the engraved metal breastplate of the military police hanging from his neck on a metal chain. The menacing black cylinder of a mine protruded from beneath the bridge. The guard was checking the briefcase of a prosperous-looking civilian in a business suit who waited patiently with a gray bicycle propped against his leg.

"What we gonna do?" Moran whispered, looking longingly at a cluster of houses across the river.

The MP apparently was dissatisfied with the civilian's papers and turned him back. The man was swearing under his breath as he wheeled his bike past the two Americans.

"Oh, hell," Moran groaned, "we just got to get over to them houses."

"Come on," said Lang.

The MP eyed them with puzzled severity.

"How goes it?" Lang asked politely in German. "We are prisoners of war from VIIA. We have parole for two hours. We would like to cross your bridge."

"Where are your papers?" the MP demanded. "You must have papers."

"What did he say?" Moran said urgently.

"He wants to see our papers."

"Offer him a pack of cigarettes."

"I've got a better idea."

Lang reached inside his shirt and took out the prisoner of war identification tag he wore on a string as he had once worn his dog tags. It had been given to him at Stalag Luft 9. He motioned Moran to do the same. The MP inspected them closely.

"Ah," he said, his attitude changing. "Officers."

He saluted and motioned them on.

362

"What a crazy frigging war," said Moran as they hurried across the bridge. "A Goon civilian gets turned back and kriegie dog tags get us over first class."

They knocked on the door of the first house. Light footsteps tapped on a wooden floor and the door opened a few inches. One bright blue eye peered out from beneath a coil of gray hair.

"Prisoners of war from VIIA," Lang said reassuringly. "We have permission to be here."

He had been rehearsing it in his mind all the way across the bridge.

The door opened and a sharp-eyed old woman looked at them uncertainly. Lang's first impression was of incredible cleanliness. Her thick gray hair, coiled in a neat braid, looked as if it had just been washed, her face shone as if freshly scrubbed and her starched white apron was spotless. He was suddenly struck speechless, painfully conscious of the stains on his wrinkled uniform, how his hair came down over his ears, that he had not bathed in more than a week and must smell like the barracks. The old woman, waiting in polite silence, gave no sign she found him offensive.

Moran nudged him.

"Ask her about potatoes, for Christ's sake," Moran said.

Moran gave her his most charming grin and she smiled.

"Dear lady," Lang began, encouraged by Moran's example. That was the way you started a letter in German, "Gnaedige Frau." "Dear lady, we have soap, coffee and chocolate which we would like to exchange for potatoes and eggs or whatever you wish."

She clapped her hand to her mouth.

"Seife!" she exclaimed. "Kaffee!"

She called out in German to someone inside the house, "Bertha, Ernst, come quickly! Young gentlemen with soap to sell."

She opened the door wider and stood back.

"Bitte," she said. "Kommen Sie herein."

Lang bowed slightly from the waist before entering, not knowing why he did so.

"Smooth," Moran whispered approvingly behind him. "You're doin' it real smooth."

The room they entered was as overpoweringly immaculate as the old woman. The floor gleamed with fresh wax and the glass covering family photographs reflected the sparkle of a cabinet filled with cut glass. Highlights danced on light and dark woods. A cat on the cushion of a rocker stared at them with solemn yellow eyes. Even the cat was immaculate, with a starched blue ribbon around its neck. It was the first time Lang had been in an ordinary room in an ordinary house in more than two years and to him it was not at all ordinary.

He was in an instant acutely aware of how accustomed he had become to prison life, accepting it as hard and constricted but with a normalcy of its own. But now, comparing his existence with that indicated by the old woman and this room, he understood how truly different it was from that of people outside the wire and that the difference between himself and this old woman was far greater than mere age, sex and nationality. She slept in a clean bed every night in a clean house, wore clean clothes, cooked on a real stove, sat down at a real table to civilized meals every day. He slept in a twelve-man tier, wore the same unwashed clothes day after day and spent as much time foraging for food as a forest animal. There were bedbug bites on his ankles and blackheads in his knees.

He had an overpowering sense of not belonging. Because he had been living like an animal he must be extremely careful not to behave like one, to show this old woman he was what she had called out to others in the house, a young gentleman. He wondered how she could have called him that. Was it because his side was winning the war?

A man and a woman had come into the room. The three Germans looked enough alike to be brother and sisters. Were they, Lang wondered, or did all old Germans look alike, like Italian colonels? The man was somewhat younger than the woman who had admitted them, and leaned on a thick cane. The second woman was older, with clean white hair, fine wrinkles and paler blue eyes than either of the others.

Lang and Moran laid out soap, tea, coffee, chocolate bars and cigarettes on a table. The three old people clasped their hands to their bosoms and made clucking signs in identical reaction.

How strange it was, Lang thought, that he and Moran, prisoners, should have things which these Germans had been denied and so found as extraordinary as he found their clean house and persons. He felt less overpowered by the surroundings now but nevertheless kept out of sight the fingers blackened by the cooking fire.

The man and the woman who let them in brought a tin basin of potatoes and a bowl of eggs. The older woman selected soap, tea and coffee from the assortment Lang and Moran had laid out. Her fingers brushed a D bar longingly and she gave the younger woman a brief, questioning look. Lang wondered why she hesitated over the chocolate. They had not bargained and she could merely have insisted on it as part of the payment. She must have already fixed a price in her mind for the eggs and potatoes. If she had been a prisoner of war she would have taken as much as she could get. He pressed the chocolate bar into her hand.

"Bitte," he said.

The man had been staring longingly at the cigarettes. Not to be outdone, Moran thrust a pack upon him. The old people seemed momentarily stunned by their generosity. Then the old man took the basin and hobbled back with more potatoes while the younger woman wrapped each egg separately in a screw of newspaper. Moran held the barracks bag open and Lang poured the potatoes into it.

The man lit a cigarette and inhaled hungrily. He coughed and his eyes teared, as if he were out of practice, and the younger woman pounded his back helpfully.

"I also was a soldier," the man said to Lang when he

was finished coughing. "In the other war. This devilish leg of mine is from the other war."

Lang made sympathetic sounds.

"Let's go," Moran said impatiently.

"He's telling me how he got wounded in World War I," Lang explained.

"I have yet my uniform," the man said. "Would you like to see it?"

"He wants to show us his uniform," said Lang.

"Ain't you seen enough Goon uniforms to last you?" Moran demanded. "What the hell time is it, anyway?"

It was three-thirty.

"We got to get back," Moran said.

They shook hands all around with polite formality and Lang bowed slightly again before going out the door, satisfied that he had made a good impression. He was pleased with himself.

"You were great," Moran said as they hurried toward the bridge. "If you can do that with used cars we're in business. They're gonna pee in their pants when they see how many Kartoffels we got."

There was a new MP on the bridge. He gave them a sharp look as they hurried toward him.

"This one looks meaner than the other one," Moran whispered.

"You are prisoners of war?" the soldier demanded when they drew near.

"Jawohl," Lang said, taking his identification tag out of his shirt.

Moran did the same.

The soldier acknowledged their credentials with a curt nod.

"You have been trading cigarettes for bread?" he demanded with what sounded to Lang like disapproval.

"What'd he say?" Moran whispered, worried.

"Richtig," Lang said, ignoring Moran to watch the MP

366

intently for indications he might intend confiscating the potatoes and eggs for which they had traded.

"Come back tomorrow at fifteen hundred hours," the MP said. "I will have a huge army loaf to sell."

Lang concealed his relief and amusement with difficulty. When they were safely across the bridge he told Moran what the guard had said.

They ran whooping down the road, staggering in helpless laughter under the awkward weight of their potatoes.

⛓⛓⛓⛓⛓ CHAPTER 23

Stalag VIIA seethed in a ferment of stimulating but taunting expectancy. The war was ending and it did not end.

Lang knew liberation could come at any time but at the end of each day it seemed no closer than before, as if deliberately loitering just out of reach beyond the wire. Since their return from the wood walk, flushed with the success of their excursion and beguiled by their fleeting view of life outside the wire, he and Moran had talked of little but liberation and going home as they had in the intoxicated but deluded days of the Italian capitulation. It was with them, as with the thousands of other prisoners in the teeming compounds, a compulsion, a diversion and a torment to speak and think with certainty of an end to their captivity.

They could not remain inside the fusty barracks a moment longer than necessary. Each morning Lang and all his combine rose early and had breakfast outside surrounded by the hundreds who shared their quarters and who, like them, could not bear to remain indoors when outside the war was ending. At night they went reluctantly to their bunks and lay awake whispering until they goaded one another into torments of anticipation.

There was a rent in the wire netting of Lang's bunk, getting larger nightly so that his rump dropped closer and closer to Jackson below him, but he did nothing to repair it. Why bother, with liberation and a real bed so near? He had divided the potatoes with Augustine, Crumbacker, Hartman and Jackson and they all ate recklessly, made ravenous by their constant seminars on the abundance that awaited them outside.

Lang and Moran planned a menu for the first day they would have unlimited choice of food and Lang recorded it all in his notebook so they would not forget what they had agreed upon. They knew it was a game but they played it seriously, adding and eliminating, arguing heatedly or agreeing enthusiastically as they attempted to get breakfast, lunch or dinner to manageable proportions. They were unable to do so and the three meals on which they eventually agreed were gargantuan.

"Wouldn't it be great if we could really eat all that?" Lang said wistfully.

"What would really be great would be if we could catch up on all that tail we've missed," Moran said. "No matter how far behind you get you can't ever catch up. It ain't fair."

"I'm not half as far behind as you," Lang said. "I never had much luck with girls."

"You're gonna have to beat 'em off with a stick," Moran said. "You wait and see."

Lang wished he were as confident of that as Moran. He had learned a lot of things in the bag but how to be successful with girls was not one of them. That would be one of his major projects when he got out.

"Hey, Bernie," he said, "you remember Serena the Butterfly Girl?"

"Who?" said Moran.

"Nobody," Lang said, embarrassed.

On a morning late in April, shortly after the wood walk, Lang heated enough water for the whole combine and they sat cross-legged on the ground behind the barracks drinking coffee and discussing the inevitable topics of home and liberation. Two P-51s thundered over the compound, bringing them to their feet in a shower of spilled coffee. They had been buzzed before by friendly fighters but never at such low level. The planes passed so close Lang could see the pilot of one of them. He was grinning and holding up two fingers in a V.

The fighters climbed sharply, slow-rolling as they gained altitude, then dived down in another pass so low that many prisoners threw themselves to the ground in fear of decapitation. The fighters repeated the maneuver again and again. More prisoners came tumbling out of the barracks and soon the compound was packed with a yelling mob throwing caps into the air and waving shirts, jackets and handkerchiefs. Lang tore off his shirt and shook it enthusiastically. The noise, the speed, the reckless camaraderie of the pilots, the nearness of men who were free and brought the promise of freedom, filled him with excitement almost cruel in its intensity.

"Christ Almighty," Moran said huskily, "what a show!"

The fighters soared up and up until they were toys in the vast clean sky and dived once more to level off far across the camp. They thundered the breadth of Stalag VIIA, rocking their wings in greeting and farewell, climbed sharply at the outermost wire and dived out of view beyond the horizon. The sound of their guns came chattering out of the distance.

"The crazy bastards," Jackson said fondly and enviously. "They took time out to give us a show."

"I wonder why?" said Augustine. "They never beat up the camp like that before."

"Probably so we wouldn't get in a flap when they

370

started working over targets so close to us," Lang said. "Wanted to show us they knew who we were."

And maybe it was also their way of saying sit tight, he thought, we're coming for you. He wondered if he could find out later who they were and look them up and thank them.

"Hey, Wings," Moran said to Hartman, "look at Jackson. I think the wild blue yonder's got him."

Jackson was staring longingly toward the sound of the strafing. He turned and smiled sheepishly at Moran.

"That's the difference between you fighter boys and us bomber men," Moran said. "Me and Wings, we got more sense than to want to climb into anything they shoot back at."

"I don't know," said Hartman. "If I could transfer to fighters I'd take another tour."

"When I get out of here I ain't even gonna fly a kite," Moran said.

He winked at Lang.

Lang was too restless to joke with Moran. He put on his shirt, feeling a little foolish at letting himself become so overwrought. Moran, Jackson and Hartman continued talking flying, illustrating tactics with movements of their hands. Other captive pilots did that often but Lang could not remember Moran ever having done so before.

Lang left them, refusing Crumbacker's offer of company, and picked his way through the crowd of men toward an open space beyond the barracks area which had been fenced off until the prisoners uprooted the posts for firewood. The barbed wire still lay along the ground and though it was down marked a sharp division between the compound and the once-forbidden territory. The earth on the compound side was barren and hard-packed. On the other side there was still grass and only here and there browned patches where prisoners had placed their tin-can stoves.

Lang walked across the springy turf, eyes down, unconsciously searching for dandelions. When the interior fence first came down he had gone into the virgin field to gather

371

them, hungry for anything green. He had never before eaten dandelion greens but knew they were edible. Remembering how his mother prepared mustard greens, he had boiled the leaves with cubes of Spam but, because he had chosen the larger plants, seeking quantity, they were too bitter to eat. He went out again and gathered only the succulent young leaves. This time the dish was a success and other prisoners, observing the experiment, quickly stripped the field of dandelions.

When he was deep in the field a machine gun burst into action outside the wire and Lang thought he heard bullets whisper overhead. He threw himself to the ground as angry as he was frightened. He had gone into the field many times and so had others. No one had said it was against regulations. They could have at least shouted a warning before opening fire. The guards had never been that trigger-happy before and lately had been positively easygoing.

Other machine guns opened up outside the camp and he heard the crack of individual rifle fire. He knew then the first burst was not aimed at him. Allied troops had reached the area and the battle for Stalag VIIA had begun.

He pressed himself against the earth, exultant but feeling exposed and vulnerable in the open sea of green. He crawled toward the compound thinking, Don't get hit now, oh God, not now. He lunged across the downed barbed wire and reached the shelter of the abort. Only then did he look about him. The compound was paved with prisoners, some of them pressing themselves flat against the ground, others half crouched and looking toward the sounds of battle. A row of wide eyes showed over a slit trench between the abort and the barracks.

"Steve!" Moran cried from the trench. "Over here!"

Crouching, Lang raced the few yards separating the abort from the trench and tumbled into it. It was jammed. He squeezed in between Moran and Jackson.

The battle mounted in intensity. Fighters flew across the compound to attack targets outside the camp. There were no aerobatics now and no rocking of wings. Heavy ground fire ringed the camp, but only a few stray rounds ricocheted among the buildings. The prisoners could see nothing of the action except the darting planes though a few men craned their heads recklessly for a better view. Lang saw Crumbacker scramble to his feet to peer toward the perimeter.

"Get down, you idiot!" Lang cried. "Crumb, get down!"

Crumbacker obeyed, his grinning lips shiny with saliva.

"How about this?" Moran said in a low voice, as if afraid of being overheard. "Steve, how about this?"

A man came running through the compound bent low over ground.

"Everybody inside," he shouted. "Colonel's orders."

The prisoners scrambled inside through doors and windows. No one risked the exposure of the upper bunks and they sat jammed shoulder to shoulder in the center aisle and on the edges of the bottom bunks. The barracks were not large enough to accommodate so many occupants except when they were arranged for the night in the three tiers of the twelve-man bunks.

Lang was between Augustine and Moran. All six members of the combine sat on the edge of the same lower bunk. Across from them, five men had sat on the paillasse instead of the edge of the bunk and had fallen through and now sprawled with their knees hooked over one side and their backs against the other.

There was little conversation. Everyone was trying to follow the course of the battle by the sound of weapons outside the camp. Firing stopped on one side of Stalag VIIA and increased in intensity on the other, in the direction of the nearby village of Moosburg.

"I hope they don't use artillery," Hartman said nervously. "What if a short round dropped in here?"

"Shut up, Wings!" said Lang.

"You don't think they'll do that, do you, Steve?" Augustine said. "They won't drop any shells near the camp, will they?"

"Hartman's nuts," Lang said reassuringly. "The Goons don't have any artillery and we're not about to use any. They know we're here."

He was reassured by his own words, for the thought had also occurred to him. He remembered the marshaling yard at Bolzano and the sound of falling bombs. Bombs and shells did not know friend from foe.

Moran shifted restlessly.

"How long we gonna have to sit here on our butts with all that goin' on outside?" he demanded.

"If you're so eager why don't you grab yourself a pranger and get out and help 'em," Jackson said.

"I'm a lover, not a fighter," said Moran.

Lang felt the same restlessness. The sounds of battle and the prospect of imminent liberation filled him with uncontrollable energy. He had to find relief in activity, any kind of activity.

"Let's brew up," he said.

"You kidding?" Moran said.

"No. You bring the wood and the stove. I'll get the other stuff."

He reached through a barricade of feet and got Nescafé, Klim and sugar from their box under a bunk. They crawled to the washroom, wriggling through men hardly aware of their passage. They crouched on the concrete floor by the window. Moran cut shavings with Lang's knife while Lang mixed the paste of Klim and water for cream. They talked in whispers while the water heated, not knowing why they kept their voices low, and peeked frequently out the window though nothing was visible from it but another barracks and a patch of barren ground. It was strange to look outside and see no one there. The compound was always as bustling as an ant colony.

They sipped their coffee silently. Swallowing was difficult. Lang hoped the others were not sore because he and

374

Moran had gone off alone. It had not entered his mind to invite any of them to come along.

The firing became spasmodic. Through the open door between the washroom and the bunkroom came a murmur of subdued sounds. Tense whispers, nervous laughter, the sharp intake of breath. Like Lang and Moran, everyone inside was listening.

From outside the barracks, in the direction of the center street, came a startling clanking, roaring, grinding noise.

"A tank!" a voice shouted. "It's a tank!"

A man ran past the window shrieking:

"They're here! They're in the camp!"

For a moment there was no other sound but the clatter of the tank outside on the road. Then everyone began yelling. Augustine, Jackson, Crumbacker and Hartman came running into the washroom, their faces flushed.

"You hear it, Steve?" Augustine cried.

"Come on," Lang shouted.

He crawled out of the window and ran toward the street, Moran and the others at his heels, colliding with other prisoners pouring out of windows, adding his voice to the din surging over the camp. With Moran at his elbow he battled his way blindly to the road. The tank was inching delicately through a sea of men, invisible beneath a blanket of cheering prisoners except for the thrusting barrel of its gun and an open turret from which protruded the helmet of its grinning commander.

All firing had stopped.

A shrill voice sounded above the tumult.

"Look! The steeple!"

From the steeple, all that could be seen of Moosburg from the center road, flew an American flag. The battle for Stalag VIIA was over.

Men yelled and cheered and shook hands and hit each other on the arms and pounded one another on the back. A few stared in stunned silence. A few, a very few, cried. There were tears in Augustine's eyes. Jackson was silent. Hartman fell to his hands and knees and kissed the ground. Crumbacker turned toward the barracks, a determined look on his face.

"I'm gonna take me a bath," he said.

"Oh, shit!" Moran yelled. "Jesus Christ, oh son of a bitch! We made it. Steve, you son of a bitch, this time we really made it!"

Lang looked at Moran's wild, happy face and knew exultation, an overpowering affection for this violent, profane Hercules, and a kind of sorrow.

Yes, this time they had really made it.

It was over.

The days of scrounging and dirt and deprivation, of want and wait, the long yearning nights, the fears and frustrations, the tedious hours, the endless scheming, the monotony, the anxiety. All over.

All over, the nights on the steps with a sensual voice singing the longings of young sentries, all over, the being needed, the camaraderie, the friendships stronger than love or family. But not all of it was over, not all the good part.

He had come long and far between the moment just now when Moran called him a son of a bitch in a delirium of freedom and love and that moment in the water beside the wreckage of the *High Flying Flora*, so incredibly long ago, when Moran had thrust the Mae West at him in contempt and cried, "Here, you son of a bitch." Long and far, a tortuous journey strewn with the bodies of Bertram and Jaybird and a pitiful little Italian and someone called Blubberbutt.

It had been worth it, the hunger and the fear, the boxcars, the cruel march, all the waiting and enduring and the two lost years of his youth.

It was worth it.

He seized Moran by the waist and lifted him in the air and whirled him, laughing and struggling, around and around and around until the cheering crowd, the peeling barracks, the barbed wire, the tank with its blanket of bodies and the distant steeple of Moosburg swam dizzily together.

376